Destination
ROMANCE

A SERENITY PRESS ANTHOLOGY

First published by Serenity Press Pty Ltd, 2018
Copyright © 2018 Serenity Press
Cover design by Monique Mulligan
Edited by Monique Mulligan

National Library of Australia
Cataloguing-in-Publication data:
Destination Romance/Serenity Press
ISBN: (sc) 978-0-6483106-1-7
ISBN: (e) 978-0-6483106-2-4
Romance – fiction

Serenity Press books may be ordered through online booksellers or by contacting:
SERENITYPRESS.ORG
publisher@serenitypress.org

Contents

Introduction

'One's **destination** is never a place, but a new way of seeing things.'
– *Henry Miller*

After holding a writers' retreat in Northern Ireland, we knew we wanted travel as the theme for our third Serenity Romance anthology. Travel awakens the soul, the senses, the mind – and for many, it opens hearts, bringing new teachers, friends and lovers our way. Why not invite writers to draw from their travel experiences?

And yet, we still wanted to continue our tradition of linking all the stories to one common place, as we did with the fictional Serendipity Bridal Boutique in *A Bouquet of Love* and the real coastal town of Rockingham, Western Australia in *Rocky Romance*. This time around J'Adore Travel Boutique in country New South Wales, owned by quirky Maggie Redmont, became that place; the brief for writers was to include the travel agency in some way, but to take the characters to some other destination.

The contributors delivered. They dreamt up delightfully romantic scenarios to draw readers in and out of J'Adore Travel Boutique, with phobias, physical challenges, heartbreak, bickering, miscommunications, and plenty of will-they-won't-they moments providing heartfelt feels. These writers brought Heart Springs and the travel agency to life, as well as taking readers to vibrant and romantic destinations around the world: Greece, London, Paris, Thailand, New Zealand … even the sand dunes of Western Australia.

To each of the contributors – we thank you and admire you for taking up the challenge. To our readers, please enjoy.

Monique Mulligan & Karen McDermott, Serenity Press

Cruise It or Lose It

CAROLYN WREN

Rose yanked up the collar of her coat as an icy cold breeze blew along the café strip. A few of the alfresco tablecloths quivered in response to the rush of air, and a couple of Tarts Bakery menus escaped their holders, dipping and soaring on the wind like paper airplanes on an unexpected adventure.

Escaping this winter weather would be great.

Rose chuckled at the irony of her wayward thought. After all, the very reason she was lingering outside J'Adore Travel Boutique wasn't to plan a vacation – it was to cancel one … again.

A quick peek through the window confirmed her worst suspicions. J'Adore hadn't hired any new staff since her last visit. Maggie was sitting behind her desk, her trademark red lipstick contrasting against the white china of her mug as she sipped her morning coffee. Izzy was on the phone, the hands-free headset almost hidden by the mass of her spiky hair. Elle was talking to a customer, leaning forward to display her ample cleavage to the suited businessman.

Maybe a temp was hiding in the wings? Some work experience junior Rose hadn't met?

Stop hovering and just get it over with.

She passed the businessman on her way in, sidestepping to give him room.

Elle looked up with a smile. 'Good morning, Miss Sullivan, what can we do for you today?'

'I'm … I'm afraid I have to cancel my holiday. I totally understand if my deposit isn't refundable this time.'

Elle flicked a glance at Maggie, who gestured to the chair in front of her. 'Rose, please take a seat. Is there anything J'Adore has done to offend you? If we've not lived up to expectations, you know you can tell us. Did you find a better quote online? We pride ourselves on matching our competitors' prices.'

'No, no, it isn't that. You've all been wonderful, and so patient with me.'

Maggie clasped her hands on the desk. 'Then forgive me, but I have to ask why you've booked and cancelled the exact same holiday three times in a row.'

Rose's shoulders slumped. 'I have a phobia. I thought I could conquer it, but I can't.'

'A fear of flying? Please don't be embarrassed, it's surprisingly common.' Maggie's tone was compassionate. 'Most of the airports run courses. The success rate is excellent. I can give you some information if you like.'

Out of politeness, Rose took the pamphlet Maggie handed her and pleated the glossy paper between her fingers. 'It isn't flying. I *love* flying. I'm scared of water, or more specifically, the ocean. Yes, I know it's stupid. A twenty-five-year-old Aussie girl scared of the sea.'

There was a brief moment of pause, as all three J'Adore staff exchanged glances. 'Did you ever think that a three-week Mediterranean cruise wasn't the best vacation choice for you?' Izzy said.

'It's the *worst*.' Rose leapt up from her chair and dragged a hand through her hair. 'I'd never have considered it if not for my best friend's wedding. I'm Deb's maid of honour, and when she suggested an exotic overseas wedding, I pictured a castle in Italy, or a camel trek across Morocco, or some insane private ceremony on top of the Eiffel Tower. I never thought in a million years we'd be a tiny, vulnerable speck in the middle of a dark, bottomless ocean.' Now that Rose had confessed her fears she couldn't stop talking. 'I can't imagine anything worse than being surrounded by miles of endless nothing. It's terrifying. There's no ground, no stability, we're just *floating*. And there's the other thing: look at my name, Rose. It's the same as Kate Winslet in *Titanic*. You know what happened to her, right?'

'She survived the sinking and lived a long and happy life?' Maggie said, a hint of amusement in her tone.

'Yeah, okay, good point, but, I bet she never, *ever* went on another cruise.' Rose flopped back in her chair. 'Sorry. I know films are not real life, and I know I sound like a lunatic. If you cancel my booking, I'll go away and never bother you again.'

'How much do you want to be at this wedding?' The look of sympathy on Maggie's face was genuine.

'More than anything. It breaks my heart that I won't be there to share Deb's big day.'

Maggie turned to her staff. 'Has that last cabin on the Epona been snapped up yet?'

'I'll check.' Elle's fingers flew over the keyboard.

'Cabin?' Rose glanced from one consultant to the other. 'Cabin as in ship? You want to cure my cruise phobia by booking me on *another* cruise?'

Maggie plucked a folder from the neat pile on her desk. 'Just hear me out. First of all, this is a three-day cruise, not a three-week one, so it's more like a cruise-lite trial run. Secondly, you're worried about being a speck in a wide ocean? With this particular trip, you'll be able to see land in the distance most of the time.' She flicked through the folder and produced another glossy brochure from its midst. 'The Straits of Malacca is a thin strip of ocean between Indonesia and Malaysia, a hot spot for short cruises because of its proximity to various tourist ports.' She spun the brochure to face Rose and pointed to a map. 'The Epona is the new premier cruise ship in the French-owned Spirit of the Seas fleet. This is its introductory trip – a long weekend cruise, visiting three ports along the way.'

'That last cabin is still available, but I bet it won't be for long,' Elle interrupted her.

'Can you slap a hold on it, please Elle?' Maggie returned her attention to Rose. 'I know this all seems crazy, but it could be a good way to see if your fear of the ocean is real, or if the *thought* of it is what's freaking you out. Here's one more incentive. The first port of call is less than twenty-four hours after you leave Singapore. If the whole experience is too much for you, disembark there, call me, and I'll change your airfares to fly you straight home. You can tell Deb you tried everything to be there on her wedding day, but cruising is simply a no-go for you.'

With her pep talk done, Maggie sat back in her chair, leaving Rose with the *last* thing she'd expected to feel today, a flicker of hope shining through her disappointment and stress. That is, until one word brought her up short. 'Wait, by an introductory trip, do you mean maiden voyage? Because the theme music to *Titanic* is playing in my head right now.'

'Rose, every ship has to have a first voyage. I'm sure you've been on brand-new airplanes in the past and never even knew. Is this any different?'

That logic is hard to argue with. 'Can I afford it?

'The available cabin is basic. That's a good thing because the Epona is top of the line and *very* expensive. This cruise has been sold out for months. The only reason I can offer it to you is because we received a last-minute cancellation yesterday.' Maggie tapped her pen on the desk. 'There is one more thing I need to mention. The Epona departs Singapore this Saturday.'

'Wait, what? *This* Saturday? Three days from now?'

'I'm afraid so.'

'That ... that's insane. How will I even get there?'

'On it.' Elle's flying fingers hit the keyboard again. 'Okay, I can do a Friday midnight flight out of Sydney, with their full transfer package straight to the ship. It'll be tight timewise, and a long road trip for you beforehand, but it's doable.'

'The ball's in your court, Rose. If all this is too overwhelming, we'll understand completely. We're offering you an option, that's all, without any obligations. Say the word, and I'll personally cancel your Mediterranean holiday right now, with a full refund of your deposit.' Maggie's quiet, professional tone cut through the whirling chaos in Rose's head.

'How did you do that? How did you take something impossible and make it possible?'

Maggie's smile was infectious. 'That's our J'Adore motto. We aim to make all your travel dreams come true, especially the impossible ones.'

Rose nibbled on a fingernail. *Can I do this?* The new school term didn't start for two weeks; logistically she *could* take off at a moment's notice without any impact to her job. 'This is nuts. I'm not a spontaneous person.'

'There's a first time for everything.'

Rose sucked in a deep breath, closed her eyes and leapt into the void. 'I'm in. Quick, do it now before I chicken out. Book it. Book it all.'

Within minutes she was clutching itineraries and tickets in her hands, standing on the threshold of a bold adventure, with butterflies performing cartwheels in her stomach. Maggie shook her hand. 'Congratulations, Rose. This is the best decision you've ever made.'

This is the worst decision I've ever made.

Rose gripped the brass railing as another roll of the ship sent her stomach lurching. Sweat ran in a line down her spine and pooled in the waistband of her jeans. *Yuck.* Her feet, encased in boots and woollen socks, were steaming in their sauna-like conditions. A family raced past her, chatting in excited tones. Rose managed a wan smile for a little girl who waved as she tore up the sweeping staircase of the main foyer in a bright floral sundress.

Rose's left bum cheek was throbbing, a result of the oversized injection the ship's medic had so kindly administered for seasickness half an hour earlier. 'It should start to take effect in ten minutes,' he'd said.

Ha, ten minutes, my arse … literally.

Streams of people were pouring in from the outside deck area, bathing her in a constant rush of tropical air, which only added to her discomfort. Rose averted her eyes from the blue ocean revealed with each swing of the solid steel doors. She knew she was creating a traffic jam by lingering on the bottom stair, but she still couldn't force her feet to move. As even more people joined the throng, the staircase became a veritable swarm of humanity. The array of different languages surrounding her was fascinating, or it would have been, under normal circumstances.

One person stood out from the crowd. A tall, utterly gorgeous man dressed in shorts and a white polo. With curly blond hair, tanned skin, and blue eyes, he belonged on the cover of a magazine. He looked to be about her age, was breathtakingly handsome and … was heading straight for her. Rose's gaze dropped to her feet as she pushed back against the balustrade, giving him room to pass. Leather moccasins stepped into her lowered point of view and stopped. A flurry of French followed, spoken in a deep voice that cut through the surrounding noise to wash over her like silk. Rose forced herself to look him straight in the eye. *Hashtag hotness!* After a few moments' pause, he began

5

again, switching from honey-smooth French to rich, full-bodied Italian with effortless ease. Or, had he been speaking Italian the whole time? Was her brain so fried she'd lost the ability to distinguish between languages, as well as speak them?

'Mademoiselle?'

Sucking in a deep breath, Rose gave herself a mental slap. 'I'm sorry. I didn't understand a single thing you just said.'

A wide grin turned his face into something mythically beautiful. 'Ah, English. Forgive me. I asked if you thought gravity was a wonderful invention?'

'Gravity?' Rose blinked, partly to clear away the sweat running into her eyes, partly because she'd obviously misheard him, and partly because no one, *no one* could be that good-looking.

'*Oui* … I mean, yes.'

'Gravity isn't an invention, it simply exists.'

'To stop us floating away?' He fluttered his fingers in the air.

'That's one reason.'

'So, using this theory of existence, we are safely grounded?'

'Of course, we are.' God, she loved that accent. The essence of it hung in the air, like honeyed wine.

'Then, you have no logical reason to keep holding on.' He gestured to her death grip on the rail.

The heat of a blush hit her face at his teasing. Because, obviously, standing next to Mr Honey Wine Hotness while sweaty and wrinkled wasn't enough of an embarrassment. She had to add blotchy red cheeks to the mix. *Could this day get any worse?*

He stuck out his hand. 'I'm Jacque.'

Jacque? As in *Jack?* Rose recoiled, stumbling backward up one more step in an effort to get away, quite an achievement considering she *still* hadn't let go of the rail. 'No, you can't be Jack, we can't be Jack and Rose on the maiden voyage of a ship.'

'Pardon?'

'The *Titanic* movie?'

Another grin lit up his features. 'Didn't Rose survive the sinking of the ship? If I am Jack in this scenario, surely I'm the one in danger.'

'Why does everyone keep reminding me she lived? It's not like she *enjoyed* the sinking. I just think we'd be better off avoiding each other. In case we tempt the fates.'

'We are safe. The Epona is a fine ship.'

'That's what the Titanic people said.'

'I'm certain your holiday will progress smoothly, even if we stand side by side.'

A bubble of hysterical laughter caught in Rose's throat. 'Considering my suitcase went AWOL, and I'm trying hard not to throw up on your moccasins, it's not going very smoothly at the moment.'

The smile drained away. 'Your luggage is missing?'

Rose gestured to her long-sleeved shirt, jeans, and boots. 'I promise I'm not wearing this winter ensemble in ninety-degree heat as an eccentric fashion statement. These are the only clothes I have. I'm trapped on a floating building on a maiden voyage with someone called Jack, homesick, seasick, and with no knickers.'

His perfectly shaped brows headed skyward at her last words, sending another flaming rush of heat to her face. *Oh God.* 'Obviously, I'm *wearing* knickers at the moment. I meant I have no spares.' She paused to suck in a breath. 'On the bright side, my bum's stopped throbbing … you totally don't need to know that.' Rose dragged a hand through her limp hair. 'I'm normally not this much of a lunatic. It's been a chaotic few days.'

The sympathy written all over his face was almost her undoing. Silly tears threatened to humiliate her even further, especially when he reached out to touch her cheek. 'My poor *bella* Rosa, your vacation is off to a rocky start.'

'Please don't call me that.' The complaint came out a little too strident, judging by the startled look on his face. 'Sorry. Belle Rosen is a character who dies in The Poseidon Adventure.' *Could I sound any more ridiculous?* 'It's a movie from the '70s. A bunch of people are on a cruise ship, and it flips upside down.'

'Spontaneously?'

'A tidal wave.'

'Ah.'

'If you want to keep walking now, I'll completely understand. I'm heading to the purser's office anyway, for an update. Or, I was, until I got lost.'

'Could they not bring the information to your cabin while you rested?'

'I'm avoiding my cabin. It has a porthole looking straight out to the ocean.'

'I see.' Clearly, he didn't. 'Would you allow me to escort you? With a small detour, beforehand?'

'If that detour is to *your* cabin. You can think again. You're gorgeous, but I'm not that desperate for a distraction.'

He threw back his head and laughed, a joyous sound that stopped everyone in their tracks, except for an elegantly dressed woman who ogled him in open admiration and walked straight into one of the foyer's marble pillars. 'Perhaps I do not have a cabin. Perhaps I am an illegal passenger, like your movie Jack.'

Rose gave him her best teacher scowl. 'It's not nice to tease a paranoid person, you know.'

'Then I shall stop. I am offering only a brief respite from your stressful day. We do have one problem, however. We cannot take the staircase with us.'

His perplexed expression made her smile, in spite of everything. 'That's a shame because I think I'm here for the duration.'

'What if we take it one step at a time?' He held out one hand, palm up.

Rose tried to be surreptitious about wiping her sweaty palm on her jeans before she wrapped her fingers around his.

He held out his other hand. 'Let me be your gravity, Rose, I promise you will not float away.'

The giggle building in her throat was born of nerves, and she bit it back, because this was the most romantic thing that had ever happened in her life, and Honey Wine Hotness Jacque seriously had a way with words. *Must be the accent.* Throwing all caution to the winds, Rose took another deep breath, and let go of the rail.

His hands were cool and steady clasped in both of hers. That very steadiness grounded her and chased away some of the churnings in her stomach. With all the chivalrous elegance of a Regency hero, he tucked her arm into his and took them down that final step, bringing them to ground level. People still swarmed around them, a blur of crisp cotton and summer clothing interspersed with Epona crew members resplendent in royal blue uniforms.

'Do you know where to go? We could ask one of the—'

Her question ended in a squeak as Jacque spun her in a half circle. In a dizzying change of direction, Rose found herself pressed against a broad pillar with his arms encircling her body. 'Wh— what are you doing?'

'I thought the crowds might scare you. On the stairs, you appeared overwhelmed.'

More overwhelmed than having sky blue eyes framed with unnaturally luxurious eyelashes staring at her from mere inches away? And why did people keep giving her extra phobias? 'I'm fine with crowds, *and* planes. The ocean freaks me out.' She put a finger to his lips for a moment to forestall the inevitable question, and *not* because she was looking for an excuse for more physical contact. 'Yes, I know I'm on a cruise ship. It's a long story.'

'You can tell me about it in the cigar room.'

'I don't smoke.'

'Neither do I. It's perfect.'

'That makes no sense. How do you even know this room exists? The Epona is massive, and we only left Singapore an hour ago.'

'I snuck in early.'

'Is that allowed?'

'Does it matter?'

'Are you going to keep answering my questions with questions?'

'Why? Is it annoying?' His smile was pure mischief.

He seemed in no hurry to move. The swarms of people had disappeared into her peripheral vision. They couldn't compete with the man holding her a gentle captive in the circle of his arms. He smelt of something spicy, a tantalising hint of fragrance she wanted to breathe in. The reminder of her own dishevelled, sweaty state was enough to break the tension swirling around them. Rose tore her gaze away and shuffled her feet. Jacque took the hint and caught her hand in his.

'Forgive me. I promised you a respite. I take it you wish to avoid the outside deck areas?'

'Yes please.'

'You are in luck. My sense of direction is excellent.'

Using a smaller, internal staircase, he led her to a lower floor, and a double-sized wooden door marked *Salon de Cigares*.

Inside, Rose inhaled the rich aroma of leather and cedar. With its lack of windows, dark panelling and dim lighting, she could have been in an exclusive gentlemen's club. Best of all, the air conditioning was a blast of frigid air, chilling her overheated skin. 'I thought it would smell smoky.'

'It doesn't officially open for business until ten tonight. By the morning, this entire space will reek of tobacco, so we must make the most of it. Why don't you relax and take your boots off?'

'Here?'

'Why not? I won't tell.' He ducked behind the wide bar and began rummaging through shelves.

With a mixture of trepidation and relief, Rose ripped off her footwear with a sigh of pure bliss as the cold air hit her damp toes. 'Are you sure we won't get into trouble for being here?'

'You paid for a cruise. This is part of the cruise. Besides, it's for medicinal purposes.' He held up several bags of salted crisps and a frosted can of ginger ale. The mere sight of them made Rose's mouth water. She almost snatched the snacks from his hands and tore open the cellophane packet, ignoring his amused chuckle.

'You are my hero, have I mentioned that?' She washed down a handful of crisps followed by a long swig of the ginger drink. Her unsettled tummy almost wept in relief.

He rested his arms on the polished marble, looking like the world's most gorgeous bartender. 'The simple remedies are often the best.'

'You sound like an expert.'

His elegant, one-shouldered shrug was pure Gallic. 'I've had the odd bad day at sea.'

'Have you been on a lot of cruises?'

'More than one.'

'I guess you've worked out this is my first. I was so obsessed with the ocean phobia, I never even considered the nausea factor. I'm such an idiot.'

'Ah yes, the long story.' He plucked a cloth from a hook and began to polish the immaculately clean surface. 'My name is Jacque. I'll be your friendly bartender for today. Tell me everything.'

Rose crumpled the empty crisp packet and reached for another as she sunk into one of the oversized leather sofas. 'It all started when my best friend Deb announced she was getting married ...'

She told him everything, from her foolish fears to the tedious eight-hour drive to Sydney, the exhausting red-eye flight and finally, her horrified realisation that her luggage had decided to take a different vacation.

'Full transfer was supposed to mean me *and* my luggage, so I have no idea what went wrong. I guess I shouldn't have boarded – I didn't want to. I stood like an idiot just looking at the ship for at least half an hour, but I didn't know where else to go. I was in my cabin on the phone to my travel agent when I realised we were at sea. Talk about panic.' Rose threw him a rueful smile and went back to her drink.

Jacque took a sip from his can; his attention focused fully on her. If her tale of woe was boring him, he was doing a damn good job of hiding it. 'You like movies.'

Rose pounced on the change of subject. 'I teach Media Studies at my local high school. Film analysis forms part of the curriculum.'

'You enjoy it?'

'Very much. I've always had an obsession with films, in case you couldn't tell.' She tucked her legs under her. A jaw-cracking yawn took her by surprise, and Rose clamped a hand over her mouth. 'I'm so sorry.'

'Don't apologise. It's a typical side effect of the anti-nausea injection.'

'How did you know I had one?'

'You mentioned a tender ... derrière. You'll feel better after a nap.'

Rose screwed up her nose, even as the heat of yet another blush roasted her cheeks at his matter-of-fact tone. 'I wasn't kidding when I said I was avoiding my cabin. It's on a low deck, and that damn ocean looks *really* close. I guess I can put up with it for a day.'

'Day?'

'I'm disembarking tomorrow morning.'

His surprise was obvious. 'Why?'

'Jacque, I have no clothes, my cabin freaks me out, and I can't even bring myself to go on deck. Let's face it. I'm a cruising failure. This whole experiment's been a disaster.'

A frown only added character to his handsome face. If she had to suffer through twenty-four hours on the ocean, at least she could take one sweet memory away with her.

The shrill jingle of a phone interrupted her musings. Rose reached for hers, before remembering it was dead, the battery flattened by the long Australian call. 'Is that yours?'

'I don't think so.'

'Where's it coming from? It sounds like it's down low.' She stood and peered over the bar to discover the noise emitting from a battered rucksack shoved into a corner. 'Did someone leave that there?'

'It's nothing, ignore it.'

Why was he so dismissive? 'If it's a lost bag, we should take it to lost property.'

11

'No need, it *is* mine.' With a muttered curse, he snatched the rucksack off the ground, rummaging through its contents. He pulled out a ship's map with some sort of handwritten notes on it, a water bottle, and finally a slimline phone, hitting a button to silence its insistent demand. 'Sorry. I told you I snuck in here earlier. Please consider staying on board. It takes most people a day to find their sea-legs.'

'You're forgetting the no-clothes situation.'

'Tell the purser to issue you a gift voucher to spend on board. I'm certain that's something he can do. I noticed several boutiques where you could purchase fresh supplies.'

'It's fine, really. I came, I saw, I failed to conquer. My travel agent was right. At least I can tell Deb I tried.' As another yawn escaped her, Rose reached for her boots. Would anyone really care if she walked around with bare feet? 'We should get to the purser's office. I'm sure you have other things to do.'

'Nothing important.' The ringing of his phone cut him off. He silenced it a second time.

'You sure?' Rose tossed him a wry look and pulled open the doors. 'Thank you, for being so kind during my scared rabbit moment. Without you, I'd still be on that staircase holding up traffic.'

Voices came from along the corridor, and more uniformed crew members, together with a bunch of men in business suits appeared, speaking in rapid French. 'That sounds urgent. Do you know what they're talking about, Jacque … Jacque?'

Her companion had completely disappeared. 'Jacque?' she peered behind the bar, even more baffled to find it empty.

'Sorry,' he whispered, a mere breath away from her ear.

Rose shrieked and clutched her boots to her chest. He'd appeared from a door panel in the wall, invisible to the naked eye. 'Don't *do* that. You scared me half to death.'

'Sorry.' This time the single word held more than a trace of humour.

She craned her neck to look over his shoulder. The small space was some sort of storeroom, piled high with wooden crates and boxes. 'How did you know this was here?'

'Lucky guess.'

She glanced at the door, then back at him. That was a lie; there was no *way* anyone could stumble across that accidentally.

12

'You—' A flicker of unease ran along Rose's nerve endings as her brain pieced snippets of their conversation together.

I snuck in here early.

Perhaps I am an illegal passenger.

In the foyer, he'd pushed her against the pillar just as crew members walked past. Not to avoid the crowds, but to avoid being *seen*?

She took a step away from him, followed by another. 'Who *are* you?'

He held out his hands in a soothing gesture. 'Rose, it's all right.'

'Are you a stowaway?' The question came out as a croaky whisper. 'Are you trying to get a freebie cruise?' Another thought slammed into her head 'What's in those crates? Did you put them there? You're not here for some nefarious purpose, are you? Because that would be *so* unfair considering everything I've been through in the last few days.' Rose curled her fingers around one boot and held it aloft.

'Why would you think that?'

'There are heaps of movies about bad people sneaking onto ships. *Juggernaut, Under Siege, Speed 2.* Plus, you have a *map*.'

Jacque huffed out a breath. 'Everyone on board has a map. They're in all the cabins. Do I look like I'm planning something bad?'

'How should I know what evil doers look like? The ones in *Die Hard* were really handsome.'

'*Die Hard* was about a building, not a ship.'

'I don't think the type of structure is relevant to this conversation.' Rose lunged for the nearest thing she could lay her free hand on, which happened to be a full bottle of alcohol sitting on top of the bar. She waved her weapon in what she hoped was a threatening manner. 'You should know, I've taken a self-defence course.'

'Rose, I was teasing you earlier. I'm allowed to be on board. I'm not a stowaway. As for what's in the boxes, I'm guessing cigars or very expensive single malt whiskey like the bottle in your hand.' His tone was placating, and still sexy as hell. *Damn him.*

'Why did you hide? Why are you avoiding everyone dressed in a ship's uniform?'

He exhaled in a sigh. 'I'm meant to be working. I lied and said I had a stomach bug.'

'What?'

'I'm supposed to be in my cabin resting. That's why I hid.'

Working? Rose's relief was so intense, and the situation so absurd, the urge to giggle bubbled up inside. Jacque wasn't a stowaway or even a passenger; he was a member of the *crew*. No wonder he knew his way around the ship. No wonder he looked comfortable behind a bar and could switch from one language to another with such ease.

Great, talk about making a first impression. Meet a gorgeous, helpful guy, hurl accusations, and threaten him with violence. *Way to go, Rose.* 'You're chucking a sickie.'

'Pardon?'

Australian slang apparently didn't translate. 'You're playing hooky.'

The familiar smile returned as he lowered his hands. 'I am. I wanted a single day to explore as an average passenger, to smell the sea air. Is that too much to ask?'

Poor Jacque. She wanted nothing more than to avoid the ocean. He just wanted to enjoy it. 'You idiot. You almost gave me heart failure. Why didn't you just tell me? I wouldn't have dobbed you in.'

'Dobbed?'

'Tattle-taled.'

He ran a hand through his hair. Yep, even that looked sexy. 'In truth, I had planned to keep a low profile, until I saw a damsel in distress on the stairs. I could not leave you there.'

The simple answer made her want to hug him. 'So, you work for a living and didn't pay big dollars to be here. That makes no difference to me. I'm still grateful.'

He dipped his head in a silent thank you.

'There's no way you can come with me to the purser's office now. What if someone sees you?'

'If you don't mind taking a circular route, I promise we will slip under the radar.'

'No ocean views?'

'Not even a hint of sea air will touch your face.'

Jacque could stop traffic with that smile. 'I'm holding you to that promise.'

Circular route was right. After at least ten minutes of negotiating long corridors and utilitarian stairwells, Rose was completely lost. Despite that, when Jacque gestured with a flourish to an office door marked Purser, she was reluctant to end this bizarre encounter.

'I'm sorry for all the accusations, and jumping to crazy conclusions.' She pulled her arm free from his.

'Don't be. Your reaction was understandable. Plus, I've never been threatened with boots and four-hundred-dollar single malt before. I'll cross it off my bucket list.'

'Four hundred dollars! Thank god I didn't break it.'

'I would have hidden the evidence, Little Rose.'

A beat of silence stretched between them. Why was she prolonging the inevitable? 'Enjoy your day of freedom, and thank you again.' Before her courage deserted her, she pressed a quick kiss to his cheek, and almost dove through the office door.

Her haste was wasted. The purser's phone rang as she walked into his office. He apologised and began an incomprehensible conversation in French while she was directed to a waiting area, which lived up to its reputation. Crew members bustled about her. Once or twice they glanced her way with worried expressions. Either the ship was in some sort of trouble – Rose shoved *that* thought aside – or her lost luggage was creating waves. *No pun intended.*

The office was much warmer than the blissfully chilled cigar room and after a few minutes, Rose's eyes began to droop. She jerked awake when the purser called her name.

'Mademoiselle Sullivan. Please forgive me for keeping you waiting. I cannot tell you how sorry we are for what has happened. I assure you the Spirit Line prides itself on customer service.'

'You found my suitcase?'

'I'm afraid not.' Rose's shoulders slumped. He continued, 'We have an alternative to help compensate for your inconvenience. If you'll follow me, I'll take you to your new cabin.'

'New? I thought the cruise was sold out.'

'Specific arrangements have been made. Your hand luggage is being relocated as we speak.'

After an elevator trip to the tenth deck, the purser directed Rose to a smaller lift – a *private lift,* requiring a four-digit code. It opened straight into an apartment. Not a cabin, an actual apartment. The living area alone was twice the size of hers at home.

'The bedroom is here, overlooking the upper promenade.' The purser pulled back lace curtains to expose floor-to-ceiling windows and a balcony. Rose hovered in the doorway until he beckoned her forward.

She gripped the railing in disbelief. A Parisian street was one level below her, complete with shops, cafés, and even cobblestones. The horizon was blocked by other balconies and cabins straight across the street, atop more shops, meaning she could see only sky, not sea. Even the tangy ocean smell was muted by the flower boxes adorning every balcony. The illusion was so flawless; Rose glanced up and down the street, half expecting to see the Eiffel Tower looming in the background. 'This is incredible.'

'The living areas and formal dining are through here, on the ocean side.'

She held up a hand before he could draw those curtains. 'Leave them, please. I prefer this view.'

'As you wish.' Her hand luggage was on the king-sized bed, together with numerous shoe bags and flat boxes. More clothing hung from a dress rack standing in the corner. 'A credit has been issued in your name in all the ship's retailers, for whatever you need. Please accept these initial supplies.'

Initial supplies? There had to be a month's worth of clothing littering the bedroom.

The purser handed her a key card with a polite bow and left, encouraging her to call him directly if she needed anything.

Rose sat on the bed, stunned. 'Am I dreaming? Is this another mix-up?' Were the J'Adore team responsible for this massive cabin upgrade? Rose had a sudden image of a high-paying Epona passenger standing in a hallway with his suitcase, utterly confused at his sudden eviction.

Even the movement of the ship seemed less pronounced here. Perhaps because the luxurious cabin was in the centre of the vast ship. Or because she was on a higher deck. Whatever the reason, Rose sent a prayer of gratitude to the ocean gods.

The bathroom door was partly open, revealing a marble wonderland that beckoned. Rose tore off her winter clothing, flinging them in all directions in her frantic haste to be clean and cool.

She purred in bliss, scrubbing at her hair and skin with high-end toiletries as the water washed away the last remnants of her ridiculous day.

The clothing rack was a treasure trove of goodies in various sizes. She pulled on lace underwear, a cotton sundress in bright yellow and slid her feet into matching sandals, securing her damp, unruly curls with a simple gold clasp. Wandering back out to the balcony, she leant her elbows on the railing and watched the streetscape below.

A familiar figure caught her eye, strolling past the alfresco tables of a café with the battered rucksack over his shoulder. Rose bit back his name on her lips. She'd almost blown his cover twice already.

'Jacque.'

He kept walking. Not surprising, considering she'd kept her voice low.

Maybe something else would work. '*Jack*. Look up. It's Rose.'

He glanced upwards, shielding his eyes from the sun and smiling that megawatt smile when he saw her. '*Bonjour*. My Winter Rose has become a Sunshine Juliet on her balcony? Are you lost again, *petite fleur*?'

'Not this time. This is my new cabin, I got an upgrade.'

'It is only what you deserve. You have your luggage?'

'I'm afraid not, but at least I have a change of … clothes.' She'd almost said knickers. 'Are you still exploring?'

'Yes,' he held out the map. 'I am about to stop for lunch. Would you care to join me?'

Did he want to spend more time with her? Instead of running away screaming like any normal person would, considering their initial encounter? *Stop analysing, and say yes.* 'Yes. I'd like that very much.'

'What do you think?' She couldn't resist a girly twirl when she reached his side, something she'd never done in her life.

His reply was in Italian, which earnt him an eye roll. 'How can I tell if you're complimenting me if I can't understand you?'

'It was a compliment, trust me.' To prove his point, he kissed her on both cheeks, cradling her face between his hands. His lips were whisper soft, with only the barest hint of stubble. The gentle caress wound its way through her body, leaving traces of heat in its path.

Don't turn into a puddle. It's just a European greeting. 'What's the plan?'

'Every real explorer needs food.' He gestured to the café. 'La Maison François is porthole free … unless you would prefer one of the main food areas?'

'As a selling point, port hole free is a winner.'

While freshly baked baguettes were being filled with *jambon* and camembert, Jacque flattened his map on the table together with a printed itinerary of daily events. Both items were strewn with handwritten notes and items circled in red pen. Jacque took his exploring very seriously, it seemed.

'I took photos. I'll show you.' He produced a tablet from his rucksack, and she shuffled closer for a better look.

'There are three separate pools. This one has a water slide. The observation deck has a panoramic view of the entire ocean, and is joined to the sky bar, here.' He pointed to a large room with floor-to-ceiling windows and miles of ocean beyond. 'I take it this is not something you wish to see firsthand?'

'Um, no thank you. I'll stick to the sea-free zones.'

'Poor Rosa,' he brushed a knuckle over her cheek. The caress was fleeting, but his touch lingered on her skin.

The flash of a royal blue uniform caught her eye. Rose stood up, blocking the view of Jacque from the counter. He sat forward and peeked around her body, watching the gate crashers with the hint of a frown marring his forehead. She jumped when he curled his hands around her waist, smoothing the thin cotton with his thumbs and keeping watch at the same time.

After a brief conversation, their voices and footsteps faded away, and Rose blew out a breath. She wasn't ready to lose Jacque's company, and she had no desire to see him carted away to some HR office to be chastised.

'My fierce protector.' He was gazing up at her with a smile and warmth in his eyes.

I could fall head over heels with that smile.

He made no effort to remove his hands from her body, and that swirling tension rose again, surrounding them. Was it just her? Was she reading a mutual attraction into every touch, every kiss, like a clichéd movie heroine?

'*Deux* baguettes.' The waitress placed two plates on the table. Rose took a step back, resuming her seat.

The rolls, fresh from the oven, tasted as good as they looked. Rose murmured an apology when Jacque reached across with a serviette and wiped a smear of mustard from the corner of her mouth. 'Did you always want to work on ships?'

He drew in a deep breath and released it slowly. 'The ocean is a cruel mistress. She summons and beguiles in equal measures.'

'I'm not sure if that's a yes or a no.'

'Neither am I. Perhaps it is the thought of icebergs that keeps me bound to the sea.'

'You're teasing the paranoid person again.'

'Please forgive my indulgence. Teasing you is enjoyable, *ora* Rosa.'

Ora, was that gold? That made little sense considering her brown hair and eyes. Maybe it was because of her yellow dress? Keeping up with his variations on her name was a linguistic challenge, one she was enjoying.

He wrapped his fingers around hers when they left the café as if strolling along the cobblestones hand in hand was the most natural thing in the world. 'Below us is the theatre, a grand place to rival anything in Europe. They perform two shows a night. Would you like to see?'

'I'd love to see a show tonight, thank you.' His hesitation sent a wave of mortification surging throughout her entire body, and she pulled free. 'Sorry, you meant see the *theatre*, of course you did.'

He put both hands on her face; his palms cool against the burning heat of her cheeks. 'I must work tonight, or else I would be proud to accompany you to the performance.'

'Tonight? You said a day of freedom. Can't you go back tomorrow?' *Did that sound needy?*

'Ships like this operate on a twenty-four-hour roster. My absence would be noted this evening and followed up.'

'How much time do you have left?'

'My presence will not be required until six or seven.'

She still had some time with him. *I'll enjoy every moment of it.*

The sound of childish laughter interrupted them. Rose twisted in his embrace, gaping at the bizarre vision of a woman dressed as the female embodiment of Blue Beard – complete with beard – leading a conga line of junior pirates along the cobblestone path. A tiny girl who couldn't have been more than five, waved her parrot hand puppet as she passed, smiling through her silver eye patch. *What on earth?* Rose turned back to Jacque in silent question.

'*Club Enfant.*' His eyes were lit with humour. 'The children's club. The Epona promises *all* its passengers a wonderful holiday, regardless of age.'

'Where are they going?'

'To see the horses in the park, I suspect.'

'Horses? Park? I think you're forgetting where we are.'

'I am not. Follow me, and prepare to be amazed.'

The jolly troupe, with Rose and Jacque in tow, danced their way down two flights of stairs and through a double glass door. Rose sucked in a breath at the enormous indoor park complete with swings, slides and monkey bars, all set in acres of grass like carpet. In the centre of the vast open space was a full-sized merry-go-round, rotating slowly, its decorated horses bobbing up and down amid twinkling lights and fairground music.

Jacque pointed to the painted clouds on the high ceiling. 'The tropical sun can be harsh on tender skin. Children need an alternative place to run and play. The park offers that option.'

Rose laughed in wordless astonishment.

He leant close to whisper in her ear. 'Admit it, you want to ride the carousel.'

'Maybe.' She gave him her version of a casual Gallic shrug which earned her a grin.

They made their way to the giant ride and hopped on while it was still moving. Jacque caught her around the waist and lifted her onto a gold and silver horse. The touch of his fingers lingered again, even through the cotton sundress. The twinkling lights played on his hair and created patterns on his white shirt. Rose's heart skipped a beat when he straddled the horse next to her and rode it with his arms spread wide. 'Are you having fun?'

'Yes.' She raised her voice to be heard over the music.

'Enough to stay on board for the entire cruise?'

'Only if you make the ship stop moving.'

'I will see what I can do.'

When the ride slowed, then stopped, he hopped off, holding out his hand to her. 'I spy an ice cream truck in the distance. Let me guess which flavour is your favourite.'

'Unless you guess chocolate, you're wrong.' Rose stepped off the merry-go-round and grabbed at him in an uncoordinated lunge when the world continued to spin. 'Whoa.'

'What is it?'

'Head spin, in a big way.'

He muttered something under his breath as he scooped her into his arms and carried her a safe distance from the ride's foot traffic, before lowering her to the ground behind a screen of potted plants. 'Lie flat, you'll feel better.'

'Did we hit a wave?'

'No, the different types of movements are confusing your inner ear. Perhaps the carousel was not a good idea.' He crouched down beside her, compassion and understanding reflected in those lovely eyes.

First her legs, now her ears. How many of her body parts had to adapt to being on the damn sea? 'I'd prefer it if you didn't see today's continuous failures as a true reflection of my character.'

'You have my word.' He lay back on the grass, facing her, and propped himself up on one elbow, giving Rose a tantalising glimpse of bare abdomen as his shirt rode up. 'Better?'

'Yes.' He was right. The cessation of movement helped. The painted clouds in the sky had already stopped their slow, vertigo-inducing rotation. 'It's official. I'm an ocean wimp.'

'You put yourself through the trial of a cruise and faced your legitimate fears of the sea. And for what? The love of a friend, to ensure her wedding day is complete. That single act makes you the bravest person I've ever met. I'm very glad I met you, Rose, while I caught a sickie.'

The beautiful compliment was punctuated with a kiss, the merest brush of his lips over hers. She was caught between swooning and laughing at his mangled phrasing. '*Chucking*. It's called chucking a sickie.'

'And still, it makes no sense.' He captured her mouth a second time, and a third, each caress deeper, more sensual and achingly evocative.

He kissed her, until she was putty in his hands, a puddle on the floor. She shivered when he pulled her into his arms, and his tongue traced the outline of her lips, seeking entry. The sensual kiss turned turbo, a fusion of her mouth on his. She clutched at his shoulders, nestling closer. His moan was music to her ears, as was the tightening of his arms around her.

Don't stop. He answered her unspoken plea with another kiss. This one was longer, slower, a daring exploration of her mouth that seared her very soul.

She murmured a complaint when he finally drew back. 'I was compelled to kiss you and I will not apologise. However, we are in a public place, *petite fleur.*'

Yep, he was right. She was engaged in a full-on make-out session in an indoor park surrounded by children. *What would my students say if they saw me now?* The thought brought a smile to her lips.

Jacque folded her against his chest, with one arm wrapped around her waist. Her breathing was rapid, but so was his. His heartbeat was a drum against her ear.

'That painted cloud looks like an *uccello* … a bird.'

'Does it?' Rose was too comfortable to turn and look. '*Uccello*,' she tried the word out on her tongue. 'I'm trying to work out if you're French or Italian.'

'Both, one parent of each.'

That explained the honeyed wine hybrid accent. 'I envy you. I'd love to speak a second language, let alone a third.'

'Stay on board, and I will teach you.'

His self-assurance made her chuckle. 'On a weekend cruise? When I'm getting off tomorrow?'

'The solution is simple. Do not disembark.'

'This argument is going around in circles.'

'Very well. I must ask a question which only someone of your expertise can answer.'

'Um, sure, go for it.'

'In the *Titanic* movie, why didn't Jack look for another piece of wood to float on? The whole ocean was littered with debris, and yet he stayed in the water and froze to death.'

Now, *this* was something she could talk about. 'I know, right?' She snuggled closer. 'I've said the same thing so many times. Why didn't Rose pull him onto her raft? She makes one feeble attempt then declares it "too small". They could have had the happy ending.'

'Sailing away into the sunrise on the rescue ship?'

'Exactly. Or she could have handed over her life jacket. They were in love, and he died. It was horrible. I would have at least tried to save him, whatever the cost.'

Jacque's laughter was a deep rumble against her cheek. 'I believe you are missing the point of the tragic love story.'

'Why aim for heartache when happiness is in reach?'

'You are a romantic with a strong protective streak.'

'You bet I am. I refuse to apologise for it.'

He murmured something in Italian. Rose let the honey rich cadence of his voice wash over her as she stifled a yawn. How long had it been since she slept? It had to be twenty-four hours by now.

Five seconds. I'll close my eyes for five seconds.

She was floating, moving up and down on a gentle swell. *Maybe the sea isn't so scary after all.* A boat approached from the distance, its vibrating engine noise disturbing the peaceful cushion of cotton under her cheek. Wait, were waves made of cotton?

Rose bolted upright, the top of her head coming into contact with Jacque's chin in a wince-inducing crack. She was half on top of him, with her arm around his waist and one leg thrown over his thighs. The vibration that woke her wasn't from an engine; it was his mobile, which he silenced while rubbing at his injured face. 'Ouch, your head is hard, *petite fleur.*'

'What time is it?'

'Almost six.'

'*Six?* Why didn't you wake me?'

'You needed the rest—' His phone began vibrating again; he jammed his thumb on the button with a mumbled curse. Someone was clearly trying to get hold of him.

His look of regret confirmed her gnawing suspicions. 'I must go soon.'

Guilt rose in her throat like bile. 'I ruined your day. You wanted to explore, and we only got to one place, and it wasn't even *on* your list. Then I topped it by falling asleep.'

'You ruined nothing.' He clasped her fingers in his.

'You wanted the sunshine and the ocean, and I kept you inside.'

He lifted their joined hands and pressed a kiss to her skin. 'There are many privileges in the world, ones that must never be taken for granted. The greatest privilege is to hold a woman while she sleeps.'

Rose had to smile, despite her overwhelming guilt. 'Do you have to be such a gentleman about it? Can't you pout and sulk like a normal person?'

'I will sulk if it makes you feel better.'

His phone rang again. 'Jacque, you have to go.'

'I will see you safely to your cabin.'

She held up a hand to halt his words as she scrambled to her feet. 'I can find it by myself, I promise.' Rose forced a smile as emotion clogged her throat. 'I can't thank you enough for what you did today. It makes no difference to me what you do for a living. I wouldn't think any less of you if you scrubbed the Epona's decks, or took out the trash.'

His reply was soft and low … and in French. Rose eye rolled him. 'That's cheating. I'm going to record all our future conversations and play them back through a translation app.'

'I only said you should go to the Captain's ball tonight.'

'I have nothing to wear.'

'Go shopping.'

The response was so logical; it made her chuckle. 'You want me to spend my ship credit on some fancy frock I'll probably never wear again? Will you be there?'

'Yes, but the circumstances will be different.'

She squeezed his hand. 'If I *do* go, and if I see you, promise me you'll at least wave. You won't pretend we never met.'

'I promise.' Jacque kissed her, a feather-light brush of his mouth over hers. He murmured something in Italian – *damn, I need that translator app* – and slid past her. Gone in a heartbeat.

As she took the private lift to her posh cabin, the loss of his company was a tangible weight on her heart. When the doors opened, Rose blinked at the extra racks of clothing standing in the main living area. Had they been there when she left? Nope, she would never have missed the vast collection of full-length ball gowns decorating the room like a flock of exotic birds.

She ran her hands over silk and velvet and lace. Where had they come from? A note taped to one of the hangers made her chuckle: 'With compliments from the Epona.'

'They must be feeling really guilty about my lost luggage.' On the bright side, she didn't have to go shopping. If there was *any* chance of seeing Jacque tonight, she'd take it. And this time she'd look her best.

After a long soaking bath, and experiments with various hairstyles, Rose perused her reflection in the mirror. The floor-length red velvet designer gown was gorgeous with its deep V-neck and shoestring straps. Mid heels in a shiny gold completed the ensemble. She blotted her lipstick and patted her up-style. *Please be there, Jacque, even if it's just for a moment.*

Standing on the last stair of the sweeping staircase gave her a sense of deja-vu. Had it only been mere hours ago she'd stood in this very spot, scared and overwhelmed?

When a waiter appeared by her side, she spun to face him, hoping to see Jacque holding the tray aloft. It wasn't him. He wasn't behind the bar either or circulating amongst the guests.

For the first time that day, Rose was lonely, in a literal sea of people.

Passengers poured in from the main deck, just as they had that morning, bathing her in cool evening air tinged with salt. The door swung closed behind them, but not before she caught a glimpse of a figure silhouetted in the moonlight.

More people joined the throng. Rose craned her neck, trying to see around them before her view of the outside was shut off again. Her second fleeting glimpse offered no further clues, until the silhouetted figure turned, and waved.

Jacque?

Her stomach churned in familiar knots at the mere thought of stepping out onto the decking. What if this was the last time she saw him? Was she really going to let her stupid fears ruin this night? One step at a time, he'd said.

I can do one step at a time.

Her grudging footsteps took her to the door. Rose grabbed hold of the steel handle and cracked it open an inch. The salty ocean breeze hit her face, making her flinch.

Jacque appeared in the narrow opening, his trademark smile in place. 'Good evening. You look lovely.'

Ditto that. He'd changed too, into black slacks and a white shirt instead of the waiter's uniform she'd been expecting. He glanced at a spot over her shoulder, and Rose could guess the reason. 'Am I holding up traffic again?'

'*Oui.*'

'Is that a French "oui"? Or a you and I plural "we"?'

'Either term works in the current situation. Are you coming outside?'

'The jury's still out.'

Jacque held out his hand, palm up. 'I am still your gravity. I promise I won't let you float away.'

And there goes my heart. For the second time that day, she sucked in a breath, placed all her faith in him, and let him draw her onto the deck.

The first thing that struck her was the moon. Without the lights of humanity, it was a dazzling white ball, coating everything around them in a pearlescent glow. The night blurred the horizon and reflected that same glow on the dark surface of the ocean. They could have been suspended in space.

'Come.' He tugged her towards the railing and stood with his arms on either side of it, enclosing her in his embrace. 'See the lights in the distance? That's Malaysia. The coastline will follow us tonight until we dock in the morning.'

The reassuring sight of land toned down the butterflies in her stomach. Jacque's warm body pressed against hers from behind was creating a different type of tension, this one *way* more pleasant.

'Look, see those lights on the ocean? It's a fishing vessel, probably from one of the local villages.'

The tiny craft was dwarfed by the moonlight ocean. 'He needs a bigger boat.'

'Was that a *Jaws* joke?' Humour rang in Jacque's voice as he turned her to face him.

'We're on the ocean. The quote fits.'

'Dance with me.' He tugged her into his arms. The resulting full body contact was mind-blowing, intoxicating. He murmured something in Italian – *damn him* – and began to move. The subtle, undulating sway of the ship was their rhythm. The lapping of the waves was their music. Just like before, everyone and everything disappeared into her peripheral vision.

'Let me know if the movement is too much.'

'It's not. I can't believe I'm doing this.'

Instead of answering, he kissed her, a kiss as gentle as the swaying motion of their bodies. And nothing had ever been so perfect.

The sound of a clearing throat cut through the thick cloud of desire. Rose jumped, both from the unwanted intrusion, and the fact Jacque's fingers had tightened on her waist almost to the point of pain.

A tall, distinguished looking man stood a few feet away, backlit by the glittering lights inside. 'I see you finally decided to grace us with your presence, Jacque, as it appears you have lost the simple ability to answer your cell. Instead I find you fraternising with the guests.'

Oh God, this had to be the captain. No one could look that intimidating and not be in charge.

'Fraternising?' Jacque's echo of that single word carried an underlying hint of anger.

Their unwelcome intruder switched to French. Her lack of understanding of the language made no difference. Rose knew a dressing down when she heard one.

Jacque's responses were cool and calm, but she could hear the growing frustration in his voice. The argument went on for several minutes. She only caught the odd universal word, like 'telephone' and 'responsibility'.

Why was he in trouble this time? Had he snuck away from his duties *again* just to dance with her? The mere thought added another heavy layer to her burden of guilt. Jacque was in trouble. This wonderful, amazing man was in danger of losing his job, and it was all her fault.

Jacque touched her cheek, bringing her attention back to him. 'I'm sorry.'

For what? A quick glance between the two men made the answer clear. Her presence was not required for this conversation. With an embarrassed nod, Rose slipped out of his embrace. She made her way to the door on feet of clay and pulled it open, leaning against the other side.

Passengers flowed around her. A couple frowned at her continued traffic-blocking abilities. Rose ignored them all. Jacque, her Jacque was getting a thorough chewing-out just feet away, and there was nothing she could do.

All day he'd been her saviour, her friend, her protector and what had she done in return? Acted like a crazy person, that's what. Forget Rose in *Titanic*; she'd been the one-woman-show version of *Snow White and the Seven Dwarfs*.

One night only, folks – let's hear it for Rose Sullivan and her constant companions, Sweaty, Shaky, Sleepy, Queasy, Swoony, Fainty and Lunatic.

Rose's hands clenched into fists at her side. Jacque needed *her* help this time, and she wouldn't let him down. Wrenching the door open, she stomped back to their side. 'Excuse me, Mr … Captain.'

Both men fell silent at her interruption.

'If you want to blame someone, blame me.'

'I'm sorry?' The captain's French accent was stronger than Jacque's.

'You're giving Jacque a hard time because he took a day off, isn't that right? Yes, well, he did that, but he didn't even get to enjoy it. He wasted half the day trying to help me. Do you know why? Because my luggage went missing, and I was stressed and scared. Did you even know my luggage went missing? Of course, you didn't. You're probably too caught up in the running of this ridiculously large ship, and that's okay, I understand that. But *he* noticed, and *he* helped me, and *he* fed me and made me laugh and made everything better. Do you know how important that is? It meant the world to me. You shouldn't be yelling at him, you should … you should *promote* him.'

27

Rose jumped when Jacque murmured in her ear. 'This isn't the captain, my fierce little protector. It's Robert Bouchard, the owner of the Spirit line.'

She spun to face him, lowering her voice. 'He owns the ship?'

'He owns the company that owns the ship.' Was that humour dancing in Jacque's eyes? Maybe it was just the moon sparkling on the ocean. *Don't look at the ocean.*

Rose averted her gaze from the dark sea, lifted her chin and faced the big boss. 'My point still stands, Mr ... Bruise Hard. You should be very proud of Jacque. He's a credit to your company.'

He folded his arms across his chest. 'I know.'

'Sorry?'

'I have a great deal of pride in my son and have been trying to promote him for some time. He has been somewhat stubborn in taking up the reigns of responsibility.'

'Son? Son? *Son?*' If she sounded like an echo, it was because her brain had shut down all complex functions.

'I take it this is Miss Sullivan, Jacque? I was curious as to why someone else had taken over residence of the second Owner's Suite, and why the entire staff in London had dropped all their regular duties to search the planet for a single suitcase.'

Like a spectator at a tennis match, Rose's attention swung back and forth between the men. 'Owner's Suite? I thought I got an upgrade.'

Jacque's shrug was as elegant as ever. 'You did.'

'Wait, the suite is yours? I got *your* bed?' The words were blurted before she could stop them.

'It is only fair. I got yours.' That mischief-filled smile was back in full force. 'The clothes?'

Another shrug. 'You needed knickers.'

Her cabin had scared her, and he'd given her a suite. She'd complained about her lack of underwear, and he'd sent her the freaking Paris Fashion Show on a rack. He had staff in *London* looking for *her* luggage. His *father* owned the company that owned the ship.

Rose swallowed. 'Why didn't you tell me?'

'I wanted us to know each other better before you found out.' He lifted a hand to her hair. 'I can see it in your eyes. You are already looking at me differently, *petite fleur.*'

Jacque turned to his father, his voice taking on a hard edge. 'I was not avoiding my responsibilities, I was facing them. I will not run this company from an ivory tower, or a board room. If we have flaws, I need to *see* the flaws from the ground level, through the eyes of our passengers, the people who are important to us. If you consider that *fraternising*, then so be it. I tried to tell you this on several occasions. You would not listen. So, I chucked a sickie to see for myself.'

'You chucked a ...?' Robert's frown was the replica of his son's. Rose stifled a laugh.

'A sickie. It's an Australian term. Rose taught it to me.' Jacque pressed a sweet kiss to her lips.

'I see.' Robert turned his formidable attention back to Rose, killing the mood. She resisted the urge to cringe. Jacque's dad made Arnold Schwarzenegger in *Terminator* look like a wimp.

'My son and I need to talk. If you will excuse us, Miss Sullivan.'

There was no arguing with *that* tone. 'I'll go and pack my stuff. Not that I have stuff.'

'No.' Jacque's brusque tone was all of a sudden very much like his dads. 'The suite is yours. The clothes are yours. I will not have your holiday ruined again because of this family misunderstanding.'

Her Jacque, the heir-apparent to some sort of vast shipping empire, was still thinking about *her* needs even in the middle of all this. She could only nod in response.

He touched her cheek, a frown crossing his face at her silence. 'You are well?'

Rose snuck a look at Robert and lowered her voice. 'I'm not the one getting a bollocking from my dad.'

'I will survive it.'

'You'll let me know how it goes, promise?'

'Promise.'

Sleep was impossible. How could she sleep when Jacque was on the receiving end of some sort of familial reprimand? Would he be fired? *Can you fire an heir?* Maybe he'd be disinherited, kicked to the kerb for insubordination. The clock ticked over the minutes in agonising slowness and still, he didn't call, didn't knock. He knew where she was. Surely he knew the number of that phone sitting on the bedside table, and yet … nothing. Was he okay? More importantly, was he sleeping in her basic cabin right now, while she stared at the ornate ceiling of his luxurious suite?

Sometime around dawn, she fell into an exhausted slumber, only to be woken by the ringing of her mobile. With clumsy fingers, she yanked it from the wall charger. 'Hello?'

'Good morning, Rose. It's Maggie Redmont from J'Adore Travel. Did I get you at a bad time?'

'No, it's fine.' Rose sat up in bed, dragging her sleep-ravaged hair back from her face.

'You should have docked by now at Penang. I'm ringing to tell you we can arrange a direct flight back to Sydney this afternoon.'

Flight? Of course. She'd discussed this with Maggie yesterday. Had it only been yesterday?

Maggie picked up on her silence. 'Rose? Has something changed? Do you still need the flight?'

'Rose?' A second voice echoed Maggie's. An achingly familiar voice, coming from outside the apartment.

Rose leapt from the bed in an uncoordinated stumble. 'Maggie, can I call you back?'

She hung up, and pushed open the balcony door, peering over the edge. Jacque, several Epona crew members, and at least a dozen children, all wearing pirate hats, were gathered on the cobblestones. Each and every one of them had a flower clutched in their hands.

'There is my sleeping beauty. I stopped the ship from moving, just as you asked.' His smile rivalled the bright sun trying to blind her.

'You mean we've docked. I'm pretty sure you can't take credit for that.'

'Nevertheless. We have come with a request.' He bent and whispered something to the kids, who looked up in unison.

'Please stay on the ship, Rose. Please don't get off the ship.' They extended the blooms in their hands.

Jacque held up his flower, a single red rose. 'I went down to the *Club Enfant* this morning to enlist volunteers to persuade you. You cannot disembark. We have so much exploring to do. Look at us. We are Jack and Rose on a maiden voyage. We have a *duty* to bring joy to the story. Would you deprive us of our happy ever after ending – are you crying? What's wrong? Wait right there, I'm coming up.'

Rose blinked away more happy tears as he flew out of the lift, across the apartment and straight into her arms, where he belonged.

'It's fine. I didn't sleep well, and I was worried about *you*.'

'Forgive me. It was very late by the time things were sorted. I did not want to wake you.'

Rose thumped him in the shoulder. 'Less chivalry and more communication next time, please.'

'Jack Bruise Hard hears and obeys, and is now most likely bruised.'

Her heart flip-flopped at his teasing. 'Stop procrastinating. What happened with your father?'

He waved away her concerns with a brush of his hand. 'We made a deal. I get to enjoy cruises as a passenger as an important observational exercise, instead of being stuck in boardroom meetings.' The smile fled from his face when she punched him a second time. 'What was that for?'

'You said you were a waiter.'

'To be fair, that assumption was yours.'

'You also assumed I wouldn't like you because you're *rich*?'

'It changes things for most people.'

'Yeah, well, I'm not most people, and what's with the battered rucksack? Is that part of your ruse?'

'No, it's just my favourite.'

Someone on the street below cleared their throat. Jacque gestured with his chin. 'They're waiting.'

'For what?'

'I may have promised them a kiss.'

'A what—' His mouth swooped on hers. Heaven. A honey-wine nectar she could so easily get addicted to.

Everyone cheered, causing Rose to stifle yet another giggle. She would *not* ruin this romantic moment.

'How much vacation time can you get?' His words whispered against her skin.

'I have to be back at work in two weeks.'

'Good. By the time you get to your friend's wedding, you will be an expert sailor.'

'This is only a three-day cruise.'

'With another longer one straight after, and several more in quick succession.'

Two weeks together, in his arms. *Who could refuse that?*

Rose had a million more questions. All of them could wait. 'Stowaway. Passenger. Waiter, Heir. Is there any other title you'd like to lay claim to? King of the World, maybe?'

He grinned at her *Titanic* joke. 'What's the name of your friend's wedding ship?'

'The Eliza. Why, do you own that fleet too?' She'd meant it as a joke, but his look of innocence gave her the answer. Her mouth dropped open in disbelief. 'You are kidding, right?'

'I apologise on behalf of my family fortune.'

'Hold on, does that mean you can upgrade her cabin?'

'Consider it done.'

'I'm not asking because you're rich.'

'I know.'

'I'm just saying. You'd better not think that.'

'I'm not.'

'She's my best friend, and it would be such a wonderful surprise for her, but if you think I'm thinking of you differently now because of the money and everything, I'm not. If you and your scary dad have another fight, and you end up getting demoted or disinherited and swabbing the decks or whatever, I'll still love everything about you—' *Dammit.*

His reply was in French, of course, but even she understood the phrase *je t'aime* in the middle of it. 'May I continue to upgrade *your* cabins too, Little Rose?'

'If you insist,' she curled her arms around his neck. 'I need to ring my travel agent back. I cannot believe I'm going to be spending a lot of time on cruise ships.'

'*Oui.*'

'You mean "oui" as in French yes? Or "we", as in you and I, plural?'

'*Si.*'

'As in Italian yes? Or seeing see? Or ocean sea? Oh, forget it, just kiss me. I'll start learning new languages tomorrow.'

He smiled as he lowered his mouth to hers. She could so easily fall head over heels with that smile.

Too late. I already did.

The Boy Next Door

TANYA KEAN

Grace's steps were light as she walked down the main street of Heart Springs. The large camphor laurel trees that had stood silently over the town for eighty-odd years offered a familiar comfort. For the first time in over a month her time was her own. She didn't have to be at the doctor's, the oncologist's, the hospital, the solicitor's, the funeral director's … anywhere. Her mother had slipped away four weeks ago and Grace felt able to face the world again. Almost.

In a place like Heart Springs you were not allowed to grieve in private – *you were public property*, Grace thought. Everyone knew your business and you knew what everyone else was doing. It was comforting when her mother was ill, but now it was stifling. Initially smothered by well-meaning concern, then overwhelmed with pity and casseroles. If she heard, '*Your mother was a saint*',

'Such a huge loss for the whole community', 'How will you cope without her?', one more time she would scream.

She couldn't stay locked away forever – life had to go on. She simply needed to work out what that life looked like. Once, a lifetime ago, she'd had goals, ambitions, dreams and enthusiasm for the future.

That was before.

Before her dad died, before her mum got sick, before Michael Barrington had broken her heart.

Grace blew out a melancholy sigh. She was relieved she was no longer required to make decisions, to be the strong one, to be the reliable dutiful daughter. But if she wasn't any of those things, who was she?

A familiar woman dressed in a billowing orange floral caftan and yellow straw hat decorated with large purple chrysanthemums ambled awkwardly along the footpath towards her. Mrs Carruthers, her high school English teacher. Grace's heart lurched; the last thing she wanted was to have Mrs Carruthers feel sorry for *'poor dear Gracie'*. Mrs Carruthers held up her hand in a wave and quickened her unsteady pace to meet up with her. Grace couldn't be rude, and now she had been seen, couldn't escape. She reluctantly made her way along the footpath, meeting her old teacher in front of J'Adore Travel Boutique.

'How are you, Mrs Carruthers?' The older woman was puffing and rested her arm heavily on Grace, trying to catch her breath. Her eyes locked with Grace's and she smiled.

'You don't have to call me Mrs Carruthers, Gracie dear, we're not in school any more. Call me Joyce.' She hesitated and frowned. 'How are you, dear?'

'I'm fine. Still have a few things to sort out, but I'm getting there.'

Mrs Carruthers sighed wistfully. 'I miss your mother every day. She had a special spark. Enjoyed her life to the full, despite the difficulties life threw at her, and at you too, Gracie dear.' Grace cringed, but Mrs Carruthers was so sweet she could only nod in agreement.

'Your family certainly has had its fair share of sadness. I think it's time you changed all that.' Mrs Carruthers looked over Grace's left shoulder. 'I still remember your Year Ten essay. You remember. The one about the Greek Islands. It held the promise of so much adventure.' Her gaze switched back to study Grace's face, devilment twinkling in her eyes. 'You should take a holiday, Gracie dear. You're far too young to rusticate in Heart Springs.' She patted

Grace's arm affectionately. 'You should be out there, enjoying the world, having fun.'

'I haven't had much time to think about a holiday. I have the farm to take care of. Besides, I love it here. Heart Springs is my home.'

'Pish. There's a whole world waiting out there, my girl,' the old dame said in her best schoolteacher voice. 'Go, spread your wings, find some young man to have a fling with, have an adventure. You will come back a different person and then you can rusticate.' Her eyes crinkled closed with amusement. 'You were forced to stay in Heart Springs when all your friends left. First your dad's tragic death and then your mum getting sick, all put a stop to you having your own life. There is no excuse now, nothing here to hold you back.'

Nothing here to hold you back.

Was there anything in Heart Springs holding her back? Fear? Possibly. Self-pity? Maybe. Money? Not according to the will. Her job? She wouldn't really miss it. What then?

'Well, you give it some thought. I'm heading to Tarts Bakery to get one of those decadent caramel swirls for my choir morning tea. Can't sing without cake! Take care now, Gracie dear.'

Mrs Carruthers gave her arm a claw-like squeeze and Grace watched her slowly shuffle up the street heading towards cake heaven.

Grace sat on the bench under the sweeping arms of a peppercorn tree in front of the travel boutique, contemplating Mrs Carruthers' words. She'd forgotten her essay. Fancy her old teacher remembering, Grace smiled bemused. It had been full of all the wistful longing for adventure her teenage self imagined. Looking up at the window of the travel agency she jolted upright. Right there, luring her like a siren were posters of azure blue water, white sandy beaches and blue and white stucco buildings. The Greek Islands.

'That can't be a coincidence,' Grace muttered to herself.

Mrs Carruthers' words echoed in her mind: '*There's a whole world waiting out there, Gracie dear.*'

Grace looked up and down the near-deserted street. Perhaps she'd go in and see. Where was the harm in an enquiry?

The sharp jingle of the bell above the door alerted everyone that a new customer had arrived. Three heads turned to Grace, smiles on their faces.

Suddenly Grace questioned her rash decision to enter – she should look online. Talking to people so soon after her grief, even in this small friendly town, was always going to prove difficult. Maggie, the owner of J'Adore Travel Boutique, rose from her chair behind a desk strewn with paperwork and approached her.

'Hello, Grace. Come in. I was so sorry to hear about your mother.'

Grace forced a smile.

'Thank you, Maggie. I appreciate your condolences.'

Grace stood in awkward silence, unsure of what to say next. She looked at the wall of brochures on the plastic shelves behind the desks. Maggie's other colleagues, Izzy and Elle, went back to gazing at their computers.

'Can I help you with something?' Maggie asked.

Grace looked nervously at Izzy and Elle, then back to Maggie.

'Ah, I'm not sure. I was thinking of taking a break. A holiday, I guess.' Grace said. 'I have no idea what to do or where to go. I thought I'd come in and see what you might recommend.'

'Well, you've come to the right place. Nothing I like more than a blank canvas.'

Maggie smiled and indicated Grace sit in the chair before the desk. She went around to the other side and tapped a few keys on her keyboard. She looked up expectantly.

'What interests you? Are there any places you have always wanted to visit?'

'I don't know, up until five minutes ago I hadn't given a holiday much thought. Bit of a spur of the moment coming in, I was heading to the café for a coffee when I …' Grace looked towards the door, 'when I came in.'

Maggie waited for a few seconds. Grace scanned the wall of brochures hoping for inspiration. What possessed her to come into the travel agency in the first place? She twisted her hands in her lap. This was a mistake. *I don't do spur of the moment*, she thought, rising from the chair.

She needed to escape; a light sweat began to bead on her forehead and a familiar niggle of panic started to flutter in her belly. 'Look, I'm sorry, Maggie. I don't want to waste your time. I'll give some thought to where I'd like to go and come back another day.'

Maggie dismissed her concern.

'Not at all, I would like to help. How about we go and have that coffee? We can talk about what interests or ideas you might have. We can take it from there,' Maggie smiled.

'Oh. Okay … I guess. Don't you need to look up stuff on the computer? Check details or whatever? Like I said, I don't want to waste your time.' Grace's voice was scratchy.

'It's fine. I'm due for a break and I'd love a coffee. Brooke makes the best skinny caps in the state, you know. Izzy, I'll be over at The Tea Lady with Grace. Won't be long.'

Izzy looked up from her computer and nodded. 'All good,' she replied and focused back on her computer screen.

Maggie reached for her handbag under the desk and stood up. Grace stood and joined her as they headed for the door.

'Come on, let's go. I can't wait to tell you about some of the amazing places you could go. The world is out there waiting for you, Grace Kennedy.'

Grace knew that was an exaggeration. The world was certainly not waiting for insignificant nobody, Grace Kennedy. Twenty-six. Decidedly single, with mousy hair that hadn't seen the inside of a salon in nearly five years. Stuck in a small town with no chance of meeting a nice guy. Most eligible guys had either left for the bright lights of the city or had been snapped up quickly and were now married. Her world was Heart Springs. Small, predictable, boring, dull and lonely.

She had been in love with a nice boy once. Back when life held promise. Back when her dad had been alive, and happy, and her mum had been well and equally happy. It was strange the difference ten years made. Michael Barrington had been the typical country boy next door – a mate, her first crush and the first boy she'd kissed. But Michael had left suddenly four years ago, after a huge argument with his dad and she never saw him again. Even his sister Katy didn't know where he was. It was eating away at their family and his dad had aged a decade in the years since Michael had left.

As they headed for The Tea Lady Café, Grace wondered if she was doing the right thing letting herself imagine she could get away. Life had proven if she set her expectations too high, chances were those dreams would come crashing down to lay in piles at her feet. Maggie's acceptance of her impetuous decision to go on a trip as commonplace gave her some encouragement that her travel dreams might be possible.

'So where do you want to go?' Maggie said a few minutes later as she sipped a frothy skinny cappuccino.

Grace stirred her caramel latte absently, unsure of how to reply. 'I don't know, to be honest. I feel a bit lost, you know, not sure of what's next in life for me. Everything I wanted to do had to be put on hold when Mum got sick. Until now I haven't had a lot of spare time to think about the future. It would be nice to do something fun and exciting though.' Grace wasn't sure Maggie needed to know the dull details of her boring life.

'Sometimes you have to step back from the ordinary to find something extraordinary. Gain some perspective. If you went on a trip, let your hair down, relaxed and stepped away from the farm and Heart Springs, you might find out what it is you want to do with your life.' Maggie smiled compassionately. 'I should know, I lived overseas for years, but realised there was something missing. I took a chance settling back in Heart Springs. Fate has a way of guiding us to where we should be. Who knows, you might end up having the adventure of a lifetime, like me.'

'That's what Mrs Carruthers said. She said Heart Springs will always be here when I choose to come back. Mum was always on at me to return to the city and pursue my career as a journalist, but I couldn't leave her here on her own.'

'Mrs Carruthers might be right, she's a canny old duck! Is there somewhere you've always dreamed of going?'

Grace mentally flipped through her memory. There were so many places she had dreamt of visiting when she had been a girl growing up.

'I've always liked the idea of a cruise through the Greek Islands.'

Maggie sighed and smiled affectionately. 'Ah, yes. The Greek Islands. What's not to love? Santorini, Mykonos, Corfu, Rhodes. We have some great deals at the moment. Small group yachts, island-hopper adventure cruises right through to big cruise ships with set itineraries, and high-end luxury cruises.'

'I like the sound of island hopping, no set timetable. I'd like to be able to stay on the islands for a few days at a time. I'd also like to go to London. Mum was obsessed with the *old country*, as she called it. Harped on about the Royal Family and England. Mum and Dad were going to go back to see where she grew up when they'd saved enough money.' Grace choked on her words and couldn't finish the sentence. The realisation she no longer had a family was still so raw. She took a deep breath.

'Sorry. It catches up with me at the oddest moments. I think I'm okay, then all of a sudden … well, you know.' Grace smiled wanly at Maggie.

'No need to apologise, Grace. It's perfectly understandable.' Maggie took a sip of coffee. 'So. The Greek Islands and London. Sounds fabulous.'

'What do you think, would four to six weeks give me enough time to see the islands as well as London?'

'I think you would get a good feel for the islands and get to see a lot of London. I can put together an itinerary and give you an idea of costs for flights, tours and accommodation, if you like.'

The flutter in her stomach was not panic this time, it was excitement. *This might actually work*, she thought. Maggie's enthusiasm for travel was rubbing off.

'Money isn't the issue. Mum left me comfortable and hey, this is my first big trip overseas so I want to do it in style.'

A wide smile spread across her face. Her dreams of travel were within reach and the longer she spoke with Maggie the more enthusiastic she felt. Maggie would work out the details and she would sort out any problems that might hold her back. She was determined, now she had the bit between her teeth, that she would make this trip happen.

Thanks, Mrs Carruthers.

'If you've finished your coffee, let's head back to the office. I'll give you some brochures, an idea of available dates and prices, as well as a couple of different options. You can take it away and read through and we can take it from there. How's that?'

'Sounds like a great plan. Thank you, Maggie, I appreciate you taking the time to listen to my ramblings.'

'It's my pleasure, Grace. It's my job, but it's also what I love to do. I enjoy making people's travel dreams come true. This is as exciting for me as it is for you. This trip is going to change you – you'll come back a different person. I can't wait to hear all about your adventure.'

Two days later, Grace walked into the cool interior of the pub. She scanned the bar and smiled as she saw her best friend.

'Hi, Katy.' She waved as Katy Barrington looked up from pouring a beer.

'Hello, stranger, how are you? What brings you into town?' Katy placed the beer in front of one of the old timers who practically lived at the pub. Grace gave him a smile and he saluted her with his beer as he walked away. Katy came around from behind the bar and embraced her in a tight hug.

'It's good to see you.' Katy continued to hold her. Grace pushed her away gently. Katy was a hugger. She'd gotten used to it over the years, but she was impatient to tell her friend her news.

'I've done something impulsive. I've seen Maggie at J'Adore and guess what? I'm off to the Greek Islands and London.'

'Wow. Really? Sounds amazing, lucky you. Good on you. I can't believe Cranky Franky gave you the time off.' Katy rolled her eyes and laughed.

'Yeah. I didn't think he would. Must have got him at a weak moment. He's holding my job for me and said to take all the time I need.' Grace didn't tell Katy she'd had to do some serious grovelling to convince Frank Simpson, the editor of the Heart Springs Times, that she needed more time off work.

'What I wouldn't give to go to the Greek Islands, meet some sexy gigolo and have hot wild sex on the beach.'

'Whoa, hold your libido. I'm not interested in meeting any foreign guys. I'd settle for a nice country boy.'

'Yeah, got that right. Unfortunately, all the nice country boys are already married to nice country girls.'

'Goes to show you, doesn't it? We're not nice country girls.' Grace grinned cheekily at her oldest friend.

'Speak for yourself, I happen to be choosy.' Katy laughed. 'Seriously. You'll have a great time, you deserve a break. Lord knows, you've had a lot to put up with over the years. About time you put yourself first, Grace.' Her voice lowered to a conspiratorial whisper. 'But in case you happen to meet a Greek god, could you check he has a brother? Okay?'

That evening Grace sat on the verandah steps watching the light fade and the first stars appear in the sky. She always loved this time of day. The sun's heat had faded, the light was soft and the sound of Louis munching on hay was comforting. It was quiet, peaceful and relaxing, and she often used this time to reflect.

'Well, you silly old goat, you're going to have to do without me for a while.'

Louis blinked slowly then put his head down and kept eating. He seemed more interested in his dinner than her exciting news. Her mother had named all the animals after British Royals. There had originally been three goats: Princess Anne, Queen Mary and Lord Louis Mountbatten. Louis was the last of her mother's goats. Her once big family had dwindled over the years. It was only her and Louis now.

'I've asked Jim Barrington to come over and feed you and the chooks. He'll come every day, so you won't be lonely.'

Louis' tail wriggled and Grace smiled. He couldn't care less – if there was food, he was happy.

'I don't want to be alone. I'm sick of feeling lonely. I want some adventure, some excitement. Don't you think I deserve to have a little adventure, Louis?'

At the mention of his name, Louis looked up. Bits of lucerne poked out of his mouth. He dropped his head and snatched another mouthful of fragrant hay.

'Who knows, I might come back with a hot, sexy Greek god.'

Louis' head shot up at her bark of laughter; his light-yellow eyes bulged and he stomped his front foot.

'Don't like that idea? Too bad, old buddy. You can't be the only thing I talk to, that's way too sad, even for me. Time to make some changes around here. I'm going to have an adventure and you, my hairy friend, will have to deal with it.'

Louis came over to where Grace was sitting. She scratched absently behind his ears. Despite her desire to head off overseas, she would miss her chats with Louis. He had kept her sane more times than she could remember when her mother's illness had been overwhelming. He'd listened as she speculated where Michael Barrington had disappeared to and if he would ever come back. His coat had held more tears than she thought possible to shed.

He rubbed his head roughly against her knee and she realised she'd been lost in her thoughts and had stopped scratching him. Louis bleated, the sound like a child's cry.

'Sorry, Louis. I was a million miles away.' His head butted hard against her leg. 'Ouch. Okay, I'm going. Nice to have your approval, old buddy.'

Two weeks later, after endless hours walking London's grey streets, Grace's feet ached. Putting aside her pain, she stared through the ornate black wrought iron gates of Buckingham Palace.

'It's not very grand. You sure this the right place, honey?' A brash American remarked to his wife.

Grace ignored the other tourists. She thought it was amazing. Standing in front of the very palace where kings and queens had held court for hundreds of years. All that history, and here she was – Grace Kennedy from Heart Springs, Australia! How could she fail to be impressed?

Her stomach rumbled loudly. Checking her watch, she realised it was mid-afternoon; she hadn't eaten in five hours. Victoria Station was around the corner. She could grab a quick bite in the food court, head over to the Royal Mews, then on to Downing Street before calling it a day. She'd worry about her painful feet tonight.

As she turned the corner into Buckinghamshire Street she felt the first drops of rain. Looking skyward, she realised she was going to get a whole lot wetter if she didn't get inside soon, but the heavens opened before she had taken a dozen steps. Typical English weather, but it didn't make it any less unpleasant. Squinting through the deluge, icy wet fingers slid down her back. She shivered and took off at a half run, hopping around the quick-forming puddles as well as other tourists, hoping to avoid the worst of the rain.

Glancing up at the sign above her head, Grace pushed against the heavy oak door of the Stag and Hound. A think blanket of warmth enveloped her and she shivered involuntarily. She took off her wet coat and slipped a hanky from the pocket, silently thanking her mum for insisting she always carry one. She dried the worst of the rain from her face and hair. The door opened behind her to admit another group of people sheltering from the rain. Moving further inside, she selected a table under the window so she could watch for a break in the weather. There was a fire burning low along the far wall; the room felt cosy and welcoming.

Looking at the menu she decided on the roast of the day. She went up to the bar to order and waited as the barman finished serving a customer at the other end. She noticed his broad shoulders, and the way his biceps flexed as he finished pulling the pint and lifted it onto the bar. He took the money from the customer and said 'Cheers, mate.' Grace's ears pricked up. The accent. It was Australian. There were thousands of Aussies in London, travelling and working casual jobs, all living the backpacker dream.

He turned towards her. 'Hi. What can I get you?'

Grace looked into familiar amber eyes and stopped breathing. *It couldn't be!* Of all the places in the world to walk into, she'd walked into some random pub in London to discover a ghost from the past. In the awkward silence that followed she blinked, wide-eyed, unable to process the cards fate dealt. The barman waved his hand in front of her face.

'Helloooo, are you all right? The deep timbre of his voice made her ache for home.

'Michael? Michael Barrington? It *is* you. Wow.'

Grace's voice squeaked as her throat tightened. She could hardly believe she had travelled to the other side of the world only to find the boy next door. He'd been missing from her life for four years and she'd stumbled upon him in a London pub. It was too bizarre to comprehend.

His puzzled eyes narrowed then flew wide as recognition dawned. 'My god, Grace. What the hell are you doing here?'

'Getting in out of the rain, and hoping to get something to eat,' she joked, trying to hide her shock.

'You're the last person I would have thought to see in London.'

She had never been considered the adventurous type. Michael seemed surprised to see her so far from home. She felt somewhat indignant.

'I've been in London a bit over a week, in a few days I'm off to the Greek Islands before heading home.'

'Home …?'

'Yep, back to Heart Springs. It is still there, you know. How long have you been in London?'

'A while now.' He looked away. 'I guess this is home, for the time being, at least.' His voice trailed off.

There was an awkward silence, interrupted when a man approached the other end of the bar.

'Hey, Skippy! What's a man gotta do to get a drink? I'm dying of thirst over 'ere.'

Michael smiled an apology to Grace, then addressed the customer at the other end. 'Hold your horses, mate. Just serving the lady.' He turned to her. 'What can I get you?'

She ordered the roast and a glass of red wine.

'Great choice. Stay right there, I'll only be a sec.'

Grace watched him as he expertly poured the guy his pint of lager. She couldn't believe she had found her long-lost childhood friend on the other side of the world. It made her homesick but also slightly nervous, seeing Michael after such a long time. Butterflies quivered in her stomach.

When the other customer had gone back to his table, content with his beer, Michael walked back and stood before Grace. 'I can't believe it – of all the people to bump into. What made you come to London?'

'I've always wanted to travel.' Grace stopped, not wanting to explain the events of the past few years. 'Until recently I hadn't had the opportunity.'

Her mind was still trying to process this unexpected turn of events.

'I'm staying around the corner in Belgravia. Funny, I walk past this pub every day and never knew you were here.'

'Yeah, weird, huh? It's great to see you, Grace.' He checked his watch. 'I finish at three ... can you hang around? It would be good to catch up.' The delight in his eyes told Grace he missed home. He seemed glad to see a familiar face. She certainly wasn't about to knock back the chance to spend time with him.

'I was going to do some more sightseeing after lunch.' She briefly looked out the window. 'But the rain looks like it's set in, so I might have to change my plans.'

She couldn't stop herself staring at him, assessing his features and comparing them to her memory. He still looked like the handsome, golden-haired boy next door, but he must work out somewhere because his muscular body had filled out to god-like proportions.

What he would look like under his clothes? Grace was sure his arms were not the only thing well-muscled. His legs and torso would be ripped, for sure. He still walked with an easy, casual swagger that made her insides dip like a roller coaster. But it was his eyes Grace remembered the most. His warm honey coloured eyes drew her in like a bee returning to the hive, irresistibly drawn closer until ... stung.

But Michael had appeal that went beyond boyish good looks. He had a wicked sense of humour. He'd always been able to make Grace laugh, despite the sadness in her life. He also had a tender side that Grace knew only too well from the years she had relied on him through the devastating sudden death of her dad. She couldn't remember exactly when she fell in love with him; it seemed like he had always been in her life.

Perhaps it was when he eventually kissed her.

One night of sublime bliss, at the town hall dance. They had stepped out for some air and in the quiet shadowy moonlight he had squeezed her hand and taken her lips. Gently at first then with more passion than she had ever encountered. From that night, she was convinced one day they would get married. Her girlish illusion was shattered in her early twenties. Michael had brought a stunningly beautiful English backpacker home to meet his family. His father and Michael had an enormous row and he'd simply vanished. He hadn't said goodbye, just disappeared from her life. She never saw him again.

'Michael, what have you been doing for the last four years? Why has no one heard from you since you left?'

She had no right to interrogate him, to press him for answers, but she'd been shocked to see him. Finding him after all this time, wondering what the hell had happened to make him stay away for so many years, made her unwilling to spare his feelings. His eyes darted left and right and he looked uncomfortable, unsure of himself. Not the confident, cocky boy she remembered.

'It's a long story, Grace and not a particularly flattering one.' He glanced down the end of the bar where a few people were waiting to be served.

'Sorry, I have to get back to work. I finish soon. Have your lunch and we can talk. I'll buy you a drink and tell you the whole sorry tale.' He brightened and gave her a huge grin. The cocky country boy was back. 'Gee, it's bloody good to see a friendly face though.'

Her lunch arrived and she took it to a table by the window, her eyes drawn back to Michael time and again, pondering all he'd said. A long, unhappy story. Well, she had one of those too. It was going to be an interesting afternoon.

ᘒ

What were the chances? Grace Kennedy turning up in London, of all places. There had been something between them growing up. Grace was his sister's best friend, and therefore off limits, but it hadn't stopped him fantasising about her and wishing things could be different. She was the first girl he had kissed; he'd been a hormonal seventeen-year-old and she'd been a year younger. That one kiss had haunted him at night and left him sweaty and frustrated. Funny to think back now.

He had tried to be there for her when her dad had taken his own life, allowing her to cry herself dry, rant at the injustice and vent her anger at her father for leaving them to fend for themselves. Now she had turned up out of the blue, bringing back those memories and highlighting the hole his own painful departure from Heart Springs left in his soul. Grace was the only person he'd seen from Heart Springs since he'd left, an angry and headstrong fool.

He was dying to ask her about home. What was everyone doing? How were his folks? His sister? Her arrival brought back with startling clarity how much he missed home. What he wouldn't give to go back in time, change the past. Take back the hurtful words he'd said to his father.

'If you can't accept Jennifer as the girl I'm going to marry, you're a narrow-minded, intolerant old goat. I'm done with you, done with the farm too.'

He still could see the shock and tortured expression as his father spat back at him.

'I can't believe you would choose a stranger over your family. You're no son of mine. Go on, leave. But don't come back. Don't come onto my property ever again. You are dead to this family.'

Michael had been the golden boy, the eldest. Feted to take over the farm. He'd never expected his father to be so vehement in his opposition to Jennifer.

He continued to glance over to where Grace sat nursing her second glass of wine. It was still raining and although it had eased off slightly, it wasn't going to stop any time soon. Michael finished up, wiped the bar down a final time and handed over to Will, the barman taking over his shift.

'See ya in two days, mate.' Michael threw the rag into the sink as he moved around from behind the bar.

'Righto, enjoy your days off, you lucky bastard.' Will winked in Grace's direction and laughed.

Michael pulled out the chair opposite Grace, placing his beer in front of him. He sat on his hands to stop himself from reaching over and grabbing her. He felt a silly lopsided grin on his face. Grace smiled wide in return and his stomach flipped as those cute dimples creased her cheeks. God, she was so gorgeous, it was dazzling.

'Good timing that you turned up now, I've got two days off. It'd be great to hang out if you don't have too much on.' Michael took a sip of his beer.

'Just sightseeing,' Grace replied.

'I haven't had a chance to see much of the city, at least not the tourist spots.' He studied her for a few moments. 'You look great, Grace. I can't tell you how good it is to see a familiar face. What made you come to London? Where are you off to after here?'

Michael was happy to see her. She couldn't know what he'd been doing for the last four years, or what events had occurred to find him working in a pub in London. The light in her eyes when she'd recognised him made his heart ache. There was pain behind her smile and he was burning to ask about home, he had so many questions. But for now, they could wait. He would simply enjoy being in her company.

'I'm having the best time, Michael. Should have done this years ago, but you know, things were hard for Mum and me after Dad died.' Her voice dropped. 'I recently lost Mum too. To cancer … she'd been sick for ages.'

Michael was shocked by her revelation. She'd suffered another blow, this time alone. She held his gaze, fighting to hide her sadness. Her lips trembled but she shook herself and smiled sadly.

'But, I'm here now, and …'

'I'm sorry about your mum. She was an amazingly strong woman. Must have been hard, I wish I'd been there for you. I'm sorry I wasn't.' He reached out and grasped her hands without a thought. Grace squeezed them lightly.

'I had more time to prepare this time. You helped me so much when Dad died, I don't know what I would have done if you hadn't got me through those first few months.'

The silence hung as both were lost in thoughts of the past. Michael sat back in his chair abruptly and cleared his throat.

'So, what have you seen of London?' His question pulled her back from where she'd retreated. She gave him a weak smile.

'The usual tourist sights. The Tower, London Bridge, Piccadilly Circus, Hyde Park. I think I've walked a hundred miles since I arrived.' Grace laughed. 'I wanted to see what all the fuss was about. Mum loved England and the Royal Family so I couldn't not come. There is so much history here – I've spent hours poking around narrow little streets, castles and old buildings. I don't want to go home.'

Michael studied her face as she rambled on about her trip. He frowned at her last comment. She caught his look and asked the question he'd been dreading.

'Don't you miss home, Michael? Why haven't you ever been back?'

How to explain why he'd never gone back to Heart Springs … *Where do I start?*

'I told you it was a sad, sorry tale. Dad always expected so much of me, wanted the perfect son, always pushing me to be the one to take over the farm. I could never do anything right. After the fight, I was so angry. I jumped on the first plane outta there with Jennifer, and headed to London. We moved in together and I deliberately cut all ties to Heart Springs. It didn't take me long to realise I'd made a huge mistake. I couldn't relate to life in England. Jennifer's toff friends laughed at my Aussie accent and thought I was so colonial. I was a boy from the bush in a city I didn't understand and hated. In the end, Jennifer moved on and hooked up with a guy better suited to her career and lifestyle.' He gave a resigned shrug.

'I was a bit of excitement for her. She enjoyed showing me off as a novelty but in the end, she settled for what she knew. But after the way we left Heart Springs, I couldn't return to Australia. I was too embarrassed and I couldn't admit Dad was right. He said I was an arrogant knob, foolish and stupid for chasing after a girl who would never accept me for who I am.'

He and Grace looked at each other, the silence drawing out until Grace's eyes dropped to their joined hands. Michael felt hollow.

She must think I'm a complete dick. He slowly withdrew his hands from her grasp and wiped them along his jeans, letting out a long soft breath. It was good to tell someone his story. He felt lighter and a little relieved to share his fears with Grace, like old times.

Grace's blue eyes pierced his and her words fell softly. 'Jennifer didn't know what she was giving up. I wouldn't have let you go for some snooty aristocrat. You've always been my prince.' Grace's lips tightened in an effort to keep from giggling and her eyes twinkled with mischief. Michael smiled and rolled his eyes.

'I've missed that dopey sense of humour.' He looked out the window. 'Looks like the rain has eased off … did you want to head out again?'

'To be honest, I'm stuffed and my feet are aching. I'd like to go back to the hotel. Come back with me, I can't let you go now I've finally found you again.'

Michael hoped he heard a proposition in her invitation. *Wishful thinking!* He drained his glass, stood and grabbed her hand. 'Sure, lead the way.'

∞

It was still drizzling lightly on the short walk back to her hotel. Grace suggested Michael grab a bottle of red wine before they left the pub, hoping it would help ease her jittery nerves. Seeing Michael was surprise enough, but asking him back to her hotel was not exactly sensible, given how she felt about him. She wasn't about to let him disappear again now she'd found where he'd vanished to all those years ago. They had history. They'd shared their hopes, dreams, heartache and fears. They'd been through good times and bad, and always together.

Grace knew she must convince him he belonged back in Heart Springs, not here in cold, lonely London. Experience told her she might well get her heart broken a second time. She pushed away the negativity, deciding to live in the moment for a change and see where fate took her.

Relaxed on the couch, feet curled under her, Grace felt a little tipsy. Sitting beside Michael in such a cosy setting had been one of her girlish dreams. Playing happy families. She winced as she shifted her aching feet to the coffee table in front of her.

'Are your feet still sore? Give them here and I'll massage them.'

Grace hesitated; it was such an intimate thing, having someone touch your feet.

'Come on, you know you want to.' He wiggled his eyebrows.

He turned to face her, picking up her tender foot and settling it onto his lap. As he started to rub the soreness from her toes and pads she closed her eyes and let out a low groan. Sinking lower into the couch she allowed herself to drift into unfurling bliss. She felt the couch dip. Michael's lips gently pressed hers and she responded with a hungry desire of her own. The kiss deepened and Michael leant over, dropping her foot gently and climbing up her body until he had pushed her fully into the couch and was stretched along her length.

Her hands wrapped around his back and she felt ripples of muscular strength as he wriggled closer still.

'Grace ...' he murmured against her ear.

Her skin reacted to the tremor in his voice. Goosebumps followed by a flush of heat. Her belly flipped with desire. He feathered light kisses from her ear, travelling down her neck. Grace couldn't escape the burning hot craving. They'd only shared one chaste kiss, years ago. That was nothing like the incendiary exploration of his lips. His hands travelled along her ribs, and gently grazed the side of her breast. A little moan escaped her lips as a ripple of electricity arced towards her core. Michael lifted his head, his ragged gasps making Grace smile.

'I'd forgotten how well you can kiss, Michael Barrington. Actually, that's a lie, I've never forgotten how well you could kiss.' Grace looked down shyly.

'You're as beautiful as I remember, Grace. I still can't believe you're here.' He was poised above her, holding his weight so as not to crush her. He rested his forehead against hers and sighed. 'Here with me.' He looked up, meeting her eyes. 'I want you, Grace.'

Grace wasn't capable of thinking rationally. Right now, all she could think about was that she was with her childhood friend and secret fantasy lover and he wanted her. She had waited years to hear those words and his declaration was a heady experience. She didn't reply, instead she pushed against him, stood up awkwardly and with lowered lids, held out her hand in a silent invitation. He placed his hand in hers and she led him across to the bed.

Michael captured her mouth in a dazzling hot kiss making her forget her own name. He pulled her against him and she felt the evidence of his arousal hard against her belly. A jolt of lust rippled through her. She'd gone from weary and footsore to raging arousal in the space of a few short minutes. She was overwhelmed by his urgent need and by her intense response to him. She forced herself to break the kiss.

'God, Michael.' She was breathless with desire, yet she struggled to allow herself to give into her craving.

Michael's eyes, darkened to rich treacle, feasted on her. They told her what words could not. Four years of longing, of regrets and missed opportunities wrapped around her armour, lured her in. She melted into his embrace. He moved her towards the bed and as her calves touched the edge, the realisation of what they were about to do made her heart leap in her chest, and she had a moment of panic. She pushed it down, for once not thinking about doing the right thing. The 'good girl' thing. She wanted to allow herself to live in the moment, just once. To follow her heart and fall into the abyss.

She splayed her hands across his chest and hit hard muscle. The sensation made her belly swoop and dive. Yep, she was undeniably falling. Michael hissed as she pulled his shirt out of his jeans and brushed her hands over warm flesh. He captured her mouth in another searing kiss. She had never felt so aroused yet so cherished all at once. She had always been in love with him, but the reality of being in his arms was so much more than she'd ever imagined in her girlish fantasies.

Michael lifted his mouth slightly, so they were barely touching. Stroking and nipping her lips with his, sending a wave of warm pleasure through her. Grace heard a low groan and was startled to realise it came from her. She felt him smile against her lips and as he lifted his head, she opened her eyes to see him gazing at her.

'Tell me what you want, Grace.'

'I want. I want you to ... to ...' She swallowed, her throat unexpectedly dry. Her mind was racing.

'To what? What do you want, Grace?' he whispered on a ragged breath.

Grace could hardly form the words. For so long she had denied her own needs – she hardly knew what it was she wanted any more. The way his kisses were snaking down her neck hardly helped to give her clarity. She let go and dived off the cliff.

'I want you,' Grace replied.

She closed her eyes and gave herself over to the heady sensation of freedom those words awakened within her.

Michael hauled in a deep breath and exhaled roughly. 'My god, Grace, you are so beautiful. So sexy. I want you like I've never wanted anything in my life.'

And then he took his time worshipping her body in ways that ensured she knew exactly how much he wanted her. As they crested the peak and shattered together, her heart soared with happiness.

ॐ

As they lay in the tangled sheets, Michael watched the woman he had thought of so many times since he had run from Heart Springs. He watched her face, illuminated with sated sensuality, dishevelled and bewitching. And he fell a little bit in love with her all over again.

Grace raked her nails softly along his back. He tucked her in close; she twined her legs over his and nestled into his arms. Michael's fingers stroked along her arm lightly.

'I can't believe we waited so long to do that,' she murmured sleepily.

'Mmm. As Katy's best friend you were always off limits,' he mused. 'We also had a great bond and I couldn't risk losing your friendship if I turned out a disappointment.'

Grace gave him a gentle nudge. 'After that performance, there's no way you could be considered a disappointment.' Her smile turned serious. 'I've thought of you as more than a mate for some time now. You just didn't know it.'

'Really? If only I'd known that before I met Jennifer.' Michael smiled and pulled her closer, placing a light kiss on her forehead. He went silent for a long moment.

'So, what happens now?' he asked hesitantly.

Grace rolled towards him, sweeping a long stroke over his chest and resting her hand on his heart.

'I'm not sure … I'm not planning on going anywhere just yet. Are you?' She lifted one eyebrow.

He reached over and ran the back of his hand down her cheek. 'I'm staying right here, beside you.'

'Good. Just hold me. I'll think about what it means in the morning.' She wiggled closer and snuggled into him.

The outside world faded away, leaving the two of them in the shadowy darkness. They held each other until their breathing became regular and they drifted into satisfied slumber.

෨

Grace and Michael woke late the next day. They'd made love again during the night, taking their time, exploring each other's bodies in leisurely intimacy. Michael held her gently, taking her slowly to the height of ecstasy until she shattered in his arms. So tender, so loving and caring – it had brought her to tears. They'd smiled impishly across at each other over the breakfast of eggs and toast Grace had made from her meagre supplies in the tiny kitchenette.

Grace tried to gauge Michael's thoughts but his expression remained guarded. Her mind was a jumble of conflicting emotions. Could she force herself to be brave and tell him what was in her heart, what she wanted? In recent years voicing her needs proved difficult. What she wanted had often taken a back seat. Her mother had needed her support after her dad died. And when her mum had gotten sick, she'd needed Grace as a nursemaid. Taking this trip had been a way to find herself, find out what she wanted to do with her life, what was important. She realised what she wanted was right in front of her: Michael Barrington.

'I leave London the day after tomorrow,' Grace said.

Michael frowned and sat slowly back in his chair.

'I figured as much. I'd guessed you would have booked your trip in advance. You hadn't planned on meeting me, I suppose.' His smile was gloomy.

'You could always come with me to the Greek Islands. Is there anything keeping you here in London?' Grace pressed her teeth into bottom lip.

'I don't have any commitments if that's what you're asking. Do you really want me to come to Greece with you? Up until yesterday you hadn't seen me for four years.'

'Are you saying I was only a one-night stand, Michael?' Grace was equal parts angry, hurt and confused.

'No way, that's not what I meant.' He jerked upright. He leant across and took her hand. 'I've wanted you for a long time, you know. Last night was magic. I want to see where this goes. I'd rather you didn't have to go anywhere but I know you've made arrangements for your trip, so I won't ask you to stay, but I would like to see you again.'

'Then come with me. You said you don't have anything keeping you here,' Grace argued. 'All you need to do is book your ferry ticket. Maggie planned my trip so I could be flexible so if I liked somewhere I could stay longer. You wouldn't be changing any of my plans.' She smiled. 'I don't *have* a plan.'

She lifted one eyebrow, challenging Michael to find an excuse to refuse her offer. Instead he squeezed her hand and gave her a huge grin.

'Okay, I think it would be fantastic to go to the Greek Islands with you.'

Grace's heart leapt and tears pricked behind her eyes. She'd never felt happier than the way she did at this minute.

After a hair-raising donkey ride up the cliff-face's cobbled pathway from the ferry terminal at Santorini to their hotel, Grace dragged Michael to the balcony of their room, unable to contain her excitement. She had someone to share this amazing view of the Aegean Caldera: blue and white houses seemingly stuck at random along the cliff face all the way to the rocky beaches below. A 'pinch me' moment. Michael wrapped her in a strong hug and she laughed.

'I can't remember the last time I was this happy. Have I said thank you for coming with me?'

'Only a hundred times.' He turned towards the ocean but kept hold of her hand. 'This is amazing and to be here with you is so special.' He leant down and took her lips; she reached up, twining her fingers into his hair, anchoring him to her mouth. Michael lifted her up and Grace squealed in surprise. He walked from the balcony into the bedroom and laid her on the soft white linen of the enormous bed. Grace was amazed how quickly he could arouse her.

Shedding their clothes, they rocked together slowly, until Grace cried his name softly as he brought her to her peak; Michael's whispered erotic curse soon followed. Grace couldn't keep the smile from her lips. It was wonderful to be in his arms.

Over the following three days, they explored the island. Hopping on buses with locals. Heading to Oia, the famous artist town a few kilometres from Santorini. Walking the narrow lanes and alleyways of the stunning town, they discovered tiny tourist shops and cool medinas to sit and watch the world go by. They also explored each other's bodies, spending long hours tangled in a sweaty and lust-filled mess. At night, they visited the tavernas and ouzeries where they ate freshly grilled octopus and drank too much ouzo with the old fishermen. Grace couldn't remember laughing so much or feeling so content.

Grace and Michael sat in the hard, plastic chairs at Athinios, Santorini's ferry terminal the following Friday, waiting for the ferry to Mykonos. Two Greek *yia-yias* discussed their purchases, wild hand gestures and laughter punctuating much of the discussion. Although Grace didn't understand Greek, it was obvious the women enjoyed each other's company. Small towns were the same the world over – laughter and gossip was universal. It wasn't so different from her quiet little town back home, and she couldn't help but smile at the friendly faces.

Every so often the pungent aroma of fish, cheese or spices made her conscious of the exotic and vibrant scene before her. Avoiding the cruise ship tourists had allowed her to experience the bustle of Santorini life in a way that made it feel like home. This was what she had wanted, an authentic Greek experience. The added delight of sharing it with Michael was a bonus she hadn't anticipated. Four years had not diminished her love for him. She hoped he felt the same, but for now she was enjoying his company.

Once they'd boarded, Michael went to stow their bags, and Grace found some seats next to the window so they could stare out across the azure water. A large woman jostled Grace as she eased herself into the seat next to her, settling her ample shape into the chair and balancing a wicker basket in her lap at the same time.

'*Yasu*,' Grace smiled a welcome, trying out her limited Greek.

'*Kalimera*,' the old woman replied.

A noise from inside the basket alerted Grace. The woman chuckled at her puzzled expression. She gently lifted the lid of the basket and two yellow bills fought to escape.

'Ducks!' Grace cried, a little too loudly. She looked up into the woman's crinkled face and they both laughed. The old woman slammed the lid back quickly before the birds managed to get out and rested her arm across the top to keep them contained.

'*Papies. Gia to deipno mou.*' She put her hand up to her mouth and indicated a chewing motion. Grace realised the ducks were destined for the dinner table.

'You're going to eat them?'

'*Nai! Fysika.*'

'Of course we will eat them.' Grace heard a man's voice and looked up to see a handsome bronze god standing next to the old woman. His accented English was incredibly sexy.

'Ah, Nico. *Edo eisai. Érthei na kathísei.*'

The old woman patted the seat next to her and the Greek god sat, still looking at Grace. He held out his hand. Grace took it and felt his strong grip.

'*Yasu*. I'm Nico. This is my grandmother, Calli.'

'*Yasu*, Nico. I'm Grace, it's nice to meet you both.' Grace shook Calli's hand, the old woman's eyes sparkled with humour. She continued to hold Grace's hand.

'It's lovely to meet you. Where are you from?' Nico asked.

'Australia.'

'Ah, *Australi* ...' Calli looked wistfully out the window.

'My parents moved to Australia in the sixties, but my grandmother won't leave the island, so we come here to see her,' Nico said. 'I'm from Melbourne.'

'Small world. How nice that you come back to see your grandmother.'

It was clear the two had a special bond. Grace felt a stab of sadness witnessing Nico's obvious love for his *yia-yia*. Would she always envy others their connection to kin?

'How long are you planning to stay on Mykonos?' Nico asked.

'Only a few days. I wish it was longer. The Greek Islands are so beautiful.'

'You've been elsewhere?'

'We've had a week on Santorini, after Mykonos we will be going to Corfu and Rhodes.'

'We?'

'Yes, *we*.' Grace looked up to see Michael glowering at Nico. She was surprised. She hadn't imagined him to be jealous.

'Michael, this is Nico. He's here visiting his family. He's from Melbourne. Small world, hey? And this is his grandmother, Calli. She lives on Mykonos.'

Michael eyed Nico warily but shook his hand. 'Hi Nico. Nice to meet you, Calli.'

'You must let me show you around. There are many places only the locals know. I'd love to show you the island's secret places.' Grace felt a little awkward when she looked over at Calli, who had a wide grin on her face.

'Nico. Good Greek boy. You like?' Grace couldn't believe she was matchmaking in front of Michael. She laughed self-consciously.

'Ah … Yes, I s'pose. But I'm already spoken for. Sorry, Nico.' Nico laughed and slapped Michael gently on the back.

'No worries, I'm actually engaged to a girl in Melbourne. Old ladies are the same the world over.'

Grace thought back to Mrs Carruthers and her sage advice to travel the world.

'They can't help themselves.' She had to agree.

Nico proved to be generous and fun company. Michael relaxed, no longer seeing Nico as a threat. In truth, Grace was delighted to know he cared enough to want her all to himself. Nico's extended family made them welcome and Grace revelled in the bond a large happy family afforded. They also made the most of their days spent alone. They rode donkeys along the rocky shoreline, stopping at secluded beaches to swim naked in the clear warm waters. Michael hired a Vespa and rode to the village of Alefkandra, passing the famous windmills on the way.

They sipped ouzo and arak in the medina, overlooking the ocean with bright magenta bougainvillea draped across weathered wooden pergolas. Grace clung to Michael's back as they sped past white stone buildings, leaning into the tight corners of the narrow island roads. Her hair whipped in the wind as the unique Mediterranean blue roof tops streaked past her vision. Nights were spent in each other's arms, dancing at the *tavernas* or walking the beach, holding hands under the stars and making love. Grace felt carefree, cherished and alive, discovering the freedom she thought she'd never find again.

'I've had the time of my life – I don't want it to end. I'm not sure I could go back to my old life.'

Grace reflected on Mrs Carruthers' words: 'going away and travelling would change' her. She felt a completely different person. Neither she or Michael had mentioned her departure, both enjoying their bubble of bliss. However, reality lurked, waiting to push the intoxication of the last six weeks into a neat little box of holiday memories. Michael broke into her thoughts.

'It might seem random, but maybe there is a reason you picked my pub to walk into.'

'I don't think it was fate, Michael. It was raining and the pub was around the corner from my hotel. Likely I would have walked in sooner or later.' The side of Grace's lips curled upwards.

They were sitting at a table outside a cafeteria beside the rocky beach. *Kaiki* fishing boats floated lazily on the moon-streaked waves.

'Perhaps I'd been waiting for something to push me out of my listless coma. After Jennifer left, I wasn't sure what I was doing or where I was headed. Then you turn up, out of the blue. That isn't a coincidence, Grace. I'd call it divine intervention.' Michael, suddenly serious, pulled in a shaky breath. He swallowed and looked out across the water.

'I wanted a grand adventure. Heart Springs felt too small, nothing to do, you know. When Jennifer and I met, it was exciting. At first.' Michael gave her a weak smile. 'After the fight with Dad, she convinced me to come back with her to London. But I can't breathe in the city. My heart's back in Australia.'

He turned back towards the ocean. When he didn't continue, Grace thought, *It's now or never.* Michael had captured her heart ten years ago with that first kiss and broken it when he left Heart Springs. He was handsome, athletic, funny and tender, *the boy next door.* He had been a part of her life during some of her happiest days and when her heart was breaking. Even when he wasn't there, she had drawn on his strength. She had lost everyone she'd ever held dear, including Michael. But now she had found him and she was determined not to let him go a second time.

She sucked in a breath and said in a rush. 'Come home with me, Michael.'

The continued silence became heavy and loaded.

'Come home,' Grace whispered, she reached across and wound her fingers into his. 'It's time to put your demons to rest.'

Michael's amber eyes turned from the ocean, resignation and pain evident in their depths.

'Ah, Grace. I wouldn't know where to start.'

'Katy reckons your dad won't admit he was wrong but it eats away at him. He knows he forced you away. He's not a well man. He's suffered not knowing where you are. If you're alive or dead. You're both so stubborn, neither willing to admit you might've made a mistake. He misses you. Katy misses you. The place isn't the same without you.'

'You're exaggerating, Grace. He told me to get the hell off his land, to never come through the gate again.'

'I miss you.'

Michael's head jerked up at her blunt admission.

Her voice lowered to a whisper. 'Do you remember what you told me the night Dad died? You said, "I'll always be with you, right here, beside you, holding your hand". A tear slowly tracked down her cheek.

Michael wiped it away. 'I remember. I love you, Grace. I think I always have, but I'm not the boy next door. Not any more.'

'You're wrong Michael. You're still the boy next door, you just got lost along the way. Anyway, we've both changed, everybody changes, it's life ... nothing stays the same for ever.'

Grace felt a little sad for the time they'd lost, but the truth was the journey they had both travelled had ultimately led them to each other. No other path would have brought them to this point. Michael was more than worth the wait, making the next chapter of their lives more powerful for their separation.

'I've discovered the hard way, Michael, there is very little in this life that doesn't require some sort of compromise. Love isn't always a soft or flowery emotion. It can be hard and painful, but the torment is forgotten with the sweet delight of losing your heart to someone who returns your love.' Grace placed her hand in his and gave it a gentle squeeze. 'I love you too. I want to always be by your side.'

Michael let out a huge sigh. 'I think it's time to go home, Grace. Your holiday is almost over, but our adventure is only beginning.'

Grace waited at the international terminal, nervous tension barely contained, checking the departure board in case there had been a gate change, the flight delayed, or, god forbid, cancelled. Each time, the information remained the same: **QF2. London to Sydney. Departing 21:35. Gate 10.**

She took the itinerary out of her Pacsafe shoulder bag, the J'Adore Travel Boutique distinctive logo a bright reminder of home. The recollection of Maggie's words echoed: *'This trip is going to change you. You'll come back a different person. I want to hear all about your adventure when you get back.'*

She glanced at Michael sitting beside her, absorbed in his iPad. Grace couldn't wait to introduce Maggie to her boy next door. The one she'd found half way round the world. He looked up and smiled. Her heart gave a little leap and her eyes prickled with happiness. He reached over and took her hand. She watched as he drew it to his lips, placing warm kisses along her knuckles. Their flight was called and she stood, pulling him to his feet and hitching her shoulder bag higher. Michael squeezed her hand tightly and gave her a broad grin.

'Let's go home,' he said.

The Next Stage

JEAN JENKINS

The air stewardess viewed the weeping woman with concern. 'Can I get you anything? A drink perhaps?'

Carol Ellington blew hard into the bunch of tissues and slowly raised her head, tears streaming down her cheeks. 'A brandy, please.'

She wiped her eyes, making them even redder. The young man sitting next to her shuffled with embarrassment and looked out of the window, apparently very interested in the cloud formation below.

The stewardess handed her a miniature cognac and plastic cup, swiftly peeling back the top of a can of dry ginger ale. A sympathetic wink and index finger to her lip as she handed her a second cognac.

'Take it easy, madam, and press the call button if you require anything else.'

Carol mumbled her thanks and tried unsuccessfully to return the smile. She took a deep breath followed by a sip of the hardly diluted cognac as she tried to collect her thoughts.

She had made a mess of things. She was no good at relationships. Why did she seem to pick men who were cads, rotters, and faithless scum? She'd certainly done the right thing in breaking up with that rat Justin after catching him in bed with Alma Smith, middle school Social Science teacher. But was she doing the right thing by herself in returning to Heart Springs after all these years? After all, she hadn't kept contact with anyone.

She had three months' long service leave ahead of her and, instead of getting married to Justin, here she was flying from one side of Australia to the other.

On impulse, she had given notice for her teaching job in Perth to finish at the end of her long service leave. She had put her apartment on the market and bought a single flight from Perth to Heart Springs. And not a single person knew she was on her way, except old Charlie, who kept the local pub.

Carol took a large gulp of the cognac as she considered the situation.

Thirty-two years old, her income coming to an end after her leave, and she was heading towards the small New South Wales country town that she hadn't set foot in for more than ten years. At least she wouldn't have to put up with any more lies from that deceiving bastard Justin. How could she have been so easily taken in?

Resisting the temptation to dissolve into tears again, Carol unscrewed the second bottle, poured it into the cup and added the remaining dry ginger ale.

It was all over with men. *She* was all over with men. It was time to put the bad times behind her and start over in a place that long ago had been a safe haven: Heart Springs.

Her eyelids grew heavy and finally blessed sleep gave her a break from the thoughts buzzing round in her head. 'Raise the back of your seat, madam. We're coming in to land at Sydney.'

Carol looked at her watch. She'd been asleep for over an hour. A quick comb of her hair and a brush of lipstick and she was ready for the next phase of her life – a phase when she would sort it all out.

Twenty minutes later, she felt decidedly woozy as she walked up the aerobridge. She had two hours before boarding her regional flight to Heart Springs. A cup of strong coffee would set her right.

She located the departure lounge and settled down to wait, coffee in one hand and the *Sydney Morning Herald* in the other.

'I'm so sorry.'

Carol gave a start as her hand holding the newspaper was jolted by a briefcase. She looked up to see it was held by a distinguished-looking man a little older than her.

'May I?' He nodded to the seat beside her.

'No problem,' Carol muttered, hoping he wouldn't want to engage in conversation.

To her relief, he merely nodded, sat down and removed a slim paperback from his briefcase. Carol couldn't help glancing at the title. *Summer of the Seventeenth Doll by Ray Lawler. Full Script.*

Good gracious!

Embarrassed to be caught peering, Carol mumbled an explanation. 'Sorry to look over your shoulder like that, but I'm an English and Drama teacher, and my senior school performed *Summer of the Seventeenth Doll* two years ago.'

'I'm hoping to get a part in my local drama society's production. Thought I'd read the play to increase my chances of putting on a good show at the auditions in three weeks' time.' The voice was resonant and friendly. It caught Carol by surprise. She had got used to Justin's carping tone.

'Robert Forbes, by the way,' and a hand was held out in Carol's direction.

Carol felt her hand enclosed in a warm, strangely comforting grip. She shuddered slightly, and her hand was gently loosed free.

'I apologise if I've taken a liberty, Miss or Missus Drama teacher.'

Carol recovered her equilibrium. She was a free woman now and no longer had to put up with Justin's obsessive jealousy. He, who was two-timing *her*!

'I'm sorry, Mr Forbes. I'm Carol Ellington and I'm delighted to hear that your amateur dramatic society is going strong and well. Where is it, by the way?'

The answer 'Heart Springs' was scarcely heard above the announcement that passengers could now board to fly there.

Carol mouthed a goodbye, and rose hastily to follow the small line of passengers heading towards the departure gate.

She shouldn't have engaged in conversation. She had broken her resolution. Still, it was nice to have exchanged a few civilised words with an obviously civilised man. Thinking about the frisson she felt at the touch of his hand reminded her that she couldn't press a delete button as far as her feelings were concerned.

As the plane taxied to the runway, Carol saw that Robert Forbes sat four rows in front of her. She couldn't take her eyes off his fine head of auburn hair.

The sixty-minute flight northwest of Sydney passed in a flash. Carol had a good view as they came in to land. The town had surely grown since she was last here.

A small flight of steps was wheeled out to the plane and Carol watched Robert Forbes descend and make his way across the tarmac towards the terminal. That, too, was bigger than she recalled.

By the time she entered the terminal, Robert was in a close embrace with a pretty blonde woman who seemed a lot younger than him.

Just as well I didn't get any romantic ideas about him, Carol chided herself. *By that age, any good man is already taken. What's more, it looks like he may have gone for a younger model.*

Carol was making her way to the taxi rank when she saw the pretty blonde driving past, Robert Forbes at her side. Carol suddenly felt deflated. She was out of place, with no idea of what she was going to do. At least she had booked herself a room at the local pub for a few days.

Besides, Heart Springs was merely a stopover to revive happy memories and come to terms with less happy ones. She could then move on to the next phase of her life, when no man would have the opportunity of deceiving or betraying her.

A shower followed by dinner in the corner of the not-so-quiet pub dining area, and Carol was ready for her book and bed.

'Carol Nolan, is that you?'

The loud female voice penetrated across the noisy bar. Carol turned to see the woman at the far end standing and waving frantically. The flicker of recognition firmed as the two drew together.

'I don't believe it. Carol Nolan, after all these years!'

'Maggie Redmont. You were overseas the last I heard of you.'

Maggie gave her a hug, her dangly earrings grazing Carol's cheek. 'Come and join us, Carol. It's been such a long time.' Arm in arm, as if time had never passed, Carol and Maggie walked the length of the bar. Carol glanced at Maggie's flouncy skirt and red high-heeled peep-toed shoes. 'You haven't changed, Maggie. Still the fashion leader, I see.'

Maggie laughed. 'There's a vintage fashion store now in Heart Springs. I can indulge to my heart's content.'

She led Carol towards a table at which two women were sitting.

Pulling up an extra chair, Maggie said, 'Introduction time, girls. Izzy and Elle, do you remember my former next-door neighbour and friend Carol Nolan?'

'Carol Ellington now. You were overseas, Maggie, when I got married.'

'And your husband not with you tonight, Carol?' interrupted the younger of the two.

Seeing Carol's expression fall, Maggie continued quickly, 'Carol, I'm sure you remember Izzy. She's now my business partner.'

Carol stared at the young woman in her late twenties, with her blonde spiky hair and eyes heavy with mascara. Could it be? Yes. It *was* Izzy, Maggie's best friend from way back. How she'd changed! She looked so confident and happy in her own skin. 'Lovely to see you again, Izzy.'

Izzy stood up and embraced her. 'Welcome back, Carol.'

Maggie turned her attention to a slightly older woman who looked in her mid-thirties, her generous bosom straining, barely contained by the low-necked satin top. 'I'm not sure if you know my other hard-working colleague, Elle. Elle, why don't you get us a celebratory bottle of champagne? Put it on my tab.'

Carol relaxed. This was the reason she had returned to Heart Springs: to remember the good times; to recoup her energy and remember that good people still existed.

Elle emerged from the throng around the bar, champagne bottle and four glasses on a tray.

'Here we are, girls. This is obviously a celebration.' Elle bent over to pour the drinks, her generous décolletage producing a soft wolf whistle from the group of men at the next table.

Elle gave a good-natured smile. 'May we all never be without a man when we need one.'

Maggie raised her glass. 'To my reunion with my good friend, Carol. It's wonderful to see you after all these years. And I want you to tell me everything you've been doing.'

All four glasses were raised.

Carol clinked her glass with all three. 'Oh, Maggie. It's so good to meet up with old friends.'

'If I remember correctly, Carol, you went off to study at Sydney Uni. Your parents were so proud of you. And you say that you're married?'

'It's a long story, Maggie. I met and married a fellow uni student, Paul Ellington. It was a marriage made in heaven.'

Carol felt in her pocket for a tissue. It was still impossible to mention Paul's name without that full feeling starting in her throat and making its way to her eyes.

'As you may remember, my parents were killed in a car crash driving from Heart Springs to Sydney. Paul and I were with them, after spending our first Christmas together. Paul suffered terrible injuries and died three months later. Miraculously, I survived with hardly a scratch.'

'I'm so sorry.' Maggie pushed a couple of paper serviettes towards Carol.

Carol dabbed her eyes. 'My tears are not for Paul. I'm over that. It's just that I've made a mess of my life since, and I didn't know where else to come to sort myself out. I've made terrible choices as far as men are concerned.'

'Haven't we all?' said Elle, as she topped up their glasses. 'But we manage to survive, eh, girls?'

Maggie stretched her hand across the table. 'You're a good-looking woman in your early thirties, Carol. You've plenty of life to live.'

'What you need is a holiday,' butted in Izzy, 'and we're the people to organise it for you.'

Seeing Carol's puzzled expression, Maggie chipped in, 'Oh, you don't know about my travel agency, J'Adore Travel Boutique? It's just a little further along the street. You know, in the trendy bit.'

Carol laughed. 'Trendy and Heart Springs are not words I'd normally put together.'

Maggie drained the last of the champagne in her glass. 'Come and see us tomorrow. Have a browse around and we'll pick the holiday that will set you right.'

Hugs and kisses all round and Carol promised the three that she would drop by the following morning.

There was a spring in her step as she made her way to the hallway and up the fine old timber staircase to her room.

She and Maggie had been good friends. When she came home to get married to Paul, Carol was disappointed to learn that Maggie was overseas. And now she had her own travel agency with groovy Izzy as her business partner and man-magnet Elle also on staff. *They* didn't seem to have any man problems.

Lying in bed and looking at the stars through the open curtains, Carol thought back at the short time she and Paul were together. Their perfect marriage had lasted only a few months. Maybe that was her problem. She had wanted to recreate it. It was time she realised that this was never going to be possible.

The shock of losing Paul and her parents had been almost too much to bear. Immediately after graduation, she had taken up a teaching post in Perth, far away from the sad memories. She had thrown herself into her teaching of English literature and, even more so, into teaching drama and producing the school plays. The professional side of her life was organised and satisfying. She had left with excellent references.

It was her choice of men that had been abysmal. After three lonely years, Arthur Beresford was the first to take advantage of her vulnerability. Twelve years older than her, he seemed a kindly father figure. Carol thought she had found the refuge she needed and trusted him implicitly. What a fool she had been. All the time he had a wife living on their farm in rural Western Australia. How convenient it had been to have Carol's affection when he was in Perth!

She should have been older and wiser when she was introduced to Justin Clarke a couple of years later. He portrayed himself as sympathetic, loving and kind. That is, until Carol caught him actually in bed and *at it* with Alma, her supposed friend.

He had the effrontery to say he didn't really love Alma and it was simply a weak moment. *Weak moment, indeed!* She later learned that Justin had been two-timing her with a couple of others, almost from the day they first met.

Thank goodness she was safe here in Heart Springs and far away from both those cheats. A shame the timing was wrong – meeting distinguished-looking and drama-loving Robert Forbes, who was clearly in a relationship.

Maggie was right. A good holiday to regain her confidence and then take her time to find another suitable teaching job.

As she slept, Carol dreamt she was floating in the clouds with Paul and he was trying to persuade her to fly back to earth. On the ground below was Robert Forbes, arms upraised to catch her.

'Tarts Bakery is *the* place to have breakfast, Carol. Try the bacon-and-egg pie, followed by a chocolate croissant. The coffee is pretty good too, although not as good as in The Tea Lady Café.' Charlie paused and leant on the mop, the bar floor gleaming after his efforts.

'Thanks, Charlie. And you say it is just a few doors before the J'Adore Travel Boutique?'

'You can't miss it. It isn't called the café strip for nothing.'

The spring in her step of the previous evening still there, Carol had taken care with her choice of clothes. Trendy café strip, indeed! She would show Heart Springs that she, Carol Ellington, was still capable of trendy. Maggie must be close to thirty, yet she looked a million dollars in her rockabilly dress style. Izzy too, with her short platinum-blonde spiky hairstyle. Carol found the last of the trio, Elle, the least easy to categorise. She seemed closer to her mid-thirties. But hey, was she a flirt!

Perhaps she, Carol, could learn something from her – to take things less seriously and even to flirt a little, to lighten up and realise the folly of trying to recreate the love of her life. Paul had been her soulmate. He was gone, impossible to replace. She must give up her search for the unattainable and relax, enjoy her life.

Thank goodness Arthur and Justin were far away. Carol was afraid Justin might try to track her down and beg forgiveness as he had done before. She had been weak, and taken him back. Never again. The spring still in her step, she felt free for the first time in years.

Carol turned the corner and gasped. The old High Street had been transformed. It was now indeed a trendy café strip. The former rough concrete pavement had been widened and brick-paved. Tubs with small colourful trees adorned the frontages of most stores.

Simultaneously, the delicious scent of freshly baked bread and pastry invaded her nostrils. In front of her was the sign 'Tarts Bakery'.

She entered. The interior was bright and chintzy with three tables set in the huge bay window.

Half an hour later and Carol could vouch for Charlie's choice of breakfast. She stepped back out to the pavement. Next door was the vintage dress shop that Maggie had raved about, then a gift shop and a restaurant. Carol noted the name – Bob's Grill. It might be a good place to have lunch or dinner. She certainly couldn't survive for long on greasy pub fare.

She gazed at her reflection in the exclusive-looking dress shop next door. No prices on the stylish frocks in the window. Obviously expensive.

My, how Heart Springs has changed.

Finally, she found herself in front of J'Adore Travel Boutique. It fitted in so well. Trendy! The travel boutique had it in spades. Carol entered. Flamenco music with castanets set a romantic mood and vintage travel posters covered the walls.

Three desks were conveniently spaced around the attractive room. All had clients engrossed in conversation with the staff. Maggie looked up and waved, her fingers indicating she'd be free in ten minutes. Carol chose a few brochures and sat in a leather winged chair to browse through.

Ah, Italy. A country she had never visited. *Florence, how beautiful.* She gazed at the statue of Michelangelo's David. That was a man with a physique to yearn for. She sighed. Pictures were all she could have now. She was finished with men.

'Can I help you? Oh, Carol. It's you.'

Izzy, dressed today in the tightest black crop pants Carol had ever seen, embraced her warmly.

'How was the night sleeping at the pub? Not too noisy, I hope.'

Carol looked up into the bemused eyes of the young woman who would have been stunning if her hair-style were less spiky.

'I slept like the proverbial log, thank you, Izzy. And here I am, as promised.'

Izzy's piercing blue eyes glanced down at the picture of the statue of David. 'You should see it for real. It's magnificent. I'm still looking for the real-life version.'

'You've been to Italy, Izzy?'

'All three of us in J'Adore Travel have been just about everywhere in the world between us. That's why we can personally recommend holiday destinations.'

Spiky hair forgotten and won over by Izzy's warmth and sincerity, Carol relaxed.

'And you've seen Michelangelo's David for real?'

'Too right, in Florence. I've seen both the original in the Galleria Accademia and the replica in the Piazza Della Signoria. You can walk past it every day and gaze in wonder at the manly physique fully on display. It's positively *orgasmic.*'

A giggle escaped from Carol. She hadn't had such fun in ages.

She closed the brochure. 'I'd like to book a holiday in Italy one day, but for now I want to go somewhere closer, where I can relax and not worry about anything. But I would like to visit new places that I've never seen before.'

'A cruise could be your answer. Somebody else does the driving, the cooking and cleans up your room – that is, your stateroom. That's what cabins are called these days.'

Carol felt a surge of excitement. 'That sounds just up my street. I'd like to get away for a couple of weeks and come back refreshed to make some important decisions about the rest of my life.'

'You can sail from Brisbane or Sydney, Heart Springs being almost half way between the two.'

Ushering her clients out through the door, Maggie overheard Izzy's last remark. She bent forward and gave Carol a peck on the cheek. 'There's no more fabulous experience than sailing out from Sydney's Circular Quay. It has to be one of the best cruising ports in the world. You've got clients due in five minutes, Izzy. Get their paperwork organised and I'll take over with Carol.'

As motioned by Maggie, Carol moved to the desk in the centre of the room. 'Have you been on a cruise before, Carol?'

'No. I thought they were mostly for retired old people.'

Maggie smiled. 'Any reputable cruise line caters for people of all ages: a nightclub, live theatre, ballroom, playroom for kids, casino, library …'

Carol cut her short. 'All right, all right. I get the message. So, which cruise do you recommend? I'm ready to go right now.'

Maggie viewed her friend with concern. This was unlike the steady, cautious Carol of her youth. She stretched her hand across the table. 'We'll organise you a cruise to remember, Carol. By the way, your passport is up to date, I presume?'

'Sure is. From Perth, the cheapest holiday is in Bali. I'm afraid that is the extent of my overseas experience. I've already decided that Italy will be my next planned-in-advance holiday. But for now, I simply need a break before I come back and get my life in order.

'There is a cruise to New Zealand with a most reliable five-star cruise line which leaves tomorrow. The Sydney agent is a mate of mine from way back. If a stateroom is still available, you would have a blast. And a last-minute booking could mean a bargain price.'

Carol clapped her hands with excitement. 'I've always wanted to visit the Land of the Long White Cloud.'

Maggie pressed a few buttons on her computer. 'You may be in luck.' She picked up the red retro phone on her desk. A few quiet words were exchanged.

She put the receiver back on its cradle. 'You're in luck, Carol, my lovely. My good friend says there is a late cancellation, plus I've got you a special deal: a cabin with a balcony on the port side and all to yourself.'

Carol's eyes sparkled in anticipation. 'Done. Book for me, please.'

Maggie became businesslike. 'I'll book you a return flight Heart Springs to Sydney. You'll leave tomorrow morning, arriving in time to catch the transfer bus from the airport to the cruise ship. You'll be in time to have lunch on board. Your paperwork will be ready for collection this afternoon.'

Carol leant over the desk and squeezed Maggie's hand. 'This is fantastic. Can I buy you lunch to celebrate?'

Maggie looked at her watch. 'Why not. I'll meet you in Bob's Grill at midday. Lunch after the cruise will be on me.'

Izzy and Elle were both busy with clients when Carol rose to leave. Izzy gave a regal wave and Elle blew a kiss. *Really!* Her cleavage seemed even lower this morning. No wonder her male clients were so engrossed.

Outside the sun was shining and Carol decided to take a closer look at the shops on the café strip. Would she need to buy any clothes for the cruise? She'd ask Maggie's advice over lunch while perusing the cruise brochure.

As she passed Bob's Grill, she noticed the 'Open' sign. She glanced at her watch. Half an hour to midday. She decided to sit inside with a quiet glass of wine while she read and waited for Maggie.

'Why, it's the drama lady – Carol, I believe.'

Carol turned, startled, waiting for her eyes to adjust to the dimmer restaurant interior. Seated at a table for two, near the door, sat Robert Forbes, a bottle of red wine, a half-full glass, and an open book on the table before him. Why, oh why, did her heart have to somersault like that?

'Come and join me for a glass of wine, Carol. As you can see, I'm battling with the script of *Summer of the Seventeenth Doll*. I'd appreciate your advice.'

Carol hesitated. She had time to kill. She'd love a glass of wine and, even if Robert were an item with a younger blonde, that meant he was safe and she could ignore her acrobatic heart. Plus, he was civilised and mature and had an inviting smile. It could be a pleasant distraction to pass the time.

'Thank you.' Carol sat on the chair opposite him.

Robert waved to the waitress and mimed for her to bring another wine glass. 'I can't make up my mind whether I should audition for the part of Barney or Roo. Either way, they are aged forty and forty-one respectively, merely two or three years older than me. How on earth did you get teenagers to play those parts?'

Carol took a sip of the wine the waitress had poured for her.

'It was a challenge, I must admit. But the kids were great and they really enjoyed taking part in such an adult play. It gave the whole Year Twelve class a base for discussion of what they could do with their lives. Besides which, most got a brilliant result in their English exams.'

'Would you allow me to read you a page or so, Carol? Have you the time before your date turns up?'

Strangely pleased that Robert presumed she was lunching with a male friend, Carol smiled back. 'That's fine.'

Robert moved his chair around the table so that both he and Carol could read the script.

Goodness, Carol thought, *he does smell good*. Why did I waste those years on fellows like Arthur and Justin? Despite her resolution, Carol felt the old familiar stirring. At least this time she already knew that he was spoken for, probably married.

As she listened, Carol was suitably impressed. Robert understood the character. His enunciation was good. He read intelligently. Oh, how she needed a man who was intelligent and sensitive and shared her interests. *Whoa*. She pulled up her thoughts. She didn't *need* a man at all.

Robert paused in his reading and Carol advised him which parts of the script should be stressed more and where he should pause to allow the full effect of the words to be appreciated and their inner meaning understood.

'Oh, there you are, Carol. And Robert too.'

Maggie swept towards them and enveloped first Carol and then Robert in her Maggie-style embrace.

'So, *this* was the table-for-two booking you made, Maggie.' Robert waggled his finger at her.

Maggie laughed. 'And I didn't know that you were already acquainted with my friend Carol.'

'Carol kindly agreed to be my drama coach for the past few minutes. And payment was a mere glass of wine. Here, let me escort you to the best table in the restaurant. You said when you booked that you and your lunch guest needed a quiet table where you could talk.'

'Thank you.' Maggie sat down and plonked her bright green bag on the seat on her right.

'Madam Carol.' Robert drew back her chair. He handed them a menu. A slight bow and he was gone.

Carol raised her eyebrows. 'Who *is* he?'

Maggie laughed again. 'Why, Bob of Bob's Grill of course.'

'You mean he's the manager? He doesn't seem the type to run a restaurant.'

'He's not. Robert owns the place. He's actually the local solicitor. It was his wife's. She died a couple or so years ago. It's just a hobby as far as Robert is concerned.'

Carol's heart somersaulted back the other way. Robert Forbes was a widower. Wait on. He was already hooked up with the young blonde of the airport embrace.

As if reading her thoughts, Maggie said abruptly, 'Don't get any ideas, Carol. Robert Forbes has vowed never to get married again. His marriage to Penny was a total disaster.'

Carol sighed aloud, and looked at the menu. Surprised at the sophisticated selection, she chose spaghetti marinara.

'I'll have my regular, thanks Mary,' Maggie said to the plump, businesslike waitress. 'And a glass of champagne each. After all, Carol, this is a special occasion.'

As they ate, Maggie explained how the cruise ship would take two days to reach the southernmost tip of New Zealand from Sydney and from then on it would be a different port every day. 'Ten exotic places to visit and finally two days cruising back to Sydney. It's a peach of a cruise.'

After Mary had cleared their plates away and they were waiting for their coffees, Maggie leant forward. 'And by the way, Carol, singles can have a *very* romantic time on board, should they choose.'

Carol's response was immediate. 'I'm through with men, Maggie. As I can't pick a decent one, I'd rather do without.'

'You must have been very hurt, Carol.'

'That's the understatement of the year. I thought I could replicate my wonderful marriage with Paul. Instead, I ended up with the two most dreadful species of malehood in the world. They were liars and cheats.'

'Would it help to talk about it?'

'I made dreadful choices. First Arthur and then Justin. Justin Clarke came into my life when I had more or less recovered from Arthur. Nice as pie he was at the start. Then he began to get jealous and wanted to know where I was and what I was doing every hour of the day and night. It got heavy going, but I believed him when he said he loved me. We each had our own apartment, but I stayed over in his sometimes.'

Carol sipped her champagne. It felt good having a friend share the bad memories.

'I got back early one day, and there he was – in bed with one of the female staff. I grabbed the couple of things I'd left in his apartment and never saw him again.'

Maggie tut-tutted, and Carol paused as their coffee arrived.

'He had asked me to marry him. I thank my lucky stars that I found out what a deceitful bastard he was. It was right on the end of term and I was finishing up the following day to have three months' long service leave. Instead, I cleared my desk completely and gave three months' notice. I went straight to the real estate agent and put my apartment on the market. My personal stuff is in storage and the agent has permission to sell my furniture along with the apartment. I booked myself a single flight to Heart Springs, phoned the pub to put me up for a few nights, and here I am.'

'Do you think you'll stay, Carol?'

'That's what I have to decide. I'll relax on the cruise and try and work it out.'

Maggie looked at her watch. 'Thank you for lunch. I'll hurry ahead to check that your paperwork has come through. Why don't you buy yourself a couple of gorgeous dresses to take on the cruise?'

After settling the bill, Carol took the opportunity to freshen up in the ladies' room. She looked at her reflection in the mirror.

'You're only thirty-two. You're not bad looking and you still have plenty of energy. You'll be fine, Carol Ellington.'

If only she had that confidence in her heart.

As she made her way to the door, Robert Forbes was nowhere to be seen.

The paperwork finalised and tickets secure in her handbag, Carol decided to take Maggie's advice and buy herself a new dress to wear at the first formal dinner on the cruise. Should she dare to try vintage or, a bigger dare, venture to enter the exclusive boutique?

Pausing again to look in at the window, she gazed at the long chiffon dress in the window. The colour was just right and the matching chiffon shawl gave it a timeless elegance. *What the hell!* This was the start of her new life. She went in.

Twenty minutes later, she emerged, exclusive shop bag in hand, eyes sparkling, and almost collided with Robert.

He smiled that smile that somehow disturbed her equilibrium. 'At least I didn't actually jolt you this time, Carol.'

No, she thought. *You merely turn up when I least expect you and rock my heart about.*

'May I accompany you? I'm going in the same direction back to my office. How far are you going?'

'Only to the pub. And yes, that's fine.'

'I'd never have classified you as a serious day-time drinker.'

Carol burst out laughing. 'I'm staying there, but only until tomorrow morning, when I leave on a cruise from Sydney.'

'In that case, may I invite you to dine with me and my niece this evening? Lesley is sick of dining with her old uncle and it would brighten her last evening, as she leaves tomorrow too.'

Carol smiled. She couldn't help but be impressed with his gentle civility.

She thought for only a moment. It was no fun eating alone. There would be safety in numbers with Robert's niece there, and presumably his pretty young girlfriend too.

'Thank you, Robert. That's very kind of you.'

Carol took care with her dressing. A long, leisurely bath and a practice run for the cruise with a pretty dress.

Walking along the café strip in the balm of the evening was pleasant. But the pleasantness couldn't prevent Carol from having second thoughts about agreeing to have dinner with Robert Forbes.

She could hardly back out at this late stage. Besides which, he had indicated that he would appreciate her presence with his niece there. Carol wondered what he meant by that. He seemed such a capable man with everything under control.

She decided that she would compromise and leave early after dinner. After all, she had only arrived yesterday and was already half-packed to fly off again tomorrow. Wanting an early night could scarcely be regarded as unreasonable.

As she neared the restaurant, Carol felt her heart quicken at the thought of sitting close to Robert again. This was ridiculous. She was going to have nothing to do with a man in an intimate way for a very long time. Possibly never. Besides which, Maggie had explained that a past disastrous marriage meant he wasn't interested in any future serious relationship. Plus, he seemed to be involved in a dalliance with a younger woman. That sealed it. She would simply enjoy his company and nothing more.

Her sensible self-talk disappeared in an instant when she saw him standing outside the restaurant. He walked towards her and, taking her hand, raised it to his lips.

The feeling went straight down to her loins. So, this was how a lady could feel when welcomed by a gentleman.

She and Paul had just been kids when they married. Raw and inexperienced. Arthur and Justin had been calculating abusers. If only this gentleman were free and they were meeting at the right time of their lives, how different things might have been.

These thoughts were over in an instant. Carol smiled and walked through the door gallantly held open for her.

Robert took her elbow and gently guided her to a private table in an alcove. Seated was the beautiful blonde woman she had seen at the airport. *Was this a joke?*

'Carol, I'd like to introduce you to my niece, Lesley.'

Lesley stood and held out her hand. 'I'm so pleased to meet you at last, Carol. Uncle Bob has done nothing but talk about this mystery drama teacher lady who has returned to Heart Springs.'

'Good evening Lesley. I'm pleased to meet you, too.' Carol meant these words like never before.

Hold on, she thought. *That still doesn't mean that Robert isn't having a dalliance with someone else. After all, Arthur never mentioned his wife back on the farm all the time he was romancing her.*

The negative thoughts vanished when, yet again, delicious food arrived and Carol took pleasure in the gentle banter exchanged between Lesley and her uncle.

While waiting for dessert to arrive, the head waiter appeared. 'Excuse me sir, you're needed in the kitchen.'

'I'll be back soon, ladies. Please order me a short black to follow dessert.'

Lesley leant forward and spoke in a low voice. 'I can see the way you look at my Uncle Bob, and I know he likes you too, Carol. I so want him to be happy. He really deserves no less.'

Taken by surprise, Carol felt flustered. 'What do you mean, Lesley. Isn't he happy? Hasn't he been happy?'

'His marriage with Aunt Penny was unhappy from the start. She and Uncle Bob separated after only a year, as Aunt Penny had met someone else and moved in with him. Two years later, Aunt Penny was diagnosed with inoperable cancer and her lover vanished. Uncle Bob took her back in and looked after her for six months. She died nearly three years ago. People seem to believe that he loved his wife and is still mourning her. The truth is, he says he can't risk marrying again and I know he is unhappy.' Lesley's voice suddenly changed in tone as Robert approached. 'Oh, we mustn't forget to order Uncle Bob's short black.'

'Forgive me for leaving you for so long. The kitchen problem is sorted. Ah, here is dessert – the specialty of the house.'

'I'm envious you are going to New Zealand,' sighed Lesley, digging her spoon into a mouthwatering mix of meringue, fruit and cream. 'I would so like to visit the sites where they filmed the *Lord of the Rings* trilogy.'

'I'm a fan of the Ring books too,' offered Robert. 'You'll have to tell us all about it when you return, Carol.'

Carol smiled at him. How this man could lift her morale. Perhaps it was just as well he had made himself unattainable.

She was shocked when she finally realised how late it was. 'I must go. I still have a little packing to do.'

'I'll drive you back. It's on our way. My house is on the edge of town on the hill overlooking the river. I moved here eight years ago and bought the country solicitor's practice. Best move I could have made.'

Pulling up at the pub, Robert got out and opened the car door for her. 'Good night, Carol. By the way, I'm driving Lesley to the airport for an early flight, so I'll pick you up too.'

He bent forward and gently kissed her on the cheek. Lesley gave a cheery wave from the car and, before Carol could recover her composure, they were gone.

It was just as well she was going to be away for two weeks. She needed to get her head straight about Robert Forbes. It was plain he wasn't in the market for an intimate relationship and she was in danger of placing too much importance on his polite civility.

As she drifted off to sleep, Carol told herself sternly that she was not to rush into another relationship. The memory of Arthur's deceit was never far from her mind and her betrayal by Justin was still raw.

Carol looked out of the window. She recognised the car. Robert was punctual. Could this man do nothing wrong?

Lesley greeted her from the back seat. Sitting beside Robert in the front of the car, Carol felt heady. What on earth was the matter with her? She was about to set forth on a dream cruise to New Zealand and sort her life out, yet here she was quivering like a schoolgirl. She was glad when they reached the airport.

'That's my plane called already.' Lesley kissed her uncle and gave Carol a hug. 'Good bye, Carol, and good luck.' A brief wave and she was gone.

'Yours will be called in ten minutes,' Robert said, glancing at his watch. 'I hope you have a fabulous cruise, Carol, and I hope you see a few hobbits and orcs.'

Carol tried to sound businesslike. 'I promise I'll give you a coaching session when I return. There'll be a couple of days before the auditions.'

The loudspeaker interrupted. 'Boarding now for Sydney.'

Robert gave her a gentle kiss on the cheek.

'Goodbye, Robert,' she whispered, as she pulled away from him. Why was this man playing with her feelings when he had no serious intent?

Seated in the plane and looking down at Heart Springs, Carol momentarily regretted the haste with which she had booked this holiday.

Hold on, she told herself sternly. *This is where you have made your mistakes before. Remember what a solid, sensible and loving man Arthur seemed to be.*

Then there was that two-timing rat Justin. *To think I nearly married him.*

Carol put all such thoughts behind her. She would relax on this holiday and not think of any man, especially Robert.

Everything went like clockwork. A shuttle bus took her directly from the airport to the cruise terminal at Circular Quay. Her passport was checked and held by the cruise ship. She was given her cruise ship card, which doubled as her cabin key and card for purchases while on board. At last she boarded the luxury cruise liner.

The entrance in the main foyer made her gasp with appreciation. It was like entering another era – the art deco days of luxury cruise liners. She followed the steward's suggestion and took the lift to the formal dining room. Ushered to a table where three people were already seated, Carol enjoyed a leisurely lunch chatting to a dutiful middle-aged daughter who was treating her elderly parents to a cruise for their diamond-wedding anniversary.

Finally, she went to her stateroom and gasped with delight. Her cabin verandah directly overlooked the Sydney Opera House.

On the table was a half-bottle of champagne and a fruit basket. There was a tap at the door. 'Good afternoon. I am Felix, your steward. You ask me for anything you need. Would madam like me to open the champagne for her?'

'Why not? Thank you, Felix.'

'In an hour, the call will come for madam to go to the lower deck for lifeboat drill. Madam must take the life jacket with her. It is on the shelf in the wardrobe. On the room door is a diagram of where you must go to assemble. You see that you are lifeboat eight.'

A slight bow, and he was gone.

Not wanting to unpack yet, Carol sat on the wicker chair on the verandah, sipping her champagne and gazing at the Circular Quay and Sydney Opera House precinct below. She was relaxed. She had the space and time to sort things out. She raised her glass and drank a silent toast to Maggie and the J'Adore Travel Boutique, banishing the niggling thought that it would be a more pleasurable experience if Robert were there too.

Her thoughts were interrupted by the ship's announcement. 'Will all passengers assemble at their designated lifeboat immediately. Please wear your life jacket.'

Four minutes later, Carol was standing beneath her allotted lifeboat, together with a mix of families and people of all ages, some still struggling into their life jackets.

'Hello, I'm Dave and this is my mate Bruce.' Two young men in their late twenties greeted Carol.

She smiled, then turned away to help a family with three young children get into their life jackets. Maggie was right. There would be plenty to distract her on this cruise. It would be good practice in keeping a cool head and not rushing into an inappropriate relationship. She needed that practice.

Their lifeboat crew leader was finally assured that all the passengers on his list were capable of assembling ready to abandon ship, should the need arise. Carol returned to her stateroom, where she unpacked and changed into a dress ready for dinner. She finished her champagne, leaning on her verandah rail, absorbed in the spectacle of the harbour as the cruise ship headed out of Circular Quay and towards the Heads.

At Maggie's suggestion, she had opted to dine in the formal dining room and being seated with different people each evening.

Carol was placed on a table for eight with two middle-aged women Dutch schoolteachers, a young American couple on their honeymoon, a retired medical doctor from Brisbane, and Dave and Bruce from the lifeboat practice.

Carol learnt that she would find the following day's programme in her stateroom. 'But don't go straight back, Carol. You must come to see the nightly show in the theatre,' Dave urged.

With the exception of the honeymoon couple, the other six strolled the length of the ship to the theatre.

They walked through the piano bar, where a raven-haired young woman was playing exquisitely on a grand piano; past a few shops, now closed, and a busy mini-casino. And finally, the theatre itself.

Carol was amazed to see that it was the replica of a full-scale theatre. The main auditorium was tiered and the dress circle above had three boxes to each side. Drink waiters were taking orders. Before long, Carol was lost in the glamour and excitement of the singing, dancing and repartee on stage.

The cast complied with the demanded encore to the invigorating grand finale, and Carol felt a joy and lightness she hadn't experienced for years. When Dave and Bruce pressed her to accompany them to the nightclub, Carol declined and instead joined the Dutch ladies and doctor in the piano bar.

This time a poetic-looking young man was playing, his hands rising up from the keys with theatrical gestures. Following the advice of her experienced Dutch companions, Carol ordered a hot chocolate.

This is the life, she thought. This was the escape from reality that she needed, and she had two whole weeks ahead. The problem was, she felt lonely.

Two days later, Carol woke to see that the cruise ship had left the ocean and was slowly sailing through what she imagined the Norwegian fjords looked like – except this was close to the southern tip of New Zealand. She had left her curtains drawn back. It had been magical to lie back in bed and gaze at the moon shimmering across the far reaches of the Tasman Sea. The vastness of the ocean, stretching beyond the horizon, helped calm her and regain her sense of perspective.

And now she had awoken to the wonders of Milford Sound. She flung off the bedclothes and wrapped herself in the tartan blanket conveniently placed on the small sofa next to the verandah glass door. She stepped outside and breathed in the crystal-cool air. Now she understood the name – The Land of the Long White Cloud. Continuous cloud stretched above the cliffs and mountains as if to say, *I am an ancient land, The Land of the Long White Cloud.*

A knock on the door announced the arrival of room-service breakfast. She took her mug of coffee and Danish pastry out on to the verandah, leaning over to gaze in wonder at the waterfall gushing from the top of the cliff to the waters below. A couple with a camera in the next-door cabin gave a cheery wave. She saw that nearly every verandah had someone photographing the beautiful scenery.

Carol's stomach knotted. Everyone else had someone to share the experience with. The thought came to her that she would have liked Robert to be at her side. She wanted to point out the little fishing hamlets nestling on the shoreline; the many small waterfalls pouring from various levels of the cliffs; the crispness of the pure air; the magic of the whole experience.

Carol told herself not to be silly. *Snap out of it.* Maggie and Lesley had made it plain that Robert wasn't willing to risk another close relationship. Robert's own behaviour was one of a friend and nothing more. She was his drama coach and a useful companion. Full stop.

Carol had a quick shower before the cruise ship entered Doubtful Sound. This time she went up on to the top Observation Deck and was with others to enjoy the unique beauty of this even longer fjord. By lunchtime she was ravenous. The cruise had certainly improved her appetite. She decided to try the buffet restaurant. It was hard to choose which of the many sections to dine in. *It's no wonder people complain that they gain weight on a cruise,* Carol mused.

After lunch, she ventured on to the circuit deck, where she found herself in the company of serious walkers and joggers and others casually ambling along and pausing to view the occasional albatross. Carol did two brisk circuit walks and then took the stairs up to the pool area where she ate an ice cream and read another chapter of the mystery novel she had borrowed from the ship's library.

A voice came over the loudspeaker. 'Ladies and gentlemen, we are passing Slope Point, the southernmost tip of New Zealand. On the port side, you can see a family of fur seals on the rocks, cheering us on.'

Joining with others and leaning over the ship's rail, Carol again felt that knot in her stomach, that aching twinge that if Robert were here to share the experience, it would be doubly enjoyable. Again, she spoke sternly to herself.

What on earth was she doing, almost yearning for Robert's presence after knowing him for less than a week? Carol gave a silent, cynical laugh. Although a university-educated woman and experienced competent teacher, her emotional common sense was sadly lacking.

Changing for dinner that evening, Carol decided she would join in the singles' activities and not hide from other men on the cruise ship. She must snap out of wanting a deep and intimate relationship. She would take a leaf out of Elle's book and flirt light-heartedly. That way, things wouldn't get out of control. Yes, and that was how she would be with Robert after the cruise.

The following day, the ship berthed at Port Chalmers. Carol booked herself a bus tour to Dunedin, delighting in the experience of a town founded by early Scottish pioneers. A tour of the local Cadbury factory, complete with tastings, rounded off the day. As the ship sailed away in the cool of the early evening, Carol joined in the singles' sail-away party, clinking glasses and laughing with other unattached cruisers. She waved to Dave and Bruce, who were talking animatedly to a couple of pretty young women.

'Do you mind if I sit with you? I'm Susan.'

'You're welcome,' and Carol smiled at the attractive woman, a couple or so years older than her. They were soon joined by Blake, an amiable man of about the same age, and the trio stayed together for dinner and the theatre performance which followed.

Afterwards, Carol played a game of backgammon with Susan and then with Blake. Smiling at Blake's clumsy attempt to invite her to the bar for a 'nightcap', she allowed him to kiss her goodnight on the cheek. She helped herself to a hot chocolate in the all-night café and, swaying slightly with the movement of the ship and the tiredness of a long day, she made her way back to the haven of her cabin.

She was too tired to think about Robert. Yes, she was getting there. She was sorting herself out.

Carol thought no scenery could be more dramatic than that of the Milford and Doubtful Sounds. How mistaken she was.

The early morning view from her verandah was breathtaking. The cruise ship was anchored in Akaroa Harbour, a huge bay surrounded by volcanic cliffs. A myriad of small craft of all sorts was there to greet them. Carol waved to a fleet of canoes circling the ship. She could see the tiny settlement of Akaroa nestling at the base of the cliffs. A hurried shower and breakfast, and she was ready to see it all close at hand.

This time, there was no exiting via the grand foyer and walking down a carpeted gangplank to the wharf. Instead she had to descend to a lower deck, just above the water line. There was her bright orange lifeboat number eight; except it was now one of the tender boats to take about fifty passengers to the Akaroa jetty.

'Good morning, Carol. I trust you slept well.'

Carol emerged from the lift to see Blake walk down the last stair.

'Thank you, Blake. I certainly did.'

They waited their turn to board the tender.

'You first, sir. Step across when I say.'

The burly crewman held Blake back by his arm as the tender bobbed up and down. It bobbed up level with the ship's platform. 'Now,' and Blake stepped across the void to be grasped by the crew on the tender.

Waiting her turn, Carol's stomach had risen to her chin. The tender seemed to be bobbing more than ever. 'Now.' She stepped forward to be grasped by the crewman on one side and Blake on the other.

'Thank you,' she mouthed, as she and Blake followed instructions and moved forward to squash up to the others sitting on the hard bench.

A brief safety announcement, and they were sailing across the picturesque harbour. Carol enjoyed sitting close to Blake, with his arm around her comfortingly.

This is more like it, she said to herself. *A flirtation with a man like Blake is just what I need.*

The tender was manoeuvred to the jetty and Blake held her arm and helped her disembark. Strolling along the jetty, Carol made it clear to Blake that serious romance was not on her menu.

Blake patted her arm reassuringly. 'That's fine Carol. I understand. I plan to do the local sight-seeing tour for a couple of hours, to get my bearings,' he added, pointing to the waiting minibus.

'I'll come along with you, and then do my own thing for the afternoon,' was Carol's reply.

They joined the small group on the bus. 'Akaroa has a population of only six hundred and twenty-four. A cruise ship in the harbour and we more than double it,' laughed the bus driver.

Carol and Blake listened enthralled as he pointed out the main points of interest in the small town, New Zealand's first French settlement.

They drove to the top of the highest cliff for a panoramic view. Their cruise ship below looked like a toy.

The driver offered bottles of water all round. 'Our tourism was virtually non-existent before the big earthquake at Christchurch. Port Lyttelton is where the cruise ships used to berth for tourists to visit Christchurch.'

'Why don't they still do that?' Blake was curious.

'The earthquake made the harbour unstable. I guess it will be repaired some day. In the meantime, little Akaroa makes all tourists and cruisers welcome. We have a courtesy bus which runs the length of the town. The jetty is one end of it.'

Having learnt that local fresh seafood was the specialty, Carol and Blake ate their fish and chips in the beer garden of the local pub.

They walked along the main street, pausing to gaze at the French-style houses with their shuttered windows. Blake stopped to buy souvenirs for his friends and Carol forgot that she had wanted the afternoon to herself.

'Look at the time!' Blake said. 'We'd better get the courtesy bus back to the jetty.'

Carol was amazed that the day had passed so quickly. 'Thank you. I've enjoyed myself,' she said, as they took the lift up from the embarkation deck.

Blake volunteered the information that he was in a quad interior cabin and the other three guys had gone on the daylong tour to Christchurch. Carol was on the point of inviting him to her cabin verandah for a pre-dinner drink, when she realized her folly. How could she, a mature woman of over thirty, contemplate being so foolish? This was going to be harder than she thought.

She ordered room-service dinner, and ate alone on her verandah as the twinkling lights of the Akaroa settlement disappeared in the distance. She no longer wanted the company of Blake. Pleasant though he was, he couldn't compare with the maturity of Robert.

Where was all this going?

Carol woke feeling at peace with herself. *Not quite halfway through the cruise*, she mused, *and I think the job is done.*

She was happy with her own company. Maybe she would find another soulmate, maybe she wouldn't. But she had woken up knowing for sure that she would never again make the mistakes she had in the past. The ghosts of Arthur and Justin and their infidelities were dead and buried.

She could have an uncomplicated, friendly and even mildly romantic relationship with pleasant men like Dave, Bruce and Blake. Things didn't need to get heavy. As for Robert Forbes, he had indicated that friendship was all he could offer her, and she should relax and enjoy the offering. Yes. She, Carol Ellington, was back in control and it felt good.

Seeing other couples on the cruise ship, she realised how fortunate she had been to have that untainted special first-love experience with Paul. The memories were precious and irreplaceable.

Recalling Robert and Lesley's enthusiasm, and adding her own curiosity, she had booked herself on the all-day *Lord of the Rings* tour from the city of Wellington.

Her tour group met in the main foyer, and were told there was a delay in their departure. The reason soon became apparent. Two paramedics appeared carrying a stretcher bearing an ashen-faced woman, followed by her anxious husband who, in turn, was followed by a crew member carrying two suitcases.

The ambulance pulled away from the foot of the gangplank as Carol and her tour party started from the top.

'That looks like the end of the cruise for those two,' said Blake.

A minibus, complete with local tour guide Marguerite, awaited the small group. The head count completed, the bus wound its way through the busy working port of Wellington and out through the security gates.

'Welcome to you all, on this *Lord of the Rings* tour,' began Marguerite. 'As you probably know, all three films of the trilogy were filmed in New Zealand, using our spectacular countryside and scenery. Regrettably, we cannot see all the sites on a one-day tour, but we can show you several.'

Half an hour later, as Marguerite walked them through a part of Mount Victoria, hardly more than a stone's throw from the city, Carol felt a sudden flash go through her. She could hardly wait to tell Robert that she had walked through the part of the Hobbiton Woods where the hobbits hid from the Black Riders.

Later, visiting the Weta Film Studios in Wellington, Carol tried to put these thoughts behind her. She knew she could do it, but something still niggled. She was unable to press the delete button as far as Robert was concerned. Thoughts of him appeared out of the blue like an unwanted pop-up on the computer.

Marguerite warned the group to eat well at the lunch provided, as they had a full afternoon ahead of them. It was good advice, and Carol and Blake shared a table, talking animatedly about the thrill of experiencing firsthand *Lord of the Rings* locations.

'I'll join you and the others this evening,' she told him.

The tour bus stopped next at the Hutt River, which was the great River Anduin of the film. Later at Harcourt Park, they visited the Gardens of Isengard. Carol made a mental note that she would tell Robert (that damn pop-up again) that she could almost see the orcs among the trees.

Their final visit was to the Kaitoke Regional Park, an ancient New Zealand native rainforest. Despite her tiredness, Carol could visualise the elves living there.

Marguerite looked at her watch. 'It's back to the cruise ship, ladies and gentlemen. We've run out of time.'

Carol had a leisurely shower to relieve her aching feet. As the warm water cascaded over her, she thought about the evening ahead with the single cruisers. It was all going well. She had scarcely finished dressing, when there was a knock on her cabin door. Annoyed that she had let slip her cabin number to Blake, Carol opened it, still towelling her wet hair. The towel and her jaw dropped, when she saw who it was.

'Why, Robert … What are you doing here? How on earth …?'

He cut her short. 'I'm here to take you to dinner tonight. It will be a change from Bob's Grill.' He offered her his arm.

'Wait on.' Tossing the towel on the bed, Carol's heart leapt as she quickly grabbed her purse. Her heart continued its acrobatic tricks and she was scarcely aware of the other people as they entered the lift. His arm protectively around her shoulder, she couldn't help but lean hard against him. 'You have some explaining to do, Robert. You're sure you are not here for extra help before the auditions?' she bantered.

The lift stopped and he guided her out, still holding her close.

Carol looked around. 'This isn't the level for the restaurant.'

'I know', Robert murmured. 'We don't want people around us this evening. I've booked an alcove in the specialty Italian boutique restaurant. Izzy told me you fancy all things Italian.'

Carol felt her face redden as she recalled Michelangelo's David in the Florence brochure, now at the bottom of the suitcase she'd left at the pub.

Sitting side by side at a table for two in a discreet alcove with a curved window overlooking the dark boiling waves below, Robert told his story. 'Maggie and I had a deep and meaningful two days after you left. I told her how much I was missing you. Maggie gave me a lecture on how I was letting my disastrous marriage with Penny blight the possibility of any future relationship. I realised she was right.' Carol's heart stopped beating. She couldn't breathe. The world stood still. She couldn't take her eyes off Robert's lips.

He took Carol's hand in his. 'What's more, I was imagining you on a cruise ship being romanced by every eligible bachelor in sight. I was afraid I would lose you.'

Carol's heart came back to life and took a leap. She forced herself to sit patiently, listening to words she had not expected to hear.

'As you know, Maggie and the cruise line's Sydney agent are old mates and talk with each other frequently. Maggie learnt yesterday that a couple were leaving the ship at Wellington, as the lady had appendicitis and needed surgery. The agent was more than happy to have a single person take over the empty cabin for the rest of the cruise. Maggie arranged an instant flight, and here I am.'

He squeezed her hand gently. 'This is not to put pressure on you, Carol. I merely thought it would give us the opportunity to get to know each other. You have your cabin, and I have mine. Of course, I'll understand if you prefer to be alone. The last thing I want is to be a nuisance.'

Carol gazed into his eyes and saw only tenderness and concern. She laughed. A weight had been lifted from her shoulders. She didn't have to rush into anything. She had found her romance equilibrium.

The reply was from the new Carol. 'It couldn't be better, Robert. I'd love to share the experiences of the cruise with you. I'm not sure where I want our relationship to go ... but I know that I would like to get to know you better.' Scarcely whispering, she added, 'I tried not to, but I missed you, too.'

And then she felt herself enveloped by a strong pair of arms and kissed gently as if a butterfly's wing grazed her forehead. She raised her face and soft lips met hers. She stayed motionless and, new Carol or not, she felt a stirring deep in her belly in as Robert's lips pressed harder with an urgency that beckoned to the very essence of her being. Her lips responded and she was suspended in an eternity of bliss – calm and simultaneously exploding with fireworks.

'Hmm Hmm.'

Carol opened her eyes to see a pair of hands holding two menus. She eased back from Robert, who smiled into her eyes and murmured, 'One thing at a time, Carol darling.' He released her slowly, yet she felt still embraced.

The meal and life beyond would be gently paced and delicious. And Carol knew already that she would not be alone when she visited Florence.

The Italian waiter smiled at them both, raised his eyes heavenwards and sighed, 'L'amore.'

Heart Swings

RENEE CONOULTY

'It's in here somewhere.' Brooke McDonald plonked her handbag on the seat beside her at J'Adore Travel Boutique. She rifled through it, pulled out an envelope and retrieved the cream card from within.

Maggie, the travel agent, stifled a giggle.

'I know. It doesn't look much like a wedding invitation. My cousin has a silly sense of humour.' Brooke ran her finger over the metallic-red embossed font — *We're going to Thai the knot* — then opened the card to check the dates.

'Chiang Mai is lovely in February. How long do you want to stay?' Maggie's nails clicked on the keyboard.

'Maybe a week?' Brooke glanced around the room. The bold colours of the vintage posters caught her eye. She'd always wanted to go to Italy or France. 'I'm a bit nervous about travelling overseas alone.'

'I *love* travelling alone … but if you're worried, I can book you in with a tour

89

group who do hotel transfers.' Maggie passed her the Thailand brochure. 'There are a few options. What kind of sightseeing would you like to do? You could do a day tour to the Tiger Temple or ride an elephant?'

'No.' A documentary on elephant training showing the poor animals were drugged or beaten had stayed with Brooke. She didn't want to perpetuate that type of tourism.

'Are you into history? You could visit the bridge over the River Kwai?'

'Not my thing.' Looking over the side of a bridge was as bad as flying – she didn't need to put herself through that as well.

'What about a Thai cooking class?'

'Maybe.' Her mum had suggested that too.

'Or trekking through the hill tribes? I found a great tour package the other day … let me find it.' Maggie opened another brochure.

Brooke studied the description. Wandering along remote mountain tracks, the birds calling from the trees, peace and tranquillity… a proper holiday. 'That sounds more like it,' she said. 'I think I'll do the overnight one.'

'There's a trek finishing two days *before* the wedding or one leaving the morning after. Which would you prefer?'

'I'd prefer the one after.' Brooke sank back in her chair as Maggie finalised her booking. Her parents would be happy. She'd given them excuse after excuse as to why she shouldn't go, but Brooke had never been able to say no to her mum and dad.

The next three months flew by in a blur of Christmas, New Year and Australia Day celebrations: food, alcohol and fireworks blended with torn wrapping paper, empty paracetamol packets and Brooke's mum nagging her dad to 'clean the barbecue, already'.

Then, all too soon, it was time to go.

'Dad, you didn't have to come. I was going to call a taxi.' Brooke's stomach dropped as they drove into the airport car park. She was really going to do this.

'Why waste money on a taxi when I can drive you? I would've driven you all the way to Sydney if you'd asked.'

'I didn't want to put you out.'

Brooke's father hauled her suitcase out of the boot. 'I'll sit with you until boarding time.'

'You don't have to do that.' Brooke popped the handle out and kissed her dad on the cheek.

'I'll just wait in the car, then. Your mother would shoot me if I went home before the plane took off.'

'Oh, don't do that. You can sit with me if you like.' Brooke slowed her pace so her dad could keep up. 'Your back playing up again?'

'Bugger of a thing.' He paused to stretch. 'Thanks for going to your cousin's wedding. I'd never cope sitting that long on the plane.'

'Wish you and Mum were coming. It'd be good for her to see something outside New South Wales.'

'We'd never get her into one of those jumbo jet things, let alone the bug-smasher you're going in today. She's even worse with flying than you are.'

'I know.' Brooke patted her dad on the arm. 'I'll take lots of photos.'

'Can you watch my handbag, Dad?' Brooke said after she'd checked in and they'd found a seat to wait. 'I'll be back soon.'

'Back in a flush?'

Brooke smiled. 'Yep. Too-da-loo.' She waggled her fingers over her shoulder as she walked away. They'd done that routine since she was five.

When she returned to her seat, a backpack was sitting on the seat beside her father. 'Whose is that?'

'Young bloke who was sitting over there.' Her dad gestured to the next row of seats. 'He asked me to watch it for him while he went to the loo.'

'Do you know him?' Brooke's brow crinkled.

'No, but he looked a bit nervous. Probably worried about flying, like you.'

'You can't just look after strangers' bags at the airport, Dad.' Brooke stood. 'It's dangerous. I'm getting security.'

'But he seemed like—'

Brooke strode away.

₮

Beep. Beep.

A car horn. Ryan Thompson glanced back up the hall towards the toilet then grabbed his bags and headed to the front door.

Dammit, the taxi's early.

'Bye, Mum,' he called as he passed the lounge room.

'See you later, darling.' She met him in the hallway and planted a kiss on his cheek.

'Are you sure Dad'll be okay while I'm away?'

'He'll be fine for a few days. You've been such a help already, getting the business back in order. You go have some fun.'

Fun. That was scarce in a tiny town like Heart Springs. Ryan couldn't wait to get out of there.

The fifteen-minute drive to the airport seemed to take forever. Ryan squirmed in his seat. Not even his Facebook feed could hold his attention.

'PayWave or swipe?' the driver asked when they finally pulled up at the regional airport.

Whatever's faster. 'PayWave, thanks.' Ryan bounced his heel while the payment processed then leapt out of the taxi.

Thank god there's no queue.

The check-in process was relatively fast. He strode through to the waiting area and took a seat, crossing his legs as he scanned the room for the toilet sign. His gaze stopped on a pair of long, milky white legs then followed the curve of calves, up firm thighs that disappeared into a pair of tight black shorts. Another biological need took over. Ryan stood. Who was she? She must be on her way home. She looked way more interesting than the country girls he'd seen around town.

He watched as she slipped the handbag strap off her shoulder and placed her bag in the vacant seat beside an older man. He took a step towards her, but as he got closer, she strode away, never once looking in his direction.

'You all right?'

Ryan looked down. He hadn't realised he'd continued walking. The older man was looking up at him, a slight frown on his face.

'Um, yes. No. I need the men's.' A bead of sweat formed on Ryan's top lip.

'It's over there.' The man waved in the direction the woman had gone.

Ryan's stomach cramped. 'Mind if I leave this here?' Ryan dropped his backpack onto the nearest seat.

'Sure.' The man nodded. 'You'll be fine. Flying is safer than driving.'

In the men's, Ryan ran damp hands through his hair and checked his reflection. Scruffy stubble covered his jaw line. He should have shaved but he was enjoying the break from his usual corporate look. He'd come to Heart Springs three months ago to help his father and the one time he'd turned up at work with a two-day growth, his father had lectured him for twenty minutes about first impressions and business etiquette. Then sent him home to shave. He'd shave for his mate's wedding but the rest of this Thailand trip would be razor-free.

Ryan dried his hands, balled up the paper towel and aimed for the bin. *Score.* He raised his hands to the empty room, grinning as he imagined a stadium full of applause. Hopefully, the woman would be back and he could get a proper look at her ... and he had a great excuse to talk to her when he picked up his bag.

Stepping through the doorway, he glanced over to the row of seats and the grin dropped off his face. Two security guards stood beside his bag, scanning the room. The older man he'd spoken to stood a few metres to the left, the woman by his side. The man pointed to Ryan.

Shit.

One of the security guards approached Ryan. 'Is that your bag over there, sir?'

'Yeah.'

'Come with me, please.' The security guard walked back to Ryan's bag and Ryan followed. 'You can't leave your bag unattended at the airport. It's against security policy.'

'It wasn't unattended. That man agreed to watch it for me.'

'He said he'd never met you before. Are you willing to show us the contents of your bag? If you refuse, we need to call the police and you'll miss your flight.'

Ryan's shoulders slumped. 'I've got nothing to hide.' He unzipped his bag.

'Not here. Take your bag over there.' The guard gestured to a table beside the x-ray scanner.

Ryan closed his bag and glanced over at the woman. She glared at him. He smiled sheepishly then followed the security guards and unpacked the contents onto the table under the watchful gaze of a guard. The guard tapped a plastic wand over Ryan's belongings, testing for explosives.

'All good. You can repack your bag and carry on with your journey. Just remember to keep your bag with you at all times in the airport.' The security guard went back to his post beside the metal detector.

Ryan shoved everything back into his backpack and stood at the back of the room, away from the gaze of the other passengers. Head down, he boarded the plane. Careful not to bump any of the other passengers, he found the emergency exit row seat he'd requested. The flight to Sydney was just over an hour, but the extra legroom would make the trip more comfortable. The last time he'd flown in a regular seat the flight attendant made a point of bumping into his leg every time she went past. He sat in the aisle seat and got settled: water bottle in the seat pocket, bag under the seat and fitness magazine in hand.

'Excuse me. Can I get past?'

Ryan tucked his legs to the side and glanced up. A familiar pair of figure-hugging black shorts filled his gaze. His eyes dropped to her toned thighs then scanned back up her body. It was *her*.

∽

'Oh, it's *you*.' Brooke edged away from her seat companion. Of all the people she could have sat next to, she was stuck with the idiot who left his bag unattended at the airport. *Seriously, who would do something that stupid?* Brooke had barely been anywhere, but even *she* knew that.

She scanned the plane, spotting a couple of vacant seats a few rows back. But why should she surrender her extra legroom seat? She glanced at the man sitting next to her. Even with the extra room, his knees almost touched the seat in front.

'Hi, I'm Ryan.' His voice pulled her attention. 'Sorry about that bag thing before. I wasn't thinking straight.'

'You can say that again.' She should have asked for the single seat on the left.

'Well, we all do stupid things, sometimes.' He shrugged. 'So, where are you going?'

'Um, we're all going to Sydney.' *Is this guy a bit thick or something?*

He pulled at his collar. 'That came out wrong. I meant—'

'Excuse me, have you both flown in the emergency exit row before?' The flight attendant interrupted their stilted conversation, showing them how to open the emergency exits before continuing with the general safety demonstration.

As the engines rumbled and the plane began to move, Brooke clung to the armrest and stared out the window. They were still on the ground. She inhaled deeply, releasing the air through pursed lips.

'You okay?' Ryan tapped Brooke's arm.

The sudden touch made her flinch. 'Yeah. Just a bit nervous. This is the second time I've flown anywhere.' Brooke plugged her ear buds into her phone, double checked it was in aeroplane mode and cued the guided meditation her mum had suggested.

'It's only a short flight. You'll be fine. Do you want to chat to keep your mind off it?'

Brooke rolled her ear buds between her fingertips as she considered. Ryan ran his knuckles over his jaw line then fiddled with his watch band. Maybe he was as nervous as she was. Her dad had said he thought Ryan was scared of flying and that's why he'd rushed off without his bag. He would want her to help Ryan. She pushed a tight-lipped smile onto her face. 'Sure.'

℘

He'd travelled with plenty of people who were scared of flying. Her white knuckles and wide eyes were a dead giveaway. Take off was the worst, except for turbulence of course, and distraction often helped. Small talk wasn't Ryan's forte, though.

'What's your earliest childhood memory?' He watched her face closely. Hopefully, it was a good memory or he might have buggered up again.

Her eyes softened. 'The earliest thing I can remember is talking to my pretend friend on the shoebox phone Mum helped me make. Mum told me I had to call her up and tell her that she couldn't come play that day because I'd been naughty.'

Ryan chuckled. 'What had you done?'

'I'd eaten all the red lollies off Dad's birthday cake. Mum had spent ages decorating it for his party that afternoon.' Brooke's hands relaxed and she turned her body to face him. 'So, what's your earliest memory?'

Ryan tapped his fingers on the armrest between them. 'Hmm.' The engines roared and the plane picked up speed. 'My earliest memory would be when I was in preschool.' Ryan felt a sudden pressure on his hand. Brooke had gripped the armrest and trapped his fingers. 'It was story time and we were all sitting on the mat while the teacher read one of those giant picture books. Did you have them too?'

Brooke nodded. Her fingers gripped tighter as the plane accelerated. He

95

stroked her little finger with his thumb.

'Well, I was sitting up the back with my best friend, Georgia, and we must have decided that the story was boring because we got up and walked outside, down to the cubby house at the back of the playground. I don't really remember whose idea it was, but we decided to try kissing. On the lips. It was only a quick peck, but when we finished, the whole class was standing there watching us. The teacher too.'

Brooke's whole body tensed as the plane lifted off. 'Did you get in trouble?'

'Yeah. We both missed out on painting that afternoon.'

Brooke wiped her palms on her shorts. 'So, you weren't scared of cooties?'

'I've never been scared of cooties.'

&

The flight was smoother than Brooke expected. Her phone lay forgotten in her lap as she chatted with Ryan about their childhoods: both were only children, had a pretend friend and had devoured Enid Blyton's Secret Seven series. They were still sharing primary school tales when the plane landed.

'That flight was okay, hey?' Ryan asked.

'Yeah, it was.' Brooke's shoulders relaxed as the plane taxied in.

Ryan picked up his backpack. 'Have fun in Sydney.'

'I'm not here for long, but it will be fun having my feet on the ground for a little while.'

They followed the other passengers into the building to wait for their checked luggage.

Ryan's bag came through first. 'Maybe we'll run into each other in Heart Springs?'

'Maybe.' Brooke's bag trundled past her on the carousel as she watched Ryan walk away. She would have given him her number if he'd asked. But he hadn't. He hadn't even asked her name. Grabbing her suitcase the next time it came past, she strode to the meeting point for the international terminal shuttle bus.

After checking in for her Bangkok flight, Brooke found a quiet corner in a coffee shop for a bite to eat. She spent a couple of hours people watching, scrolling Facebook and daydreaming. Now that she'd finally slowed down, her career dilemma pushed into her thoughts. What should she do?

She loved working at The Tea Lady café – she was their best barista – but she couldn't work in a café forever.

She'd almost finished the business degree her parents wanted her to do. The part-time online course had been dragging on for years, but once it was done, her Mum planned to train her up to take over the family nursery business. She'd been learning about plants since she was born.

Her best friend, Lisa, left Heart Springs right after high school and had been bugging her to move to Sydney ever since. She called a couple of weeks ago to offer Brooke a management role and a room in her inner city flat. Her one-woman business was rapidly expanding and she said it was an opportunity Brooke couldn't refuse.

Lisa knew her just as well as her parents did and they each swore their suggestion was the best. But which one was? The pressure to choose was doing her head in. After the wedding, she would have two days in the blissful peace and quiet of the Thai mountains where she could stroll along the track and figure out whose advice to take.

The wedding was in two days. There were no direct flights to Chiang Mai, so she was staying overnight in Bangkok then catching the connecting flight the next day. Her cousin had already arrived and had a girls' pamper day planned. By the time she got there, she'd be in need of pampering. Brooke glanced at her chipped nail polish. Hopefully, she'd make it through the wedding without breaking a nail. It was a minor miracle that they were all relatively the same length. She'd never manage that working in the nursery.

When she boarded the plane, she couldn't help wishing Ryan was there to hold her hand during take-off.

∞

Ryan lugged his bag out to the café near the Arrivals entrance.

'Hey, Thommo!' The man stood and slapped Ryan on the shoulder. 'Ugly as ever.'

'Your mother never thought so.' Ryan dropped the suitcase handle, returned the shoulder slap and pulled up a chair at the table. 'How've you been, Clarky?'

'Yeah.' Clarky shrugged. 'I'll shout you a coffee and we can catch up. Still drinking double shots?'

'Yep, double shot cappuccino would be great.'

'Back in a tick.' Clarky ambled up to the counter, returning soon after with their coffees.

'So, how you coping back with the olds?' Clarky asked.

'It's not so bad. Need to get my own space soon, though.' Ryan scooped up a spoonful of foam then took a sip.

'Dunno if I'd cope going back home. But, I think I'd give it a good go if I had the family business handed to me on a platter.'

'It's not on a platter, mate, and I'm not sure I'll take it.'

'You'd be an idiot to knock that back … but then you are a bit of a knob, sometimes. Heard you and Janette broke up.'

'Yeah. She refused to leave Sydney and wouldn't consider long distance. Said she'd go insane in a boring country town like Heart Springs. I'd rather be back here too. But, I couldn't say no to Dad after his business partner died. How do you say no to a grieving man?'

'I hear ya.' Clarky sipped his coffee. 'Wish I was going to Thailand with you. Heidi's due any day now, so I'm not game to leave town. Make sure you send my best to Fitzy for me.'

'Will do. Still can't believe you're gonna be a dad soon.' By this time next week, Ryan would be the only one out of their uni trio – Clarky, Fitzy and himself – who was still single.

'Yeah, I can hardly believe it. I still feel like a kid myself.'

Ryan tugged at his own thick hair. 'You don't look like a kid.'

Clarky touched his balding scalp. 'Eff off.'

Ryan grinned then glanced at his watch. 'I've got an hour until I need to check in at the international terminal.'

'No worries. I'll give you a lift over when we're done.'

∞

The flight from Bangkok to Chiang Mai was quick. Brooke had booked a room in the same hotel the bride, her cousin Nicola, was staying in. All the female wedding guests were staying in that hotel and the men were booked into one down the road. Even though Nicola and Todd lived together, they wanted to maintain some traditions, like not seeing each other before the wedding.

98

Brooke was relieved. She didn't know Todd's family and she'd never met Thommo, Todd's mate from uni, so she was happy to hang out with the girls.

The afternoon pampering session couldn't come too soon. The respite from the heat in the air-conditioned massage room itself was bliss, let alone the talented masseuse's hands. Chiang Mai was a tad cooler than Bangkok but the unfamiliar humidity was harder to bear than the hottest New South Wales summer.

'I could do this every day.' Brooke struggled to speak, her cheeks compressed against the edges of the massage table peephole. The floral scent of the massage oils filled her lungs, finally overpowering the traces of pungent Bangkok air that still clung to her hair.

'Mmm.' Nicola's voice drifted through the closed curtain. 'I had one last night too.'

Forty-five minutes later, the six women sat side by side, feet soaking and fingers outstretched. The Thai beauticians chatted among themselves, every now and then asking about nail polish colour preferences in heavily accented English.

Brooke blew on her nails, holding her fingers out stiffly. The French manicure made her nails look even longer and the hand-painted white flower on her ring finger was stunning. The women had all got matching manicures, each with a feature nail. The bride-to-be had diamantes on hers.

'Now back to the hotel for pre-dinner cocktails,' Nicola announced when they were all done, 'then I'm going to bed straight after dinner. I have to get up before the sun tomorrow.'

'Why so early? You told us we're getting picked up after lunch,' Becky, Nicola's sister, asked.

'It's part of the Thai traditions. We're going to the markets to buy food for the monks who come past every morning so they'll give us their blessings.'

'Well, you can go to bed and I'll send you blessings from the bar,' Becky laughed.

Brooke had never seen a bridal mini bus before. Limousines, vintage cars and regular sedans decked out bridal-style plenty of times, but the white ribbon stretching up from the short bonnet was almost comical.

'Hi, girls. Jump in. We have to pick up the boys, then we're heading to the temple,' Nicola called from the first bench seat, where she was perched next to Todd.

Brooke clambered into the back of the van and sat next to her aunt.

'We're already married!' Nicola held up a colourful certificate. 'We signed all the papers at the city hall. At least, I hope we're married.' She giggled and passed the certificate back to her mother. Brooke could only read their names; the rest of the certificate was in Thai.

'You're married, I promise,' Jit, the wedding coordinator, reassured.

Last night, during pre-dinner drinks, Nicola had relayed the story of how she'd met Todd at a swing dancing class she'd been going to with her friend Janette. He'd taken Thommo as his wing man to meet women. And it worked. The four of them began double dating.

Janette had confided she was a bit nervous about seeing Thommo again. She'd dumped him because he was moving back to 'some boring little town in the middle of nowhere' and she'd refused to leave the city to follow him. She'd confessed that she was seriously considering hooking up with him at the wedding, though. For old times' sake.

The van stopped to pick up the rest of the groom's party. Brooke waved to her uncle and cousin as they boarded. The next two men had to be the groom's brother and father. They all had the same widow's peak, though the older man's had receded more than either of his sons'. That meant the last guy would be Thommo. Brooke watched Janette sit up straighter, thrust out her chest and look out the window. Brooke smirked then looked up to see Thommo's reaction.

Her smirk dropped.

That wasn't Thommo, it was the guy from the plane.

Ryan.

❧

Ryan hesitated at the bottom step. He was over Janette – she'd been lots of fun, but that's all it was. Convenient and fun. Right? Maybe they could do convenient and fun again, for old times' sake?

'C'mon, Thommo,' Nicola beckoned, her face radiant.

Ryan forced a smile on his face and continued onto the bus. 'So, can I call you Mrs Fitzy yet?'

'Yep.' She waved a colourful certificate at him.

'Onya, mate.' Ryan reached past Nicola and shook Todd's hand. He scanned the bus for an empty seat, spotting one in the back row directly behind Janette. She was staring determinedly out the window, obviously trying to ignore him. Or maybe playing one of her games. He'd never really figured her out. They were better off apart. He needed someone uncomplicated.

He took another step down the aisle and froze. The woman sitting across from Janette looked up and their eyes locked.

It was her. The woman from the plane.

Her eyes widened.

'What ... what are you doing here?' he asked, wiping a bead of sweat from his hairline.

'Um...' She pointed to the bride and groom. 'Going to a wedding.'

Suppressing a smile, he sat behind Janette. He leant across the aisle and tried to get plane-girl's attention. 'Hey.'

Janette turned instead. 'Oh, hello, Ryan.' She practically purred as she swung sideways and placed her hand on his knee.

Nicola clapped. 'Attention!'

Ryan slid back into his seat and Janette's hand dropped off his knee. He looked up to see what the bride had to say but his gaze never made it past plane-girl.

'I've got a surprise for everyone,' Nicola announced as the bus pulled up outside a shop. 'We've organised traditional Thai outfits for all of you so we can all match. We're stopping here, then onto the temple.'

A destination wedding is one thing, but a fancy-dress wedding. Really?

A few minutes later, the bus pulled up and everyone got off. Plane-girl rolled her eyes at him as she followed the women into a side room. Ryan shook his head in return then continued, with the other men, into a room at the back of the shop. The wedding would carry on for the rest of the day. He'd get a chance to talk to her soon.

෨෧

Brooke followed the bride and groom into the teak Buddhist temple. She hitched up the form-fitting pale blue silk skirt, exposing her ankles, as she climbed the timber steps. Nicola had bustled everyone back onto the bus as soon as they were dressed so Brooke hadn't had the chance to talk to Ryan yet.

101

'They look like peasants,' Janette whispered, nodding towards the men, all dressed in identical brown fisherman's pants and beige shirts. She nodded at Ryan, who looked uncomfortable in the unfamiliar get-up. 'I reckon those baggy pants will look better on my hotel room floor tonight.' Janette raised her eyebrows then giggled.

Before Brooke could respond, Jit called for attention. 'Everybody, it is time. Please sit here.' Jit pointed to the wooden floor in front of a flower covered dais. She helped the bride and groom get settled on the floor, then sat down beside them.

Brooke copied her, tucking her legs around to the side.

'Oh, I can't get down on the floor like that,' Janette said. 'Thommo, can you help me?'

Brooke rolled her eyes at the blatant ploy. It wasn't like Janette had to balance on those ridiculously high heels she'd worn – everyone had taken off their shoes before they entered the temple.

Ryan held Janette's hand to steady her as she lowered herself to the floor.

'Thommo, you can sit here. I'll need a hand to get back up too.' Janette patted the floor next to her.

He did as he was told, a sheepish look on his face. 'Is it your ankle?'

'Yeah. It's healed but the flexibility hasn't come back.' Janette trailed her fingers over her ankle.

'Can you dance on it? I'd love to see you dance again.'

Brooke's gaze slipped over to Ryan. Was he really going to fall for that?

'I can dance if you're gentle with me.' Janette looked up over her lashes at Ryan. 'Oh, I'm being so rude. Thommo, have you met Brooke?'

'Brooke.' Ryan reached out to shake her hand.

'Ryan.' His handshake was firm, his fingers enveloping hers. He brushed his thumb over the back of her hand, just like he had on the plane. And just like on the plane, she didn't want him to stop.

'But I didn't tell you his—' Janette said.

'Sh, sh, sh.' Jit hushed everyone as a man wearing orange robes sat cross-legged before the newlyweds.

Brooke sighed inwardly. Once again, they had missed their chance to talk.

The ceremony was beautiful, though Brooke couldn't understand a word of it, apart from Jit's brief whispered translations. A blessing for this, a blessing for that. Lots of rituals – pouring water together, drawing white dots on their foreheads and tying strings around their wrists. The monk flicked water everywhere, blessing the whole wedding party. He placed a necklace over Todd's head but practically threw one at Nicola's head with a stick.

There was a movement in Brooke's periphery. She glanced over to see Ryan covering his mouth, his eyes crinkled at the sides. He dropped his hand and mouthed 'cooties'.

Brooke snorted.

Jit turned sharply, holding her finger to her lips.

ᘓ

The blessings continued after the temple: releasing birds and fish blessings; blessings from village elders; blessings of banana leaves and sugar cane; knotted string blessings; and viewing the nuptial bed blessings. Ryan was blessed out – apart from food and alcohol blessings.

Barefoot, he followed the village elders down the stairs. The two-storey traditional stilt house had been converted into a wedding reception venue, and local elders had been invited to the last part of the wedding – to give their blessings, of course. The Thai elders sat in a circle on the floor; Ryan joined the group of Aussies in their own circle, surrounding a Thai feast of vegetable and meat dishes to share and individual bowls of sticky rice for each guest.

'Where are the forks?' Ryan asked.

'No forks, mate,' Todd said.

Dammit. Not chopsticks. I suck at chopsticks.

'You eat like this.' Jit spooned some curry into her bowl of rice then scooped it up with her fingers.

You've got to be kidding.

Apparently not. Ryan tilted his head back and dropped some food in. He stopped chewing when he saw Brooke huddled with the women on the other side of the circle, mimicking Jit's actions. She giggled, licked the sauce from her fingers then scooped up another mouthful. Sitting on the floor, eating with her fingers and she was having a ball. Ryan dug his fingers into the bowl, snagged a slippery bit of chicken and shoved it in his mouth.

Strange, but fun.

After dinner, Todd and Nicola took centre stage for their first dance as a married couple. The whole wedding had been traditional Thai Buddhist, but the wedding dance was swing, with moves perfectly choreographed to the music. It seemed like they were gliding around on a perfectly polished sprung floor, rather than barefoot on tiles.

Janette sidled up beside him. 'Want to dance the next one?'

'Sure.' Ryan's naked toes were twitching. He hadn't danced in months. Not since he'd left Sydney.

The next song began. Ryan took Janette's hand and led her out onto the dance floor. He wrapped his right arm around her back and waited for the intro to finish. He breathed in coconut and nectarine. His feet danced instinctively, his arms swept her around the dance floor. Ryan didn't think about the dance moves, they just happened. When they danced, Janette felt like an extension of him. Connected.

Why weren't they still together? Ryan almost had the business sorted. If he could find someone else to partner with his father and take on half the client base, he could move back to Sydney. To the city, the beach, the fun. Where he could dance again. Would she wait for him? Was he just trying to convince himself she was just a bit of fun?

Ryan wrapped Janette in his arms, dipping her low as the final beats of the song played. As he lifted her back onto her feet, he glanced over her shoulder. Brooke was staring at them, eyes wide.

He remembered feeling like that the first time he saw people swing dancing. The rush of endorphins the first time he danced a whole song. Suddenly, he wanted to share that feeling with Brooke, to see her face light up, to hold her hand again. He would ask her to dance.

As the music faded, he pulled away from Janette. 'Thanks for the dance.'

Janette stretched up on her toes and whispered, 'I need to talk to you.'

Ryan looked at Janette, then over to Brooke. 'Okay. Can it wait till later?'

Janette looked over her shoulder then back to Ryan. Her eyes narrowed. 'No. I need to talk to you now.'

Giving Brooke a what-can-you-do look, he followed his ex into the darkness of the night.

ॐ

Brooke tapped her foot in time to the music. She knew Nicola and Todd met at swing dance classes but Brooke had no idea what swing dancing was. She could line dance and two-step at the country dances back home but this was something else. The bride and groom stepped and tapped and twisted and kicked in what seemed like random rhythms, their bodies moving fluidly together. Then Janette and Ryan.

Wow.

The way Janette moved. Her hips twisting, a flirtatious pout on her face, the way she ran her fingertips down Ryan's arm. Brooke wanted to dance like that and she wanted to dance like that with Ryan. Hopefully, he'd ask her. She thought he was about to when she caught him looking at her over Janette's shoulder.

He didn't. Instead, he disappeared with Janette.

The music changed to a more modern mix and a couple of people got up to dance. Brooke wandered over to the drinks table and poured herself another glass of bubbly, keeping an eye out for Ryan. Maybe she could ask him to dance when he came back? She didn't feel comfortable asking the groom to dance and it would be a bit difficult with Nicola attached to his side.

Jit turned down the music and clapped her hands. 'Time for Nicola and Todd's fireworks. Put your shoes on and come out to the front.'

A Catherine wheel spun and fireworks shot into the sky: reds and yellows and greens. The noise must have caught Ryan and Janette's attention. They wandered over from the tropical garden at the side of the house. They'd probably been making their own fireworks. Janette's hair looked tousled.

Maybe she'd got what she wanted. Brooke felt like that one firework that had misfired, sputtering around in the dirt.

୫

'For old times' sake?' Janette purred, pressing her body up against Ryan.

Now that they were off the dance floor, the endorphin rush of dancing subsided and reality kicked back in. 'I don't do casual sex.' He caught her hand and brought their clasped hands up as a barrier between them.

'It doesn't have to be casual. Find another accountant to be your dad's partner and then you can come back to the city, where you belong. I miss you.'

Ryan's parents had taken a tree change a couple of years back, moving away from Sydney once Ryan had finished his accountancy degree. Four months ago, his father's business partner, Frank, had a stroke and had been left with

105

permanent damage to the fronto-parietal cortex, which meant he couldn't process numbers. Ryan stepped in to help keep the business running and his father had offered Ryan the partnership, after a trial period. Joining the business when Frank retired was always on the table, but Ryan wasn't yet sure if it was the right move.

'I miss you too.' The words rolled off his tongue without a thought. Did he really miss her? Or did he just miss the dancing?

'A position's opened up at my uncle's firm. It's yours, if you want it.' Janette trailed her finger down his chest.

Ryan perked up. He was already bored in Heart Springs and this was the perfect excuse to go back to Sydney.

Family or fun?

Janette ran her other hand down his chest and under his shirt. She grappled with the folds of fabric at the top of his pants. 'Where's the button on these things?'

Ryan pushed her hand away. 'Not now. I need to think about it.' He didn't want to let his dad down, but he didn't want to be stuck in a boring little country town forever, either.

Red and green lit up the sky.

'Oooh, fireworks!' Janette looked up.

'C'mon.'

They joined the crowd at the front of the house to watch the rest of the fireworks. But Ryan's gaze strayed from the colourful sky and Janette, to the woman in the pale blue silk dress.

℘

The fireworks ended. Brooke kissed her cousin goodbye then boarded the mini bus to go back to the hotel. Ryan stepped on board. He looked her way and their gaze met. Brooke had an empty seat beside her. She wanted him to sit with her and chat like they had on the plane. To make her laugh again. To find out what other mischief he'd gotten up to as a kid.

'Ryan, darling, come sit with me.' Janette patted the vacant seat beside her.

He'd have to walk past Janette to get to Brooke.

Brooke dropped her gaze.

He sat with Janette.

The driver dropped off the women first, apart from Nicola, who'd stayed with Todd in the bridal suite at the reception venue. Brooke made her way to the front of the bus, sidestepping past Ryan so she didn't brush against his leg. He didn't fit very well in these tiny seats either.

'Bye, Brooke.' He looked up.

She stopped. 'Bye, Ryan.' She looked from Ryan to Janette, then back to Ryan. 'Are you coming, Janette?'

He moved his knees to the side to let Janette past.

'Not just yet.' Janette ran her finger down Ryan's arm. 'I need to do some more convincing. Ryan's dream job has just come up but for some silly reason, he's thinking of staying in some boring little town with his parents.' She turned to Ryan. 'Heart Springs is their dream, not yours. You'll go nuts there with nowhere to dance and no decent coffee.'

'No decent coffee' – what a load of rubbish. She's obviously never been to The Tea Lady. 'See you round, then.'

Brooke stared at the bus as it drove away. Her brow furrowed. Was Ryan the mysterious new guy in town people were talking about? Bob and Joan's son who'd come to help after Frank had a stroke? Not that it mattered – it didn't sound like he'd be around Heart Springs for long.

Disappointed, Brooke went straight to bed – she had to be up early for the trek's courtesy bus. She pushed thoughts of Ryan out of her mind but fell asleep running her thumb across the back of her hand.

Brooke suppressed a yawn as she stepped onto the courtesy bus. She was looking forward to this trek. Strolling along the quiet mountain paths away from all these damn mini buses … space and time to think. About to claim the window seat next to the woman in the first row, she noticed a familiar face a few rows back.

Ryan.

Part of her longed for the chance to stare out the window and daydream, but she couldn't resist the safety of sitting with someone she knew, even if he was back together with Janette.

'Hey, stranger.' She slid into the vacant seat beside Ryan.

'What are you doing here?' he asked.

'Um, going on a trek.' She smiled.

'Are you following me?'

'Of course not. I booked this trip months ago. Did you book yours in Heart Springs too?'

'Mmm hmm.' Ryan nodded.

'Well, we would've both used J'Adore, it's the only travel agency in town.'

'I saw the chick with the Bettie Page hairdo.'

'Bettie Page?' Brooke's brow furrowed.

'Yeah. She was a pin-up model in the '50s. Janette has a poster of her and often does her hair like that when she goes dancing. You know, dark hair, short fringe.' Ryan tapped the middle of his forehead. 'That '50s Rockabilly look.'

'I'm not sure what Rockabilly is, but I booked with Maggie and she had some kind of vintage dress on. And she did say she'd looked up this trekking tour recently. I'll bet it was her.'

'Small world, hey?' Ryan smiled.

'That's small towns for you.' Brooke wrapped her arm across her body. 'What do you think of Heart Springs? Are you planning to stick around?'

'Honestly,' Ryan angled his body towards her, 'it's boring. There's nothing to do. I think I'll head back to Sydney soon. There's nowhere to dance and I miss all the cafés and bars.'

'But there's always a band on at the pub on the weekend. It's a great place to dance.'

'I don't do country music.'

Snob. 'And there's an excellent café in town.' Brooke crossed her arms.

'The Tea Lady Café?' Ryan raised his eyebrows. 'I don't drink over-brewed pot coffee.'

Pot coffee? The café had an espresso machine and Brooke could make it sing. 'You've never even been in there, have you?'

'No offence, but country people can't make decent coffee.'

Any sentence that begins with 'no offence' is offensive.

'Whatever.' Brooke fished her phone out of her bag and plugged her ear buds in. 'I'm gonna chill for a bit.' She'd rather spend time with the psychopath in her audio book than talking to the arrogant arse beside her.

&

After lunch at a small restaurant, the driver dropped the group off in a small mountain village. This was the cushiest kind of hiking Ryan had ever done. He didn't even need to carry a proper pack. The driver was delivering their bags to each village they spent the night. All he had to carry was a small day pack with his water. The group set off at a moderate pace, spreading out along the track into small clusters. Brooke strode ahead of him, joining a couple of Swedish backpackers. The three women fell into step. Ryan longed to join them, just to walk beside Brooke. There was something about her that captivated him. Her long, toned legs, striding out in chunky boots and tiny shorts. Yes, those. But there was something else.

A spark. The way her eyes lit up when she was talking about dancing at the pub. He'd love to take her out in Sydney, to one of the huge swing balls to see hundreds of people dancing all at once. To teach her how to swing dance. To take her out for a *real* coffee. To see her eyes light up when he showed her what real fun was.

He'd have to get her to talk to him again first. She'd been avoiding him since he made those remarks about country people and coffee.

His feet crunched on the gravel track. Leaves rustled in the light breeze and unfamiliar birds called from the trees. Ryan barely noticed any of it, his mind occupied with Brooke.

The tour leader stopped and waited for everyone to gather. 'The village we stay at is some minutes' walk on other side of river,' he said. 'There is bridge ahead. It is strong, but only two at a time.'

Several bamboo poles spanned the river, lashed together with rope. A rickety bamboo handrail jutted out on one side.

Bridge? It looked like something the local boy scouts had whipped together.

The two Swedish girls crossed, shrieking as it swayed under their weight. They jumped down on the other side, then Brooke stepped onto the bridge. She edged across the river. She was almost halfway when she stopped, clinging to the rail with both hands.

This was it. His chance to rescue her, to win back her trust. And maybe she would hold his hand again. He stepped onto the bridge.

The tour guide looked him up and down then held up his hand. 'Maybe one at a time for you.'

∞

Brooke exhaled through pursed lips. Why had she looked down? This was worse than flying. She'd stepped onto the bridge without processing what she was doing. She'd seen Ryan getting closer and was trying to keep her distance. She was still mad at him for being rude about her job – not that she'd told him she was a barista. She clung to the railing with both hands.

I should have booked the cooking class like Mum suggested.

'Brooke.'

She turned. Ryan was standing on the edge of the bridge, towering over the guide who stood between them.

'I can't.' Her voice cracked. 'Help me.' She pried one hand from the railing, reaching towards Ryan. She needed him to hold her hand again and guide her to safety.

'You can do it. Look how far you've gone already.'

She kept her focus on the lengths of bamboo. She was almost halfway across. Why wasn't he coming to help her? She was distressed, dammit, and she needed to be rescued. She shuffled towards him.

The tour guide waved her away. 'No. That way.'

Chastened, Brooke took a step away from Ryan, glancing down to check her footing then screwing her eyes shut when she realised what she was doing. She felt safer holding on with two hands, so side stepped the rest of the way across the bridge, counting her steps to keep her mind busy.

Thea and Ingrid, the Swedish girls, embraced her when she reached the riverbank.

'You were so brave. If I know you were scared of heights, I would walk with you,' Ingrid said.

'Yah.' Thea nodded. 'I did not see your trouble until Aussie man call your name. I thought he would help you, but the guide would not let him. I was coming to help but then you ...' She gestured to the bridge.

So that's why he left me stranded.

'Here.' Ryan appeared beside her, holding out a bottle of water. 'You look like you need something stronger but that's all I've got.'

Brooke took a swig and gathered herself. 'Thanks.'

They continued to the village as a foursome.

After a simple dinner of rice, vegetables and chicken (she hoped it was chicken), Brooke wandered over to join the group at the campfire. The nights had been warm in Chiang Mai but up here in the mountains it was much cooler.

'I'd love to go to Sweden one day,' Ryan said. 'The biggest swing dance camp in the world is held in Herrang every year. Have you heard of it?' Ryan looked at Thea and Ingrid.

'Yah, we went last year,' Thea said.

'Can you Lindy?' Ingrid grabbed Ryan's forearm, her face glowing in the firelight.

'Yeah, a bit.' Ryan shrugged.

'He's amazing. I saw him dance at the wedding last night. You guys should dance.' Brooke said.

'But there's no music.' Ingrid frowned.

Ryan took Ingrid's right hand and bounced on the spot. He began to sing, making up nonsense words, and twirled Ingrid around.

'Want to try?' Thea held her hand out to Brooke.

'I don't know how to swing dance, but I can two-step.'

'I don't really know how to lead, so we can make up our own dance.' Thea took both Brooke's hands and they stepped side to side, in rhythm with Ryan's scatting.

'My turn,' Thea said after a few minutes, cutting in to dance with Ryan.

Ingrid danced with Brooke. She was better at leading and twirled Brooke around.

'So, are you and Ryan together?' Ingrid asked.

'No. We went to the same wedding and we both live in Heart Springs but we only met this week.'

'He's sexy. You should date him when you get home.'

Brooke glanced over Ingrid's shoulder at Ryan. Joy radiated from his face as he spun Thea.

'There's no point, he's moving back to Sydney soon.'

'Well, you should have a holiday fling. You were looking at him all day.'

Ingrid was right. Even though Brooke had been avoiding him, she'd been stealing glances every chance she got.

'Brooke's turn.' Ingrid grinned as she pushed Brooke towards Ryan.

He caught her hand and pulled her closer. 'I'm not doing any boot scootin'.' He twirled her around then took both her hands in his.

'Well, I can't swing.'

'We'll have to compromise then and just dance.'

He spun her again then held her close. The campfire warmed her back as they shuffled side to side on the dusty dirt dance floor.

Brooke rested her cheek on Ryan's chest. His heart thudded as fast as hers. He ran his thumb over the back of her hand, sending her heart rate racing. His hands felt so good. She lost herself in the moment, imagining him running his thumb over her jaw, over her collarbone, over her nipple ...

Maybe I should have a holiday fling like Ingrid suggested.

ဆ

Brooke sank into his arms. Her hair smelt like apples and wood smoke. They swayed side to side in the firelight, slowly dancing in circles to keep warm.

'Good night, you two. We're going to bed,' Ingrid said, linking arms with Thea.

'I'm not tired,' Brooke said, stifling a yawn.

Ryan didn't want to let go either, but they had a big day of hiking tomorrow. 'I saw that yawn. Come on, we'd better go too.'

Ryan released her hand but left his arm slung around her waist. They followed Ingrid and Thea into the communal sleeping quarters. An open plan timber room, the central walkway set lower than the sleeping surface. They passed closed curtains sectioning off other trekkers who were already asleep.

'Here's my stuff.' Brooke pointed to her bag.

'I'm in here.' Ryan nodded towards the cubicle next to Brooke's, his arm still around her waist.

'Well.'

'Yeah.'

They stood in silence for a moment longer. Ryan let his arm drop to his side. Brooke stepped up onto the raised floor and turned to pull the curtain closed. Her eyes, now level with his, were pools of black in the dim light. Her lips, slightly parted. So close.

No. I shouldn't.

Brooke paused, the curtain almost closed. 'Goodnight.'

He leant forward, closing the gap between them and pressed his lips lightly on hers. 'Sweet dreams.' His dreams would be more spicy than sweet tonight.

He stepped into his sleeping area, closed his curtain and sat on the thin mattress to unlace his boots. The curtain beside his rustled and he imagined Brooke peeling off her clothes. The urge to pull back the curtain and join her struck him but he pushed it away.

One kiss. That was it. He couldn't take it any further. He was going back to Sydney soon, there was no point starting anything with Brooke. She belonged in Heart Springs and he didn't.

℘

Brooke rolled her lips together, savouring his taste. That wasn't a night of passion kiss, it was a beginning kiss. She pulled back the hand-woven blankets and sat on the lumpy mattress, glad it was dark enough that she couldn't see them clearly. Beautifully crafted they may be, but she wasn't sure they were beautifully washed. She slipped off her boots and lay down.

'Don't let the bed bugs bite,' she whispered, sliding her hand across the floor and under the edge of the curtain.

Ryan ran his fingertips over her palm. Brooke closed her fingers over his, but his fingers slipped away and he was gone.

Brooke wanted to crawl under the curtain to reclaim his hand, and his mouth, and his... That was her hormones talking. She wrestled control of her mind back and looked at things rationally. He'd be going back to Sydney in a few weeks. Maybe she should take Lisa up on her job offer? Lisa and Ryan would be rapt, but her parents would be so disappointed. She resolved to talk to Thea and Ingrid in the morning and see what they thought. They could give her some unbiased advice.

Brooke peeked under the curtain when she woke, but Ryan wasn't there.

'Wake up sleepy, it's time for breakfast.' Thea and Ingrid poked their heads through the gap in the curtains.

Brooke rubbed the sleep from her eyes. 'Hey, can I ask you guys something?'

'Yah.' Thea and Ingrid nodded.

'You know how I'm trying to decide between working with my friend in Sydney or working with my parents ... well, now I'm even more confused. Ryan kissed me last night.'

Thea and Ingrid clambered through Brooke's curtain and huddled on her bed.

'Oooh. It's a sign.' Ingrid bounced. 'You have to work with your friend.

You can learn to swing dance and kiss Ryan every day.'

'No. It doesn't change anything.' Thea shook her head. 'Your family is more important and you love the country life. I can tell by the way you talk about your home.'

Brooke looked from Ingrid to Thea. 'So, what should I do?'

'Whatever makes you happy,' Ingrid said.

'Food makes me happy.' Thea pulled open the curtain. 'Let's eat.'

'Okay.' Getting breakfast was the only decision Brooke felt ready to make.

Brooke bought twenty beaded bracelets from the local village children, swayed by their big brown eyes. How could she say no? She shoved them into her bag, with no idea what she'd do with them all.

Brooke swallowed; the lump remained in her throat. Thea, Ingrid and Ryan were continuing on the extended trek. She'd become so close to all three of them in such a short time. It would be hard to say goodbye. Perhaps she'd see Ryan in Heart Springs … maybe in Sydney.

Brooke picked up her pace, trying to catch up with Ryan but he was too far ahead. A sharp pain pulled in her side, slowing her down. Her thoughts tumbled around. Should she stop and wait for Ingrid and Thea? But they hadn't solved her problem. Working with Lisa or the family nursery? Neither option made Brooke's heart zing. Ryan made her heart zing, but she shouldn't make career decisions over one kiss. Especially when he was avoiding her.

Brooke plodded up the track. Her brain felt fuzzy. She hadn't had her morning coffee today – only a double shot cappuccino would help clear her mind and figure out what to do. The scent of roasted coffee beans in the grinder. The gurgle of frothing milk. The regulars at The Tea Lady Café. A smile crept onto Brooke's face. Carla's daughter's baby was due any day. And Brooke planned to take in some rose powder for Enid, after spotting some aphids when she'd walked past the other day.

She couldn't go to Sydney. High-rise buildings, peak hour traffic, chain store coffee. Why did she ever think she could deal with that? She was a country girl. She'd never cope in the city for longer than a weekend.

Bags of fertiliser, dirt under her fingernails, eight hours a day with her mother. She couldn't cope with that either. She loved her Mum, but she would micromanage Brooke's every move. The nursery was a great opportunity, but it was her mother's dream, not Brooke's.

Brooke paused as the track flattened out. There was a break in the trees and she could see across the valley to the small village below, the river winding alongside. The world lay open before her and she could see what she wanted. She didn't need to be rescued. She didn't need someone else to tell her what to do.

It was time she listened to herself. She knew how to be happy.

ॐ

One kiss, that's all it could be.

Ryan strode to the front of the tour group – the best way to keep Brooke out of sight. His brain muddled when she was near. Just the sight of her stepping into the sunlight this morning, hair tousled and squinting, had him wondering if he could stay in Heart Springs a bit longer. Taking over his father's business had always been the plan, but in five years or so, when his Dad neared retirement. After he'd lived a little and was ready to slow down. When he was in his thirties and looking for somewhere to raise a family. Not now. It was too soon.

'Stop,' the tour guide called. 'You're walking too fast. You don't know where to go.'

He's got that right.

'Sorry.' Ryan shortened his stride.

They stopped for lunch at a secluded waterfall. Ryan settled on a flat rock and pulled the packed lunch out of his backpack.

'Is there room for me?' Brooke stood before him, her backpack clutched in both hands.

Ryan's appetite waned, his breakfast felt like a rock in his stomach. He'd let her down gently.

'Sure.' Ryan shuffled over. They both unwrapped the banana leaves and pinched some noodles.

'Think my mum would freak if she saw me eating with my fingers.' Brooke tucked the noodles into her mouth.

'Mine too.' Ryan slurped a noodle dangling from his lips.

Brooke nodded towards the waterfall. 'It's gorgeous.'

Not as gorgeous as you. 'Yeah. I love waterfalls.'

'I think the one in Heart Springs is shorter but the rock pool is larger. I reckon this one would be warmer, though.'

'Probably. I haven't seen the one in Heart Springs yet.' His mum had suggested going a few times but he'd kept making excuses. Like he was trying to be miserable there, just to prove that Sydney was better.

'I could take you when we get home?' Brooke looked up at him, her eyes soft and lips parted.

Ryan stiffened. 'I don't think that's a good idea. I'm going back to Sydney in a few weeks.'

'But—'

'Kissing you was a mistake. I shouldn't have done that. I'm sorry.'

'It's Janette, isn't it?' Her voice quietened. 'That's okay, I saw how well you two were reuniting at the wedding.'

He looked away. He hadn't got back together with Janette. The time away had given him the space to see how wrong they were together – away from the dance floor. Maybe it would be easier to let her think that. 'I—'

'You don't need to explain.' Brooke scrunched the remainder of her noodles up in the banana leaf, hoisted her backpack onto one shoulder and stood. 'Well, I'll say goodbye now, then.'

She sat on another rock with Thea and Ingrid, who both turned and glared at him.

Damn.

❧

Brooke finished the day's hike with Thea and Ingrid. She might as well have been walking in a tunnel the way her churning thoughts about Ryan monopolised her attention. She'd always been a good judge of character. How had she got it so wrong with Ryan?

It didn't matter, she told herself, she didn't *need* a man to be happy. She just needed a place that felt like home and a job that made her smile. A simple life.

Brooke embraced Thea and Ingrid. 'Make sure you look me up when you get to Australia.'

'Yah, of course,' said Ingrid.

'I'd love to swim in your waterfall.' Thea tucked an air-dried ringlet behind her ear.

'It'll be colder than that one.' Brooke scribbled her email address onto a scrap of paper she found in her bag. 'Here.' She passed the note to Thea. 'I'll friend you both on Facebook when I get back into range.'

'Bye.' The three girls waved as Brooke climbed into the mini bus. She caught a glimpse of Ryan as she boarded the bus and chose a seat on the opposite side so she didn't have to look at him.

It took the best part of a day, between all the transfers and connecting flights, to get back home. The whole time, Brooke struggled to decide how to tell her parents her career plan. But it could wait until the next day. Or maybe the day after that. She needed a holiday to recover from this holiday.

Her father was waiting at the gate when she arrived. 'Sweetheart, you look awful! Did you catch that mosquito thing?'

'No, I don't have malaria. I'm just tired. I couldn't sleep on the plane.'

'Come. Your mother will make you a hot Milo. That always helped you sleep.'

'I'm a barista, Dad. I can make myself a hot drink.' She hugged him back.

'And you're a very good barista.' He patted her forearm. 'Melinda next door was just asking when you'd be back. "No one makes my chai latte like Brooke. Everyone else puts too much cinnamon on top," she said.'

'That's because I love it.' She met his eye. The moment was now. 'I don't want to work in the nursery, Dad. Plants are Mum's passion. Mine is coffee.' She grabbed her bag from the carousel.

He looked down, a frown furrowing his chin. 'Your mother will be disappointed.' Then he looked up, eyes crinkling. 'But she'll get over it. Just like your grandma did when your mother started working with plants. Grandma wanted her to be a nurse, not work in a nursery.' He shrugged. 'You can't please everyone. You have to please yourself.'

'Thanks, Dad.' She kissed him on the cheek then hauled her bags towards the car park.

'You've gotta tell her, though. I'll be in the garage.' He opened the boot and put her bags in.

'Can it wait until morning?'

He nodded and opened the passenger door for her.

∽

117

Dust billowed behind the once white vehicle as Brooke was driven away from the tiny mountain village. She was out of sight but Ryan's mind was filled with images of her. The tiny gap between her front teeth when she laughed at his childhood stories. Her wrinkled nose as she licked sauce off her fingers at the wedding reception. Her big, brown eyes, only centimetres away, as he leant in to kiss her.

A squeal of laughter drew him back to the present. A small child ran past chasing a chicken. The hen zigzagged, squawking and flapping, remaining just out of reach. The little boy made a dive for it but the chicken flew up into a tree. Nonplussed, he sat under the tree, cleared a patch of dirt and began drawing pictures with a stick.

Ryan wandered back through the village to join the rest of the tour group. Three women waved as he passed. '*Sa wat dee*,' they greeted, smiles filling their faces. Sitting on the bare floor of an open shelter, weaving and chatting, they seemed to find joy in the company of their friends.

These villagers led a simple life. They appeared happier than most people he passed on the streets of Sydney. They didn't have much but they made their own fun. Ryan sat by the unlit campfire and scraped his boot back and forth in the dirt. He closed his eyes and could still feel Brooke in his arms as they danced beside the fire the night before.

'You look,' Thea sat beside him, '*vemod*.'

Ryan turned to face her. 'What?'

'Your mouth is smiling but your eyes are sad. Because of Brooke?'

Ryan nodded. 'Last night was. But now she's gone and,' he slumped, 'it's over before it really started. I never gave us a chance. I never gave Heart Springs a chance.'

'It's never too late.'

'But she's gone and I'm stuck on this trek for two more days.'

Thea shrugged. 'Go to her when you get back home.'

'But I don't know where she lives. I don't know how to contact her.'

Thea slipped a crumpled piece of paper from her pocket then shoved it back in. 'If you really want to, you'll find her.' She walked away, leaving him to his churning thoughts.

Maybe he could make his own fun in Heart Springs. He'd love the slower pace of working with his dad. He'd miss swing dancing in Sydney but he could go back for the big functions.

Maybe he could run lessons in Heart Springs? That travel agent already had the right look – maybe she'd like to dance too. And his parents would come to support him. He'd need a venue and to get the word out. If he put flyers up, maybe Brooke would come to him. He would put up with second-rate country coffee if he could hold Brooke in his arms again.

Jetlagged as he was, Ryan couldn't sleep when he got back to Heart Springs. It was too late at night to inquire about a venue so he researched the legalities of running a dance class, picked out a selection of music perfect for beginners, and planned out half a dozen lessons. He'd called in a favour from Clarky, who'd met him at Sydney airport again, this time with a portable sound system.

'Mum, do you know where Brooke lives?' Ryan asked, between mouthfuls of scrambled eggs.

'Brooke who?'

'I don't know her last name, but she lives in Heart Springs.'

'Heart Springs is small but it's not that small,' she chuckled.

He told her all about Brooke and his plans for teaching swing classes.

'I'm sure she'll forgive you.' She patted the back of his hand.

'So, has Dad got—'

'Have I got what?' His father dropped the roll of junk mail on the table and sat.

'Have you got a new partner yet? I'd like to take you up on the offer.' Ryan sat tall as his father's eyes widened.

'What brought on this change of heart?'

'A girl.' His mum placed a steaming mug of tea in front of his dad, fetched her own cup, then joined them at the table.

'Ahhh. And what happens if things with this girl don't work out? You can't just walk away from a partnership, it's a serious commitment.'

'Um ...' That possibility hadn't even occurred to him. What if she didn't forgive him?

His father smiled. 'You're impulsive, like me. How about you try really living in Heart Springs for a while. You've been staying here for a few weeks, but hiding away in the office is not living. We'll give it a trial for six months and if we're both satisfied, then I'll offer you the partnership.'

'Okay, that's fair.'

'Now, what are you going to do about this girl?'

Ryan ran through his plan with his parents. All he needed now was to find a venue. His dad gave Pastor Burns, the Baptist minister he played golf with, a call and by mid-morning, Ryan had secured the church hall on Tuesday nights for free.

By lunch, he'd printed out fifty flyers advertising his swing dance classes. He made a special one for Brooke. He considered calling Todd to get her contact details but he didn't want to interrupt the honeymoon. He had another idea and it started with J'Adore Travel Boutique.

'Can I help you?' A woman with spiky white hair gestured to the vacant seat in front of her desk.

Ryan stepped closer but didn't sit. He peered at her nametag. 'Hi, Izzy. Is the other lady here?'

'Elle or Maggie?'

'I'm not sure. I booked my holiday with her. She's got a fifties look.'

'Nobody who works here is that old.'

'No, she didn't look *in* her fifties, she dressed Rockabilly – 1950s style.'

Izzy nodded. 'That's Maggie. You know a lot about vintage fashion.' She looked him up and down.

'I'm a swing dancer.' He passed her one of the flyers.

'Oh, Maggie would love that. Maybe I'll come along too. Did you want to put this on our wall?'

'Yes, please. And do you know where—'

'Maggie's on her lunch break.'

'It's not really Maggie I need.' He thumbed the stack of flyers. 'I'm looking for Brooke. Maggie booked her holiday to Thailand too and I'm trying to track her down.'

'Why do you want to find her?'

He stifled a yawn – 'Sorry, I'm jetlagged' – and held up the flyer he'd made for Brooke.

'Awww. I want to help you but customer details are private.' She paused. 'I think you need a cup of coffee. Maybe you should go to The Tea Lady Café?'

'I'll be fine.' He stifled another yawn. 'I'll make one when I get home. They can't make decent coffee.'

'You can't have tried it, then. I've drunk coffee in Paris and Venice, and the barista at The Tea Lady is just as good. You should go over, right now.'

'Maybe they'll put a flyer up for me.'

'Off you go.' Izzy shooed him out the door.

ᔕᴑ

Steam hissed as Brooke finished frothing the milk. She poured two lattes, placed them on the tray and stepped out from behind the counter to deliver them. The door swung open and a man walked in. She faltered. *What is he doing here?*

Steadying the tray, she continued to the corner table and forced a smile on her face.

'Here you go.'

She walked wordlessly back to the counter and crossed her arms. 'Would you like an over-brewed pot of coffee?'

'*You're* the barista?' Ryan looked down at the stack of papers in his hand. 'That kinda screws up my apology.' He turned the top flyer facedown. 'Could I please have a double shot cappuccino while I think up a new one.'

That was *her* drink. 'Are you sure? It might be crap.'

'I'm sure.'

'What have you got there?' Brooke pointed to the stack of papers.

'Some flyers. I came over to see if I could put one up in the window.'

'Show me.'

He passed her one of the dance class flyers. There was a cartoon image of a couple dancing surrounded by text.

Heart Springs Swings

Learn to dance the Jitterbug

Come along and cut a rug

Bring a friend or two or three

Your first lesson will be free

Tuesday nights 7 p.m.

Baptist Church Hall

'You're going to teach *dance* classes?' She tilted her head to the side. 'Show me the one you're hiding.' She waited, palm up.

He rubbed his jaw with his free hand, then handed her another flyer, the same dancing couple surrounded by text.

Brooke, You Swing My Heart

Sorry I was such a lug

I'll drink bad coffee from a mug

You make me laugh, you make me smile

I want to live here for a while

We'll have fun, we can make our own

Simple things like ice cream cones

I'd like to teach you how to dance

Can I please have a second chance?

Every night

Wherever you are ...

'I might just burn your coffee for that.' Her gaze was icy but at his hopeful face her resolve softened like a double scoop choc mint chip on a sunny afternoon.

She placed the flyers on the counter and turned to the espresso machine.

'I'm sorry. I'm sure you make—'

She drowned out his words with jets of steam. A smile crept onto her face but she kept her back turned to make him sweat a little longer. That poem was so corny, just like the ones she'd written for her secret crush in high school but had never been brave enough to send. But if he was willing to give Heart Springs a chance then she was willing to give him a chance. She loaded two double shot cappuccinos onto a tray and nodded towards the table at the back of the café.

Ryan followed, sitting opposite. They each scooped some froth off the top before they took a sip.

'Mmm. *Excellent* coffee.' Ryan took another sip. 'I mean it. It's really good.' He drank some more and took a breath. 'I gave your coffee a chance. Will you give me a chance?' He looked up, eyebrows raised. A dollop of froth clung to his top lip.

'I don't think one cappuccino is enough of a compromise.' Brooke pressed her fingertips together, as an idea formed. 'I'll come to your swing class next week *if* you come boot scooting with me tonight.'

Ryan didn't hesitate. 'It's a deal.'

'I'm not done yet. You need to make an effort with the town, too. I want you to tell me the names of half a dozen people in town by the time you pick me up, and your parents don't count.'

'I don't need till then. I know Dad's old partner, Frank, and Pastor Burns, who is letting me use the church hall. Maggie, who booked our holidays, and Izzy, who is working there today.' He tapped his fingers in turn. 'I passed Bob's Grill on the way here, so Bob? And Brooke. You said my parents didn't count but you didn't rule out yourself.'

The blob of froth wobbled as he spoke. Brooke couldn't resist. She leant over the table and scraped it off with her finger. She was about to pop it in her mouth when Ryan caught her hand.

'Hey, that's mine.' His gaze locked with hers as he licked the froth from the tip of her finger. Heat bloomed deep in her belly then spread lower as he ran his thumb over her knuckles.

She dipped her finger in her own cup, scooped up a little froth and wiped it back on Ryan's lip. 'And that's mine.' She leant closer and kissed him, sucking his top lip gently and running her tongue over his bottom lip. The tips of their tongues met, dancing circles around each other.

Brooke's heart began to swing.

When Love Breaks Down

LISA WOLSTENHOLME

Gill's hands clasped each cheek and she rolled her eyes as Jim's hammering picked up pace. The walls in the kitchen trembled from his onslaught.

'Oh Jim,' she sighed. He was only meant to be hanging shelves, yet with every hammer on nail, another piece of magnolia plaster was freed, and the wall now resembled a target practice.

Jim had retired in the December two months prior, and already the cracks in their relationship were widening as much as those on the wall. Everywhere Gill went, Jim tagged along, or at least wanted to know where she was going and when she'd be back. The routine was getting tiresome, and Gill was more than regretting encouraging Jim to take early retirement from his plumbing business.

She'd tried everything to get him out from under her feet. Driving him to the Heart Springs Men's Shed for one, but afterwards he complained that the men in the group were a bunch of old cronies who just liked playing with power tools. *Ironic*, Gill thought now. She'd also suggested he join the local community centre and enrol in some activities and courses. He could learn Italian, she'd said, or pursue his liking of chess. But it was to no avail. Instead of finding his own things to do, he spent most of his time interfering in hers.

Life had been so easy for Gill before Jim had retired. The grass seemed much more lush then, with Gill regaling in how much fun and freedom she'd had until Big Brother Jim started watching her every move. The ladies at her local church group commented on how surprising it was that Jim had taken a sudden interest in all things spiritual, but their cocked eyebrows and whispers in the kitchen confirmed Gill's suspicions that Jim was an unwelcome guest. She missed the days when he would come home late from work, slurp through his dinner, then fall asleep on the couch while watching whatever sport he could find on Foxtel. But what could she do? Until he established his own hobbies and weekly routine, she had to tolerate him being part of hers.

Deep down, Gill knew Jim was an honest man who worked hard to give them both a good life, and appreciated that it gave her freedom other wives longed for. But their status quo had been rocked since he'd retired, and her only respite came each morning when Jim, under duress, took the dog for a walk or dropped in on their daughter Maggie at her travel agency, J'Adore Travel Boutique.

Gill bought the dog for Jim on the premise that it would keep his mind and body healthy, but really it brought her much-needed time apart. It was obvious for all to see that Jim was none-too-keen on his four-legged *friend*.

'It's not a man's dog, is it?' he'd complained when Gill brought the pooch home.

'Maybe not, but she's loyal and adorable,' Gill replied, squishing the fluffball's face as Jim scoffed in disgust. 'She's called Foofie, and she's a LaHenryoodle, you know. Quite a prized cross-breed.'

'I don't care if she's the Heart Springs P&A Society Supreme Champ, she's a bloody yapper! And if you think I'm going to yell out "Foofie" if she buggers off into the bushes, you can think again.'

Jim was adamant he and this dog would *not* be best walking buddies, but Gill knew how to wear him down, threatening him with household chores. It

was just enough to guarantee an early morning river walk, a time when her proud husband seemed convinced he wouldn't be seen and so avoid becoming the town's laughing stock, especially if Jim's long-standing fishing 'mate' Henry Masters, saw him with Foofie.

It was Friday night, the time when Maggie came over for dinner. Her travel business in the centre of Heart Springs kept her busy and made Gill and Jim proud, but it meant little time for home-cooked meals and pyjama days. Friday night, the end of her working week, became the time when she could kick back at her parents' place and be waited on for a change.

Gill had made Maggie's favourite meal, roast and vegies with lashings of thick, meaty gravy. She always liked to make a fuss of their only child.

When the doorbell dinged at just after 7 p.m., a flustered Gill closed the oven and rushed to the door, knowing full well that Jim would not be uprooted from the couch while the golf was on.

Exhausted from all the running around she'd been doing trying to get Jim from under her feet, Gill was desperate for some time alone. She patted down her greying auburn hair, wiped her hands over the front of her 'The Better Half' apron and opened the door.

Maggie also looked flustered. 'Sorry I'm late, Mum,' she gasped, half-smiling. 'We had some last-minute hiccups with bookings. The Bali hotel we've been using for our honeymooners has gone bust.'

'Oh, you poor thing,' Gill soothed, hugging her pretty daughter and ushering her in. 'Dinner's almost ready. Go and say hello to your dad.'

Maggie kissed her mum on the cheek and headed into the lounge room where her father was sprawled out on the recliner. Gill adored her daughter, but knew that Maggie was the apple of Jim's eye and would always seek out her dad whenever problems arose. Sure that Maggie wouldn't want to be lumbered with her tales of woe about Jim, she resolved to keep quiet and be her usual smiling self throughout their evening together.

But halfway through the meal, Gill's composure began to wane. Jim and Maggie were deep in conversation about all-things J'Adore and Gill felt distanced from the yakking pair.

Maggie glanced at her frazzled Mum. 'Where's Foofie?'

Gill tutted. 'In the laundry. Your dad locked her in there so he could watch the golf in peace, apparently.' Sarcasm tinged her final word, and Gill threw Jim a look of scorn.

'Poor Foofs,' Maggie continued.

'Poor me, more like,' Jim cut in. 'Bloody thing does nothing but yap. I can barely hear myself think.'

'Oh Jim,' Gill sighed, rolling her eyes.

After dinner, Jim and Maggie retreated to the lounge room while Gill made cups of tea. While stirring the tea, her mind drifted to a long, sandy beach lapped by crystalline waves and not a single soul in sight. Her lips curled into a longing smile.

'Is the tea ready yet?' Jim called, pulling Gill from her reverie. 'Maggie's got to go soon.'

'Oh Jim,' Gill mouthed, shaking her head as she placed the cups on a tray and scuttled into the lounge.

As Maggie put her coat on to leave, Gill hoped her daughter hadn't noticed the tension between her parents, or the frown lines she felt sure were becoming a permanent fixture on what she prided herself as an otherwise youthful face.

'You all right, Mum?' Maggie whispered, once Jim had disappeared to let Foofie out of the laundry.

'Yes, darling. I'm fine,' Gill replied, feigning cheerfulness. 'Been busy, that's all.'

'Dad's not been doing your nut in, then?'

Gill gawped, surprised that her daughter had noticed. 'Of course not,' she fibbed. 'Why would you think that?'

'Well, he's been doing *my* nut in every time he passes the agency, coming in, chatting to the girls, rearranging brochures, and generally getting in the way.'

'Oh. I hadn't realised.' Gill suspected that Jim might be interfering where he shouldn't now that he had all this free time, but was secretly glad of the time apart.

Maggie leant in towards Gill. 'Between you and me, I think the two of you need a holiday. A break from the rut you've got into, because you seem to be getting on each other's nerves. You know?'

'I really don't,' Gill replied, forcing a chuckle and ignoring the line forming between Maggie's perfectly plucked brows. *Clever, that one*, Gill thought.

'Swing by the boutique and I'll sort something out.' She hugged and kissed her mum goodbye and then headed off.

Gill pondered Maggie's comments. Yes, perhaps a holiday would do them good. A change of scenery and a break from the day-to-day things that were getting her down. Perhaps it was the best thing for them both. They could recharge their batteries and stop getting so bogged down. But Jim was a stingy old bugger when it came to money, and liked to be the one with the great ideas. Gill would have to use her cunning to swing this.

'You didn't have to come with me, you know,' Jim said to Gill as he untangled Foofie's lead from around a bush.

'I know, but I fancied a bit of fresh air this morning. It's been ages since we had a stroll by the river together.'

The pair walked on, with Foofie pulling relentlessly on the lead, stopping and sniffing every patch of grass, or lamppost, or bush they passed.

'Bloody dog!' Jim huffed, tugging at Foofie's lead.

'Oh look, Tarts Bakery's open,' Gill said, pointing across the road to the main street. A small group of people sat outside in the cool morning sunshine, sipping drinks and chatting. 'Let's stop for some breakfast, Jim.'

'With this thing?' he retorted, yanking Foofie.

'It'll be fine. I've seen people with their dogs there many times.'

Jim shrugged and followed Gill. The bakery was a few stops down from Maggie's travel agency, and as they crossed the road, a plan formed in Gill's mind. It was only 7.40 a.m., but she was sure she could stretch out a breakfast stop until 9 a.m., when Maggie opened shop.

Two cups of coffee and three croissants later, and with Foofie yapping at every person and dog passing by, Jim was fidgeting, as if itching to be on his way.

He's probably worried that he'll be seen with Foofie, Gill thought, and tittered under her breath. 'I just want to pop in and see how Maggie is,' she announced. 'She seemed a little stressed on Friday night, so I want to check she's okay now.'

'S'pose so,' Jim shrugged, 'But what'll we do with the mutt?'

'We can leave her tied up outside the shop. She'll be okay for a few minutes. It'll be fine.'

Jim shrugged again, and followed his wife. But Foofie, eager to get going, stood, shook herself, and then ran around Jim's feet, causing the lead to wrap around his legs. He tried to move forwards and tripped, thumping down onto a nearby chair, clipping the table as he fell. Empty cups clattered onto the floor.

Foofie yelped.

Jim swore.

Embarrassed, Gill glanced around to see if anyone had noticed.

'Jim!' came a cry from across the road as Jim untangled his legs and pulled himself up. 'Is that you causing a racket?' It was Henry.

'All right, Henry,' Jim replied.

Gill knew Jim hadn't seen Henry for years and had complained many times about the, 'pedantic, old fart who yakked too much'.

'How ya going, Jim? Been a while,' Henry said, striding over towards Jim.

'Yeah, not bad, Henry. You?'

'Yeah, good. Been busy, ya know. Caught a bloody huge Jewfish the other weekend with the boys. Any bigger and we'd have had to throw it back!'

Gill glanced over at Jim's scowling face as silence deafened.

'Nice dog, Jimbo.'

'It's the wife's,' Jim replied quickly.

Gill closed her eyes, shaking her head.

'Anyway, we'd better be off. Got a lot to do, ya know.'

'Right-o mate. Call me sometime and come out fishing with the boys.'

'Right-o,' Jim replied, pulling on Foofie's lead, and grabbing Gill's hand. 'Bloody boaster,' he murmured under his breath.

They arrived at J'Adore and nosed through the window. Maggie looked up and waved them in.

'Can we put a bowl of water out for Foofie?' Gill asked, popping her head around the door.

'Sure can,' Maggie beamed, ruffling Foofie's face and giving her a fussing over.

After tying up Foofie outside the door and placing a freshly filled water bowl in front of her, Gill and Jim took seats at Maggie's desk.

'Hi,' Izzy called from her adjacent seat, beaming a smile at Gill and Jim.

'Hello, Izzy. Elle. How are you both?' Gill replied, smiling back at the younger women who were stacking brochures on the stand.

'Great. Busy, as usual. She keeps us on our toes,' Izzy replied, tossing her head in Maggie's direction.

Maggie smirked, shaking her head and sat behind her desk.

'So, how're things with that hotel in Bali?' Gill asked, flicking mindlessly through a brochure.

'More-or-less sorted,' Maggie replied. 'We managed to secure another hotel. Unfortunately, we haven't checked it out for ourselves, but it's been recommended by a colleague so we're hoping it'll work out. Just means I'll have to take a short break to Bali to check it out properly.'

'What a burden,' Jim smirked, as Gill's eye's widened with interest.

'It's a relief, for sure,' Maggie continued, 'but at least it's sorted ... for now.'

Gill smiled proudly at her daughter, once again marvelling at Maggie's determination and ability to get things done.

'So how are you two?' Maggie asked.

'We're fine, love,' Gill replied, throwing Maggie her well-practiced, all-is-right-with-the-world smile. 'I just wanted to check *you* were okay.'

'Your mum came to walk the dog with me this morning,' Jim stated, as if it were a blue moon occurrence. 'Even made me have breakfast with her at the bakery before coming here.'

'Well, it's nice that you are spending quality time together,' Maggie offered.

'Yeah, with that bloody mutt causing no-end of trouble. Showed me up in front of Henry, she bloody did.'

'Jim ... language,' Gill scolded. 'Maggie doesn't need to hear that.'

'Sorry,' Jim mouthed, as if it was a well-practised routine.

Gill ignored him, wondering how they had managed to stay together for so long. Like chalk and cheese, many of her friends had questioned what she, a petite and prim girl from a well-to-do background, saw in farmer's boy, Jim.

But Gill knew. Jim was still a handsome and rugged man. A hard worker who, throughout his life, always strived to better himself. Charming, with a 'no flies on me' attitude, Jim had worn Gill down with his warmth and wit, and his relentless pursuit of her. Back then, Gill fell head over heels for the roguish Jim, and their love and destiny was consummated in the back of Jim's dad's four-by-four ute a short time after. Jim had certainly made Gill's toes curl that night, and the very next day he'd proposed, making her feel like the luckiest girl alive.

'You're the sun that warms my tepid heart and sets my loins on fire,' Jim often said as he nuzzled her neck, causing the butterflies in Gill's stomach to loop-the-loop.

But while Gill loved Jim dearly, recent times found her digging deep when it came to many of Jim's nuances: his prolific use of swearing; his childish need to be the better man; and most of all, his incessant prying into her day-to-day affairs. Oh yes, life had been a much smoother ride when Jim was working.

'So, Mum, Dad … while you're here there's something I want to show you,' Maggie said, interrupting Gill's daydreaming.

'Oh?' Gill replied, curious.

'Back in a minute.' Maggie pulled out a brochure from a drawer in her desk.

'Better be off soon,' Jim whispered to Gill, picking dog hairs from his shorts. 'Foofie'll be getting hot.'

Gill chuckled to herself at Jim's concern for the dog he disliked so much.

Maggie thrust the glossy brochure towards her parents.

'What's this, love?' Gill asked.

'Well, we've just struck a deal with a coach operator who do Australian tours for the over-sixties. They're not your usual coach-tour company, a bit more high-brow, you know?'

Jim glanced up from his grooming routine. 'That's nice, love, but why are you showing them to us?'

'Because you're both over sixty, and I thought you could have a look through and see if the itineraries, hotels, and such would be of interest.'

'Oh, right,' Jim replied, grabbing up the brochure and flicking through. 'We can have a look and let you know what we think.'

'That'd be great, Dad. It's always best to check these things thoroughly before we unleash a new operator on the paying public. Might even be a trip in it for you.' Maggie's smile was more hopeful than anything, but Jim didn't seem to notice and continued browsing.

'We'd best be off,' Gill said, rising from her seat. 'Your dad's worried about Foofie.' She smiled a knowing smile at Maggie as the two made their way to the door.

'What the bloody hell has that mutt done now!' Jim yelled just as Gill passed through the door. Foofie rushed over to greet them, but instead of her fur being the usual shade of gun-metal grey, it was coated in brown splodges. As Jim reached down to click on her lead, he shot back.

'She stinks! What the hell has she been rolling in?'

'I'll get a towel,' Maggie offered, leaving Jim shooing Foofie away for fear of getting his newly fur-picked shorts covered in god-only-knew what.

All the way home, Jim muttered and cussed *that bloody dog*, knowing full well he would have to bathe her when they got back. Gill knew it'd make him a moody bugger for the rest of the day, so decided not to mention the brochure until he'd calmed down.

'You know, love, we've never been to the Pinnacles,' Gill announced as Jim poured himself a beer.

'What, love?'

'I said, we've never been to the Pinnacles. They look intriguing.'

'Where the hell are the Pincles?' Jim asked, plonking himself down on the couch next to her.

'Pinn-a-cles, Jim. In Western Australia,' she replied, holding up a picture. 'Come to think of it, we've never even been to WA together.'

'Why would we want to go there? There's nothing in WA except for Perth and hoons. Most isolated state capital in the world, you know.'

Gill sighed. Jim had such a narrow view of the world, being born and bred in rural New South Wales. In all the years they'd been together, his sense of adventure only extended to a trip up to Cairns to see the Barrier Reef on a glass-bottomed boat, and a couple of breaks in Bali after she'd threatened divorce.

'Jim! How can you judge? You've never been there!' Frustration bubbled under her skin.

'Never going there, either,' Jim replied gruffly.

Gill flicked through a few more pages. 'Well, I think it looks really interesting. There's so many different things to see. Look.' She held out the brochure again.

Jim folded his arms. 'I am not going half-way across 'Straya to sit on a bus full of old cronies to look at a few rocks.'

'Oh Jim.'

It was another three days before Gill broached the subject of the coach tour with Jim. She'd have been impressed by his resistance to even discussing it, had it not been for his silly excuses like, 'I get claustrophobic on buses', 'WA water tastes salty' and 'What if we get stranded in the desert?' Gill had a fight on her hands and she knew it.

By the time Maggie arrived for her usual Friday night dinner, Gill and Jim were butting heads. Jim had continued to dig in his heels about coach tours, which made Gill even more determined that they should go.

She had a wildcard up her sleeve, though – Maggie. If anyone could convince Jim it was a good idea, it would be her.

As the family settled down to a sumptuous meal of Jim's favourite slow-cooked lamb shanks, Gill and Maggie were ready for him.

'So, did you get a chance to suss out that brochure for me?' Maggie asked casually.

Gill looked over at Jim, who dropped his knife and fork onto the plate, sat back and folded his arms again. *Oh boy.* This wasn't going to be easy.

'Dad?' Maggie continued. 'Is something wrong?'

'Your dad is not the least bit interested in coach tours,' Gill sighed.

'That's not true,' Jim countered. 'Your mother has been trying to convince me we should go on one. To WA of all places!'

'Isn't Mum's family originally from WA?' Maggie asked. Gill nodded. 'Well, perhaps that's why she wants to go there.'

'If we're going to go anywhere, it will be somewhere on the Eastern side where there's more than camels and rocks to look at,' Jim tutted. 'I mean, a coach! Full of *old* people. What if I need to fart?'

'Dad!'

'Jim!'

The two women yelled in unison. Gill threw Maggie a despairing look.

'Dad,' Maggie soothed, 'there are toilets on board, and you're not on the coach twenty-four-seven. You'll be staying in lovely hotels, as well as having day trips and activities.'

Jim muttered something under his breath.

'It's only ten days, Jim.' Gill was just about at the end of her tether.

Maggie stepped in. 'You'll have premium-class flights to and from Perth, and the food and beer is all-inclusive.'

'All-inclusive beer, you say?' Jim's interest suddenly piqued.

'Yes, Dad. All-inclusive beer.'

'And how much would this coach trip cost me?'

Maggie smiled. 'On this occasion, it wouldn't cost you a cent. You'd be doing me a favour by going instead of me, too. All I ask is that you provide me with a blow-by-blow account so that I know if this is the right tour company for J'Adore.'

'Maggie, we couldn't possibly—'

'Mum, I insist. I would've had to go anyway with this being a new contract, but it's not aimed at the under-sixties. You'd be doing me a *huge* favour.'

'Oh. Well in that case,' Jim said, rubbing his hands together. 'Maybe it won't be so bad after all. Free beer, eh.'

Maggie retrieved her bag from the back of the dining chair, fishing out some paperwork. 'Well, that's a relief because I've already booked you on the next WA tour. It's in three weeks' time,' she said, handing the details over to Gill.

'You crafty little bugger,' Jim scolded, but this time with a smile plastered across his stubbled face.

Gill reached over and squeezed Jim's hand. 'This'll be good, Jim. I promise.'

'Better be,' he replied. 'WA, eh? I'd better get myself some new thongs. Will we need any shots before we go?'

'Oh Jim,' Gill sighed, her eyes crinkled from a broad smile.

Gill gave Maggie a final hug as she and Jim approached security at Qantas Domestic Departures in Sydney Airport.

'Don't forget you can use the Business Lounge,' Maggie called, waving them goodbye. 'And I promise to take good care of Foofs.'

Gill prayed this break would do them good, giving a much-needed break from the boggy routine they'd got into since Jim had retired.

'Don't worry if you accidentally lose her,' Jim winked.

Once through security, Gill and Jim made their way to the Business Lounge.

'This is nice,' Gill cooed, as an attendant checked their tickets and showed them past the wood-panelled reception to a small table with high-backed, grey marle chairs.

Jim, wearing a smart pair of blue corduroys and a crisp white shirt, far removed from his standard issue khaki shorts and T-shirt, fidgeted as they ordered drinks and a sharing platter. If only Jim would relax a little, Gill thought. Their flight wasn't due to board for another hour, so they had plenty of time to enjoy their surrounds. She pulled out their itinerary from her cabin bag, hoping it might help.

'We'll be picked up by our tour guide when we arrive in Perth, then transferred to our hotel overlooking the Swan River in the CBD.' Her face lit up as she read aloud the next few stages of the trip: a river cruise to Fremantle; a trip to Albany to take in the Brig Amity Replica and Anzac Memorial; an opportunity to snorkel at Greens Pool in Denmark; and wine tasting in Margaret River. The final leg of their tour would take them up north to Wave Rock; then back down the coast to Perth, taking in the Pinnacles and the sand dunes of Lancelin. Gill could barely contain her excitement.

Her glee was interrupted by low-rumbling snores. She looked up, and to her horror saw Jim slumped in his chair, away with the fairies. Glancing around, Gill's eyes fell upon a couple sitting a few tables away. The man grinned across at her, his eyebrows raised.

I'm not even going to say it, she thought, quickly turning her head and helping herself to the seafood platter in front of her.

By the end of the flight, both Jim and Gill were flagging. They'd barely spoken during the whole four-and-a-bit hours. Jim had spent most of the time watching re-runs of *iFish*, only pausing for the complimentary food and drink, while Gill had settled down with a rom-com.

'I see you managed to avoid farting,' Gill said in a hushed voice as they disembarked.

Jim ignored her sarcasm and sped up, as if his life depended on being the first one to the baggage carousel.

'Jim! Slow down!'

'I'm not letting some larrikin sneak off with our luggage,' Jim huffed, showing no signs of easing up.

After waiting nearly forty minutes to retrieve their two neatly packed cases, they looked for a sign reading 'Golden Oldies Coach Tours', spotting it surrounded by a sizable crowd.

'How many people are on this bloody thing? Jim exclaimed.

'It's a tour, Jim. There's bound to be a fair few people on it otherwise it wouldn't run.' Gill tried not to roll her eyes, and failed.

Jim tutted as they joined a small queue of 'oldies' checking in with a tour guide dressed in brown slacks, pink shirt and a purple spotted bow-tie.

'Jim and Gill Redmont,' Jim informed the guide.

'Welcome, Jack & Gill—'

'It's Jim,' Jim interjected in a gruff tone.

'My apologies, *Jim*,' the guide replied, ticking off their names on his clipboard. 'Welcome Gill and *Jim* to our tour. I'm your tour guide, Tom, and I will be with you throughout this wonderful journey taking in the delights of Western Australia. If there's anything you need, please let me know.'

Gill smiled and shook Tom's free hand. Jim threw Tom a faux grin as they were directed to the gaggle of waiting oldies. Moments later, they all clambered onto the bus that would take them into Perth.

'It's a bloody service bus,' Jim announced, scoffing as he shuffled awkwardly down the aisle.

On cue, Tom, twiddling his bow-tie, announced, 'This is just the bus taking us into Perth. Our tour coach is a much grander beast.' His eyes glinted as if he was referring to his most prized possession. 'It'll be about a twenty-five-minute journey, so make yourselves comfortable.'

Jim sat down near the back of the coach, and Gill slinked in next to him.

'I thought it was you!' came a cry from behind. Gill and Jim's heads turned in unison.

'You were the guy snoring in the lounge at Sydney.' The man's booming voice turned to chuckling. 'Bob Wilson,' he said, offering his hand between the seat gap.

Jim's face reddened. Gill patted his knee for reassurance and Jim begrudgingly shook the man's hand. 'Jim and Gill Redmont,' he replied, quickly yanking his hand away.

'Well, hello, Jim and Gill,' Bob replied, lingering a look over Gill that exceeded a polite glance.

Gill's cheeks flushed. 'Hello, Bob, and...' Gill said, nodding towards the woman sitting next to him.

'Oh yes, this is Pam, my darling wife.'

'Nice to meet you, Pam,' Gill said, smiling. When Pam smiled back warmly, Gill sensed that she and Pam would get on just fine.

Bob was a larger-than-life, smartly dressed man, who looked as if he was going to a business lunch rather than on a coach tour. In the twenty-or-so minutes it took to reach the hotel, Bob had told Gill and Jim all about himself, pausing only between breaths. He was a car dealer, but 'not just any car dealer – *luxury* cars, HSV's and such-like'.

'Luxury cars, my foot,' Jim murmured in Gill's ear. 'Everyone knows Fords are the *only* cars for real men.'

Pam, prim with black bouffant hair, full make-up, and a burgundy skirt and jacket suit, said very little during the bus ride, except for the odd comment and sideways glance with Gill about Jim's clipped responses and Bob's enthusiastic dialogue.

By the time they reached the hotel, Gill could see by Jim's pursed lips and stiff body that he was becoming increasingly uptight, especially when Bob kept referring to him as 'Jimster'.

'It's Jim,' he had corrected, only Bob seemed oblivious, each time patting Jim's back saying, 'Sorry, mate.'

Gill checked them in, and she and Jim headed off to their room to freshen up before dinner. But all twenty-eight couples on the tour were on the same floor, and Bob and Pam were a mere two doors away. Gill hoped Jim hadn't noticed.

'Flaming idiot,' Jim said in the confines of their hotel room. 'Anyone would think he was the only *luxury* car dealer in the world.'

'Pam seems nice,' Gill said, as she set about powdering her face in the plush en-suite.

'Shame she's married to a bigger!'

'A *bigger*, Jim?'

'You know, mine's bigger than yours,' Jim said, mocking Bob's tone. 'Well, one thing's for sure, we're not sitting anywhere near him on this trip!'

'Oh Jim,' Gill sighed, shaking her head in disbelief.

The following day, after a lavish breakfast of eggs and bacon, Tom ushered the travellers onto their coach. 'Oohs' and 'ahhs' filled the air as they found seats and marvelled at the luxury interior.

Jim led Gill to the back of the coach, securing a table and four seats far away from Bob and Pam, much to Gill's disgust. She'd enjoyed chatting with Pam after dinner that previous evening. But Jim, after several hours listening to Bob's incessant nattering, had declared he'd had more than his fill of Boaster Bob.

'Right. Where's the dunny?' Jim asked, looking around the coach.

'There.' Gill pointed at a small door tucked behind some seats.

Jim barged through the embarking couples towards the toilet, returning several minutes later, declaring, 'It'll do.'

He sat down and fished around in his backpack for a copy of *The Age* as Gill pulled open the floral curtains hanging on the windows.

But as she and Jim were settling in, Bob's grating tone boomed nearby. He'd somehow managed to squeeze past the couple about to sit with Gill and Jim and asked to swap, claiming that they were 'great mates with Jim and Gill'.

Gill nudged Jim under the table just as his mouth opened.

Chastised, Jim slumped back in his seat, tight-lipped.

'Morning,' Gill said, welcoming their new friends.

'You all right, Jimster?' Bob asked.

'It's Jim,' Jim snapped. 'And yes, I'm fine.'

Gill's leg met Jim's in a swift kick.

'Sleep all right did you, Gill?' Pam asked, offering Gill a Jaffa.

'My favourites,' Gill said, her eyes twinkling as she took a few from the packet and popped them into her mouth, determined that Jim's sour mood would not ruin the start of this holiday.

'Jim?' Pam thrust the packet towards him.

'No thanks, Pam.'

'He's not a fan of lollies,' Gill quickly replied, hoping Pam hadn't noticed Jim's curt response.

'Looking forward to the cruise, Jimster?' Bob asked.

Through gritted teeth, Jim forced a smile. 'Suppose,' is all he managed, then picked up his newspaper from the table.

'Not a morning person, eh Jimster?' Bob chuckled.

But to Gill's dismay, Jim just shook his head, flicking through the pages as if looking for an article of interest.

All through the coach journey, on the river cruise, and again at dinner, Gill and Jim listened to Bob raving on about his car (an HSV V8), his business (the *only* luxury car dealer in northern NSW), his hobby (golf, of course, with a handicap of sixteen), and his home (double-storey, with a *huge* pool in the upmarket part of Greenhaven, NSW).

Gill suspected that Jim would be reeling from that last snippet because Greenhaven was a mere forty-two kilometres from Heart Springs. Spitting distance, in driving terms. But she was delighted by the fact that she and Pam, who were getting on well and had discovered a shared passion for sewing, lived close. And with Pam being just down the road, future meet-ups were definitely on the cards.

When Bob then started going on about his other pride and joy, Gill could see from Jim's scowl that he'd just about had enough. Even Pam started rolling her eyes at Bob's boasting, especially when he raved on about Monaro and Torana, his prized, pure-bred bulldogs that had cost him a small fortune.

'He names his dogs after bloody cars!' Jim scoffed when Bob and Pam had gone up deck on the ferry to take photos.

'For heaven's sake, Jim. Just try and get along, will you,' Gill had snapped in reply.

But when Bob asked Gill if they had any pets, Jim's face flushed with embarrassment as he told Bob about Foofie, and was less-than-subtly kicked in the shins by Gill when he claimed Foofie was *her* dog.

When Bob wasn't talking about himself, which Gill realised was most of the time, he was complimenting her on her hair and clothes, and clung to her every word.

'What are you doing with a rough old dog like Jim when you could have any pure-bred you wanted?' Bob had said to her, laughing, while casting admiring glances over her trim figure.

Flattered by Bob's comments and not reading anything into them, Gill wondered if that was what was bothering Jim.

'Well, she wouldn't be interested in a mongrel like you!' Jim had fired back, confirming Gill's suspicions that the green-eyed monster had reared its ugly head.

By the time they docked at Fremantle, Jim's mood had become more sour than a lemon, so much so that when the group congregated at E-shed to start a walking tour, Tom took Jim and Gill aside and whispered, 'He's bit overbearing, I know, but please try to enjoy yourself. You may never get another chance at a trip like this.' He gave Jim's arm a squeeze.

But it did nothing to lighten Jim's mood, and Gill became increasingly worried.

When the coach arrived back at the hotel, Jim barely spoke for the rest of the day. Gill was exhausted from trying to keep the conversation flowing, not being one to sit in silence for long.

Jim headed straight to their room, with Gill in hot pursuit.

'Jim! Are you going to tell me what this is all about?' she asked as he flung himself down on the bed like a two-year-old throwing a tantrum.

'Bob! Need I say more?'

'Don't you think you're being a bit silly?' Gill said, hands-on-hips like a scorning matron.

'He obviously fancies you 'cos he was all over you like a rash! And don't even get me started on his boasting! *I've got a big car, and I've got a fancy house, and my dogs are better than yours,*' he said, mimicking Bob again.

'This is ridiculous, Jim! I can't believe you're getting your pants in a twist over someone like Bob. He's only joking around, I'm sure.' Gill's anger boiled. 'This is supposed to be a break for us, and you're acting like an idiot!' She turned about foot and headed to the bathroom, slamming the door shut behind her as Jim uttered a string of expletives.

She left him to stew for a while as she freshened up and changed her clothes.

'Are you going to get ready for dinner?' Gill called out a short while later.

'You're joking!' Jim yelled back. 'I'm not going anywhere near that flaming moron!'

A few moments later Gill emerged. 'Well you stay here and sulk if you want, but I'm going to dinner!' she shouted, her mind made up. 'And I might even have a few drinks in the bar after, too!' And with that, she grabbed her purse, strode out of the room and banged the door closed, point made.

The first days of the tour were tense. Barely a word passed between Gill and Jim, and she found herself spending more and more time without Jim as he continued to sulk. And Bob was enjoying the rift way too much for Gill's liking.

Her friendship with Pam, however, blossomed, and she found herself enjoying much-needed time away from her grumpy husband. But it worried her that the rut developing since Jim had retired had widened into a bloody great ravine.

By the time the coach reached the Pinnacles, Gill was ready to throw in the towel. She hadn't yet confided in Pam about what was going on with Jim, but figured she needed to do something soon or else the whole holiday would be ruined.

After the coach pulled up at the Information Centre, Gill took Pam aside.

'Do you mind if you and I go for a walk? Alone?' Pam was happy to oblige – was Bob getting on her nerves too?

As they strolled through the rock formations, leaving Bob and Jim to fend for themselves, Pam and Gill discussed all-things husband related, with Gill admitting that Jim's continuing bad mood and absences from group activities was due to his jealousy of Bob.

'Really? I thought you'd both figured out that Bob has a tendency towards, how can I put this, *exaggerating*.' Pam rolled her eyes. 'He's always like that, especially when he has an audience.'

'I didn't realise,' Gill replied, grinning.

'Between you and me,' Pam said, mouth behind hand, 'because Bob would be so embarrassed if anyone found out, I think it's because he had a rough childhood. His parents didn't have much and he struggled for years to get that business of his going. He's only really started bringing in the big dollars since he switched to luxury cars. For a long time, it was my salary as a nurse that kept us afloat.'

'Oh. I see,' Gill replied.

'I retired a few years ago, but Bob roped me into helping him out at the office. I'm barely getting any time for me now,' Pam said, shaking her head.

Something else we have in common, Gill thought.

Gill pondered Pam's words for a few moments; a lightness came over her, but she chose her next ones carefully. 'Um ... I think Jim's also a little jealous of the attention Bob's giving me.'

'I had noticed,' Pam replied, chuckling. 'Don't worry, he's always been a flirt. But when it comes down to it he's more faithful than the dogs, even though he's had ample opportunity.'

'How do you put up with it? I know I couldn't.'

'Honestly? He only does it to make himself feel good. And I think he realises that I'm a rarity when it comes to women who will put up with him. Besides, I had a word with him last night and told him to rein himself in or I'd invite my mother to come and stay for a month. You should've seen his face!' Pam's face resembled a frightened ferret.

As they laughed, Gill felt a surge of relief. She hadn't wanted to rock the boat, but knew that something needed to be done to salvage what little there was left of the trip. Now, she had something concrete to take back to Jim that might help lighten his mood and allay his fears.

After what turned out to be a pleasant and reassuring walk around the Pinnacles, a stark desert-like landscape littered with limestone spikes in various shapes and sizes popping up out of the ground, Gill spotted Jim and Bob in deep conversation outside the toilets.

That's odd, Gill thought, slowing her pace. Pam winked at Gill. As the two women approached they could hear the mention of cars, only the men weren't talking about Holdens or Fords. No, they were going on about four-wheel-drives, and something about the sand dunes in Lancelin.

'Jim?' Gill said, her tone hesitant.

'Here they are,' Bob butted in, greeting both women with the kiss on their cheeks. Ignoring the stern look Jim threw at Bob, she planted a chaste kiss on Jim's lips.

'Is everything okay?' Pam asked.

'Oh yes, everything is fine,' Jim replied, his broad smile belying his earlier mood.

As the foursome returned to the coach, Gill took Jim aside to find out what he and Bob had been discussing.

'Let's just say the puppy came around with his tail between his legs.'

'I see,' Gill replied, still reserved. 'And have you apologised for your silly mood?'

'Bloody oath,' Jim said, smirking.

'So, what was that about four-wheel-drives?'

'It's a surprise. You'll have to wait until tomorrow,' was all Jim would say, and she caught him throwing Tom a wink as they got on the bus. She wanted to press him, but didn't want that to ruin Jim's newly-acquired good mood.

The coach headed off for Lancelin, pulling up outside the Beach Hotel as the sun was setting over the azure waters of the Indian Ocean, throwing out a kaleidoscope of pink, orange, and purple. The weary travellers checked into their rooms, and Gill seized the opportunity to find out more about Jim and Bob's conversation.

'Have you two finally called a truce, then?' she asked, unpacking her toiletries and placing them in the bathroom.

'What do you mean? We weren't at war.' Jim seemed flabbergasted by Gill's remark, as if there weren't something strange about his complete about-turn with Bob.

'For the past four days, you've been a wet blanket. Not speaking, not joining in activities, and skipping meals. Right after you made that comment to Bob about him being a mongrel, if I recall.'

'Silly misunderstanding,' Jim replied with a boyish grin. 'Are we going for dinner? I'm starving.'

Gill shook her head. Whatever had gone on with Bob today, Jim was keeping it close to his chest.

Jim was in fine form over dinner, sharing stories and jokes with his 'buddy', Bob. He seemed unfazed by Bob's boasting, and didn't even react when Bob still called him 'Jimster.' Gill was bewildered, but let it wash to enjoy the sudden upturn in events.

'Maybe it's something they put in the tea up here,' Gill commented to Pam as they sipped their wine while Bob and Jim played pool.

'Jim seems much happier now,' Pam remarked, as happy with the bromance as Gill was.

'Whatever has gone on, I'm not rocking the boat. I want to enjoy the rest of this trip.'

'I'll drink to that,' Pam said, clinking her glass next to Gill's. 'But I'm damned if I know what those boys have got planned for tomorrow. Did you get anything more out of Jim?'

'Not a thing. Whatever it is, I hope it's legal and moral!' The two women chuckled and chinked their glasses again.

The next morning, Tom seemed more excitable than usual as he ushered the oldies onto the coach.

As Gill and Pam took their seats, they realised that whatever this activity was, it hadn't been listed on the itinerary.

'What are we doing today, Tom?' Pam asked as she took her seat and smoothed down her pants.

'All will be revealed shortly,' Tom replied, clapping his hands with glee.

Bob and Jim sat down, grinning like two little boys who'd just been given new bikes.

'Jim, what's going on?' Gill asked sternly.

'Wait and see,' was all he offered in return.

A sense of foreboding sat like a rock in Gill's stomach. She didn't like surprises, especially ones Jim had a hand in – they often turned out to be something that only boys masquerading as men would enjoy. Pam seemed equally worried, casting Gill anxious looks.

Within minutes, the coach pulled up outside a portacabin surrounded by dusty LandCruisers and a couple of mini buses. Gill's stomach knotted.

'Oh no,' she said, shaking her head. 'I'm not going in one of those.' She pointed to the four-wheel-drives and scowled at Jim.

'Why not? It'll be a laugh,' Jim replied.

Bob nudged Pam, egging her on. 'You're up for it, aren't you, love.'

Pam smiled and nodded.

Gill's heart began to race.

'Don't worry,' Pam said reassuringly. 'Bob's an experienced off-roader. We used to be part of a four-wheel-drive club. He'll look after us.'

Pam didn't seem at all fazed, and it did little to ease the butterflies performing acrobatics in Gill's stomach.

'Jim hasn't driven a four-by-four for years!' Gill protested.

'It'll be fine,' Jim cut in. 'Bob and I agreed to go in convoy. Safety in numbers.'

'We're here, everyone,' came Tom's high-pitched call from the front of the coach. 'Welcome to your sand dune safari!' He clapped his hands, clearly excited, and stood. 'If you could all make your way to the portacabin, one of the guides will come and brief you all about what we're doing today.'

The hum of conversation was rife as the oldies dismounted and headed to the cabin. Once they were all assembled, a bearded, bald-headed man, dressed in camouflage khakis and sporting aviator glasses, gathered them around.

'Welcome to Lancelin Safari 4x4. My name's Colin and I'll be your guide for today's activity.' Clearing his throat, he continued. 'We have two options available for you good folks today. You can either join one of the gentler tours of the dunes on our custom-made four-by-four mini-buses, or for those feeling a little braver, you can drive our LandCruisers and follow a convoy around the dunes.'

Mumblings spread around the group.

'For those deciding to go on the bus tour, please head over to Mini-bus A where Greg, your driver, will get you on board and let you know what you'll be doing and seeing. For everyone else, follow me into the office and we'll sort out the paperwork and go through the safety procedures.'

'Are we doing the bus tour?' Gill asked, hoping Jim would agree.

'As if!' Jim retorted. 'We're going in one of them.' He pointed to the LandCruisers and grabbed Gill's hand.

'Are you sure that's a good idea? You haven't been in anything like that for a long time.'

'It'll be like riding a bike,' Jim replied, pulling Gill towards the office.

Oh god, Gill thought.

After they'd filled in all their details, had their licences copied, and gone through all the safety procedures, they were ready to rumble. Kitted out with safety helmets and walkie-talkies, Gill and Jim headed to their assigned vehicle.

As Gill climbed in the passenger seat, she looked down and noticed the manual gear stick.

'Have you ever driven a manual before?' she asked Jim.

'Course!' he replied, unfazed. 'The tractors on the farm were all manual.'

This did nothing to allay the kangaroos performing high-kicks in Gill's stomach.

As Jim buckled up, Colin's voice came over the airwaves. 'This is Colin here. Before we start, make sure you are strapped in, your helmets are securely fastened, and you know which number you are in the convoy.'

'Number five,' Gill mouthed, referring to the big, black number painted on the bonnet.

'Ten-four,' answered Jim, giggling like a girl.

'Oh Jim,' Gill sighed.

'Okay. Start up your engines, stay in line, and keep an eye on the cars in front and behind you,' Colin announced as engines roared into life.

'Where's Bob and Pam?' Gill asked.

'In front, of course. We made sure to stay together.' Jim turned the engine key and started up, then started up again after he stalled the first time. After a few bunny-hops, he made his way to the convoy.

The drive was plain sailing at first. Everyone stayed in line and Colin regularly checked in with the drivers. Jim was still having issues with the 'sticking shift' when he struggled to change gears, but somehow managed to keep up.

The group had been safely going up and down the dunes for about forty-five minutes when Colin announced that they could have some free time for the next hour, and follow some of the designated tracks on their maps.

Jim's face suddenly beamed, alerting Gill.

Bob pulled up next to Jim and climbed out. Jim joined Bob, and the two men strode a few metres away from the cars, maps in hand. They seemed deep in discussion, pointing at the map and nodding, with grins as wide as Kangaroo Valley.

When Jim returned, Gill was already picturing them stranded in the middle of nowhere, never to be seen again.

'You okay, love?' Jim asked.

'What are you two up to?' she demanded, pointing to the map.

'Nothing, love,' Jim replied. 'Just deciding which track to follow.'

Gill was not convinced. Jim was acting like a kid about to light a fire the way he was in cahoots with Bob.

'Ready?' Jim said as he buckled back in and started the engine.

'You better not be doing anything stupid,' she warned as Jim pulled off, ignoring her.

He followed Bob to an uphill track, but as they approached, instead of pulling up behind Bob, Jim stopped alongside. Gill stayed quiet, eyes wide, sensing the men were about to do something very, very stupid.

Bob and Jim exchanged cheesy grins and simultaneously revved their engines.

'Jim?' Gill yelped. 'What are you doing?'

But before an answer came, the men nodded at each other, released their hand brakes and sped up the track, side-by-side.

'You're racing?' Gill shouted above the din of the engine and crunching gear changes. 'Are you out of your mind?'

'Hold on,' Jim shouted, dropping a gear as the vehicle climbed.

Gill was frantic. *How could he be so stupid and put them both at risk?*

But Jim was loving it. His ear-to-ear grin was a reminder of the dashing smile she used to love about him. But the memory quickly flitted away as Jim and Bob went neck-and-neck … until Bob went off-piste just over the crest of a dune. Jim tried to follow, but over-steered and pinged a rock, slamming on the breaks in a panic. Both he and Gill were thrown forward as the car came to an abrupt halt and then stalled. Bob and Pam were nowhere to be seen, leaving only a sandstorm in their wake.

'Jim! You idiot! Why the hell did you do that?' Gill screamed.

'It was Bob's fault!' Jim complained. 'He went off the track at the last minute, so I swerved to follow him.' He cussed under his breath as he restarted the engine.

'Well, you'd better hurry up and catch him because I'm guessing you haven't a clue where we are.' Gill was seething.

'I *know* where we are. Besides, we can follow Bob's dust trail.'

Gill crossed her arms, as Jim pulled down the hand brake and pressed in the clutch to pull off. But as he did so, the wheels juddered and began to spin. The more he accelerated and tried to move forward, the more the wheels spun.

'Jim? We're not moving!' Gill yelled.

'I know we're not bloody moving, woman. Give me a minute and I'll find out what's happening!' Snorting, Jim put the gear back into neutral, pulled up the hand brake, unbuckled his seatbelt and hopped out of the car.

Gill stayed put, arms crossed, glaring. She waited while Jim walked around the car surveying the situation, scratched his head a few times, then got back in.

'We're bogged down,' he announced, pursing his lips.

'I could've told you that months ago,' Gill bit back. 'So, what are you going to do about it?'

'I'm going to get us un-bogged, obviously,' he replied, mirroring Gill's tone.

'Well, let me know when you've done it.' Gill turned her back on Jim, anger seeping through her pores.

'Fine.'

'Fine,' she replied.

They sat in silence for the next few minutes, Gill mentally cursing Jim's idiotic behaviour.

'Why don't you try the walkie-talkie, or don't you know the call sign for being bogged?'

Jim tutted and picked up the handset, pressing the 'call' button. It crackled several times as he spoke. 'Hello, er … this is Jim Redmont. Um … we've got a bit of a problem. We're bogged.' He waited for a response. And waited. The walkie-talkie crackled some more, but no other sound came.

Gill gasped. 'Are you telling me we're bogged in the middle of god-knows-where, and there's no one around to help us? Jim! Do something!'

'Do *what*? No one can hear us!'

'Well, dig us out then!'

Jim muttered under his breath, riling Gill further, then clambered out of the car. He opened the boot and began rifling through the safety gear.

'Bingo!' he announced, pulling out a pair of bright orange tracks. 'We can use these!' He looked pleased with himself as he shoved each track under each of the back wheels, and climbed back in the car. 'That ought to do it,' he said, restarting the engine.

It didn't do it. No matter how many times he scooped out sand and adjusted the tracks, the wheels kept on spinning. And the more they spun, the more bogged they became.

Beside herself with panic Gill lashed out with the force of a sandstorm at her clueless husband. 'I can't believe you brought me on this stupid safari!' she shouted. 'I should've known you were incapable of being sensible. I mean, you couldn't even organise a bun fight in a bakery!'

'How was I to know Bob was going to speed off like that? We were supposed to be going in convoy!' Jim fired back.

'It's not *Bob's* fault, Jim. You agreed to do this, knowing full well you hadn't driven a four-by-four, let alone a manual, for years.'

'I didn't think we'd end up like this, did I! And I didn't mean for it to happen!'

'Well, it *has*, and now we're stuck here. God only knows if anyone's going to find us and dig us out!' Gill was beyond mad, infuriated that Jim was taking no responsibility for his actions. 'Face it, Jim, *you* got us into this, so *you* need to get us out!'

'What do you want me to do? I've tried the walkie-talkie. I've tried the tracks, and neither has worked. We've sunk into the sand, and unless you can help me dig us out, we'll be staying put until someone comes to rescue us.'

'*If* they come to rescue us. They probably don't even realise we're missing!'

Arms folded, lips pursed, they sat for what seemed an eternity until Jim jumped out, found a shovel in the back of the LandCruiser and set to work.

The afternoon sun was searing. As Jim dug, sand immediately filled the holes. He dug and re-dug until he threw down the shovel, swearing and kicking the back wheel, before he bent over to catch his breath.

The sight of her sweating, sand-dusted, exhausted husband thawed Gill's iciness. In that moment, she realised he was doing everything he could to get them unstuck.

She got out of the car and approached him.

'Come to gloat, have you?' he said, standing upright and wiping his dripping brow with a handkerchief.

'No, Jim, I haven't,' she soothed, reaching over to touch his arm. 'I've come to help.'

'Right-o,' he nodded, and went to retrieve the shovel. 'I'll use my hands, you use the shovel.' He passed it to Gill, who began shovelling the sand from behind one of the back wheels as Jim crouched and did the same from the other side. For several minutes they shovelled sand, only to see it slide back like a waterfall.

'It's no use,' Jim said. 'We're flogging a dead horse.' Mopping his brow again, he looked like the weight of the world was now on his shoulders. 'I don't know what else to do,' he rasped.

'But ... Jim, we have to do something. We can't stay out here all night!' Panic rose from her gut at the thought of spending the night out in the wilds of the Lancelin dunes.

'What, Gill? What can we do? The sand isn't shifting, and neither is this truck.' And with that, Jim grabbed a water bottle from inside the LandCruiser and took a long gulp.

'That's right, Jim. Give up, why don't you?' Gill's momentary softness took a sharp about-turn.

'What else can I do? We're stuck. Face it.'

'Try the walkie-talkie again. Anything. Just do *something*.'

'Why don't you do something? Every time we get in a rut, it's always me that has to fix it!' he yelled, his sweating face reddening.

'That's because it's *you* that always causes it!' Gill screamed, convinced Jim would soon realise that it wasn't just the truck that was sinking in the sand.

Jim shook his head and started walking away, stumbling through the shifting sand.

'Jim!' Gill called out to him, puzzled. 'Where are you going?'

'To get help,' he barked back.

'But you don't know which way help is!'

'I'll follow the track.'

'It'll take you hours, and you'll run out of water.' Gill's concern escalated.

'I don't care!' Jim yelled, not even turning to face her.

Gill fell silent as a myriad of awful thoughts swam in her mind. Would they be rescued? Would Jim make it to the portacabin before the searing heat took him? Would he have enough water? Would *she* have enough water? It all became too much, and tears trickled down her cheeks like river tributaries. 'Please Jim, don't go,' she called out.

Gill waited with bated breath, as if the world had suddenly ceased spinning.

Jim stopped. Slowly he turned, staring into Gill's crystalline eyes. All at once, his jaw unclenched. A smile spread. He strode back to her, arms outstretched, and Gill rushed into them, nestling into his chest.

'Oh Gilly,' he soothed, stroking her hair as she sobbed against him. 'I'm sorry. I'm so sorry.'

As he held her tightly, Gill began to feel safe. He hadn't held her like that for so long, and she wanted to stay in his embrace forever. When her sobs waned, she gazed up at her husband, who planted a soft kiss on her forehead, smiling as she took in his still-handsome face. 'I guess we'd better wait it out,' she sniffed, dabbing her nose with a tissue.

Jim released his hold and took Gill's hand, leading her to the car. He held open the rear passenger door and helped her in. The sun was still beating down, the car hot like a sauna. Jim reached into the driver's cab, turned on the engine and set the air con running, then closed the driver's door and clambered in the back next to his wife. They nestled onto the back seat, Jim's arm clutching Gill's shoulder, pulling her into him.

'It's a bit of a pickle,' Jim said, almost in a whisper.

'It is,' Gill nodded, clasping Jim's other arm as if she were about to fall. 'But I'm sure it won't be long before someone realises we're missing, though, and Bob'll be able to show Colin where he last saw us.'

'If he even realised we'd been left behind,' Jim scoffed, still laying at least part of the blame on Bob.

'Oh well, we can always play I Spy in the meantime.'

'How about we just talk,' he said, gazing into his wife's still watery eyes. 'I think we've got a fair bit of making up to do.'

'That sounds good,' Gill replied, snuggling in closer, inhaling his musk-like scent.

'I've been a pain in the arse lately, haven't I?' he admitted.

'That's an understatement,' Gill replied.

'Well, say it like it is, why dontcha!'

Gill laughed.

'That's something I haven't heard for a while,' Jim said. 'I miss it. And I miss you.'

'You do? But we've been together most of the time since you retired. How can you miss me?' Gill asked, eyes furrowed.

'Well, maybe it's because I now realise that being close to you is not the same as being with you all the time. I miss the times when we are *really* together, not just in the same room.'

'That's the nicest thing you've said to me for quite some time,' Gill mused. 'I miss you too.'

Jim pressed his lips against Gill's forehead. She closed her eyes, giving silent thanks for this precious moment.

Gill's eyes glistened and as Jim's embrace tightened, her heart strings felt like Jim was plucking them with a feather-light touch. He bent his head and planted a soft, sweet kiss on her welcoming lips. Gill surrendered, as if Jim's kiss was thawing her icy body.

When her eyes fluttered open, Jim was gazing at her as if seeing her for the first time. He kissed her again, his tongue probing her mouth as if hungry for a sweetness only she could satisfy. He pressed hard against her and she felt the desire in his loins reaching an inferno.

'Oh Jim,' Gill sighed, curling her toes as the ache of desire flowed through her.

It was another fifty minutes before Gill and Jim heard the low rumble of a vehicle approaching, but the most productive fifty minutes they'd spent together for a long time.

'There you are!' Colin boomed. 'We thought we weren't going to find you!'

Quick as a flash, Jim called back, 'You couldn't give us another hour or so, could ya!' and winked at Gill.

Dusk was fast approaching by the time they were pulled out of the sand and drove in convoy back to base. As they neared the office, the coach party gathered round and let out a huge cheer.

After Jim and Gill parked, and Colin snatched the keys, Bob and Pam approached.

'Thought you were out for the night,' Bob said, laughing.

'Well … you know how it is when you want to find a quiet spot to do the things your kids don't want to think about you doing,' Jim said and winked at Gill again.

'Oh Jim,' Gill sighed, gently shoving him with her shoulder.

Back in Perth, and with the spark between them well and truly reignited, Gill finally relaxed, enjoying candle-lit dinners and romantic strolls along the Swan River with Jim, not to mention time spent watching in-house movies in their hotel room. It was as if they were newly dating.

The night before, Tom informed the weary travellers that their final day was designated a shopping day, but Jim and Bob, whose truce seemed to be holding, had decided that a fishing excursion down the river was a more fitting end to their trip, leaving Pam and Gill to shop in the CBD.

Gill was suspicious when Jim and Bob didn't leave for their excursion until well after breakfast. And why did Jim want to know which shops the women were intending to visit? She shrugged it off as Jim reverting to his post-retirement ways. Hopefully it would be a one-off.

Suspicions aside, she and Pam spent a lovely morning traipsing around the shops on Hay Street and through the arcades, settling in at the Dome on St Georges Terrace for a much-needed cuppa and cake.

They were surprised to find the boys in the hotel bar, already several beers in, by the looks of things, when they arrived back at the hotel, laden with bags.

'Catch any fish?' Pam asked a sheepish-looking Bob.

'Nah ... should've gone yesterday when they were biting.'

Jim nodded in agreement. 'Not good fishing around here,' he added, casually sipping his beer. 'Buy anything nice?'

'Oh, just some gifts for Maggie and the girls, and some necessities.' Gill grinned at Pam, who glanced away to hide her smirk.

After dinner, the foursome took the opportunity to have one final night together in the bar. Bob was back to full boast-mode, but Jim managed to resist the temptation to call him out or bite back. Gill was pleased he seemed happy enough to kick back and enjoy those final few hours.

The coach collected the oldies early that next morning, with Jim, Gill, Bob and Pam taking up their usual seats at the back of the coach. As it made its way back to Perth's Domestic Terminal, spirits were high – Tom, sporting a newly acquired red polka dot bow-tie, had them all joining in singing classics such as 'Shakin' all over,' and 'Love is in the air'.

When it was time for them all to disembark for the last time, Tom took up his trusty microphone and gave an emotional parting speech: 'Well, ladies and gentlemen. It has been an absolute pleasure to have taken this journey with you. I hope you have all had a wonderful time. I know I have. It is with great sadness that I have to bid you all farewell. On behalf of Golden Oldies Coach Tours, I thank you for travelling with us and hope to see you all again in the future. So long. Farewell. Auf wiedersehen. Goodbye.' And with that, he took a flamboyant, final bow.

Gill could swear there were tears in his eyes as the tour party gave him a rapturous applause.

Five days after their return, Gill and Jim were settled back at home, working on a new and improved day-to-day life, including a ramped-up bedroom routine. Jim had returned to the Men's Shed, sparking an interest in restorations, leaving Gill plenty of time and space to get back into her own hobbies. But much to Gill's dismay, he'd tracked down a beaten-up old Nissan Patrol, intending to make it his first restoration project.

'What are you planning to do with it when it's finished?' Gill asked, after he'd brought it home and housed it in their sizeable shed.

'Dunno,' he replied, but the niggle in Gill's stomach told her he was planning something she probably wouldn't like.

Later one evening, and after a fine roast and veg meal with Maggie to celebrate their thirtieth wedding anniversary, Jim and Gill snuggled up together on the couch.

'It's been quite a month,' Jim said, wrapping his arm around Gill's shoulders.

'Hmmm … it has,' Gill replied, pondering how she could've ever thought of giving up on this wonderful man of hers, warts and all.

'Oh … I almost forgot. I've got something for you.' He scuttled off to the bedroom, returning with a small, gift-wrapped box.

'Just a minute,' Gill said, mirroring him, coming back with a slightly larger wrapped present.

They swapped gifts, wishing each other a 'Happy Anniversary', and lingered over a kiss far longer than Maggie would want to witness.

'Open it, then,' Gill urged.

With a twinkle in his eye and a wide smile, he tore at the paper. '*Four Wheel Driving for Dummies*,' he exclaimed. 'What d'ya mean *For Dummies*? I knew exactly what I was doing up at Lancelin!'

'Of course you did,' Gill replied, deadpan. 'So, what are you going to do with that old banger?' she continued, cocking her head to the side.

'I think you know, my love,' he replied with a wink.

Gill tutted, shaking her head. 'You'll definitely be needing that book then,' she replied with a snigger.

'Go on. Open yours.'

Gill carefully unwrapped her gift, revealing a black velvet box. She snapped it open – inside sat a large, shimmering opal pendant on a silver chain. Its multi-coloured facets refracted under the lounge room light, creating a myriad of colours.

'When on earth did you get this?' she asked with a smile as wide as the Sydney Harbour Bridge. 'Actually, I can guess – the so-called fishing trip in Perth?'

Jim beamed, took the necklace from the box and fastened it around his wife's slender neck.

'It's a national treasure, just like you,' he gushed.

'Oh Jim,' Gill sighed. Only this time, it was a sigh of rekindled love for her roguish husband.

Living in the Past

MELANIE PAGE

Nae hauled back the heavy glass door and breezed into J'Adore Travel Boutique. She dropped her battered carryall on the floor and sketched a wave before dropping into one of the swanky vinyl chairs. Izzy grinned around the computer monitor at her.

Maggie Redmont sat up straighter and her lips made a perfect, red 'O'. Her eyebrows had gone into hiding under her fringe. 'Naomi Carpenter!' Nae watched as shock shifted to wide-eyed approval. 'Look at you. Have you done something with your hair?'

Nae gave an impish grin and ran a self-conscious hand through her jet black hedgehog coiffure. 'I mighta.'

Izzy, in the far chair, fluffed her platinum spikes and broke into a huge smile. 'I like it. But weren't you growing it for the wedding?'

'I sure was.' Nae heard the echoes of ironic finality in her statement.

Maggie and Izzy had the sense not to touch it with a ten-foot pole.

Elle, on the other hand … 'What happened between you and that toffee-nosed …?'

Nae offered a dismissive shrug and ran her suddenly clammy hands down her black T-shirt. 'We had a big row. Well, to be honest, quite a lot of rows. He wanted me to ditch my medieval history studies and do political science or economics. Something with a future. Then we could go live in Point Piper, do cocktails with the high-flyers … be somebody.' She rolled her eyes, then frowned. 'It was all about him. Never about me. By the end, he was angry all the time.'

'Sounds like you made the right choice.' Izzy's voice was calm.

'Yeah, I know.' A slow, sombre sigh. 'And it wasn't great, but I don't regret it.'

'When did this happen?'

'Just after I got back to uni.'

Maggie reached across the desk in a gesture of sympathy. 'Oh honey! But that was weeks ago.'

Naomi lowered her eyes and studied her short, black nails. 'I know. But I just had to suck it up and get through the term. I mean, with work and study, I haven't had time to think about it much.'

'So, you just back for Easter?' Izzy changed the subject and Nae was grateful.

'Got home yesterday!' Nae chewed on her lower lip, then leant forward and took the plunge. 'I think I'd like to go overseas for a bit. For the last couple of years, I've been saving and planning for a future that isn't going to happen now. I just want to get away for a while, really away. Not just to the coast for a week.'

'Sounds like a plan.' Izzy nodded approval.

'Mum doesn't get it. Oh, the break up with Travis, sure. And she doesn't mind about that. I guess she imagines I'll be happy to come home and settle here once I graduate, teach history up at the school.' She shook her head.

The business woman in Maggie stepped to the fore. 'What can we do for you, Nae?'

'I want to see something of the world.'

Maggie chuckled. 'We thought maybe you did. Where exactly? And more importantly, when?'

Nae considered the glossy posters adorning the wall. It was a smorgasbord of all the exciting places she'd dreamt about and she was so hungry. But … 'I don't know. Can you do time travel? I want to visit the past.'

Maggie smiled. Elle chuckled. Izzy followed Nae's gaze upwards to the poster of the Colosseum. 'Are you thinking any particular country?'

'England, France, Germany. Somewhere around there.'

'A tour?' Elle pulled two brochures from the vibrant wall display and passed them over. 'There are some good ones that do a lot of historical sites.'

Nae picked them up and flicked through them. 'I don't know that I can afford a tour. I mean, I've got the money I put aside for the wedding, but it's not a fortune. Besides,' she shrugged and met Elle's eyes, 'I'd sort of hoped to, you know, actually do historical work.'

'You mean like, join the dig at Vindolanda, something like that?' Izzy leant forward on her elbows, her chin on her folded hands.

'You know about the Roman dig up there?' Without meaning to, Nae's voice rose in excitement.

'Hey, I watch the History Channel sometimes.' Izzy laughed and shook her head. 'I went there when I was in Hexham a few years ago. They found a Roman belt buckle; I've never seen historians so excited. Is that what you want to do?'

Naomi sat up a little straighter. 'Yeah, kinda. Except that Vindo and most of the other sites are purely excavation. I'd rather do experimental archaeology, see how the other half lived.' There was a pause and a shrug as she remembered that this was just a possibility. 'Or something else. Maybe I'll just do a bit of backpacking or something.'

Maggie rose. 'How soon do you want to go, Nae?'

Nae met the calm look and considered. 'I've got no exams in June, so I'll have about six weeks. I'd go at Christmas, even though Mum would kill me, but most of that kind of thing shuts down for the European winter.'

Maggie came around the counter Nae felt a warm hand on her arm and sensed her eyes prickling at the warmth of the gesture. 'Do you have to rush off? We can look at a few options.'

Nae felt the diffidence rise, the lack of self-esteem that persistently put her own goals and dreams last. She shrugged, demurred. 'Yeah, I'd like that. But if there isn't anything suitable, that's okay. Mum says I should save the money, and she could be right.'

'Nae.'

She could feel Maggie's warm brown eyes burning into her soul. 'Yeah …'

'Do you want to go?'

This was the moment of truth. She could play it safe, or she could go for what she wanted, what she craved. 'Yeah.' Her voice was soft … And then it wasn't. 'Yes, I do.'

'Well good!' Elle leant over the desk. 'You deserve to live a little, Nae. Sometimes you have to do something just for you.'

'Nae …' Izzy's voice cut in. 'Have you seen this?'

She turned the monitor and Naomi watched as the promo for the documentary played. Then she grinned. Then she laughed aloud. 'Are you serious?'

'Sure am.'

Nae felt Maggie's eyes on her. 'Let us look into it, Nae, and we'll let you know.'

Izzy laughed. 'Yep. Consider us your three fairy godmothers.'

On a Monday evening in early June, Nae finally dragged herself away from the Louvre. Dizzy with tiredness, she fought her way back through the metro and then to St Martin's hostel, across the way from the Gare du Nord. With the addition of three new arrivals, two of them obviously backpackers, the tiny foyer was crowded.

'Miss Carpenter?' Among the polyglot babble, the cut glass English accent stood out.

Naomi turned. No one except her curmudgeonly maths teacher had ever called her Miss Carpenter. A tall-ish, fair-ish, young-ish man, in a well-fitting indigo suit jacket over an open-necked shirt, was holding out his hand. His baby blue eyes twinkled, and his close-cropped reddish beard failed to disguise mobile lips and strong white teeth.

'Yes?' Realisation hit. 'Oh, you must be Phillip. I'm sorry. I must have my days muddled up. I wasn't expecting to meet you until tomorrow. Hi, I'm Naomi.' She connected with his grip. It was warm, and firmer than she'd expected. He looked like the captain of her school debating team but had the hands of a tradesman.

He also had a lovely Hugh Grant smile. 'Indeed. I hadn't booked my tickets then. I've been home to Norfolk for my brother's twenty-first. I hope you don't mind that I suggested we travel to St Valery together. When your travel agent contacted Michel, she mentioned that this was your first visit to France.'

She flushed. 'No. That would be wonderful. It's my first visit anywhere. I've never been further than Sydney before.'

A swift smile set her at ease. 'I've never been there at all, so you'll have to tell me about it. I'd quite like to visit.' He nodded in the direction of the small bar across the street, neon sign glowing pink. 'Would you care to get a drink?'

Nae nodded and followed. While a wild night on the town, even if she were so inclined, was out of her reach, a glass of wine wouldn't break the bank. He pulled out her chair and waited beside her until she sat.

'They have some Australian wines and beers here, if you'd like one.'

She shook her head. 'I'd rather have a local wine please. Something not too dry.'

'Excellent suggestion.' He stepped away for a moment to place their order, then returned.

Nae cast about in her mind for something unexceptional to say by way of conversation. 'Do you come here often?'

He was kind enough not to laugh, but his eyes lit up with amusement. 'Naomi, I'm fairly certain that was my line.'

Nae flushed pink. 'I can't believe I said that! Sorry. I must be more tired than I realised. And please, Nae is fine. Only my mum calls me Naomi.'

'Don't apologise. I shouldn't tease you.' He paused and considered. 'If you mean Paris, I've passed through perhaps half a dozen times in the past year. Before that I have visited once or twice. I haven't stayed at St Martin's before.' He waited. 'How long have you been in Paris?'

'About thirty-six hours.'

The barman put two glasses of a vibrant red on the table. Phillip lifted his. 'Santé.'

'Cheers.' She took a sip to steady her nerves. 'We have to wait until seven for the night bus to St Valery, don't we?'

He nodded.

'I've been to the Louvre today and yesterday, after the plane got in, the Musee de l'Armée at Les Invalides. Do you have any suggestions for what I should do tomorrow?'

He ran a finger around the base of the glass. 'What would you say to a medieval walled city?'

Despite the exhaustion, her eyes lit up. 'Seriously? Where?'

'About an hour by train. If you'd care to meet me down here tomorrow morning, we could go together. I haven't been since I became involved in the St Valery project and I was planning to revisit.'

'I'd love to. Thank you.' She yawned. 'Oh, I beg your pardon.'

'Not at all. I'd be surprised if you weren't tired, it must have been quite a flight.'

A nod and another sip. The wine was disappearing fast. 'Twenty-seven hours. How long have you been at St Valery?'

His eyes glinted over the wineglass. 'I've been receiving a stipend since the end of last year, but I've been involved for three years, since I finished my Masters. And you? What do you do, Nae?'

Nae felt her shoulders tense, the way they always did when she was obliged to justify her academic choices. At least Phillip probably wouldn't curl his lip like Travis had. 'I've just finished undergrad studies in medieval history. I've started a post grad in museum curatorship. It was either that or teaching – there's not a lot of work in medieval history in Australia, as you can imagine.'

He nodded and stopped swirling his wine. 'You must be an extremely imaginative thinker.'

She blinked. 'Well thank you. But why?'

'You live in a place where there are no buildings older than two hundred and what, fifty years, no medieval artefacts or literature. Yet you set yourself to understand a world that is as alien as can be from everything you've known. I call that imagination.'

She felt the blood rush to her cheeks and took another sip to cover her confusion. He seemed sincere, but if this was flirting, she could get used to it. 'You're too kind.' A pause. 'And what about you? What is your role at St Valery?'

'I'm researching for my doctorate, so the hands-on experience I'm able to get there is priceless. For the most part I cast a scholarly eye over the experimentation and write it up. I also write the work-safe procedures, so I'm the one responsible if it all goes bust.'

'Oh.' Nae drained her glass. 'Does that happen often?'

He grinned. 'So far, we've narrowly avoided fire, flood and dismemberment. I hope they can keep it up for another few months, and then it will be back on Michel's shoulders.' He took the last sip from his glass. 'If you're not too tired, would you like to find a restaurant and have some dinner?'

She looked at him through lowered lashes and considered. She was tired; he was a stranger. They were in a foreign city where she was flat out asking the way to the ladies. A sensible person would be wary. On the other hand, he was not much older than she, he was great company, and he was hot, in a studious kind of way.

'That would be great. Thank you.'

Provins was at the top of a hill. They embarked at the Gare L'Est just after nine o'clock, narrowly avoiding the worst of rush hour, or so Phillip said. To Nae, it looked worse than the Boxing Day sales.

She gazed eagerly out the window at her first glimpse of French countryside until they disembarked, an hour later, at the end of the line. Nae stood stock still, eyes bright. Even here, within sight of the railway station, quaint little stone and half-timbered houses sat among roses. With a gentlemanly flourish, Phillip ushered her over to a narrow path that wound up, and up, and up. They passed over a burbling stream that ran between the houses, bulbs and sedges along its banks.

It wasn't the fairy tale village of her imagining, but it was real. Houses were weathered to a soft grey, with brown shutters and tiny, wrought-iron balconies. The roads curved to follow the shapes of the houses. Ground floors were remodelled into shopfronts, with the original structures still above. Late model cars and bright neon signs stood in front of crazily timbered and plastered medieval homes. Tiny alleyways of grey stone stairs rose at almost forty-five degree angles between the houses to her left and dropped just as sharply to the right.

After a few hundred metres, Nae stopped short. The corner of the limestone façade in front of her had weathered away, exposing the wattle and daub structure. It was a method of building she could describe in detail. To see it in real life was overwhelming.

Phillip turned. 'Is anything the matter?' Then he caught where she was looking.

She turned, her face alight. 'Oh, no. I just ...' She waved a hand in the general direction of history.

He came back and stood beside her, put an arm around her shoulders. 'I understand.' A pause. 'Funnily enough, I envy you this moment.'

'Why?'

He smiled wryly. 'I've been surrounded by the past all my life. I struggle not to take it for granted. This moment that you are experiencing now; the amazement, the wonder, the thrill of seeing the past come alive for the first time …' He shrugged. 'It's something special.'

She tilted her head and considered. 'You mean I'm a history virgin.'

He blinked and then his cheeks creased into a broad grin. His shoulders shook.

'Oh, God, I'm sorry! I did it again, didn't I?'

Now he laughed aloud, dropped his arm from her shoulders and waved a dismissive hand. 'Don't worry. Your secret is safe with me.'

'You mean the fact that I can't open my mouth without swallowing my foot and leg?'

'That too, if you insist.' He took her hand. 'Come on. The fun is only just beginning.'

Walking along the wall of a medieval city, complete with the traditional crenellations, towers and arrow slits, was the most exhilarating thing Nae could remember doing. With sparsely occupied land stretching in all directions, it was easy to imagine smoke rising from thatched villages and a bevy of knights galloping up to the fortified gate. A stone's throw away, across a deep ditch, the bitumen road ran along the top of an earthen embankment. It was one thing to see a diagram of medieval defences, another entirely to stand on them and imagine trying to mount an attack.

She stood on the top of one tower and turned one-eighty degrees, a hand on her head to keep her hat from flying away. 'They didn't miss a trick, did they?'

Phillip apparently had no difficulty interpreting this cryptic utterance. 'No indeed. Everything was deliberate, even the curves in the road to slow down the fellows with the battering ram.' He started down the stairs and offered his hand. 'Come up to the citadel. That will blow your mind.'

The twelfth century Tour César, set high in concentric stone rings, was something else. From the moment Phillip obligingly translated the sign out the front, to climbing the cramped stone staircases, Nae couldn't stop grinning. It was beyond her wildest dreams and yet she persisted in feeling stubbornly at home.

Phillip stood with one hand on an ancient beam, the original rafters of the conical tower above their heads, the world at their feet. 'Are you glad you came?'

She seized his free hand without thinking. 'It's just incredible. Thank you for showing me this.'

'It's been my pleasure.' He stood for an awkward moment, as though he wanted to say more but thought better of it. His eyes met hers … lingered. 'If you've seen enough, we should have a late lunch before we go back. The night bus doesn't get to St Valery until supper time.'

At the restaurant on the town square, the immaculate waiter pulled out her chair. At a distance, somewhere off to her left, there was cheering and applause. 'What's that? Do you know?'

Phillip picked up the menu. 'In the tourist season, there is a falconry display. It's worth going to, if you've never seen it before.'

'I've seen falcons. I went up to The Abbey Tournament a couple of years ago with a friend.' She kept her voice deliberately level. Travis had been utterly bored. She hadn't bothered suggesting they go the following year.

'Tell me about it.'

It's a medieval history re-enactment event. Groups from all over Australia go. It's held just north of Brisbane in Queensland every year, about three weeks from now.' She gestured. 'When I was there, they had people come from England and other places to joust.'

'Really?'

She nodded. 'It's big. Thousands of people go. I've got friends in the Knights Templar and the Society for Creative Anachronism. It's actually something I'd like to get involved in once I graduate and can afford to go.'

'It's expensive?'

She shrugged. 'Not really. It's mainly the travel. It's about three hundred kilometres up the coast road. But I don't have a car or much of an income. Just my student allowance, a couple of shifts a week at the local supermarket, and what I earn when I'm home on the holidays.'

'What sort of work do you do?'

She lifted a hand. 'This. I do table service in the tavern in Heart Springs. Mum and Dad bought it thirty years ago.'

'That's where you live? You said you'd been to Sydney.'

'Yeah. We're in New South Wales, in the southern part of the New England Area. There are a lot of sheep and wheat fields. And wineries. I live on campus at Macquarie University.'

'What do you enjoy about your study? What are you passionate about?'

Nae put her hands in her lap and fiddled with her napkin. 'I guess, making sense of why people acted the way they did. If we just look at events, we miss the point. We need to understand why people thought that crusades were a good idea, or that the plague was caused by witches. I suppose that's why I'm here.'

Phillip looked at her as though she were a particularly bright pupil. 'Bravo.'

Her heart sped up at his obvious approval, but she mentally pinched herself. Hard. Hopefully she wasn't so pathetic that she would misconstrue polite interest as admiration. 'What about you?'

He considered for several moments. 'I don't have a job, as such. I'm supervising a project at St Valery which is related to my thesis. After that I suppose, I will look for a place within one of the universities.' He looked down. 'Or there are other options. I've got a couple of irons in the fire, but I don't know yet how they will pan out.' He gestured to the menu. 'Have you thought about what you might like?'

'Well sort of. '*L'agneau* is lamb, right?'

'Sorry?' He looked down at the bill of fare and realised her confusion. 'I see. As I recall, the lamb *navarin* was very good.'

'Sounds great.'

The night bus rattled into Ville de St Valery just after nine. Much to Nae's surprise, it was still broad daylight. Standing at the bus stop was a slender blonde, somewhere shy of thirty, in form-fitting jeans and a silky blouse that matched her lipstick to perfection. She needed a Jag or a Lamborghini to set off her sheer physical perfection, but instead she was standing next to an old Volvo sedan.

Phillip obviously recognised her, because with a quick '*Merci*' to the bus driver, he had their cases out and headed straight for the blonde.

'Good evening, Candace. Thanks for coming out to meet us. Was Michel tied up?'

'I volunteered.' Her voice, like Phillip's, was unmistakably English. She looked from him to Nae and performed a lightning assessment. Nae recognised the glance for what it was, and also the cool smile. She had been deemed no threat. Fair enough too.

'Miss Carpenter, welcome.'

Naomi stuck out her hand. 'Naomi. Or Nae. Hi.' Candace took it almost in self-defence.

Phillip put the boot up and quickly heaved their bags in. 'Nae, I'd like to you meet Dr Candace Coalhaven, the oracle of medieval textile research. She will probably be putting you to work from time to time.'

'Cool.' The Nordic blonde could be as snooty as she liked, if she was prepared to share her knowledge.

'How are your family, Phillip?'

'They are well.' His voice was composed. Nae recognised that tone. It was the male equivalent of a woman saying 'fine'. Phillip held out a hand. 'Would you like me to drive?'

She flashed him a slow, close-lipped smile, said 'Absolutely,' dropped the keys lightly into his palm, then got into the driver's side. Nae blinked. No. It was the passenger's side. That took some getting used to.

Phillip opened the rear door and smiled at Nae.

'Thanks, Phillip.' From the front seat, Candace was looking back at her in the rear-view mirror. If looks could kill …

When, twenty minutes later, the Volvo turned the last corner, Nae was not surprised to see a small group of stone and timber dwellings arranged around three sides of a central garden. Two of the houses had flowers planted in front of them, but the next two were devoid of ornamentation, and the last two were unfinished. About thirty metres away was a large rustic workshop, also built of wood, with a shingle roof. Two smaller out-buildings, covered in thatch, were on the edge of the cleared land.

Set apart from the rest was an ancient stone building. A small church, the colour of soft ash, it was the focus of some of the noise and movement. Here and there, the building showed signs of structural repair. Despite the gathering dusk, two men were hammering the last shingles onto the roof, another was clearing up the site. The rounded arches on the windows, subtly different from splendidly gothic structures like Notre Dame, suggested it was Norman.

'We've put you in one of our newer buildings.' Candace unfolded herself from the front seat and gestured to the third house, the one in the centre. 'At the moment there is only Yvette. Louise is off site at present.'

'I'll take you up then we'll come down for supper and do the paperwork.' Phillip pulled Nae's bag out of the car.

'Honestly, there's no need.'

Nae didn't need Candace looking any more daggers at her. Presumably the blonde felt she had some kind of dibs on Phillip Day. And there was no way she was going to get into a turf war over a man, even a particularly sexy man, especially one who she would only be around for a few weeks. She hefted the case.

'If you're sure?' Surely that wasn't disappointment in his tone?

'Take the back room on the left.'

She nodded an acknowledgement and then forgot all about the catty blonde, every thought driven from her mind by the sight of her home for the next four weeks.

Nae stepped through the banded oak door into a wonderland. The lower floor of the house was as authentically medieval as painstaking research and local planning laws could make it. The floor was of compacted earth, thickly strewn with straw. The left internal wall of the house was all white plaster. It held a large fireplace with flagstones all around it and iron hooks hanging above. Nae could have stood upright in it without difficulty. Near her left hip was a table that could seat eight, with two benches as seats and some wooden preparation benches. Nae ran one mesmerised hand over the thick oak table top.

On the right-hand wall was a smaller fireplace. This was a work area. There was a tall loom by the window and a spinning wheel in the other corner. Baskets of dull-coloured yarn sat beside both. There was a room behind and a piece of coarsely woven cloth hung in the door space. The room was lit and warmed by the workroom fire. There were four small oil-burning lamps strategically placed on mantelpiece and table.

Nae left her case at the foot of the rough-hewn stairs and went to peek behind the curtain. A hip-high wooden tub stood there, with a thick linen curtain hanging around it from a central ring. There was another door in the corner. A solid one this time, with enormous bronze hinges. She breathed a sigh of relief when she saw a conventional white porcelain toilet and basin.

Upstairs was a small landing, with heavy beams higgledy-piggledy under the thatch, which led to the sleeping quarters. Off it were four identical door curtains, two on each side of the staircase. As instructed, she took the back left, which had a modern foam mattress on a wooden bed frame. It was made up with a rough sheet and a dusky pink blanket. When she lifted a corner of the mattress, she was not surprised to find it resting on a lattice of taut ropes. There was also a small chest against a wall.

Naomi left her suitcase beside the bed and went back outside. Light filtered out from the translucent windows of the second house.

'Ah, Nae. How did you find your accommodation?' Phillip held out a hand as she entered. There were a number of people she didn't know who all turned.

'Amazing!'

He grinned. 'I should have known you'd take it in your stride. We've occasionally had volunteers turn tail and run when the reality of living in the past sinks in.' Phillip gestured to the man at his right. 'This is Michel. He is the owner of the land and the one who came up with the idea of the research village.'

Michel was no more than five foot eight and robustly built. He was older than Phillip, but not excessively so. Despite the threads of grey at the temples, Nae would have put him just shy of forty.

'Mademoiselle, welcome to St Valery d'Arles. I am Michel de St Valery.' He smiled. His English was very good but his accent still deliciously French. 'I'm hoping you will call me Michel and count yourself welcome here. We were all new here once.' He gestured to the people beside him. 'My wife, Marguerite. Yvette, who is sharing the house with you. Carl, Paul and Guy, who are working on building five. Henri who is at the church with Phillip and Lorraine, our cook and quarter mistress.'

Lorraine handed Nae a pottery mug which steamed gently and gestured to something that looked suspiciously similar to Anzac biscuits.

'We'll do the paperwork tonight if you don't mind.' Lorraine, unlike the others, wore a linen coif and medieval gown. Her face was quite lined, her English thick and guttural. 'I shall be busy in the morning.' The others moved into the work space to give them privacy and Nae sat at the heavy table. 'We have the insurance policies. There's also an undertaking not to publish anything without our approval, and the roster.'

Nae signed her life away without a qualm.

'We have rostered you on for twenty days, which is our minimum volunteer agreement. You will be rostered on for five days at a time, with two or three-day breaks. Is that acceptable? That will give you a day or two to enjoy Paris before you fly home.'

'Sure.' It was a no-brainer, really. Izzy and Maggie had already checked the details when she booked. Nae knew them too well to think there would be any nasty surprises.

She sipped her pottery mug. It wasn't tea, or coffee. It was hot spiced wine, which kind of made sense. No one in the middle ages had ever heard of tea or coffee, but mulled wine was common. Oh well, her coffee addiction would keep.

'In the coffer in your room, you will find two chemises and a kirtle. There is also a sewing kit in case you need to adjust a hem, but we do ask that you don't remodel the dress extensively as we will need to reuse it. We dress in costume as part of the experience, so whenever you are rostered on, if you could do so, please.' She looked up and Nae caught a reassuring smile. 'Think of it as a uniform.'

Nibbling on an oatcake and sipping her wine, Nae sat down alone at the end of the long bench and tried to absorb it all. Then she laughed quietly to herself, washed out her mug and made her adieux.

When Nae wriggled into the linen chemise the following morning, she found that it fitted well, but given that it was essentially a long shirt, that wasn't difficult. The soft green kirtle was made of woven wool, as sheer as a lightweight jumper. It was also about two inches too long. The promised sewing kit was long skeins of fine linen thread, wound around a soft cloth, through which were poked two bone needles. It took Nae the best part of an hour to tack it up, during which time the girl across the hall, Yvette, had stuck her head in twice.

When she came back for the third time, Nae had just dropped the kirtle over her head and was twisting her way into it. Yvette, dressed in a fetching thirteenth-century ensemble, tugged the garment down and dragged a narrow leather belt from the coffer. This went around Nae's waist and a rectangle of fine white linen was draped over her hair, held on with a stiffened circular band.

'Thanks.'

'*De rien.*'

Before following, Naomi slipped her phone out and took a selfie. She couldn't post it, but she didn't have a mirror. With her black hair covered and her black clothes gone, the girl on the screen looked a lot like the old Nae. Uncertain about what was to come? Sure. Timid? Perhaps a little. But she felt buoyed up with enthusiasm, happy again in her own skin, as though she had shed indecision and heartache with the twenty-first century. Holding up her skirts to keep from tripping on the stair, she laughed aloud as she headed down.

Breakfast was porridge, along with a dark grain bread, butter, honey and apricots, washed down with a small beer. Then Nae endured a guided tour with Candace before being handed over to Lorraine for kitchen duties for the rest of the morning. This consisted of grinding grain between two large stone wheels. It was a trifle monotonous, but at least Nae could look out the open door across the garden to where two builders were laughing as they lime-washed the upper storey of the newest house. After a while, Phillip appeared. There was a great deal of arm waving, then the man on the ladder put on a bright yellow safety helmet that clashed horribly with his tunic and hose, and went back to plastering.

Nae finished grinding and was in the strawberry patch picking fruit for lunch when a tall, dark and presumably handsome shadow fell across her. Phillip squatted on his haunches beside her, his hose taut across strong thighs.

'How are you getting along?'

She smiled up at him, eyes shielded against the sun. 'It's … educational.'

'What precisely?'

She pulled another berry and considered. 'I guess the thing I'm struggling with the most is the clothing. Aussies don't wear heavy clothing, except in winter for a couple of months. Having to be aware of my dress all the time is different.'

'Yes, that makes sense.' He pulled two juicy berries from the nearest runner, slipped one between his teeth and held the other to her lips. It was a curiously intimate gesture and Nae felt a timid flutter in her chest as she bit down on the ripe fruit. Could this be – flirtation? Without more ado, he drew her to her feet. 'That should be enough fruit. I'll come with you when you make your deliveries, and we can go and check on Michel. I think you'd like to see the mill.'

Lorraine gave Nae a large basket, rather like the one Red Riding Hood took to Grandma's house, with chunks of bread, cheese, berries and large jars with a wax and cloth stopper in the top, and comprehensive instructions. They dropped lunch at house five for Carl and Paul, and went on, up a narrow track and into the forest.

Here the sounds of industry were chased away by birdsong as they walked through a verdant paradise. With the swish of her gown and Phillip in his long grey tunic and hose beside her, Nae felt as though she had been dropped bodily in the thirteenth century. Mildly awed, Nae felt her foot strike against the rough path. As she corrected her stumble, her gait hitched slightly.

Phillip misinterpreted the motion. 'Where are my manners? I should be carrying that basket.' He reached out to take it from her.

She laughed and swung away. 'No way, mister. No self-respecting peasant would relieve a woman's burdens.'

He closed one hand around the handle and they stopped. There was a hush as though the sounds of the forest had been suddenly muted. Their eyes met and held. 'No self-respecting peasant would slip away with a lovely woman and not make the most of it.' And then he bent his lips to hers.

It was the most tentative of kisses, as if he were shy, or uncertain of his reception. After no more than a handful of heartbeats he pulled back. Nae stood still, a trifle surprised.

'I do apologise …'

'For stopping?' The words came out of their own volition, but she couldn't regret them.

He looked at her. Really looked at her. 'Ah, no.'

'Well, good.' She carefully set the basket down and closed the distance between them, tilting her face up and drawing his head down. After a second he wrapped both arms around her and deepened the kiss, employing his mobile mouth to great effect. When they broke apart, Nae took a deep breath and slowly raised her eyes.

'I guess you could call that making the most of it.'

'You could indeed.' They looked at each other, a little wary. Nae could feel the inevitable query on the tip of her tongue, but she didn't want to hear the answer. Better to enjoy the moment.

Phillip leant towards her and Nae closed her eyes again, but then she felt him lift the basket at her side. Apparently he was no more anxious than she to ask that particular question. She fell in beside him, only slightly bemused, as they walked the final hundred metres to the riverbank.

The next two days passed in similar fashion to the first for Nae. A communal breakfast, followed by cooking and a trip to the mill with some kisses as garnish, then an afternoon carding wool with Candace and practising her French on poor, unsuspecting Yvette. However, on Saturday afternoon Lorraine decided to initiate her into the mysteries of medieval cookery.

Dinner had always been adequate, stews and the ubiquitous bread, nuts dipped in honey and baked, fresh fruit, and delicious wine, but on Saturday a goose was turning on the spit over the fire and a dazzling array of vegetables was being prepared. After the daily grind, where she and Lorraine took turns milling the flour, Nae sat down with a small bowl of blanched almonds and a mortar, and proceeded to turn the nuts into marzipan.

'How are you enjoying your holiday?' Lorraine was pummelling the bread dough into submission.

'It's amazing. It feels so real.' It did. Nae hadn't looked at her phone for days.

'Is there anything that you want to experiment with, something that you could do here?'

That was a question. 'Ah, candle-dipping, soap making ...' Now that her brain started making a list, it wouldn't stop. 'I've seen wooden construction but you aren't building with stone. It would have been great to see that.'

Lorraine paused with her hands in mid-knead, flour to the elbows. 'You have two days' leave on *Lundi*, yes?'

'Monday. Yes.'

'Ask Phillippe to take you to Guédelon, to the castle there. It is only an hour or so from here and he goes there often to consult with stonemasons and carpenters.'

'Do you think he would?'

'Of course. He admires you greatly. And I think perhaps he pleases you also. No?'

Nae pasted on a bright smile. 'Phillip is great. Thanks for the hint. I'll ask him.' She would. Eventually.

The opportunity came earlier than she had hoped. Phillip and the house-builders downed tools at twelve and came in for lunch, instead of waiting on Nae's usual delivery run. Michel and the other men who had been working at the mill came in about fifteen minutes later, laughing and full of self-congratulation.

'It works, my friends.' Michel walked straight up to Lorraine and kissed her on both cheeks.

Although she was enjoying the sight of all the French speakers talking excitedly at once, Nae turned to Phillip for translation. 'The mill?'

He held out a hand, drawing her closer without shifting an inch from his position against the staircase. The heat from where his body pressed lightly against hers made her skin prickle with an unnamed sensation. 'Indeed. The mill race is flowing well and the wheels turn easily. We'll have the great unveiling after lunch. I think, barring disaster, you've ground your last grain by hand.'

She laughed despite the tingle of desire. 'Hooray.'

'I thought you wanted the authentic medieval experience?'

Her glance flickered up. 'Don't get me wrong, it's been amazing. But I say, long live mechanisation.'

'What's been the highlight of your first week?'

'You need to ask?'

She would have sworn he blushed. There was loud laughter and cheering behind them. He listened and then translated. 'Michel says the dedication will be at three and after dinner tonight, we'll celebrate.'

'Can't wait.'

So after dinner, heart fluttering, Naomi pinned a small corsage of lavender to her kirtle and went down to her first medieval ball. They were using the lower floor of the fourth house, where Henri and Guy were living because it hadn't been taken over by Candace's loom. Instead there were three chairs by the hearth and that was the sum of the furniture. Other benches had been borrowed for the occasion, however, and placed against the walls. Yvette, like herself a short-term resident, had but one kirtle, a lovely madder rose, but Phillip and Michel had put on their best hose.

Just as Michel picked up an instrument that was the love-child of a flute and a trumpet, Candace appeared in the doorway. She wore a form-fitting white *bliaut* falling softly from the waist, the long sleeves lined with pale blue linen and the *ceinture*, of blue and gold cord, knotted around her hips. Her veil was translucent white linen. While the style was similar to the cheap medieval replicas beloved by Nae's fellow goths, this was a work of art. Nae opened her mouth and closed it again. The gentlemen were impressed too.

'Candace, *cherie. Tres magnifiqué.*' Michel was all Frenchman tonight.

Phillip took her hand and bowed over it in courtly fashion. 'You look positively regal, Candace. Exceptional work.'

She preened. 'Thank you, gentlemen.'

Phillip offered Candace his hand and they moved into the middle of the room. The music started, a stately dance, paced very much like a minuet but with simpler movements. Paul led Yvette out and Carl offered Nae his hand. In spite of the excitement she'd felt coming down, there was a hollowness in her stomach as they took their places. She told herself it was nothing to her whether Phillip danced with Candace. Of course he'd dance with others. But even though everyone seemed to realise that she and Phillip were an item, it was as though Candace felt she had the right to expect his attention.

Nae had never stopped to think about Phillip's relationship with others. After the first delicious surprise of his kiss, she'd decided to enjoy the moment. She was going home in a few weeks. If something happened, well, they were both adults and unattached. But was he?

She shook off the feeling and smiled up at Carl. He was a genial guy, with a sweet nature and shaggy blond looks, like an unusually friendly Viking. From somewhere near Stuttgart apparently, and with good, basic English; she could talk to him better than to Paul or Guy.

One of the dancers shouted a suggestion to Michel and the music paused. The dancers lined up in two lines, ladies on the left, gentlemen on the right. This dance apparently consisted of sidling, turning, crossing, and for the lead couple, a procession down the centre, then repeat. Once she got the hang of it, and in spite of the nameless pang she felt when Phillip and Candace did their procession, it was fun. The dance ended and there was an exchange of partners. Phillip appeared at her side.

'May I have this dance?' His voice was warm and low.

'What is it?'

'It's a branle, like a circle dance. Lots of sidesteps.'

'Um, sure.'

It was faster than the previous, rather stately *basse danse.* Nae laughed, fumbled her feet and laughed harder. 'No more for me. I'll just watch. I never was any good at this.'

Phillip looked down at her. Two dimples appeared just above the neat whiskers and her heart skipped in time to the music. 'Come for a walk with me.'

'Nonsense. You can't leave.'

He shook his head, waved at Michel and drew her out into the cooler evening. It was still daylight, despite the relative lateness of the hour, the sun glinting visibly through the trees to the west. 'Of course I can. I've wanted to get away with you all day.'

She took his hand silently. Her stomach was doing tiny backflips. She had to know. If he was fancy free, all well and good. If someone ... she admitted it to herself ... okay, if Candace had a claim on him, no more kissing.

He led her up through the forest towards the mill and the river. Around them the day was becoming quiet. One star, Venus she assumed, hung in the sky and there was the faintest wisp of a moon in the east. All around her, trees – which she now recognised as larch, spruce and oak – rustled and chattered. The clearing beside the river where they often lunched was set in deep green shadows. He drew her down beside him and lifted the veil and circlet from her hair.

'Good evening, my lady.'

A delusion of hope bubbled through her. 'Am I?'

He ran his fingers through the soft spikes at her temples. 'Is there any reason why you shouldn't be?'

She captured his fingers; his touch was affecting her like strong wine. She wanted to turn away, play coy, tease him a little, but his open, honest eyes were beguiling. 'I don't know. Do you have a secret wife hidden away, like Bluebeard?'

He laughed. 'Neither living, nor dead.'

'Not a girlfriend, mistress, light o' love?'

'Not so much as a secret admirer.'

She met his eyes. 'I don't know. I would have called Candace a not-so-secret admirer. You wouldn't even have to whistle. She'd come running if you so much as puckered.'

'Miss Carpenter, are you jealous?' His voice had deepened. He was still teasing, but she heard the serious question under the banter.

A long pause. 'Maybe. Just a little.'

He ran a hand over his beard and looked down at her. 'For the record, it has been almost a year since I kissed any girl but you. Sure, Candace showed an interest in me. But we're just friends. She went to school with my sister. And we have a few acquaintances in common, quite apart from our work here, so I guess we have a history. But no … we are not, and never have been, an item.'

Nae lay back on the grass. She couldn't recall the last time she had walked with someone, purely for the pleasure of walking. Or lay on the grass by a river. Evening was a time for TV or work or assignments. Even at home in Heart Springs, there were always things to be done. She reached up, ran her fingers along Phillip's jaw until they covered his lips. 'Then yes. I'd love to be your lady.'

He intertwined his fingers with hers and moved so her hands were raised behind her head. 'I suppose I should ask if there are a score of besotted swains at home, panting for your return.'

'Well, not a score.'

He kissed her lips. 'Temptress. A dozen then?'

'Not that I recall.'

'A mere handful?'

She shook her head.

'Well, more fool them.' He lay, stretched at full length beside her, resting on one hip. One elbow dug into the grass and his head was propped on his hand as he looked down. 'I was wondering if you would care to indulge in a traditional pastime of the medieval peasant.'

'And that would be?' She raised her lips to his, fairly certain she knew the answer.

'Swiving.'

Nae grinned and wriggled. 'Shame on you, my lord. And on the eve of the Lord's day. What would the priest say?'

'I'm sure he would understand.'

With her hands occupied, she hooked her ankle around his leg and drew him closer. He released one hand to steady himself. She ran hers down his tunic and past his belt.

'Hmmm, is that a cod-piece, or are you just pleased to see me?'

Phillip chuckled and raised an eyebrow. 'You want my cods, do you? Brazen wench.'

'Yes, please.'

Between laughing, kissing and rather a lot of fumbling with unwieldy garments, Phillip managed to expose a good deal of Nae's skin and proceeded to sample it. It was half an age before she could get her hands beneath his tunic and wrestle with the laces on his hose. There was a cod-piece, but the size and shape owed nothing to fashion.

Gradually the frivolity gave way to a rising passion, teasing to dedicated sensual exploration. As the light began to fade, Nae turned him on his back. She took the small foil packet from his hand and sheathed him in some very modern protection, then straddled his hips, sinking and rising in an age-old rhythm. The sky was full of stars when they finally bathed in the river, gathered their discarded clothes and made their way back to the houses, hand in hand.

'Oh my goodness.' It was impressive. The size alone was remarkable. She'd expected to be fascinated, but this exceeded even her wildest hopes.

'So you like it then?'

'Thank you!'

'Believe me, it's my pleasure.'

Nae looked up at the vaulting and the incredible stonework. Guédelon was spectacular, and she could see where Michel had taken his inspiration. 'Who'd believe you could build a castle today using medieval techniques?'

It was Tuesday, the second day of Nae's first break, and a week after their trip to Provins. It seemed like an eternity, but in the most wonderful way. Back in her jeans, and a T-shirt she'd picked up in Paris, she felt like herself and yet not. A change had taken place in her perspective.

At Michel's suggestion, she'd spent Monday at his manor house with Marguerite, half a mile from the St Valery site. She'd taken a long, hot shower, savoured a coffee and called her mother. Heart Springs was apparently right where she'd left it and everyone was eager to hear about her adventures.

Today Phillip had brought her to the sister site at Guédelon where he had to consult with the foreman about his pet scheme.

'You saw the old medieval church at the edge of the site back at St Valery?'

'Sure.'

'Archaeology suggests that it was Norman, abandoned after the plague went through. There are no new burials after that. Michel had a thorough dig done and now he wants to restore it as part of the project.'

'And that's your role in the place?'

He nodded, radiating boyish excitement. 'Exactly. We've bought clay from the local sources that have been supplying for millennia and built forms in the end shed. Now that the weather is good, we can make the tiles and dry them before they are fired.'

'You're making replica tiles to pave the church. Is that authentic? I thought floors were stone.'

'Absolutely authentic. York, Winchester, a thousand places … Glastonbury even had tiles. It's my main area of research.'

'Sounds riveting.'

He shrugged. 'I can give you my thesis to read. It's a sure cure for insomnia.'

She leant lightly into his shoulder. 'I can think of a better soporific.' He bent and gave her a light kiss.

When Phillip squeezed her hand and turned his attention to the foreman, Nae wandered off to watch the workmen. She was amazed by the detail they brought to their craft. She was so accustomed to seeing images of aged, fragile structures that, to see the medieval art in fresh bright detail, was a revelation. Robert, the foreman, only spoke French, so Nae quickly lost interest in the conversation. Instead she watched the stonemason chipping away at a grotesque for the roof, the wild hair, leering features and popping eyes coming eerily to life. Each stone took countless hours to shape and yet here was the castle, rising almost before her eyes.

This was where she was meant to be. Here, or somewhere like it, where she could do the work that fascinated her. And yet Nae felt the visceral pull of Australia; she had roots Down Under going back five generations on her mother's side.

As they walked back to the car, Phillip took her hand. 'Penny for them.'

'I'm sorry?'

'It's an old saying. Penny for your thoughts. There something on your mind.'

She laughed, but it rang false. 'Oh, nothing. I guess I was just wondering how many pieces I can cut myself into. I want to live in the past and the present, here in the medieval world and still keep a foot in my own.'

He didn't answer straight away. 'Only you can know what you want, Nae. But you're new here and intoxicated.' She looked up sharply and he rephrased.

'In love with the experience. Sure, it's rustic and uncomfortable, but it's new and exciting for you.'

He opened the door and ushered her in, then started the engine. 'I guess you could compare it to camping. You might like roughing it for a week or two, but I'm sure that, after a year, you would be longing for a return to civilisation.'

She crossed her arms. Phillip looked at her quizzically.

'What's the matter?'

'What about you? You've been doing this for a year, you said. You aren't longing to get back to the real world.'

'I'll admit, doing work I'm passionate about makes the discomforts worthwhile.' He gave a slow nod in the direction of the towering walls and paused. 'But my time here is almost finished. And I'm involved in a very specific project, researching the old church and restoring it using traditional methods. Once that's done, I'll be going on to the next part of my life, whatever and wherever that is.'

She paused. What he said made sense. Life was lived in phases. She was almost finished at university, and then that amorphous thing called 'real life' would commence. Her month at St Valery was a phase. It would change her, just like school and university and Travis had changed her. But Phillip too would pass out of her life; she was suddenly loath to miss any part of him.

'Let me help!' The words popped out.

'With the tiles?'

'Yes. And the restoration. I'm going to learn weaving and a couple of other things in the next few weeks, but when I'm not busy, let me come and be part of your project.'

'If you'd like to, I'd love to have you.'

The next week passed almost in the blink of an eye. Nae had less time than she'd expected, for despite the amazing technological innovation of the new water mill, she still had to carry the grain up to the mill to be ground, take the flour back and assist with lunch. Yvette showed her how to render fat, distil fragrance, and make a hard soap that would apparently last into the next century. Candace unbent enough to teach her to spin, first with a distaff and then with an old-fashioned spinning wheel. For the first half-hour she felt like a Disney princess. After that, the excitement palled. But in the late afternoons,

Nae and Phillip sat side by side and smoothed brown clay into forms, stamped it carefully with traditional motifs and laid it out to dry.

For her second spell of leave, Phillip took two days off and drove her to Orléans. They visited museums, walked in the *Jardin de Plantes*, and made delicious love in the comfort of a luxury hotel. He was incredible. He was the best tour guide she could have imagined, taking her to little-known historical places, such as the south bank of the river where Joan of Arc lifted the siege to become the Maid of Orléans. They walked hand in hand through the *Place du Martroi* and Nae had not a care in the world.

When they returned, it was late morning. Phillip went straight up to the earthen kiln that Guy and Henri had been constructing. They'd been collecting and stacking the three tons of wood they would need to fire the tiles. After they were glazed, they would be fired a second time. Nae donned her kirtle and trailed downstairs to where the loom was kept.

She had developed a respect for Candace without being able to like her. The woman was a genius with cloth, experienced enough to tell the tension of the thread by touch. Under her precise tutelage, Nae had carded, spun, dyed and was now weaving.

Candace was sitting on one of the chairs, a finger loom in her hands, shuttle flying. Nae could see a patterned ribbon taking shape. Its silver and cobalt would set off Candace's blonde loveliness to perfection.

'Good afternoon, Naomi. Did you enjoy Orléans?'

'Very much. Have you ever been?'

'Oh yes. It's quite gorgeous.' She gestured to an envelope on the kitchen table. 'Marguerite sent that down. It arrived for Phillip yesterday, marked urgent. I was going to pass it to him when he popped in, but I suppose it will have to wait.'

Nae walked over to the table and picked it up. It had an American stamp. And there was something unusual about the address. 'Did Marguerite say what it was about?'

'I've no idea.'

She turned, sick disillusion in her stomach. 'Please excuse me. I'll just make sure he gets it.'

She left the house at a purposeful walk, envelope in one fist, skirts gathered in the other. Phillip was packing tiles at the long bench in the back workshop. Henri glanced up and quietly sidled out.

Nae dropped the envelope on the table in front of him. Anger at herself, at daring to hope, welled up in her voice. 'Apparently, this letter is for you. But it can't be, can it?' She stabbed her index finger directly above the address. 'It says, "The Hon. Mr Phillip Stratton-Day". I don't know who this guy is.'

She watched as Phillip read the address, considered for a moment and met her eyes. He offered his hand.

'Hi, I'm Phillip Stratton-Day. And you must be Angry.'

Nae gave an involuntary choke of laughter at his response, which brought the temperature down a bit. Inside she was still reeling. She shook her head and refused to be diverted. 'So who are you? Are you like, nobility?'

He shook his head. 'No, I'm a commoner, just like ninety-nine point nine percent of the population. But my father happens to be Viscount Hargrave, which makes me an honourable.'

Nae took a step back and put a hand on the bench to steady herself. Phillip followed as if on a string. He put a hand over hers and she let it lie there.

'Sweetheart, it's nothing more than an accident of birth.'

'You could have told me.' She would have known better than to get her hopes up then.

He ran a hand over his hair. 'I guess I could have. Perhaps in future I'll introduce myself to people with, "Hi, I'm Phillip and my dad's a viscount".'

She choked again. She wanted to be angry with him, she really did. 'Perhaps you should open it.'

He looked at her carefully and tore open the envelope, slipping out two folded sheets. He spread them out on the bench and smiled. Peeking over his shoulder she recognised the corporate logo.

'Good news?'

'The best! They like my proposal for a medieval educational experience as part of a new theme park attraction. They want me to put a detailed presentation together and come to Los Angeles.' He wrapped both arms around Nae and lifted her off her feet, spinning her around.

'When?'

He put her down. 'I would imagine in the next two months. If I work night and day I can have the church finished and the conclusion of my thesis written by then.'

'I'm very happy for you.' She reached up and kissed his cheek. But it was a kiss laced with sorrow. Not only was he way out of her league, but he was going places where a little Aussie girl had no admittance.

The following week left little time for moonlit strolls by the river. When the kiln was fired, Phillip and Henri sat up through the night to keep it under careful observation. It wasn't as dangerous as charcoal burning, which took four days, but there was no margin for error.

When she wasn't weaving, Nae helped with the cooking. On Thursday night she stood in the communal kitchen and stirred the cracked wheat in the pot hanging from the iron ring. Phillip came in humming *Clair de Lune* and, resting his chin on her shoulder, kissed her neck.

'It smells good. What is it?'

'Frumenty.'

He grinned. 'You've come a long way, if Lorraine is trusting you to make that.'

She stuck her tongue out. 'Make yourself useful and bring me the milk please.'

He brought over the bowl brimming with milk and beaten eggs and placed it on the table. Nae added more cinnamon to the pot and checked the temperature then slowly stirred the mixture in, blending carefully. She could feel him at her back.

'How are the tiles?'

'Cooling. It looks like we've relatively few cracked.' He picked up a spoon, scooped out a generous dollop of frumenty and popped it into his mouth.

'I saw that.'

'I simply appreciate your work. I love a woman who can cook.'

'Do you now?' Her tone echoed with gentle mockery. 'Should I be jealous?'

She felt a hand squeeze her rump. His lips met hers and his arms went around her. His mouth tasted of sweet spices. Lorraine came bustling in.

'Phillipe! *Zut alors.* If you make the frumenty to burn, then you can crack the wheat and grind the spices to make more. Leave Naomi alone if you want your dinner.'

After the community had eaten, Phillip laced his fingers through Nae's and drew her off towards the mill. It had become their spot. Although it was early summer, the woods were still cool and the river inviting. He sat with his back to an ancient oak, one that must have been a sapling when the old stone church was still in use, and chewed on a long grass stem. Nae rested between his legs, her back against his chest, her head nestled into his shoulder, listening to the cricket serenade.

'Next week I have to go to Paris for a couple of days.'

She felt something lurch inside her. It could not be her heart. That had stopped.

'Business?'

'Mmm. Hartley is coming over from LA. He's passing through Paris and would like to see me, just a preliminary meeting, that sort of thing.'

'Will you be gone while I'm on leave?

He shook his head and enfolded her in his arms. 'Absolutely not. I have great plans for those three days.'

She half turned and reached her mouth up to meet his. 'What exactly?'

He slipped one hand into her chemise and kirtle to play over the satin flesh. 'Now that would spoil the surprise.'

'I'll get over it.'

He bared her skin and lowered his mouth. 'Patience.'

'Look who's talking!'

It was some time before either of them was interested in mundane conversation. Phillip helped Nae back into her kirtle and tightened the laces. He had become quite adept with them.

'I'll be going the day after we get back. Can I ask you, if you have time, to help Henri with glazing the tiles? If they're ready to go soon, we can have the second firing in the next couple of weeks and start laying them.'

This mattered to him. He was entrusting her with a big chunk of his project. As much as she ached at the thought of him not being there, there was a certain thrill in his request. That and another crack in her fragile heart.

For her third leave, he stunned her completely. He hired a car and they left before breakfast on Tuesday morning, driving three hours to a small house by Château d'Yvoire on the shore of Lake Geneva. For Nae, the sublime beauty of the Alps, lifting rugged white peaks to the clear blue sky and dominating the tranquil waters, took her breath away.

But it was not just the scenery that left her dazed. There was only a week left and she would be leaving Phillip for good. Going back to Paris, flying to

Singapore, then home. Resuming her old life. She wasn't ready to lose the most wonderful man she'd ever imagined. He was funny, gentle, sweet and incredible. But he lived on the wrong side of the world, and she came from the wrong side of the tracks.

As they walked the edge of the lake and climbed into the foothills of the mountain, explored the sleepy little village and dined in quaint cafés, Nae found herself hiding her sense of impending loss, like a fox under her cloak. The final night in Yvoire she lay, at once replete and desolate, in his arms. Juliet had famously declared that parting was sweet sorrow, but she hadn't had a clue. For Nae's heart was on a rack, slowly being stretched to breaking point.

But for all that, she could not bring herself to say anything. What was there to say? 'I love you' had no future, held no promise of a happy ending. Because he had never said he loved her. And she … she couldn't presume that her feelings were reciprocated. It wasn't quite like her doomed engagement. She and Travis had such different desires that, by the end, they couldn't even communicate them. She and Phillip shared aspirations so closely they might have been one heart or one mind.

Yet, for all that his future was already unfolding in brilliant promise, it wasn't hers. She couldn't, wouldn't cling to his jerkin as he stepped into his destiny. He didn't need her. And he had said nothing. Perhaps there was nothing to say?

Nae spent much of her last week sitting in the open doorway of the second hut, watching the bustle of the little hamlet, carefully painting and glazing Phillip's gorgeous tiles. Paul and Guy finished the last house, and two volunteers arrived from Denmark to become part of the project. Phillip returned from Paris with a day to spare, and they walked along the riverbank on Monday night. There, on the cool grass beside the mill, he loved her to dreamy satiety. On Tuesday night, Nae helped Lorraine serve a fantastic feast. Michel kissed both her cheeks and wished her well; she was apparently welcome any time. On Wednesday morning, instead of pulling on her kirtle, Nae slipped into her black jeans and her most comfortable T-shirt. It was over. Her month as part of a grand experiment was at an end. She was going home.

Phillip carried her suitcase down for her and stood quietly as she hugged Lorraine. He held the door as she slipped into the passenger seat of the old Volvo and shut it gently after her. She looked out the window with a sense of profound regret as they turned the corner. St Valery disappeared into the thick forest like an echo of the past.

'What are your plans?'

She looked at him. There was a constraint about Phillip today that she had never noted. He'd always been so much at ease. She drew a crumb of comfort from the thought that he might miss her.

'I'll do my final semester and look at options for post-grad research. It probably means I'll come back to Europe.'

He gave a nod of agreement. 'This is where the work is.'

'I don't know what I want to research, what areas still have questions that need answering.'

He shook his head. 'That's not the most important thing. Don't do what is logical, or convenient. If those were the only things that mattered, an Aussie girl wouldn't be interested in medieval history in the first place.' He turned and looked over his shoulder to enter the thick commuter traffic heading into the city. 'Follow your heart, Nae. In the end, it's the only thing that counts.'

At the station, he drew her close. Not with the passion that had become so signal in their relationship, but he enfolded her to his heart and simply held her.

'Do you have everything?'

She looked up at him and refused to blot out her last sight of him with tears. 'Yes.'

'Your ticket?'

'Yes.'

His voice was thick and dull, as though he was carefully censoring his words. The train pulled to a halt and people began to stream past them down the platform.

She looked up, her eyes impossibly bright. 'I want to thank you …'

She didn't finish. He stopped her lips with his for a few eternal seconds, then kissed her cheek and stepped back.

She looked up at him one final time. She would say it. She owed herself that. 'Goodbye.' The words wouldn't come, better that her heart break silently. She touched her tongue to her dry lips and forced the words out. 'I love you, Phillip.'

He stood, woodenly smiling at her, as the whistle blew. After a second or two of silence, Nae turned. It was what she had expected after all, but the disappointment was still a knife to her heart. With slow, dragging steps, Nae boarded and sat down in the rear-facing seat with her number on it, swallowed the boulder in her throat and let the first tear fall.

On the SCNF train to Paris, Nae watched the Gare d'Orléans, St Valery and the most wonderful experience of her life slowly accelerate into her past.

'Follow your passion, Nae.' She scrubbed at her cheeks. They were his last words to her. And he was right. She laughed at herself. Of course he was. When was he not?

Phillip Day was more than a holiday fling. He was more than a rebound romance. He was part of one priceless, perfect moment. Before she had felt stupid about following her passion. Travis had been chipping away at her for months and Mum's pragmatism didn't help. Okay, so she couldn't have Phillip; but she could make her craziest dreams come true.

She was going back to Australia to do her final semester, and Naomi Carpenter was going to blow Macquarie History Department out of the water. Then she was going to plan a future where she could live her dream. Mum would understand and Heart Springs would still be there when she visited. Other people did it, she could too.

Her pocket buzzed and for a second she had to think why. She pulled the phone out, looked at it and swiped the screen. A text came up: **I probably should have mentioned, I love you too.**

Nae's heart began to hammer. She closed her eyes. Ridiculous man. He couldn't have said it on the station platform? Or last night at her farewell feast. Or when he made love to her by the river. No. The man who was right at home in the thirteenth century had sent her a text.

Her hand flashed across the screen. Thank goodness her thumbs remembered how to text. **Really?**

Come to LA with me.

I would but I have a plane to catch, remember?

Then I'll come to you after LA

Are you crazy?

I'd be crazy not to – the past is my life, but you are my passion

The end door of the carriage whooshed open, but she didn't hear it. A tallish, fairish, youngish, completely impossible man stood beside her, but she didn't see him. Her eyes were full of tears. He bent, took the phone gently from her unresisting hand and drew her to her feet.

He said nothing. She said nothing. There was no need, and his lips were busy anyway. The rest of the compartment erupted in spontaneous applause.

On Track for Tomorrow

MEL A. ROWE

It was so beautiful and yet so dangerous. Among the ebony tiger stripes, gold shone like pineapple slices under a tropical sun. It didn't belong on the black tar, stretched across a country road. Yet Jessica couldn't stop staring at it.

There was a knock on her car window.

Jessica jumped, covered her lips to stifle her screech at the man wearing a black beanie as her heart sprinted at the intensity of his stare.

'You okay?'

Jessica nodded and wound down the window. His spiced outdoor aroma of pure male filled her small car's interior. 'Fine,' she croaked and faced the road that rolled out like a black carpet while her car remained obstructed.

'Tiger snake.' He stood tall, rubbing the snug-fitting woollen beanie on his head as if adjusting a baseball cap. With lips pursed, his dynamic denim eyes squinted at the snake that lay across the asphalt. 'Did you toot the horn?'

'Yes. But it wouldn't move.'

'How long have you been sitting here?' His sideways grin seemed to come easily.

Jessica shrugged.

'Most people would've run over it and checked their mirrors to see it hadn't flicked up into their axles.'

'Hey, being run over hurts, you know.' Her words were louder than intended. 'They're a protected species.'

'See,' she said, raising her chin higher, 'I was doing the right thing.'

'Stopping in the middle of the road?'

'It's spread out centre stage, not me.'

'You're the one blocking traffic.'

'I'm protecting the wildlife.'

'It's sunbaking.'

'I noticed. But there's no way I'm leaving the safety of my seat when I have no idea how to shove off a snake.'

'*Yah!*' He stamped his boot and clapped his hands, chasing the snake into the yellow wildflowers that grew along the verge.

'You herded it like a cow.'

'Cows don't bite.' Again, sharing that easy side-grin. 'You're free to go, *please*. Coz I can't pass when you're causing chaos to our peak hour traffic flow.'

Jessica looked back at his ute loaded with lumber and realised her parked car was obstructing the deserted highway amid open farmlands waving new velvety growth of a future harvest.

Another car appeared from behind.

'Everythin' all right, Brett?' called out the elderly driver.

'Just a sight-seeing tourist causing a roadblock.' He thumbed towards Jessica and tilted his head to see inside her car. 'You lost?'

Sure, he'd redefined the term working man's rugged good looks. His tight long-sleeved T-shirt outlined muscular arms crossed over a well-toned chest and his flat waistline disappeared into the best set of thigh-hugging jeans on the planet – but he was rude.

'No.' Jessica had to look away, and engaged her car into gear.

'You gonna thank me for saving you?'

'What? You saved no one. All I was doing …' *Ugh*, he was right. She had been playing tourist, gawking at a snake spread out across the road. 'Thank you, Mr Snake Charmer,' she said and began to drive away.

'Snake charmer? I'm wearing a beanie, not a turban.'

Through the side-mirror she spied him leaning down to the other car, pointing towards her. Great, now the locals had someone new to talk about.

Damn, why did she daydream while staring at a snake?

Because she hadn't slept, too busy going over mental checklists for her escape to rural New South Wales.

Lush poplar trees framed Heart Springs' main street, where shops on either side exuded the tasteful blend of a trendy café scene mixed with cottage crafts. Promises of homemade jams and warm bakeries made her tummy rumble, and the sweet scent of juicy plums displayed in the grocer's cart beckoned her.

Jessica spotted J'Adore Travel Boutique and parked out front, smiling with hope at the posters showcasing a long-gone romantic era of mysterious exotic getaways.

This was her gateway to freedom, if only her damned leg would wake up.

She thumped her numb left thigh. The mechanical joints surrounding her knee shifted as she flexed her foot, and she was forced to bite down at the intense burst of pins and needles. A good sign it still worked.

She reached for her walking sticks, pulled herself out, elbowed her door shut and scoped the store.

Damn. Stairs. No ramp. No hand rail. But huge front steps.

Again, Jessica scanned the sidewalk for easier access. Across the road, it was a simple slight step to enter the other shops, except the pub had a balcony she wouldn't visit in a hurry. But J'Adore was set higher above the kerb.

'I can do this.' She had to. Swallowing hard, she gripped her crutches. Gone was the full-leg restrictive brace. Now it was the Loftrand calliper-crutch and half-leg brace around the knee that always caught on her clothes.

Jessica freed her long skirt from the brace, having dressed to impress for a reason. She blew at the stray strands that fell from her top knot, and shunted towards J'Adore Travel Boutique's door.

Each step was another crucial step forwards. She had their wish list and prayed they had hers.

'I made it.' Jessica beamed wide as the door shut behind her.

'Can I help you?'

'Maggie Redmont?' She grinned at the woman with shoulder-length brown hair. Her rockabilly stylish skirt swung as if preparing to perform *Grease* on stage. With a wide smile and bright red lipstick, Maggie's look was fun and just what Jessica needed. 'Hi, I'm Jessica Pedersen, we spoke on the phone.'

'My website guru.' Maggie's infectious smile widened and her eyes shone. 'Please come in. Did you climb those front steps?'

'Um, yeah.' Jessica grinned at accomplishing another challenge to her day. 'You need a handrail out there.'

'My god, the amount of foot traffic I've lost because of our lousy entrance.'

'I wouldn't worry—'

'I worry, because it's my business. I've never thought of wheelchair access before.'

She raised her chin higher. 'I don't have a wheelchair.' *Not anymore.*

'Please, have a seat.'

'Can I stand to de-numb my bum first?'

'Sure.' With a rustle of skirts, Maggie walked and talked while looking outside her store's entrance. 'I understand why you rented Kimmel's cottage, it'll be perfect for you. It's got plenty of handrails and ramps.'

'It's not permanent.' Jessica refused to believe her injuries were lifelong.

'No, only six weeks. Here's the key.' Maggie placed a tagged brass key onto her desk. 'I'll draw you a mud map. Brett assures me you've got enough wood to last the next five winters.'

'Who?'

'Brett's your neighbour. Super yummy to look at, but not much for conversation. He's one of the partners in the local gym. They're glad you're here too.'

'I'm allergic to gyms, they fight against my chocolate addiction.' They reminded Jessica of rehab with their sterile settings and shiny machinery.

'When I bragged that my IT guru was coming to remodel my website, they wanted you to do the same for them. Also, Tart's Bakery, Bob's Grill, and I think the pub wants you to update their sites too. When you're done here, go and introduce yourself.'

'Wow.' Jessica dropped into the visitor's seat. 'I will. Thank you.'

'It's a small town. When talent arrives, we share, especially for the tourists.'

'Tourists, huh.' A name she'd been called twice today.

'I'm all about the tourist trade.' Maggie waved her hand around the boutique.

Jessica admired the antique posters, proud she'd made the effort to come. Now she had to convince Maggie of her personal request. 'Have you completed the brief?'

'Most of it.'

'We can schedule in a time—'

'First, let's get you settled. No dramas with the road trip?'

Besides a sunbaking snake and a He-man boot-stomping wannabe hero. 'No dramas.' Jessica giggled behind fingertips that tapped against her lips. 'So, is my other trip booked?'

'Hey,' Maggie sat straighter behind her desk, 'are you capable—?'

'I can walk.' *And getting better every day.*

'Can you go hiking?'

'Maggie.' Jessica smoothed out her skirt and corrected her posture. 'I'm here to do your website, and any other work available. I also want to use the walking tracks along the river and surrounding country roads to build up my endurance.' And to get away from her parents, who wanted her strapped into a full-body armour of blankets to soften any blows from life.

'You can train in the city.'

'I don't need witnesses until I've perfected my stride.'

'The outback's a tough place.'

'I'm aware of that.'

'The Larapinta Trail is a six-day, hundred-kilometre hike.'

'I'm doing this for a reason. I need this, Maggie.' She held her breath in hope.

Maggie's chin lifted and her confident smile grew. 'Then you'll have the best time out there too. But,' she leant closer, 'I'll be making sure there's enough specialised provisions for you.' She held her palm up. 'It's my job.'

Jessica sighed with a smile. 'And that's why I'm here, for the excellent service.'

The door swung open and the breeze carried a familiar scent of spiced outdoors and male that made Jessica's head turn.

'Hey, Maggie, got that wood you wanted for your shelves.'

'Brett, perfect timing.'

'It's the Snake Charmer,' blurted Jessica, as the heat rose as fast as her pulse. She blinked at the way the sun shone behind Brett through the open doorway, as if he were a gift from angels.

'Oi.' He frowned down at her.

'That's what you did, right?' Jessica couldn't help but stare at the tall tower of male with his wide muscular shoulders.

'Sounds like a story I want to hear.' Maggie giggled at the pair. 'Considering you're both new neighbours.'

'*What?*' Both Jessica and Brett gaped at Maggie, who shrugged from behind her desk.

'Did I miss something?' asked Maggie.

Brett pointed down at Jessica. 'This one was sitting in the middle of the road and couldn't be bothered getting out of the car—'

'Hey,' Jessica picked up her crutches and pushed herself upwards. 'I didn't want to run over that snake, okay. I told you, getting run over hurts like hell.'

'Aw shiiiiit,' Brett hissed under his breath as his shoulders slumped.

There it was, the pity look. Like she was some wounded thoroughbred destined to never leave the racetrack alive. Well, she wasn't beaten. She swiped the key and map from Maggie's desk. 'We'll talk soon, Maggie.' No more quick exits these days, which sucked.

'Back door's easier, Jessica.' Maggie scooted for the kitchenette in her peep-toe shoes. 'Brett, how fast can you make me a handrail for the front, and what about a ramp?'

Jessica followed Maggie through the office. 'Not for me?'

'You'll be my counsel for what my customers with disabilities might need. Sorry, don't take offence.' Maggie pushed open the back door and Autumn sunlight streamed inside.

'I won't, and I'm not offended.' All prudish pride disappeared from daily pokes and prods by medical teams who never remembered her name. 'I'll be back tomorrow.'

'I'll make sure Izzy and Elle are here.'

'Can't wait to meet them and it's nice to meet you face to face, Maggie.'

'You too, Jessica.' Maggie reached over and hugged Jessica. 'You'll love it here.'

'Hope so.' Jessica shuffled forwards as fast as her crutch coordination allowed. If she avoided her neighbour for the next six weeks – no matter how good looking he was – it'd be perfect. Besides, men who looked like Brett never bothered with women like her. She didn't need the pity, she needed to focus on completing her goals and had six weeks to do that.

Was she asking too much?

∞

Maggie swivelled back into the shop. 'Well, you put your foot into it, didn't you, Brett.'

Brett, with measuring tape in hand, hovered by the wall. 'How was I supposed to know? She was sitting in her car in the middle of the road watching a snake.' The woman with the warmest coffee-coloured eyes mixed with flecks of caramel stirred up the sweet tooth he didn't know he had until that first sight back on the road. What were the chances he'd see her again? 'Sorry to tick off your customer, Maggie.'

'You did worse than that, Brett. That's my IT guru, who's booked to update your gym's website too.'

Brett groaned and rolled his eyes. Women were always organising things for him. Why couldn't they leave him alone?

'I'm here to do the final measurements for your shelves.' No, he'd followed the mystery woman and now had to stick with his lame excuse. With tape in hand, pencil tucked behind his ear, he checked his figures against the plans he'd spread over Maggie's desk.

'How fast can you do a handrail for the front steps?'

'I'm not your wood-slave.' But he guessed who it was for.

The stranger who'd made a fool of him. Normally Brett avoided conversation with most people. Yet he'd seen her sitting in the car, with those warm eyes and lush red lips hidden behind tapping fingertips. 'How long is she staying, Maggie?'

'As long as it takes to update the website and to finish her training.'

'For what?'

'You've trekked the Kokoda?'

'Yeah. With some of my mates. Jessica's not …' He turned to face Maggie's cheesy grin.

'Jessica's doing the Larapinta trail.'

'The what?'

'Starts in Alice Springs and goes right through the red centre.'

'Do they have facilities for people like Jessica?'

'I'll make sure they're ready.' Maggie sat down and tapped away at her keyboard. 'Can you offer her any tips?'

'Yeah, go to the gym where the crew can look after her.'

'Jessica doesn't like gyms.'

'That makes two of us.' He folded the sketched plans and wound up his measuring tape with a recoiling click.

'Why own a gym when you don't like it, Brett?'

'Not my choice.' He turned with a scowl and walked out the door.

∞

Sunrise had yet to fully stretch out across the horizon as dew dripped from the cottage's corrugated roof. Jessica stepped out in her hiking boots, her crutches replaced by lightweight trekking poles. She struggled with her backpack's loose shoulder straps as her back hunched from its shifting weight.

Jessica looked towards the dark driveway as her poles staked the dirt, then watched her left leg slide forward. Head up, she looked to the path ahead, then back down to the ground and slid her leg forward. Her step was unsure on the rocks, her new boots were too tight with blisters forming, and her toes tingled from lack of circulation. The backpack dug into her lower back, her beanie blocked her view, and her grip slipped on the tall trekking poles. But still, she kept going.

A wallaby leapt across her path. She screamed and jumped back, losing her balance as her leg gave way and she landed on her back like a turtle. All while the wallaby jumped the fence and bounded away.

'Bugger.' Jessica groaned and huffed in the many layers of clothing. First too cold, now too hot.

She stared at the light she'd left on at the cottage and realised she hadn't even made it to the main road yet. *Damn.*

A low engine rumbled and the slash of headlights travelled down the dirt track from behind. Who was coming to share in her shame now? Surely it was too early, even for farmers.

'Morning,' called Brett from the open driver's window, as he stopped his ute and peered at Jessica lying in the wild grass.

Typical. Of all the people who had to witness her wallow in the wilderness it had to be Brett.

'Need a hand?'

'I've got this.' She tried to roll from side to side, but her pack wouldn't budge. She unclipped it, slid out of the shoulder straps and sat upright. 'Nothing to see here.'

'Ah huh.'

Damn his smug expression. 'No snakes here, so you might want to keep moving or you'll be the next one accused of stopping traffic.'

'It's my lane and I can stop here if I want to.' He jumped out of his cab. 'We share this track. My place is over the hill.' Brett picked up her trekking poles and held out his hand. 'Come on.'

She frowned up at him. 'I said—'

'Your arse is getting wet sitting in the dew.' He pulled her upright before she had a chance to react. His combined aroma of soap and shampoo tickled her senses.

'Hey, I can do this.' How strong was Brett to pluck her off the ground so effortlessly?

'Sure you can. But these poles are too high for you. Didn't they measure you up?'

'I bought them online.'

Brett lined up the trekking poles against her frame, lowered them a few rungs and then held them out. 'How's that?'

Jessica reached for the handles, avoiding his strong hands. 'Okay, I guess.' Another flush crept from her neck for forgetting the basics. She would've worked it out. Eventually.

Brett scooped up her pack by the straps. 'This is too heavy. What's in here?'

'A brick.' She pressed fingertips against her lips to stop drooling at the way his jaw-dropping biceps bulged from doing an arm curl with her weighty pack.

'You're meant to start small and then add to it.' He pulled out four bricks and threw them into the back tray of his ute.

Now he was being rude again. 'What do you care?'

'Heard you're attempting to do the Larapinta trek.'

The brute smelled way too good, and was hotter than a tropical summer sun. He was upsetting her already overheating internal thermostat. Yet Brett knew what he was doing with her hiking gear. 'Have you done that trek?'

'No. Did Kokoda.'

'Woah, that's hard core. Larapinta's only medium grade.'

'Have you ever hiked before?' He held out her pack to her back and shoulders.

'I'm learning.' All part of her re-learning how to walk programme. Her teeth snagged her bottom lip as he slid the straps over her shoulders.

Brett walked around to face Jessica, making more adjustments. 'Ah huh. You a walking sauna, too?'

'Well, I'm not gonna wear a ball gown and stilettos to go jump fences in snow country, am I?' When she was meant to be breaking a sweat without witnesses.

Brett gave a zip-tight tug on the shoulder straps that snapped her spine straight, then clipped the band around her waist as if he was strapping a baby into a car seat.

'I don't need help, okay?' she said. 'And I don't need you to babysit me.' Not like her parents. The only one who'd given her space was her brother, who avoided her as if she had some contagious disease.

'I'm not babysitting, I'm adjusting the gear to suit your body build before you ruin it.'

'Um, thanks.' Why did he make her so flustered? Were the straps too tight making it hard to breathe?

Brett squinted at her, as he adjusted his beanie. 'So, you're out here to use this place as a training camp?'

'It's not a prison camp.' She pushed away from his solid wall of muscle and shuffled onto the track. 'Is this a country, neighbourly interfering thing you're doing?'

'Don't worry, I won't be in your face. I like my privacy.' In a few long-legged strides, Brett jumped into the driver's seat. The cab's door creaked shut, and he rested his elbow on the open window. 'There are easier walking tracks in town you should try first. You'll need to walk long distances if you're thinking of hiking for six days. It's obvious you've got the upper arm strength from using crutches, but you'll need to focus more on your legs.' Head tilted, his eyes slowly scanned over her entire body.

Even with layers of leggings and a lumpy leg brace, she felt naked under his stare. 'I'm trying.'

'The way those boots are laced they'll give you blisters and cut off the circulation in your toes.'

Were there tricks to lacing boots no one had told her about? 'But—'

'You look like you're running a cross-country skiing marathon without snow. Why put yourself through it?'

Jessica straightened as she raised her chin. 'Because I can.'

She speared her pole-tips into the soft dirt and shunted forwards. She didn't need charity, especially not from her bantering body-beautiful neighbour, when she hadn't even had her first coffee.

℅

Brett shook his head at Jessica's determination and stubborn streak that drove those hiking poles into the ground. He had to admire her spirit – few able-bodied people would bother. Still, it irked him. Here was this woman walking alone in the dark. Normally he'd never interfere, but she had a handicap – not only physically, but also her inexperience with the rural environment.

Not to mention that he didn't know how to speak or think properly around her, let alone use the correct terminology for her condition.

Sure, he'd done Kokoda, training along with his mad mate Mick. They'd done it together to help cope with losing other mates, where those ghosts still whispered in his ear.

Tucking the beanie over his ears he put the ute into gear. He hated opening the gym in the mornings, but it was a part of life he hadn't let go of and didn't know how.

Watching through the rear-view mirror, he shook his head at Jessica's technique. That woman was causing herself a whole lot of pain with her posture alone. He doubted she'd make it to the weekend.

℅

Jessica sighed with envy at the woman pounding miles on a treadmill at the local gym. Still, she was proud she'd completed day two of her self-torture tour and made it half-way down the shared track towards the main road. But her progress was slow. Was she doing it wrong?

She didn't dare ask her neighbour for advice, preferring to wait until Brett drove past to start her morning walk. She couldn't picture Brett, the rugged working man in grease-stained jeans, boots and work shirts, as the owner of a gym. Brett didn't need to work out. He'd fixed the potholes in their shared

197

driveway, without a shirt, and she'd stared at his tanned, toned torso until her tea went cold.

But she was here now because Maggie had made this appointment. With word-of-mouth daily work queries, Heart Springs was proving to be a gold mine for her business.

'Can I help you?' asked the woman with the mega-toned body, bouncing on the balls of her feet.

'Are you the manager?'

'No, I'm Kelly.'

'I've got a meeting with the manager?' She hoped it wasn't Brett.

'Nicole, our new client's here,' Kelly shouted at the open office doorway behind the counter.

'I'm not a client.'

'Are you sure?'

'I have my own routine.' Which was killing herself at dawn, and had never slept better.

Jessica was shunted into the office filled with cartons of assorted drink bottles. 'Hi, I'm Jessica, here to help with your website.'

'Welcome, I'm Nicole. Care for a drink?' Nicole rose from behind the desk that faced the wall.

'I'm okay, thanks.' Jessica shuffled to the offered chair and smiled at Nicole's open warmth.

'You look okay too.'

Strange for someone she'd just met to say such a thing.

'Maggie called.'

'I see.' Magical Maggie was fast becoming Jessica's BFF. 'Did you complete the emailed brief?'

'I've been waiting for Brett's opinion.'

'Your partner?'

'Business partner. My husband and I bought this place with our daughter, Fiona, and her husband, Brett. This is them on their wedding day.' Nicole passed a photo of Brett beside a beautiful blonde bride.

'I haven't met Fiona.' Of course he was married. She swore never to perve on the man again.

'She died.'

Jessica's stomach dropped for Nicole, but mostly for Brett. 'I'm so sorry.'

'Me too.' Nicole sighed returning the frame to her desk. 'This was Fiona's dream, helping people become healthier, yet she ended up sick herself.'

Jessica hugged her laptop bag closer, not sure what to say.

'Maggie tells me you're training for the Larapinta trail. That's such an exciting goal.' She patted Jessica's arm. 'You should speak with Brett – he did Kokoda soon after Fiona died. I'll call Brett to return to town. If he didn't open in the mornings I'd doubt we'd ever see him leave that farm of his, so this'll be a bonus.' Nicole picked up the phone and dialled.

'I can come back another day.' Preferably when Brett wasn't around.

'Brett won't be long.'

'Great.' *Not.*

Yet, grateful for her new clients, Jessica slid her chair closer and pulled out her laptop. Her fingers itched to play because she didn't need legs to dance across keyboards. This was the part of her that just got stronger, and she loved it.

ℰᴑ

The gym door swung open and Brett's boots clomped along the floorboards as loud music masked the grunts of those sweating in air-conditioning.

'Good morning, Brett, how are you today?' Kelly beamed at him as she waved enthusiastically from behind the counter, like a window-cleaner on speed.

'Only saw you two hours ago, Kelly, nothing's changed.' He walked past the gym instructor who practically lived there, into the office and straight for the coffee pot. 'You rang, Nic?'

'You've met Jessica.'

With cup halted half-way to his mouth, he looked over the steam at Jessica, who was seated at the desk with the perfect posture of an Olympic equestrian rider. Her rich milk chocolate hair twirled into a knot on her head that defied gravity. Soft stray curls fell around her slender neck and framed her delicate facial features. She peered at him through honey-framed glasses that highlighted the caramel in those coffee-coloured eyes. The woman was stunning, and Brett had to sip his caffeine to quell his dry mouth.

'We've met.' Jessica gave him a nod then turned back to the screen.

199

'What do you want?' He ignored Nicole's frown for his uncivil behaviour towards the beauty who brought out his inner beast.

'Jessica's giving our website a makeover, remember?'

'You don't need me then.' Putting his cup down, he moved to escape.

'Yes, we do.' Nicole pointed to the spare chair.

'Why isn't Bob here?'

'He's gone fishing.'

'Where's my invite?'

'Bob gave up asking when you always say no.'

'Had pot holes to fill.' *And new neighbours to avoid.*

'Always an excuse. Now sit, young man.'

Brett winced as he rubbed the beanie on his head. He had no choice, so he sat down, crossed his leg over his knee and sipped his coffee. 'What do I have to do?' He took sneaky glances at Jessica powering over the office keyboard like a wizard.

'We answer these questions for Jessica.'

'Hold on, what qualifications does Jessica have to access our website? There's sensitive material on our system.' He flinched internally as her fingers hovered over the screen and she turned to face him.

'I did my IT internship with the government, managing their websites. I've worked with lots of highly sensitive data and I'll gladly sign any confidentiality agreement. Besides, I'm not bored enough to hack into your personal porn collection.'

'Oi.' *Not in front of the mother-in-law.* He glared at Jessica, who was again staring at the monitor, tapping fingertips across her lush full lips. Even annoyed with her, he wanted those eyes on him, just to drink in the view.

'Okay then.' Nicole giggled, patted Brett on the knee and turned to Jessica. 'What questions do you have?'

'Besides an obvious upgrade, what's your site's main purpose?'

'To catch the tourist trade. The locals know us from word of mouth, but we need to be more accessible to visitors,' replied Nicole.

'Word of mouth is good here. I've got work lined up for me, when I've only spoken to Maggie.'

'And me,' said Brett, not that he'd call it a conversation.

'Do I have you to thank for the extra business?' Jessica glanced sideways through her glasses.

Finally, she looked at him.

'Me, no. I, ah, don't talk to anyone,' he blurted out, and caught Nicole's frown. Great, now he'd be expecting daily visits of mothering for the rest of the week. 'How's your training going?'

'Okay,' mumbled Jessica, head down, as the colour crept into her fair cheeks.

'How are you training?' asked Nicole.

'Jessica's walking the lane in the mornings.'

'Are you helping her, Brett?'

'No!' Jessica and Brett said, glaring at each other.

'I don't need help,' said Jessica.

'Hey, hold on.' He sat forward, facing the stubborn female. 'I didn't offer. And I'm busy.'

'I'm fine doing what I got told.'

'Who told you to carry ten bricks in an unsecured backpack? Lemme guess, same place you got those poles from.'

She shrugged and faced the computer screen.

'Do you have someone helping you, Jessica?' asked Nicole.

'I have a plan from—'

'Not some random online guru's plan for the masses,' interjected Brett, leaning back in his seat, frowning.

Jessica turned fast, scowling at him. 'Do I interfere with your business?'

'Yes, you're doing our website.'

'Do I need to put you both into a boxing ring?' Nicole eyed the pair.

'Jessica could do with the hand and leg combination work.' Brett cocked his head and eyed her slender figure. Didn't want her muscle-bound when she was perfectly proportioned with soft feminine curves.

'Leave me alone. I'm only here to help.' Jessica reached for her crutches. 'Maybe I should go.'

Nicole placed her palm on Jessica's shoulder. 'No, don't, please. We need this site. Brett, behave. It's not Jessica's fault you hate change and don't want to be here.'

Brett grunted, frowning at the female duo. *Women.* He couldn't go against them if he tried. When they ganged up on him it was either walk away or sit silently and take it like a man. So he shut up and waited for them to forget he was even in the room.

ॐ

Jessica couldn't concentrate in his presence. Normally, she dealt with customers by phone or email, where house calls were rare. But the plan was to do the initial visits and gain an understanding of her clients' needs, then go back to being the voice over the phone. She could do this gig with her eyes closed – but not with Brett in the room. He was everywhere.

'Fine, do the site.' He tore off his beanie and raked fingers through his short hair, the colour of cinnamon and cedar that perfectly capped off his masculine features. Dark facial growth shaded his cheekbones and strong jaw-line like a charcoal sketch destined for museum walls. Trapped by his gaze, she struggled to breathe the same airspace. *Not good.*

She pinched her thigh, turned to the screen, pushed up her glasses, and tapped her fingertips across her lips. *Focus.* 'I'll optimise keywords for the SEO. So, what other features would you like?'

'I'm not sure,' Nicole said. 'What do other people have?'

'Class times, upcoming events, that sort of thing. I've created a list of the highest-ranking gym websites for you. See what appeals and answer the questionnaire. When you're ready, call or email me and we can set up another time.' Jessica gave an exaggerated flourish on the keyboard like a concert pianist at a symphony battle-off. She slid her laptop into her workbag. Gave a tight smile to Nicole and a stern nod to Brett. Trying to control her hand tremor as she left her business card on the desk, she picked up her crutches and headed for the exit. Fast.

'You're leaving,' complained Brett.

'Decide what you want, and when you've finished call me. It's no rush. I'm flexible.'

'Yeah, right.'

'Brett.' Nicole slapped Brett's denim-clad leg.

'I didn't mean her handicap thing, I meant—'

'*Brett.*' Nicole frowned at him. 'I'm so sorry, Jessica.'

'It's okay. Nice to meet you, Nicole.' His words stung. Handicap. Invalid. Words regularly thrown in her face. Her cheeks burned as she turned to hide her anger and shame, and shunted out the door as fast as she could.

ဢ

'Don't say it, Nic. I know I'm an arsehole.' Dodging the death stare from his other-mother, Brett chased after Jessica.

'Hey, Jess?' He was amazed how fast she hiked in those crutches toward her sedan. Why didn't she park in the vacant disabled parking spot by the front door? 'Jessica, I'm sorry.'

'Go away.'

'Let me help.' He reached for the driver's door.

'I don't need your help.' She tried to shove him aside.

'I'm sorry.'

'For what? If I wasn't crippled, would you still give me grief?' She threw her crutches onto the passenger seat.

'Yes. No. Shit, I dunno?' He stepped back, raking fingers through his hair. 'Why do you confuse the hell out of me?'

'What?'

He felt sucker-punched at the depth of sorrow in her eyes. *Idiot.* 'Sorry, okay. Look, I've got best mates missing limbs and I'm fine around them, but you—'

'I'm not made of glass. I may be broken but I don't shatter that easy,' she said with a lowered tone as she slid into her front seat.

'What the …?' He stopped all movement at the flash of her creamy thighs while she fought with her skirt caught in the brace. Long, soft, supple legs that no doubt led to paradise. 'I'm, ah, trying to apologise,' he stuttered, inhaling her invisible wave of heavenly sweetness.

'No need, Snake Charmer. Go find something else that slithers to scare away.' She slammed the door shut and drove away.

Brett watched until her car disappeared, then turned towards the gym where Nicole stood waiting for him at the doorway. 'Why did you leave me with this crap, Fiona?' he whispered to the grey sky, then plonked his beanie back on. He didn't need the drama.

But if he didn't deal with Nicole now, she'd follow him home. *Women.* He only talked to the few he'd grown up with, who were so familiar to his landscape he never saw them.

So why was Jessica here, ruining not only his serenity, but his sanity?

&

Jessica gloved up and opened the cottage door where a blast of icy air stung her cheeks in the pre-dawn morning. With winter coming, she was tempted to return to bed. Instead, she locked the door, hitched her pack to find that sweet spot on her spine. She gripped her hiking poles and was soon swallowed by the darkness.

The only sound was the gravel crunching beneath her boots on the driveway. She dodged the fresh-filled potholes on the shared track and turned right towards the main road. Never left to Brett's place that was hidden behind the small rise where the glow of lights hinted at his existence.

'You should have a torch.'

'AUUUUUGGHH!' Her scream echoed as she jumped back, her leg crumpled, and in a flash, Brett grabbed her upper arms and held her upright.

'I'm sure our other neighbours heard you.'

'Brett?' Her heart almost burst out of her chest, licking her dry lips, staring at the man who'd been crashing her dreams. 'What're you doing here?'

'Here's a torch.' He plonked the headlamp's elastic band over her beanie pushing it down to blind her.

She tore off her beanie. 'Wh-what?'

'Can't you speak this early in the—'

'Stop.' She raised her hand like a traffic sign. 'Why are you here?'

'To help.'

'Why?'

'Because I was an arsehole yesterday after what I'd said, and …'

She tilted her head, squinting at him. 'The whole truth.'

'Okay…' He sighed and rubbed at his beanie. 'I had Nic on my back for being rude to you, and—'

'Do you have nits?'

'What?'

'The way you scratch your head as part of your thought process?'

'No.' He went to scratch and frowned at her grin. 'Do you?'

'No. Although talking about it makes me itch.' She giggled scratching her scalp, slipped on her own beanie and adjusted the headlamp. 'Thanks for the torch.' She turned her back on him and shuffled forwards.

Brett stepped in beside her. 'You're welcome.'

Jessica frowned at Brett's long stride to her two-and-a-half steps.

'Stop staring at the dirt and watch the path ahead.'

'What?'

'The torch will light the way if you didn't look down all the time.'

'I do not.'

'You do too.'

How long had he been watching her? 'I …' She sighed, watching her boots shuffle across the dirt. 'I don't want to fall.'

'What happens when you do?'

She bit her lip and kept walking.

'Not a trick question. Yesterday you said you're not made of glass. Are you worried you'll hurt yourself?'

'Nothing worse than what I've been through.'

'So, you're still adjusting?'

Wincing, she shrugged, too embarrassed to speak.

'So, if you fall, you pick yourself up, right?'

She tried to, and gave him a nod.

'You said it hurts to get run over.'

'It does when you end up with a crushed pelvis and nerve damage.'

'Meaning?'

'Femoral nerve damage impairs movement and creates a loss of sensation in the thigh muscle. It's weakened my left leg, so I don't trust it because it collapses on me.'

'Which is why you have the brace?'

'Yes, Doctor Do-Good. Any more questions before dawn?'

His slow side-grin looked better than the sunrise.

Damn.

Brett strolled with hands in his jeans pockets, watching her stride. 'Your lower leg and foot are still okay?'

'Yes, but there's this gap that mixes messages for movement. But I'm getting better.'

'I get it. So, because you're worried it won't work, instead of trusting it, you look at the ground getting ready for it to break.'

'Are you a physio or something?'

'No. What happens if you trusted your body to hold you and move like it's always done? So what if you fall?' He walked ahead of her. 'You'll pick yourself up, dust yourself off and keep on walking.'

'You're ruining my serenity, and I don't need a personal trainer.' She shuffled onwards even if it was impossible to pass the guy in his thigh-hugging jeans.

'And you've disturbed my sanity since you arrived, but I can help you.'

'Don't need it.'

'Fine, I'm just walking my track on my land.'

'You don't have to do it this time of the morning.'

'How do you know this isn't my normal time to check out my track, but I've been avoiding you instead?'

Which is exactly what she'd been doing, and felt the flush flow to her cheeks. 'Thought you opened the gym?'

'Kelly's doing an early yoga class.'

'Kelly's a yoga instructor?' Was Kelly Brett's girlfriend?

'That and a personal trainer, and the bouncer.' He chuckled, springing up and down on his toes.

'I noticed.' She giggled.

'Wow, you do smile.'

'I smile.' She frowned again. 'You don't need to do this.'

'I know.'

'You can go.'

'I could.'

'Why are you still here?'

'Because I am. Can I ask you something?'

'Do I have any choice?' He owned the track so she couldn't shake him.

'Why do the Larapinta trail? Why train here and not where you're from?'

'Because,' – she focused on her steps, looking anywhere but at Brett – 'my family wouldn't let me.'

'Why not?'

'They won't let me do anything for myself, since …' She looked away. Why was she babbling out her secrets?

'So, this condition's only recent?'

'Almost a year ago.'

'What happened?'

'Hit and run. All I remember is I'd finished work and somehow this van cleaned me up in the car park.' She was used to these questions from the police, the rehab staff, her mum, her mum's friends ...

'Did you quit that job?'

Jessica shrugged.

'Do you think they'd treat you differently at work because of your physical impairment?'

'Swallow the handicap dictionary, did we?' Her smirk was matched by Brett's easy side-smile.

'Rang my mate last night, we served together as combat engineers.'

'Dangerous?'

'Worked with explosives, yeah. Mick lost his leg from a landmine.'

'Where were you?' She stopped in her tracks.

'Here, with Fiona while she ...' He cleared his throat.

'I'm sorry about your wife.' Jessica moved forwards, noting Brett didn't wear a wedding band.

'Me too.' He shrugged as he adjusted his beanie and caught her grin. 'I don't have nits, it's a habit. Just like you tap your lips with your fingertips as if you're playing the piano.'

She stopped and stared.

'Have I pissed you off again?'

'You irritate me.' She shunted forwards.

He stopped and grabbed her arm. 'I'm trying—'

'I'll say.'

'You're not helping.' He sniffed and looked down the dark track as if trying to find his patience while she shuffled past. 'Okay, I'll tell you something I've never told a soul.'

'I don't need to know your secrets.'

'It might help.'

'Help why, when you're leaving?'

'I've forgotten how to talk to people.'

'You talk to people.'

'I've forgotten how to have a conversation with new people, because ever since Fiona died I found it easier to avoid people in general.'

That killed her inner fight. Jessica continued with her dirt-shuffle down the track. 'Nicole said if you didn't open the gym in the mornings you'd never leave the farm.'

Again, he stepped in beside her. 'That's true, I love it here. Do you hide behind your screens? Look up.'

Jessica frowned because Brett was right. She looked towards the track, illuminated by the glow of her headlamp. Fair's fair, Brett was trying. She couldn't hate him for it, when she could relate. 'Most of my conversations are via phone or Skype and no site visits. No one sees what's under the table and take me for my intellectual skills and not the physical.'

'Are you ashamed of the way you are?'

'I don't want their pity.'

'Anyone here treat you like that?'

'You did.'

'Shit.' He winced. 'I'm sorry for what I said in front of Maggie. And Nic.'

'Apology accepted. Now, thank you for the offer but I don't need your help.'

'Yeah you do, and I'm trying to hold a conversation.'

Oh man, why? She rolled her eyes at the awakening skyline.

'How come you aren't going for a smaller hiking adventure closer to home instead of travelling to the Northern Territory?'

'Because it's in the heart of this country, and far removed from any mobile service, guaranteeing I'll be IT-free.' She scanned the obscured landscape surrounding them. 'I need to prove to myself that I'm more than a torso behind a table, that I'm still me.'

'What does your family say about this?'

Jessica stepped forwards.

'Stop looking down, look ahead.'

'Yes, sir.' She giggled.

'They don't know, do they?'

She didn't reply.

'What would they do?'

'They'd try to stop me.'

'Do you have medical clearance?'

'Yes. I showed Maggie the paperwork before she confirmed my bookings. Don't worry, she's made sure there's suitable amenities for me to complete the trek that week.'

'What's so special about that week to push yourself so much?'

'It's my hell week.' She looked away, moving forwards.

'That's a basic training term.'

'For me, it was waking up after the accident. It'll be my first anniversary in six weeks, and I don't want it to be miserable like last year.'

'Well,' he lifted her chin with his fingertips, 'keep your chin up and you'll make it.'

She stopped and looked at him as tears threatened to form.

'What did I say wrong now?'

'Um—' She swallowed her emotions. 'No one's said that to me since the accident.'

'If you want this bad enough, you'll do it.'

'Easy for you to say,' she mumbled, 'you're like this pre-dawn guru. Are you smoking some pipe you've been fine-tuning to charm more snakes across the road?' She giggled and stepped onto the asphalt. 'Wow.'

'What?'

'First time I've made it to the road.' She grinned wider at the silent countryside. 'Okay.'

'Okay, what?'

'I'll accept your help, only if we agree to be brutally honest with each other. No sugar coating. If it helps me reach my goal, I'll use you.'

'Copping your crap before sunrise there's gotta be better ways to greet the day.'

'I'll be nice, I think. It's rare.'

'I'd believe it.'

'Hey.' She slapped his muscular upper arm. 'Stop picking on the walking wounded.'

'You did not just say that?'

'I have a sense of humour.'

'Lose that with the accident?'

'Like lots of other things.'

'Like what? Besides your independence?'

'I'm getting that back too.'

'I can see that. Now, gimme that.' He snatched one of her poles.

'Hey.' Her balance teetered and she grabbed Brett's shirt; the hard muscles under her palm sent a rush of heat through her body.

'Put your hand higher.'

At least he didn't say lower, down to his jeans. 'Why?'

'Rest your hand on my shoulder. I won't bite … much.' He guided her palm higher. 'It'll force you to keep your head up. Don't worry, I won't let you fall. It's how I helped my mate, Mick, train for Kokoda and he has no lower left leg. Come on, let's keep going to the end of my front fence line.'

'Where's that?'

'I'll tell you when.' With a coy grin, he strolled beside her. 'I should bring the ute out and follow you like I'm herding cattle. At least I'd have coffee in the cab, a heater …'

'You're cruel.' *Cute but cruel.*

'The desert's colder.'

'Which is why I dragged myself from a warm bed to do this. What's your excuse?'

'My body clock is used to being up so early, and someone's gotta give you grief. You can shout me breakfast after this. Consider it my fee. You can cook, can't you?'

'Ah, yeah, can't kill breakfast.'

'I dunno, but I've got an iron stomach from surviving on rations.'

'I'm not cooking for you.'

'Reckon I'll talk you into it by the time we make the neighbour's fence line.'

'Where's that?'

'That way.' He pointed to the darkness, and side by side they greeted the dawn.

Jessica grunted as she tipped over a tractor tyre in the paddock and stood hunched over with palms resting on her thighs, catching her breath. 'Do you do this at the gym?'

Brett leaned on her hiking poles, supervising. 'No. I'd have Bob on my back for staining his floor.'

'You don't like the gym, do you?'

'I know you don't.'

'I'll admit it's true.'

'Because of your leg?'

'I've never enjoyed the whole gym experience. My thing is sweating in silence outside because I sit inside all day. But not lately with you watching over my shoulder.' She elbowed his ribs, pleased for his laugh.

Brett had been there supplying daily drive-by training tips on his way to the gym; they'd share breakfast and talk with ease. Sometimes they'd listen to the morning sounds of the expansive countryside, when Brett didn't open the gym, and he'd stroll beside her. Over the past six weeks he'd become a good friend. 'Thank you. Even though I hate you at times, I've improved heaps under your regime.'

Brett shared his slow easy side-grin that made her catch her breath, which forced her to turn away.

Jessica squatted to grip the black rubber edge of the large disused tyre. Dirt scraped under her nails as she lifted, groaned, moaned, and grumbled under its weight.

'Use your legs, trust them.'

Boots dug into turf. Her legs trembled as she strained and shouldered the heavy rubber, until it keeled over, bounced on the ground, and then settled. There she plonked onto its top edge in the middle of the paddock.

'Here.' Brett passed her a water bottle.

'Thanks.' She took a long drink as he sat beside her on the tyre.

'You okay?'

'My arms are burning and so is my bum.'

'Glutes.'

'Whatever. You do this field torture well.'

'Basic training flashbacks.'

'You don't strike me as the gung-ho Army type.'

'I didn't mind it. I enlisted to keep this place going through the drought. This farm's been in the family for generations.'

She admired the soft sloping hills and lush emerald valley peppered with cattle grazing in the distance. 'Where are your parents?'

'On the Gold Coast. I'd bought this farm from my parents, and as soon as I was eligible to receive the Army pension, I'd planned to play here.' He loved the farm the way his eyes shone looking at the scenery and the pride she heard in his voice every time he spoke about the place.

'Why do you work at the gym if you don't like it?'

Brett frowned as he pulled at a tuft of grass. 'Fiona wanted it.'

In all their conversations Brett always clammed up about his wife. But she'd never pried, until now. 'Were you married before you joined the Army?'

'Can't remember when we weren't together.'

'Really?'

'Yeah. Most of my childhood memories have Fiona in them. But she hated shifting when I'd get posted to a new base. She got homesick and came back here.'

'To the farm?' Jessica gazed at the homestead nestled among fertile farmlands.

'Fiona never stayed here. We had a house near the gym where she recruited her parents and me to help her buy the business. She loved it.'

'You didn't?'

'Nope. Being a personal trainer was Fiona's thing, where she'd run the classes and I'd maintain the machinery. Her dad, Bob, was content to push a broom at night, being semi-retired. Nicole did admin. It worked well when I wasn't here too.'

'Where were you?'

'In the Army, on overseas tours.'

'To war?' Her words echoed as fear pushed her heart rate.

'No.' He grinned at her sideways. 'I did humanitarian tours following natural disasters. I was part of a specialised group of engineers who helped restore basic facilities like bridges, water pumps, and shelters.'

'You got to be a hero?' The man was already legendary.

'Kind of. I was in Sumatra after the earthquakes when I got the call about Fiona being sick. I caught the first plane back and stayed until …' He halted and peered across the paddock as a crow cawed in the gum tree.

'How long were you married?'

'Two weeks.'

'I'd assumed you'd married sooner?'

'We'd planned to marry when I finished with the Army and we'd moved in here. But I kept extending my time, making good money, where I enjoyed making a difference on my overseas tours. Fiona wanted to stay at the house near the gym, and my parents were happy to keep living on the farm. It kept getting pushed back until Fiona was at the hospital and all our plans changed.'

'I can relate. Hospitals have a way of changing people's priorities.' She stared at the blue skyline dotted with white clouds.

'We were married in the hospital gardens just before Fiona died. We didn't even have time to choose wedding rings, and only our parents and some hospital staff were witnesses. But we'd always planned to marry. Grow old together, and to pass this farm onto our children. Now ...'

'I'm so sorry.' She squeezed his strong shoulder.

'Not your fault.' He gave her hand a pat. 'I'm a complacent prick who should've married her sooner. Not when it was too late to enjoy it.'

She removed her hand and they shared the silence, where the breeze carried rich earthy scents of growing grains.

'How come you don't have someone?'

Jessica shrugged, picking at her bootlaces. 'Thought I did.'

'Don't tell me you pushed him away like you've done with everyone else trying to help you.'

'Hey, I'm getting better.'

He mirrored her grin. 'You are.'

'I wasn't always like that. I had a boyfriend and when I was messed up he couldn't cope. My brother reacted the same way.'

'This guy didn't dump you?'

'We agreed to split up so I could concentrate on my healing.'

'Tell me he did not walk away?'

'You could see how relieved he was when I told him it wasn't a good time.'

'How'd you take that?'

'I accepted it then that I'd always be alone. My brother still avoids me, and I don't blame him.' She could never blame them, and watched the breeze caress emerald grasses that shone under the Autumn sun.

'Everyone copes with trauma differently.'

'But you never left Fiona, that's so rare. Sure, I had my parents, and work sent flowers but no one else missed me.'

'Someone must've missed you.'

'My fault. I was such a geek, focused on my work. Where, in the end, I was just a voice on the phone fixing IT issues, stuck in a windowless office staring at a screen. Except my boss, he freaked out.'

'Good.'

'That was more to do with the Workers Compensation paperwork. I realised then I was just another number and decided to work for myself. Haven't regretted it. I love my job, and with my credentials I know I'll be okay.'

'What about after Larapinta?'

'Back to my parents, I guess.' Which felt like a step backwards. 'My focus is to complete the Larapinta trail. I came here to train and prove to myself I can still do it for me. I didn't expect so much work.' But grateful for it.

'You're charging me a fortune on the gym's website.' He gave her a gentle nudge with this elbow.

'If you hadn't been such a prick I'd might've given you mate's rates.' She poked his arm.

'Hey, I've been nice to you.'

'This being nice? Making me roll tractor tyres over your muddy paddock.'

'You wanted to go hike in the desert, not me.'

'Thank you, Brett, because of your help, I know I can do it.' Jessica kissed his cheek. But he turned and their lips were just a breath apart. 'I'd, um ...' Clearing her throat, she pushed herself up and her smile widened. 'Look, no sticks.'

'Well done. Think you can walk across the paddock without them?'

'I'm too sore, which isn't going to look pretty hobbling for a few days. Can't believe I'm having a farewell dinner tomorrow.' Maggie and Nicole had organised with a few others to meet at the pub.

'I'll pick you up at six.' Brett held out her sticks that she gripped tight as part of her comfort zone. With a fingertip, he tucked stray hair behind her ears. 'You've always looked beautiful. Even with dirt on your face.'

He was so close.

Breath held, her gaze locked with his and everything around them paused as he drew her closer with his palm cradling her cheek.

'Don't.' She stepped back. 'We're friends, okay? I can't.' She stabbed the hiking poles into the earth with more force than needed as she turned away from him. 'You deserve better and I'm leaving. I'm sorry.'

Why hadn't another woman in town snatched him up? Brett was gorgeous, funny, smart, gentle, and almost perfect. Her body ached near him. Missed him when she didn't see him. But in her dreams of shared passion, she was always whole. She'd never be good enough for Brett, or for any man, and accepted that.

And with all those memories he still carried of his wife, Brett wasn't ready for anyone else, and certainly didn't need the extra burden of looking after someone with a disability.

She'd come out here to train for her trip to Alice Springs and needed to focus on the destination ahead. In two nights, she'd be standing in the heart of Australia.

Why ruin a friendship on something that wouldn't last?

Her hair wouldn't sit straight, her make-up was wrong and she'd tried on everything in her suitcase twice. It was just dinner with friends for her last night in Heart Springs.

Why am I so nervous?

Because it felt like a date.

Giving up, she let her hair tumble free past her shoulders. Slipped on her flat shoes and looked at herself in the mirror. Her blue woollen dress hugged her body, toned from all the work Brett made her do. It was the fittest she'd ever been.

She heard Brett's ute pull up, soon followed by a knock and the creak of the front door opening. 'You ready?'

'Yes.' *No.*

'Wow.' Brett's jaw dropped.

'It's all wrong, right?' She tugged at the hem of her dress, praying it wouldn't catch on her leg brace.

'No. Come on.' He wrapped her hand around his arm, grabbed her coat and bag.

'My crutches.'

'Not tonight.' Pocketing the key, he shut the door behind them.

'But …'

'Relax,' he said, opening her car door. 'It's just dinner with the crew as your *bon voyage*.'

'This feels like a date,' she blurted out as she climbed into her seat.

'I've never really *dated* so I wouldn't know.'

'But what about you and Fiona?'

'I've always known Fiona. Our idea of dating was sharing lunch in the school yard. Besides, if this *was* a date, you wouldn't go because *you* don't date.

Now relax, you look beautiful, always do.' He closed her door and ran around to take the driver's seat.

Jessica blushed and cracked the window open for the cool air. Brett was just being polite. *We're friends, nothing more.* 'I could've driven and then you'd be free to drink.'

'You'll be doing enough driving tomorrow to the city, let me do this. Have a few drinks, you deserve it.'

'But, I've—'

'Stop.' He grabbed her hand and made her face him. 'You've worked your butt off to achieve your goals, so be proud of yourself, okay.'

'I should tape your little ego-boosting speeches for when I'm on the track.' He'd helped her achieve more than expected. 'How can I thank you for all you've done for me?'

'You cooked. And you're shouting dinner tonight.'

'Yeah, but …'

'Just enjoy it.' He pulled up at the Heart Springs Hotel. Before she'd unclipped her seatbelt, Brett was there, holding her door ajar.

'I've always wanted to see the view from that balcony.' Gripping his muscular arm for balance, she inhaled his aroma of soap and shampoo. Still too damned sexy for a friend.

'Do you want to try those steps before dinner?'

'Thought we agreed I'd reserve my strength for the hike.'

'This isn't hiking, it's a set of stairs. Come on.'

Brett always encouraged her to step beyond her comfort zone. 'Well, it is my last night in town, why not?'

'That's my girl.' He grinned, giving her a wink.

His girl? No, she wasn't. Yet hearing him say it made her heart bloom. If she could skip, she would. Besides, Brett was all about assisting mates with their achievements.

'I'll be right behind you.'

She felt safe with Brett being there, but he wouldn't be there forever, and her heart squeezed at the thought. Jessica grabbed the bannister's cool wood and gazed upwards. 'I miss my pole.'

'I'm here if you need me. You can do it.'

'You say that a lot,' she said, taking the first step.

'Look up, not at the stairs. And what do I do?'

'Push me.' The gentle touch of his palm on her lower back gave her all the encouragement in the world.

'Is that a bad thing?'

She stepped again, and again, and onto the landing with a huge smile on her face. 'Today, it's a good thing.' She stood tall, and fisted the air with pride. '*I did it.*'

Brett shared his easy side-grin. 'You sure did. C'mon, view's this way.' He led her out to the balcony.

The winter breeze was invigorating as she gazed over Heart Springs' main street. The closed shops were familiar; the owners she now knew by name had become clients, even friends. Something pulled inside her heart. 'I'll miss this town, and its people.'

'We'll miss you.' Still holding her hand, Brett's thumb brushed her skin, sending shivers across her body. 'I'll miss you.'

Admiring the fine lashes that outlined his delicious denim eyes, did she dare believe him?

'I know you can't see past the walk and I get that. But you can come back.'

'I'm not planning to.'

He sighed and frowned at the town spread out below. 'After Fiona died and I left the Army, everyone did all the planning for me. Except you. You let me plan your training and weekend hiking trips, which makes me want to plan my future and not have others do it for me.'

'Are you ready to move on?'

'It's been three years since Fiona died, and I'm still hanging onto something that doesn't make me happy. While you're here doing something amazing for the first anniversary of your accident. You've moved on, turning a negative into a positive. I want to do that too. So, I'm selling my share of the gym to Kelly.'

'But what about the mornings you open?'

'I got used to you being here, giving me grief in the mornings. I don't like change, but I like how much you changed my world the minute you entered it, and I want you to come back.' His warm palm cupped the side of her face.

'I can't.'

'Why not?'

'I'm …'

'There you are,' said Nicole from the top of the stairs.

'Brett got me to do the stairs.' Nicole had stopped an awkward conversation.

'Well done, Jessica. And you look so beautiful tonight. Brett, good to see you got rid of that beanie. Now let's get you back down, we're all waiting.' Nicole hooked her arm around Jessica's and with Brett on the other side, they escorted Jessica downstairs.

'I'm scared,' Jessica whispered as the sun shone through the kitchen windows. Brett sat opposite at the dining table, sharing their last breakfast together – her payment for trek-training. This morning he'd been there banging at her door for coffee, as per usual, but without the training. Her car was packed and the cottage cleared as if she'd never been there.

'Want me to come with you to make sure you board that plane?' asked Brett.

Jessica wanted to say yes. But this was hard enough without prolonging the pain of leaving him. 'I'm dropping my car at my parents' and my brother's taking me to the airport. He owes me.'

'The brother who won't talk to you?'

'Yeah, I'm going to use the drive time to sort out our issues.'

'Good for you. Maggie hasn't rented this place out yet. You can come back.'

'Not making any commitment to anything except this trip.' She sighed with an all-over body sag, staring at the grains within the worn wooden table top. 'Am I kidding myself?' Was her question about her hike in central Australia or how she felt about Brett?

His hand covered hers. 'You'll do great. Maggie's sorted the tour guides out and I've told them not to treat you like an invalid, just a stubborn arse who's quite capable.'

'You did not?'

'I wanted to make sure you were prepared and they gave me tips to train you.' He reached out and pulled her to her feet. With her sticks in hand, Brett escorted Jessica towards her car. 'You will do this. I believe in you to do this.'

'Why?'

'Because I'm hoping once you see how magnificent you are, you'll let others in too.'

'Like who?'

'Me.'

ॐ

Brett couldn't resist any longer and pressed his lips to hers. A soft, delicate feathery dance upon the lips he'd dreamt of kissing for so long. He deepened the kiss as he pulled her into his chest and enveloped her with his arms. She tasted better than he imagined.

He pulled back and gazed into her eyes. His fingertip traced her beautiful plump lips, memorising every intricate detail.

He didn't want to, but he had to let her go. She needed to do this for herself, and watched her climb into her seat. 'Drive safe. Text me when you get to the airport and when you arrive in Alice Springs. Don't forget, send me a snapshot at the start of the hike, like you promised, before you lose reception.' But would she? Was this the end of all their communications?

'I will.'

'Be safe, please, and remember to look at that bigger picture.' He hoped she would. Which made him think harder about his own future too. 'And don't you dare take that laptop.'

'I won't.'

'Enjoy it. Okay.'

'I'll try.'

'You will.' Holding her door open, he leant down and brushed her lips with his. 'Go or you'll miss your flight.' If he didn't let her leave now, he doubted he ever would, and she'd hate him for missing her goal. This week was Jessica's. To focus on completing this hike to make her hell-week anniversary a good memory.

ॐ

'Thank you, for everything.' The tears welled in her eyes; her heart was heavy in her chest. Her lips tingled, his taste lingering, and her body was cold away from his embrace.

'You can thank me by sending me a selfie on top of that mountain on your anniversary date.'

'I will.' *Hell, yeah.*

He closed her door and stepped back. His delicious denim eyes, the chiselled cheekbones shadowed his features like a charcoal sketch destined for a museum wall. With the sunrise spreading across lush farmlands behind him, it was just the way she wanted to remember him. Even wearing his black beanie, Brett looked glorious.

Jessica's smile faltered. Her excitement for her future dimmed. Giving a limp-wristed wave, she watched him from her rear-view mirror as she drove away from the cottage.

She needed to do this trek. If she stopped now, she'd always wonder if she could.

Yet leaving Brett behind hurt more than anything she'd ever physically been through.

Checklists checked and rechecked. Boots polished, her day-pack loaded and strapped into that sweet spot on her spine. With poles in her hand, Jessica faced the start of the trail where the desert wind nipped at her skin and the sunrise started below the biggest cloudless sky she'd ever seen.

The guides checked over each hiker's pack, straps, boots, while talking about the day's trek ahead. And they were off. One guide led, one was in the middle, and another trailed in the back.

One step after the other, Jessica followed their lead. Excited as she was to finally be doing this, something was missing.

What have I left behind?

Pink bottlebrushes dripped with honeyed dew. Low grass grew in clumps between red dust and shoal, as darkness was broken by a ribbon of colour that crept across a horizon that stretched forever. It was a place of pure air, of no cars, no phone towers, no buildings, just space and the story of its people.

The untouched beauty beckoned her as she took a photo of the setting, but knew it'd never do justice to the magnificence before her. But she had promised Brett she'd take the photo at the start of her journey.

Her heart squeezed. *I miss him.*

But she couldn't do anything now, so she gripped her poles and took that first step into the wilderness.

The end was in sight. Jessica gave a weary grin. Her body ached, leg muscles burned, her hair damp from morning dew. Yet, she was delighted to be here, even if she was suffering under the steepest final climb panting the sweet scent of sunrise that was her victory calling. She'd made it.

She wished Brett were here. Every morning, and night, she'd wished he was here to share the experience, to talk to her, to share that comfortable silence walking side by side.

But I always planned to do this on my own.

And yet, she'd never been truly alone. She'd walked among a group of people she'd met as strangers; after six days of sweat, muscle aches and consistent fly swatting, following blue arrows that marked the dusty trail ahead, they'd become friends.

She'd shivered through icy morning frosts that stiffened bones and clothes. Sweltered as the noon-day desert dust covered her boots that crunched upon ochre rocks made from towering jagged mountains.

She'd laughed at the antics of lizards frolicking upon the rocks, and was envious of brush-tailed rock wallabies that leapt across boulders like springboards.

They'd discovered secluded waterholes where eucalyptus gums reflected in glistening mirrors within the cool natural swimming holes, where pitched tents were a welcoming oasis promising a good night's sleep. Distant dingoes serenaded fiery desert sunsets, where she'd listened to tales around campfires as camp oven aromas filled the air. And here, she whispered her wishes to falling stars among the billion-star skyline of silence.

Always at the back of the parade, Jessica stepped steady. She'd skinned her knees and bruised her shins. Boots slipped on sand, and her poles got trapped between rocks. Yet, every time she tripped, she heard Brett's voice telling her to get up, dust herself off, and keep moving forward. And she missed him.

Jessica had begun this climb at 3.30 a.m., scrabbling over rocks like ants on the track.

Her reward – an endless view.

The MacDonald Ranges was an open ocean of golden russet waves trapped in mid motion, kissing a cerulean skyline, where a lone eagle's stretched winged glide greeted the day.

It was purely magical. And again Jessica wished Brett was here to share it with her.

She'd reached her goal.

Now what?

'You did it.'

'Brett?' She spun towards the familiar voice and swiped at the dirt around her eyes. 'Am I hallucinating?'

'No.' Chuckling, he hugged her warmly.

'What are you doing here?' She inhaled his familiar scent, his heartbeat strong beneath her palm.

'I've been waiting here to shake your hand.'

'Huh?' She stared, mouth open as he shook her hand, giving her an easy side-grin that filled her chest with warmth.

'Congratulations.'

'Stuff the handshake.' She threw her arms around him. 'I missed you so much.' The words spilled out before she could stop them.

'I missed you too.'

His safe embrace made her body-aches disappear. But had she heard right? He missed her? 'How did you get here? Why?'

'Nicole saw how upset I was, and had a chat with Maggie, who booked my flights and organised everything. My folks drove over to look after the farm, and I've been waiting for you, hoping you'll be okay with what I have to tell you.'

'Tell me what?'

'I love you, Jessica, and I want to take you home with me.'

'You do?' Her eyes widened at this male-mirage.

'Yes. And I know you love me too.'

She wanted to. Instead she whimpered, 'Just—'

'Don't you dare believe your leg is an issue. Not after this. You did this trip on your own.'

'I had help. These people helped me, and you did too because you were with me every step of the way.'

Brett stepped closer, cradling her cheek with his warm calloused palm. With their noses barely apart, he said, 'Everyone needs help. You've helped me too. And just seeing your smile is worth being by your side, especially when you achieve your goals.'

'I don't want to stop smiling, now you're here. A year ago today was the—'

'Stop.' His thumb brushed her lips and she stared into his delicious denim eyes. 'Today is the beginning of a new life, and I won't delay living my life with you.'

'I'm dreaming?'

'Let's make it a good dream then.' His lips pressed against hers.

As the sun chased away the night's shadows of yesterday, she allowed herself to believe in today and their many shared tomorrows. 'I love you too, Brett.'

'Don't ever stop telling me and I'll never stop walking beside you.'

Her heart opened to become as light as the eagle that gracefully circled the sunrise. She felt like a migrating bird that had headed north to find where her heart truly belonged – with him. 'I won't.'

'Good. Now, let's take a photo of this moment as the first day our future.' With their arms wrapped around each other, the phone's camera captured their wide smiles while the world spread endlessly beneath their boots.

She'd found her happiness, her soulmate and herself in the heart of the country, and Jessica knew her next destination was back home in Heart Springs with Brett.

Forever.

Escape to D'Amour

MICHELLE BEESLEY

Lavender stood behind the counter of her pretty little teashop, The Tea Lady Café. In the centre of Heart Springs, the flower-filled and inviting store sold exotic teas, quirky teapots and was attached to a café stocked with mouth-watering baked goods – scones, apple teacake, lavender biscotti and some of the best coffee in town.

The last customers were on the verandah eating Devonshire teas with clotted cream, so Lavender nodded at her two young assistants to begin cleaning up, before choosing some ingredients for her own aromatic tea. The tea was filled with everything she found soothing – the South African rooibos, ginger, mint and orange – and a large dollop of Manuka honey for energy. Breathing in the fragrant blend, she tried to calm her ratcheting nerves.

The counsellor sent by the Army had explained that there would be many stages to her grief – anger at losing her husband too soon, despair at going it alone (they were newlyweds with big plans that would now never come to fruition), and even hatred towards the Army for sending him to Afghanistan. Today all Lavender felt was a well of tiredness. Her eyes were tired. Her body was tired. Her mind was tired.

She slumped onto a stool. After gulping down two big sips of piping hot tea she relaxed. The sweetness of the honey coursed through her veins, sparking any reserves of energy she had left. And then she groaned as a little bell tinkled, signalling that her peace was not to last. Another customer had arrived.

'Izzy!' Lavender brightened when she saw her bubbly friend from J'Adore Travel Boutique. Izzy was always happy and sunny; with her shock of cropped blonde hair and endless legs she would not look out of place on the cover of *Vogue* or strutting the catwalks in Milan. Yet she always said, 'I'm happy right here in Heart Springs.'

This might have been helped by the fact that her boyfriend, Ayden, was also a local. He arranged sightseeing tours around the area in his little helicopter, Nellie. He'd gone to J'Adore hoping to advertise his business and it was love at first sight for both he and Izzy. Their little foursome had always gone on double dates together – Izzy and Ayden, Jake and Lavender.

Ayden and Jake had been planning big things together once Jake left the Army for good. They were hoping Ayden could fly helicopter tours out to Jake's family lavender farm. Lavender's face clouded and she sighed as she remembered their plans for picnic baskets filled with her sweet treats and local delicacies to cater for Heart Springs' growing tourism industry. They'd even considered branching out into country weddings on the farm.

Those dreams were now shattered, but Lavender dismissed her black thoughts by pasting on a welcoming smile for her friend.

'What a morning,' groaned Izzy, 'I can't believe the bookings we've taken for Christmas ski holidays. The whole town will be in Niseko, Japan for Christmas. I don't know why you'd want to go to the snow when you live here in paradise.'

'I think that's the idea,' laughed Lavender. 'They all want to escape the hordes of holidaymakers who come here for Christmas. My mum and dad are coming up from Sydney to help this year. Mum's scones are even better than mine. I just don't think I could manage another busy Christmas like last year on my own.'

'Yes, but only you knew that tea would make such a comeback in the last few years. Business has been great. Remember how I thought you were bonkers opening a tea shop in Heart Springs?'

'Yeah, The Tea Lady Café is doing better than I'd ever dreamed it would,' sighed Lavender. 'I just seem to have no time for me, what with owning the farm as well.' She shrugged. 'Something's got to give. I was hoping to introduce high teas this year but I haven't had time or the energy.'

'Come on, now. Are you in the doldrums again?' Only Izzy could get away with saying that. 'Come to the pub for dinner tonight. I've got a plan.'

'I was planning on binge watching *Game of Thrones* and putting my feet up for the day.'

'Now you're acting like a grandma. You're only twenty seven. It's been ages since we caught up properly. Ayden's away on a golf trip with the lads, so it's perfect timing.'

'All right, I guess. Just for you. So, what's this plan of yours?'

'No, you'll have to wait. I'll tell you tonight. Now, I need three cups of green tea and some of your heavenly teacake for the travel troop. Everyone needs a little pick-me-up before the afternoon onslaught of travellers.'

Lavender looked shocked, 'What, no coffee?'

Izzy laughed. 'We're trying something different. Maggie's naturopath said we were drinking too much coffee and should replace it with green tea in the afternoon. Maggie's on a bit of a health kick, which means we are too.' She rolled her eyes.

'Coming right up,' said a bemused Lavender as she busied herself with the order.

Yes, it would be good to talk to a friend.

Oh Jake why did you have to leave me? I miss you so much.

And why in heaven would you leave me with your lavender farm to run? I know nothing, nothing *about plants or farming.*

'Earth to Lavender. You drifted off for a minute there, honey. See you at six for a drink before dinner?'

'Why not?' Lavender replied with a weary smile, placing three cups of steaming green tea in a flowery cardboard drinks container. Three huge slices of apple teacake were gently placed in her signature lavender-coloured cake boxes.

'You're a doll,' laughed Izzy, with a wink. She juggled the tea and cake in one hand and inhaled the spicy apple smell. 'Mmm, I'm feeling better already.' The little door tinkled happily as Izzy left with her prize.

At five o'clock Lavender turned the 'Closed' sign around for the day. She smiled at Regina and Becky, her young staff who'd survived another busy day and had already tidied the shop and mopped all the floors. Her barista Brooke was already ensuring the coffee machine was sparkling clean ready for the next day.

'Thanks, girls. You've earnt your money today. Why don't you take some leftover apple teacake home to your families?'

'Thanks, Lavender. My dad loves taking your cake for smoko. All the boys on site are always jealous of him.'

'Great to hear, Becky. You're such a trooper. It's the least I can do. Remember to tell your dad it's because I appreciate all the hard work you do.'

'Thanks, Lavender … anything else need doing before I go?'

'No, all done for today. I'll even have time to go home to change before meeting Izzy at the pub.'

'All right, night then,' chorused the three girls, scurrying out to do some shopping together before heading home.

Before she locked up, Lavender looked around the spotless shop, making sure everything was perfectly in order for the next day. The girls had done a great job. She was proud of the café. Jake would've been proud too. She and Jake had only just put the last lick of lavender paint on the front door when they got the news that he was to make one more tour of duty to Afghanistan. They'd just been married and started the business, and were in their own little bubble, planning their lives.

'This'll be my last tour. I'll be discharged for good after that. We won't need the extra money any more. I'll come home and help you with the shop, help Dad with the farm and get busy making beautiful babies with luscious dark hair and lavender eyes,' he'd pleaded.

'No,' she said, 'I want lots of mischievous little boys with your blonde hair and twinkling blue eyes.'

'Be careful what you wish for,' he'd laughed, swinging her around until she was dizzy. Lavender overbalanced and fell to the newly polished floor as Jake flopped beside her, covering her with kisses, promising her he'd stay safe. He lived under a lucky star, didn't he?

But her darling husband had never come home. His unit had been peacekeeping in one of the villages when a rogue sniper's bullet had felled him. Her beautiful, twinkling husband had been dead before he hit the ground. Jake was now buried on the hill above Heart Springs in a plot overlooking their little shop. Her guardian angel.

'Mercifully quick,' said the kind soldiers who'd been with Jake that day, trying to give her some solace.

At twenty-five, she was a widow. Two years had passed since then. Two years of heartache. Only the busy days kept her sane. She and Jake had built this dream together. She wouldn't – *couldn't* – let him down.

At home, Lavender had just enough time to shower and don a crisp white shirt and jeans before heading back into town to meet Izzy for a counter meal. At the last minute, she'd slicked on some berry lipstick, brightened her eyes with mascara and unravelled her topknot so a glossy, dark cascade fell down her back.

How Jake had loved to run his fingers through my hair.

Jake, Jake, my one and only love.

Her mobile beeped, bringing her back to the present.

Already here

What's your poison?

She quickly texted back:

Sav blanc

LARGE

Moments later, she gazed around the pub, nodding at customers and old friends, scanning for Izzy's shock of blonde hair. *Oh, good, she's nabbed a booth. Much easier to talk there.*

Izzy spotted her at the same time and enthusiastically waved her over. A giant ice cold glass of New Zealand sauvignon blanc was placed in front of her. Lavender took a large gulp, nodding her approval.

'See, isn't this better than sitting at home alone?' Izzy asked.

'Yes, it's just the getting out in the first place. I'm so tired all the time, physically and emotionally. When I stop for the day I suddenly realise Jake's gone forever and it's hard to move again.'

Izzy reached over and squeezed Lavender's hand. 'I know. He was your very best friend, as well as your husband. Listen, I do have a proposition for you. I've run it past Maggie and she agrees with me.'

'Sounds mysterious.'

'So, Maggie's mum has a friend called Katerina who married a Frenchman and is now running a chateau in Provence. They want someone to try out their new gastronomy tour and we thought of you.'

Lavender started to shake her head but Izzy held up a hand to stop her. 'Don't say no just yet. It will be a five-star experience, all paid for, flights as well. Katerina is Australian so she wanted another Aussie's perspective on their experience. We don't know anyone who knows as much about food and flavours as you and I know you've been wanting to get some new ideas on lavender farming. Provence is famous for its lavender.'

Lavender's eyes widened in surprise. She let out a long, deep breath before tilting her head to the side. 'Wow. I did not see that coming. But have you forgotten I have a business to run?'

'Yeah, well, that's all sorted too. I spoke to your parents and they would happily stay an extra two weeks. You keep telling me that Brooke could practically run the place by herself, so why not give her the chance?'

Lavender's eyes narrowed in suspicion as she sat back in her chair, 'Is everyone in on this?'

Izzy looked guilty. 'Please don't be mad. We've all been worried about you. It's been two years since Jake died and it's as if all your happiness died with him.' She grabbed Lavender's hand again. 'It's time, sweetie … time to move on.'

Lavender could hardly believe it when she was ushered from the airport lounge into seat 1A. Izzy had been right when she said it was five star all the way. On the leg from Dubai to Paris she'd even been offered a shower. Lavender had politely declined, thinking she didn't want to be naked if the plane fell out of the sky. Maybe she'd be braver on the way home.

At Charles de Gaulle airport, a driver holding a sign saying LAVENDER JONES was waiting to take her to Gare de Lyon, where she sank gratefully into a first-class seat on the fast train to Aix. The rocking of the train lulled her into a light doze as the scenery whizzed by, but it seemed like no time at all passed before the guard was signalling Aix-en-Provence, next stop.

A tired and rumpled but still curious Lavender hopped off the train, disoriented by the rapid-fire French speakers bustling all around her. A tall auburn-haired woman towered majestically above the crowd, and, spotting Lavender, smiled warmly. She strode over to plant two kisses on each of Lavender's cheeks.

'Well, I hope you're Lavender Jones. I don't usually go around kissing strangers. Katerina de Castile from Château d'Amour,' the woman said, with the slightest hint of Australian twang. 'I'd know you anywhere. Maggie sent some photos and links to the website for your dear little café. So pleased you could come.'

'Thanks so much, Countess de Castile. I wasn't expecting you to come and meet me.'

'Enough of the "countess". Hardly anyone calls me that. It's Katerina and of course I came. I was so excited to see another Aussie after all this time. I hardly ever get home these days. Did you bring me my secret stash?'

'Of course. Vegemite, Tim Tams and Musk Sticks are all carefully stowed away in my luggage.'

'Hooray! And all for me. My husband detests Vegemite, although I'll have to hide the Tim Tams. He inhales those. Come on, let's get you to the chateau so you can freshen up and I can get my hands on those goodies.'

Before long, they were on the road; Lavender watched as Katerina expertly manoeuvred her white Range Rover on the high-speed motorway.

Katerina noticed her gaze. 'I know, it feels really weird at first driving on the wrong side of the road, but I'm used to it now. My husband used to have me chauffeured everywhere. Some of the roads can be quite narrow and tricky. But I learnt my way around in a little yellow Renault, and these days I actually prefer the bigger car for highway driving.'

Turning off the highway, Katerina drove them through a quaint little town with a fountain in the centre, some wine caves, restaurants, *tabacs* and an inviting looking *chocolaterie*. As if reading Lavender's mind she added, 'Yes, you must visit Thierry's chocolate shop. Best in Provence. He also has a factory just outside of town which is part of our tour. People from all around the world come here for his chocolate, although like most great artists, he's a temperamental soul. His family have lavender farms outside of town, which Maggie told me you're also interested in.'

'Yes, my late husband, Jake, grew up on a lavender farm. He'd always wanted to be a soldier, to see some action after growing up in a sleepy little town. He had so much energy,' Lavender said quietly, eyes growing misty, 'He always said he was fated to marry a girl called Lavender with lavender eyes. He and his dad were planning to expand the lavender farm when he was discharged from the Army. Since they'd lost his mum a few years ago to breast cancer it had become all too much for his dad. They planned on doing some travelling to find new products to make from lavender, modernise and expand the farm again … and then Jake died. His dad suffered a stroke not long after. I think he died from a broken heart. They were so close. So, now I have a lavender farm *and* a café to run.'

'Oh, Lavender, I am so sorry. Maggie did tell me you'd been run ragged. I hope the healing air in Provence will help you. I came here with a broken heart myself and found my one true love.'

Hastily, Lavender shook her head and cupped her trembling hands to steady herself. 'But I'm not looking for anyone else. Jake was the only man for me.'

'Of course not. It's just that Provence has a magical quality and …. well, you'll see. Ah, here is our magical little chateau now. Welcome to Château D' Amour.'

Lavender was dizzy from admiring the twisting drive lined with pencil pines which kept winding up, up, up. She gasped as they wound around the last corner, where a majestic turreted chateau rose from the ground on the hill above. It looked more like a fairy tale castle with its age-old stone walls and creeping ivy. Jaunty blue and white umbrellas waved happily in the cobblestoned courtyard by the pool and enormous pots of lavender stood sentry outside the oak door. For the first time in two years Lavender felt the strangest feeling of coming home.

Lavender clapped her hands in delight. 'It's just beautiful.'

'*D'accord*, that is exactly the reaction I was hoping you'd have.'

The countess expertly parked the car. Bellboys whisked Lavender and her luggage up to a sunny, yellow room on the second floor. Moving aside the heavy damask curtains, Lavender spied vineyards as far as her eyes could see and in the distance, a city.

'Yes, we are high enough here to have a glimpse of the beautiful town of Avignon,' Katerina said behind her.

'A marvellous view,' breathed Lavender, 'And what is that on the next hill over?'

'Ah, that is my dig site. I was originally an archaeologist and what you see up there are the ruins of the very first papal palace to be built in France. It was burnt down and rebuilt in Avignon. I am still finding treasures and there is now another reason for history buffs to visit our special region of France. Roman colosseums and amphitheatres are dotted throughout our region. I'm pleased to say that I'm now the world expert in this area and have written a number of books on the subject. You will find them in our library downstairs.'

'Wow, and I thought *I* was busy,' said Lavender.

'Phfft, it is a labour of love for me. But now, you freshen up. I hope you're hungry. We have the first of many *gastronomique* experiences for you this evening.'

Moments later, Lavender drew a steaming bath, adding lavender-scented bath bombs. She enjoyed the citrusy scent of the body wash provided; after washing the smell of travel from her hair she loosely dried it, tousling her hair with sea salt spray, a reminder of home. Pulling a bejewelled hair clip from her jewellery bag, she scooped back a handful of the luscious locks, accentuating her razor-sharp cheekbones.

From her luggage, she pulled a plain black shift dress, a black Mimco clutch, and a pair of orange sandals. After carefully re-applying her make-up, adding a smoky eye and burnt orange lip gloss for a night-time effect, she slipped into her carefully chosen outfit and surveyed herself in the mirror.

Not bad after all that travel. Wish me luck, Jake … I do so want to make Izzy and Maggie proud.

Lavender descended the staircase and was ushered into a beautiful book-lined library. Tables had been set with starched tablecloths and the view from the French windows showed nearby vineyards softly lit by carefully placed fairy lights. The lights of Avignon twinkled in the distance.

The countess bustled in, russet hair piled into a topknot, wearing a cream silk shirt and a pair of black palazzo pants atop towering heels … *The epitome of chic*, Lavender thought.

'Ah, Lavender, *très bien.* You look much more refreshed and ready to tackle the feast our chefs have whipped up. Come onto the terrace. I have assembled some of our local artisans to join us.'

Lavender followed in the regal woman's footsteps and was handed a glass of champagne from a glittering silver tray. Katerina introduced her to Mariet from the local *boulangerie*, cheesemakers Audette and Marcel, and lastly, a suited gent who had his back to her. He appeared to be gazing intently at the vineyards beyond.

'Thierry, stop being so rude,' scolded the countess.

He turned with a scowl and sauntered over as if he would rather be anywhere other than here at this moment. Lavender waited awkwardly, embarrassed to be the centre of attention.

So, this is the famous Thierry Boucleuse, Master Chocolatier.

'Thierry Boucleuse, may I introduce our guest from Australia, Lavender Jones.'

'Good evening, *mademoiselle*,' Thierry drawled laconically.

Lavender blinked fiercely as she returned his gaze. Her stomach fluttered as she looked into a pair of dark, piercing eyes. *Come-to-bed-eyes,* she thought.

'Thierry,' he said curtly.

Lavender felt a frisson of energy flowing between them as their hands touched and she pulled her hand away sharply as if she'd been scalded. Her breath caught as she looked deep into his dark brown eyes.

Lavender felt dizzy, but the feeling quickly faded as she was greeted by the other artisans. The jolly red-faced pâtissier Mariet kissed her on both cheeks and the others followed suit.

She glanced at Thierry surreptitiously from under her lashes. Heat rose in her cheeks at the thought of him kissing her hello.

Would I feel that same strange jolt of electricity again?

Lavender watched Thierry move away from the group and into the shadows. He leant against the low wall of the stone terrace, still seemingly part of the group, but detached. She saw his gaze follow the meandering of the guests before seeming to seek her out in the crowd. A slight nod and a sardonic smile made her smooth her skirt before placing her hands in her hair to pat down some non-existent flyaways.

She smiled politely at Mariet, trying to focus on what the pâtissier was saying, nodding in all the right places. But she was acutely aware of Thierry. Her glance slid back in his direction and she wondered if those now-hooded eyes were gazing back in boredom or disdain. He wore an air of sadness under his rather dashing façade. Lavender hugged herself as a sudden chill and a shiver of what could have been fear or desire shook her body.

Shaking herself, Lavender now gave her full attention to Mariet, who was asking about her apple teacake.

'The secret,' whispered Lavender conspiratorially, 'is in the spices I sprinkle on top. It's a blend of cinnamon and nutmeg but also a special smoked tea I source from North Queensland. The climate there is just right for growing tea, and being such a young industry in my country they are not afraid to experiment with new flavours. I can send you some if you'd like to try it in your own baking.'

Mariet laughed. 'I don't know how the locals would feel about tea-flavoured croissants?'

Lavender chuckled along before looking back at Thierry. She felt sure she saw the smallest hint of a smile on his face as he took in the women's laughter.

Polished waiters were now offering hors d'oeuvres along with the champagne that had been putting a glimmer back into her cheeks. Katerina was certainly showcasing the freshest of local produce – sharp goat's cheese tarts with melt-in-the-mouth pastry came first, followed by slices of baguette topped with the creamiest of Brie and the local delicacy, *foie gras*. Lastly, wafer-thin sesame crackers laden with the finest of caviar. Biting into one, Lavender groaned in delight.

A smiling Katerina emerged from the library, urging her guests into the room for dinner. The library was now filled with scented flowers – pink, purple and white. Flickering candles gave an intimate golden glow to the room, as a violinist played unobtrusively in a corner. Lavender clapped her hands in delight as she realised there were sprigs of lavender dotted around the tables in her honour.

'Thank you,' she murmured in Katerina's direction as she clasped a beribboned bundle of lavender to her chest.

The countess fondly motioned for Lavender and Mariet to join her at a table set for four. She felt Thierry's presence behind her before he'd even sat down, reluctantly it seemed, in the only vacant chair, which was right next to her. Her senses were on high alert as a manly, woody fragrance with an undertone of chocolate teased her nostrils. She paused mid-sentence, flustered by her body's response to his proximity. Thierry sat ramrod straight in his chair, answering any questions in monosyllables. His behaviour was sharply in contrast with the chirpy and friendly Mariet's.

The room stilled as the waiters returned with the first course: Castile salad served with a poached egg and snails in their shells on top. Lavender choked down a gasp of surprise before asking her hostess about the origins of the delicacies on display, especially the snails, which she hoped hadn't been procured from the local gardens.

Thierry turned his body and full attention towards her as she eyed the snails suspiciously. 'You don't eat snails in Australia?'

'No, not really. They are only in really high-end French restaurants at home. There aren't too many of them in Heart Springs, which is where I'm from.'

'Here, let me help you,' offered Thierry, placing his hand over hers to help extricate the snails from their shells.

There it is again.

Lavender's hand fluttered under his like a butterfly trapped in a jar. She looked up and as her distinctive lavender eyes locked with his chocolate-brown ones Lavender felt a sudden falling sensation.

Katerina rescued her from the moment. 'It's fine, Lavender. They are an acquired taste. That's exactly why I brought you here to test our gastronomic experience. Perhaps the first night is too soon for snails.'

'Don't worry there's a lovely duck *magret* with cherry sauce next. You'll love that,' said Mariet, with a wink.

After more delicious courses the piece de resistance arrived: a delicately layered opera cake, each layer perfectly formed and the top decorated with a gold leaf pattern.

Thierry watched Lavender as she raised a forkful of the decadent cake to her lips. Her mouth made a little O of pleasure. 'My goodness, I've never tasted anything quite like this.'

A satisfied smile crossed Thierry's handsome visage.

Katerina nodded, exclaiming, 'I knew you'd love it. It's made with Thierry's gorgeous chocolate.'

Thierry bowed his head, seeming embarrassed. 'Plus a bit of chef's magic as well. But yes, it is the best chocolate in the world.'

Lavender straightened. 'Woah, that's a big call. The Swiss make some beautiful chocolate and our Tasmanian chocolatiers are doing some pretty amazing things.'

'*Phfft*,' replied Thierry, as only a Frenchman could. '*Non*, my chocolate is the best in the world.'

Lavender blinked and her face heated.

Really, the arrogance of the man. It was super delicious but to discount the rest of the world …

As if Katerina sensed the tension building, she jumped in. 'And that is why, Thierry, we will visit your shop as well as Mariet's *boulangerie* tomorrow. Is two-thirty okay for you?'

'Perhaps,' he replied, with a shrug of his shoulders.

Lavender spluttered into her wine, aghast.

What a cheek! She'd come all this way to try out the gastronomique delights for her friends from J'Adore and this man couldn't even commit to a time.

She gently pushed her chair back and stood up to her full height. 'Don't worry, Thierry. I'll probably be so busy gleaning all Mariet's baking secrets that I won't have time for you tomorrow. We'll see if we can fit you in. Now, I think jet lag is catching up with me, so I'll head to bed.'

She turned to Katerina. 'Thank you so much for a lovely dinner.'

'My pleasure, enjoy your rest. We have a busy day tomorrow.'

Lavender turned on her heel and sashayed up the stairs, trying to affect an air of confidence that she did not feel. Inside, her emotions were spiralling.

Upstairs, Lavender's hand shook as she removed her make-up.

I don't know why I let that man get to me like that. What was I thinking?

I'm sorry, Jake, that man is stirring up all sorts of feelings inside me that I thought were buried away.

She felt a quiver of longing as she tried to replace the memory of Thierry's smouldering dark eyes with Jake's twinkling blue ones. Her hand stilled as she took several deep, calming breaths.

Yet, as she wearily snuggled into the cosy down of her bed, her last thoughts were not of Jake, but of an arrogant Frenchman called Thierry Boucleuse.

Lavender woke with a start before remembering that the sunshine streaming through the cracks in the curtains was not the Australian sun.

I'm really here, in the South of France, with no shop to open, no bills to pay and no one to answer to.

Today she would be in her element, baking with an experienced French pastry chef. The girls from J'Adore hadn't given her this trip because they felt sorry for her, but because she did know about food. She could imagine the awe other Australian foodies would feel after a dinner such as she'd been privileged to sample last night.

She dressed quickly in a pink-and-white striped button-up shirt, her trusty Levi jeans, and her comfortable soft pink Converse sneakers – her preferred footwear when working. A touch of BB cream to illuminate her skin, a slick of pink lipstick and some black mascara was all the make-up she needed. After tying her hair up, a mist of pink Miss Dior perfume, and a quick glance in the mirror – *no lippy on my teeth* – she was ready to go.

Katerina was already downstairs, dressed from head to toe in chic navy and black. Lavender marvelled at how French she seemed. It was sometimes hard to believe the woman had grown up in Australia.

Outside the *boulangerie,* delicious smells emanated, proof that Mariet had been hard at work despite her late night at the chateau. Katerina waved hello to two older men hunched over a game of chess in front of the *tabac,* arguing over their next move; small cups of espresso were by their sides and they coughed as they smoked, sending swirls into the air. Taking note, Lavender decided to have some board games on hand at The Tea Lady Café for rainy days. It looked like a cosy way to while away the morning, especially when holidaymakers were looking for something to do.

A little bell, similar to the one Lavender had at home, tinkled their arrival. Mariet hurried from the back of the shop; cheeks ruddy from the heat, flour smeared on her forehead. There was a twinkle in her eye and a smile in her voice as she embraced both women heartily before handing them little cream aprons and prompting them to wash their hands ready for work.

First, they made little fruit flans with custard, popular the world over, before moving onto *pain aux raisins,* and lastly, the chewy macarons which were new to Lavender and required all her concentration. They flavoured them with raspberry, pistachio, and *chocolat.* Every so often, Lavender made little notes in her notebook of things to tell Izzy and Maggie when they skyped that evening.

Customers came and went with the tinkling of the door, arms laden with baguettes, croissants, pastries and quiche. Mariet's pretty young assistant Bridget seemed to pirouette around the shop at lightning speed, filling orders cheerfully while Mariet served her customers with a smile, all the while haring back and forth to oversee the baking.

'*Alors,*' sighed Mariet finally, 'and now we taste. Bridget, can you look after the shop while we have *un petit* rest?'

'Mmm.' It was the only sound the women made for a few minutes as they sampled the treats.

Lavender sighed with contentment while nibbling at the corner of a perfectly formed fruit tart. Its glossy glaze gave a sheen to the sweet fruit arranged on top. An idea was forming.

'This would be a perfect experience, Mariet. J'Adore Travel Boutique has a lot of requests for cooking experiences and classes. You made this such fun. And I've really learnt so much that I can take home and use in the café.' She leant towards Mariet. 'Have you thought of offering a picnic basket full of goodies for young couples keen to explore the area but not so keen on the baking?'

'Great idea,' said Katerina, clapping her hands. 'Local cheese, fruits and paté and, if you are willing, Mariet, you could provide us with the baked goods.'

'*D'accord*, a lovely idea. The locals would enjoy that too. I'll get some things together and you can try one out tomorrow.'

Katerina wiped her mouth daintily with a crisp, white napkin and reluctantly vacated her eyrie on the stool. She placed her hands on her friend's shoulders and planted two quick kisses on her rosy cheeks. 'We have to let you get on with your day, Mariet. Hopefully, Thierry is waiting for us. Do you think you have a little room for chocolate, Lavender?'

'Always, but I suspect Thierry won't show up. He didn't seem that keen on our little venture last night,' Lavender grimaced.

Mariet laughed. 'Yes, Thierry does seem a little angry with the world. It's just the armour he wears. He does not trust any more.'

Lavender looked at the baker questioningly.

Katerina leant in conspiratorially. 'I shouldn't say, but Thierry was once such a happy young man. He and his high school sweetheart Lisette opened the *chocolaterie* together. They were so young, so in love, and their chocolate soon became a sensation.' Katerina paused searching for the right words. Mariet nodded her head in agreement. 'A billionaire Swiss chocolate manufacturer came to town and wanted to buy them out, but Thierry didn't want to sell. They began quarrelling endlessly and one night Thierry came home to an empty house. Lisette had packed up and run off with the man from

Switzerland. She took all their recipes with her and poor Thierry was absolutely heartbroken.'

Mariet took up the story, sadness in her eyes. 'He developed a, how you say, a ... a shell like an armadillo. He worked night and day to be the best again. I guess that's where the arrogance comes from. Lisette was wrong – you can't just replicate the chocolates Thierry makes in a factory. He uses the freshest of ingredients, plays around with the measurements and his *chocolat* is filled with love and sunshine. I guess that is where all his love goes now ... into his chocolate.'

Lavender's heart went out to him. At least Jake had never betrayed her. Their love had been pure and sweet. It just hadn't lasted for long enough. His death had signalled an end to her happiness and at times she had wanted to end her own life too. Now, hearing someone else's story, she realised it was time to be grateful for all the good times and the love she and Jake had shared.

'You're looking very wistful there, Lavender,' prompted Katerina.

'I was just thinking that sometimes it's better to take a chance on love while you can before life throws one of its curve balls.'

'Yes, none of us know what's just around the corner.'

'Ah, but we do,' exclaimed Mariet, lightening the mood, 'Thierry's chocolate shop! And it's after two-thirty so you two better hurry. *Allez!*'

Chatting happily about the morning, Katerina and Lavender stopped short as they rounded a corner and observed Thierry pacing in front of his shop, glaring at his watch.

Katerina raised a quizzical eyebrow in Lavender's direction just as Thierry spotted them. His tense face softened a little as he raised a hand in greeting. Katerina led the way, but Lavender hung back a little, shy after last night's behaviour.

Thierry welcomed them more warmly than expected. '*Bonjour* ladies. Welcome to Boucleuse Fine Chocolates.'

His voice was proud as he led them inside, where his professional looking staff were smiling warmly as they stood behind gleaming counters filled with every kind of chocolate imaginable.

Lavender's excitement grew and her tastebuds tingled as her gaze wandered around the store. She marvelled at the intricate decorations adorning the chocolate. Some were based on an Egyptian theme: glossy mounds finished off with tiny likenesses of Tutankhamen, Cleopatra, the Sphinx or hieroglyphics.

'Why, Thierry, these are works of art!'

'Ah. You've spotted my archaeological range, suggested by the countess. They are some of our bestsellers.'

'They look far too pretty to eat.'

One of the staff extended a platter of exquisite chocolates towards the women and Lavender's curiosity got the better of her. She had no idea what Thierry's flavour choices would be. Greedily, she popped a Sphinx chocolate into her mouth and an earthy explosion of hazelnut teased her taste buds.

Thierry's concoctions were filled with the best of fresh produce from Provence – apricot, red wine, a rich praline, and to end, the most heavenly peppermint flavour Lavender had ever tasted.

'So, do you have a favourite?' asked Thierry, smiling.

'You know my love for your chocolate. I think perhaps the hazelnut today,' replied Katerina.

'Lavender?' he asked, dark eyes probing.

A shiver fluttered up Lavender's spine at the way he'd said her name.

She mirrored Thierry's serious expression. 'I agree the hazelnut is sensational, but the mint is so refreshing. It dances on my palate.'

'Ah, good,' smiled Thierry. 'That's exactly the effect I wanted you to have before tasting this.'

A lid was whipped off a tiny jewelled box covered with a glittering mosaic of mauve, lavender, aubergine and lilac.

'Wow. It's beautiful.'

'Yes, but the real gems are inside,' Thierry said, coaxing her hand forward.

Lavender teased a chocolate from the box and took in its aroma before popping it greedily into her mouth. 'Why, it's lavender flavoured,' she gasped before licking her lips. She swallowed before speaking again. 'Thierry, I have never tasted anything like this. It tastes like sunshine and the earth with a hint of fragrance. This one is definitely my favourite.'

'Good, I was hoping you'd say that.' He grasped her hand. 'Forgive my rudeness last night. I hope you'll accept them as my gift. They were just made for a girl called Lavender with beautiful lavender eyes.'

Now he's sounding like Jake.

Maybe I'm drunk on this chocolate. I feel a bit wobbly.

Get a grip!

Tucking the little box carefully in her handbag, she reached for some honeycomb-flavoured chocolate. It was a little more intense than her favourite Violet Crumble at home.

'He keeps his own bees so that the honeycomb he uses is flavoured by the flowers of Provence,' Katerina whispered.

Thierry's eye for detail and care in sourcing local ingredients mirrored Lavender's own choices at the café. She had to know more.

'Thierry?' But he was gone. She found him in a spotless and very organised office, scribbling furiously in an overflowing notebook. 'Thierry?' she began again.

Without looking up, he raised his hand to silence her question.

The man is maddening. So rude.

The awkward silence stretched on. Finally, he stabbed the pen with a flourish to show he was finished.

'I'm sorry to be rude. When I get an idea for a new chocolate I must write it down straight away or poof, it is gone,' he said, with a snap of his fingers.

Lavender's frown disappeared. 'I know exactly what you mean. I do the same with my new tea blends or a new cake recipe for the café.'

They shared a smile. The moment went on and on.

'May I ask what it is?' asked Lavender.

'It's not quite right yet, but when I have perfected the flavour, you'll be the first to try it. Now ladies,' he said, nodding at Katerina who'd entered the room, 'it's your turn. Would you like me to teach you how to make chocolates of your own?'

'Yes, please,' they chorused.

Lavender watched carefully as she was shown the process for tempering chocolate, adding the fillings, and finally, piping on the designs when the chocolate was the right temperature.

'*Et voila*, now it's your turn.'

Lavender looked skywards and bit her lip before looking around the room searching for ingredients.

'Do you have any coconut?'

'But, of course,' replied Thierry reaching into a nearby pantry.

Stray wisps of dark hair escaped from the hair net Thierry had given her and her cheeks coloured with exertion as she bustled around the kitchen.

She had so many questions: 'At what temperature is it ready? How long will it take to cool? Can I add the gelatine for my strawberry gel now?'

As she worked, she noticed how comfortable Thierry seemed in his natural habitat. There was no trace of arrogance when he was doing what he loved. They worked together well, chatting companionably, passing ingredients and even laughing when Lavender made a mistake.

Cleaning up together, Thierry complimented Lavender: 'You're a fast learner.'

'Yes, I'm always happiest when I'm creating something in the kitchen.'

'Me too.'

'*Bon appetit,*' said Lavender, trying a French flick of the wrist to invite Katerina and Thierry to sample her creation.

No more prompting was needed. There was silence as they all tasted Lavender's chocolate.

'Mmm. Beautiful,' Thierry said. 'This is not a flavour combination I am familiar with but it works. What do you call it?'

'It's Lamington flavoured. Lamingtons are one of the cakes we eat all the time in Australia. After my apple teacake and scones, they are a bestseller in the café,' replied Lavender, locking her shining eyes with Thierry's.

'*Alors,* look at the time,' Katerina interrupted. 'We must go home and change. We have dinner at Papa Goose tonight, although I don't know where we are going to put it. We've been eating all day.'

Lavender touched Thierry's hand, lightly skimming the tiny dark hairs and carefully trimmed nails. 'Thank you so much for a lovely day, Thierry, and for not getting cross when I made mistakes.'

'You're a natural,' he replied, smiling and gently rubbing her slender shoulder.

'No, really, I can't remember when I last had such a lovely day.'

'Me too.'

They dropped hands as Katerina began speaking again. 'Now, Thierry, don't forget you are taking us to visit your parents' lavender farm tomorrow. Then Lavender will see where those delicious lavender chocolates came from. And no need to worry about lunch – Mariet is organising a picnic hamper for us too. Can you pick that up as well?'

'Great idea, although *Maman* will expect us to stop in for coffee.'

'Of course,' replied Katerina. She looked distracted. Lavender wondered why.

Thierry lifted Lavender's hand to his lips to bid *au revoir*. This time she welcomed the little shiver his kiss invoked.

The next morning, Lavender was awake and ready early, anxious to be on her way. She was on the balcony in the sunshine having her second cup of coffee when Katerina bustled in wearing a smart business outfit.

'You don't look like you're dressed for the farm,' Lavender said, rising and giving Katerina a quick double peck hello.

'Yes … so sorry to do this to you, but my husband's business dealings in Lyon are not going very well so I'm just going to drive down there and talk to the accountant myself.'

'That's okay. Do you want me to postpone the lavender farm for another day?'

'No,' replied Katerina, a little too adamantly, Lavender thought. 'It's all arranged. Thierry's a very busy man. We don't want to take up too much of his precious time.'

'I guess,' said Lavender suspiciously. But her heart quickened a little at the thought of being alone with Thierry all day.

'Well, I'll be off before the traffic to Lyon gets too heavy. *Au revoir*, enjoy your day in the sunshine. Thierry's coming at nine so keep an eye out for him.'

After Katerina left, Lavender fixed her make-up and hair one more time before Thierry's arrival. Not wanting to look too eager, she sat on the sunny terrace overlooking the pool, trying to read a novel but re-reading the same sentence over and over again. At the sound of a car off in the distance she pulled out her compact to check her face once more.

All good.

At nine on the dot she heard the thrum of a four-wheel-drive making its way up the winding driveway. As Thierry parked and stretched his long legs out of the car, she studied him surreptitiously from behind tubs of lavender. Today he sported the darkest of jeans, some sturdy Timberlands and a blue-and-white checked button-up shirt. A large silver watch was his only adornment. His dark hair, she noticed, had the tiniest wave and his skin was a deeper olive than she remembered. It echoed the milk chocolate he created so lovingly. Everything about him showed strength – blunt capable hands, a strong jawline and broad swimmer's shoulder which tapered down to his … Lavender blushed at her next thought.

Lavender smoothed her hair and checked her outfit. She'd been observing Katerina's style and had dressed more carefully than usual this morning. She'd found a Breton-style red-and-white striped long-sleeved T-shirt which accentuated her trim figure, paired it with her dark straight-legged denim jeans and added long boots with a wedge heel. At the last moment she'd tied a jaunty navy scarf around her neck and was pleased to see how it drew attention to her face. She'd even put on some fiery red lipstick and was surprised how much it suited her. Her hair tumbled free.

These French know how to make the most of their assets.

She rose from her chair in greeting as Thierry walked towards her and raised his hand, mouthing '*Bonjour*'. His expression was quizzical.

'Just us today,' said Lavender shyly. 'Katerina has some business she needs to attend to in Lyons.'

'*D'accord*,' replied Thierry with a funny catch in his voice.

'I hope that's okay with you?' Lavender looked into wide eyes fringed with thick, dark lashes.

Gosh, he makes me feel like a schoolgirl again.

He took his time to reply. 'But, of course. We could take ten of us with the size of the picnic basket Mariet has prepared. And look at you all ready and waiting. I swear you are becoming more French every day you are here. *Maman* is looking forward to some female company.'

She followed him to the car, impressed when he scooted around to hold the door open for her.

Mmm … a gentleman. I love it when a man opens doors for me.

'All set,' he smiled helping her to buckle in.

Their hands brushed and the now familiar tingle spread warmth up her arm, suffusing her face with colour. Thierry expertly manoeuvred the car down the drive, through the village and out onto the motorway.

They travelled in silence and Lavender glanced over from time to time to drink in his handsome profile. Her body heated with the awareness that his long strong hands were close beside her, nestled on the gear stick. She noticed again that he kept his nails short and neat, as did she, as it made it much easier with all the kneading and baking she was usually doing. And then, thinking of home, she began wringing her hands.

There will be so much to do when I get home. It's been easy to forget about being sad in this beautiful place.

He broke the silence. 'So, Lavender, you have a lavender farm in Australia. What came first, the chicken or the egg? Were you named Lavender after your farm or perhaps because of the colour of your eyes?'

'I was named for my eyes. This shade runs in the family. My mother's name is Violet,' she paused. 'And the farm … I inherited it after my husband, and then his father, died. There was no-one else to take it on. I felt I had to. The farm employs lots of people in our area and it's a really important industry in keeping our town alive. But I'm really not much of a farmer. I don't know what I'm doing.' Her voice quivered.

'I understand,' he said, reaching over and clasping her hand to comfort her. She startled before realising that, no, she did like the comforting way he was caressing her hand, urging her to share her story.

She poured it out: her shattered dreams, unending grief and her determination to make it all work to honour her late husband.

Thierry nodded and shook his head from time to time, urging her to continue, acknowledging her sadness. 'And now how do you feel? Has it made it any better coming to Provence?'

'Yes, it actually has. By putting some distance between me and everyone who knows me, meeting new friends, learning new things. The days are so full I'm sleeping better. Also, eating better,' she said patting her tummy. 'You see, it's tough at home in such a small place. Everyone means well, of course, but I do see the pitying looks, their worried glances. They all walk on eggshells around me, except for my dearest friend Izzy. She's the one who convinced me to come here.'

'A wise friend indeed! I almost wish I had someone like that around. I have also known heartbreak but have coped with the sympathy by developing a prickly shell,' he glanced at her, 'but around you my spirit feels lightened. I'm melting like one of my chocolates in the sun,' he laughed. 'Perhaps we were meant to meet, Lavender, to become friends, to help each other.' He paused. 'Or perhaps … more than friends.'

Lavender blinked rapidly and held her breath before whispering, 'I feel it too, Thierry. It's like … like a magic growing between us.'

He nodded but was silent a moment. She held her breath when the words came. 'Yes,' he paused again, jaw working. 'I have been fighting myself about you. It's too soon. It's moving way too fast. I know nothing about you ... and yet ...' He looked across at her. 'I ask myself, am I finally ready for someone else in my life?' He looked back at the road and then at her. 'And even though it's fast, I can't help myself. Being with you, Lavender, feels like ... when the sun comes out after a shower. You make everything brighter.'

She gaped at him. 'Thierry ... that is so ... so sweet.' She fanned her face. 'You're making me blush.'

'Sweet like my chocolate, no?'

'Sweet like your chocolate, *yes*,' she laughed. 'How do you know I'm not just hanging around to try some more of the best chocolate in the world,' she teased with a wink, smiling when Thierry reddened.

'Our house is only fifteen minutes away now,' Thierry said, clearing his throat as if he were suddenly nervous.

Turning onto a nearby roundabout, he gasped. Lavender echoed his reaction as a black car came speeding towards them on the wrong side of the road. Thierry wrenched the wheel, turning the car so that he would take most of the impact. But at the last millisecond the other car shuddered to a halt, missing them by millimetres.

A middle aged English couple hopped out, looking shaken but relieved. The woman stepped behind her husband, as if prepared for a barrage of abuse.

'Sorry, mate, that was too close,' the man said. 'I'm just getting the hang of driving on the wrong side of the road and the roundabout tripped me up.'

Lavender thought Thierry was going to rip the man's head off. His jaw clenched and he narrowed his eyes, but after a sharp intake of breath he extended his hand.

'We're all fine. You must think carefully next time. You don't want to hurt yourself or anyone else.'

'Thanks, mate. I really am so sorry. I will ... I'll be more careful.'

Thierry waved a hand in farewell as he reversed onto the shoulder to let them through. He placed his hand once again over Lavender's.

His eyes bored into her. 'You're okay? You are not hurt?'

'I'm fine, a little shaken up, but fine.' She grasped for his hand. 'Thierry, you would've taken the full impact of that car if it had hit. You were protecting me.'

He placed his hand over hers and pulled her closer. 'I would do anything for you, Lavender. I … I have never met anyone like you. It seems I am a hopeless romantic around you. I have not felt ready to let another woman into my life … until now. If something had happened to you …' He shook his head as if to banish the thought.

Lavender's eyes welled. 'I feel the same way about you.'

A honk from a car behind brought them back to reality. It was time to move on. Reluctantly tearing his hand away from hers, Thierry indicated and drove carefully along an oak-lined road before turning down a narrow lane.

She said nothing, lost in thought. Moments later, he stopped and gestured ahead. 'And here we are.'

Lavender's eyes misted over. An ocean of lavender waved gently in the dappled morning sun.

'No wonder all your great French painters came to Provence. The light and the colours, they are just breathtaking.'

'Yes, you are right,' he turned to her musing. 'It was an idyllic place to grow up. The lavender provided us with everything we needed – antiseptic, beauty, fragrance for our soaps and perfumes. *Maman* even has a little potion she used to place on our pillows to help us sleep.' He drove on. 'Ah, and here is my family home,' he replied with a smile in his voice. 'Perhaps Lavender Jones, the healing properties of the lavender will also extend to broken hearts.'

Lavender digested his words as she looked at the beautiful yellow farmhouse. Its rustic red roof was the perfect foil for the lavender grounded in the rich, dark brown earth. She felt like she'd been transported into a Renoir painting.

A curtain moved and seconds later a tiny woman waved merrily from the doorway, before racing out to greet them. The woman – Thierry's mother, Lavender guessed – wrapped Thierry in a warm embrace before casting her eye towards Lavender, waiting for an introduction.

'*Ma mère*, may I introduce you to Lavender Jones, who's come all the way from Australia.'

'*Très, très belle,*' the little woman said, making Lavender colour. '*Je suis* Claudette, Thierry's *maman*. Welcome!' she said before kissing her heartily on both cheeks. '*Café au lait?*'

Later, as Thierry was lifting the bulging picnic basket from the boot of the car Lavender confided, 'She's so lovely.'

'Yes. She loved meeting you.'

'Everyone's been so kind. Where is that French arrogance we're always hearing about in Australia?'

'I think you'll find that more in Paris. We southerners are generally more …' he appeared to search for the right word, 'laid back, as you say.'

Laid back was the last word she'd have used a few days earlier. But here, on his farm, and in the sunshine, she could see the tension leaching from his body. Maybe he was right, maybe the lavender did have healing power.

Lavender was pondering this thought when her wedged heel caught in one of the drainage holes lining the side of the path. She thudded to the ground and Thierry gasped, running to her side. 'Lavender, are you okay? Have you broken anything?'

'No, no, I think I've just wrenched my ankle. I shouldn't have worn these silly boots. I was just showing off for you, trying to look chic.'

Thierry bent down and eased the offending boot off her foot. He scanned her ankle carefully, face full of concern. 'It does look like a slight sprain. Can you put any weight on it?'

Lavender tried, but grimaced in pain.

Thierry scooped her up, looping the picnic basket over his left wrist, cradling her close with his right.

'Thierry, it's too much! You can't carry me *and* the basket.'

'*Phfft,*' was his reply. 'It is not far now. We'll see how you feel after some food and a rest.'

Lavender wound her arms around Thierry's neck, enjoying the sensation of his muscled body against hers. Being in a man's arms again felt good. It had been so long … She inhaled his piney scent and her pulse quickened.

He must have felt it. 'Are you okay, Lavender? Are you feeling faint?'

Only faint at the thought of being so close to you.

'No, no, I'm fine just where I am.'

He carried her across the purple field, resting occasionally, before stopping under an ancient oak tree. Thierry gently propped Lavender up against the gnarly trunk as he expertly spread out a checked picnic blanket. Within minutes, a feast was spread before them – a crusty baguette, peppery paté, a pungent wedge of Roquefort cheese, a round of milky Camembert, pears, apricots, plus a tumble of strawberries. And for dessert, tiny lemon tarts and macarons were rounded out by a bottle of chilled champagne and some champagne flutes.

'My mouth is watering,' sighed Lavender.

'Mariet has excelled herself, but she forgot just one thing.'

Puzzled, Lavender looked at the lavish feast before them.

'*Voila!*' cried Thierry theatrically, drawing a pretty pink box of chocolates from the bottom of the basket.

Lavender laughed and reached over to snatch them, but Thierry was too quick for her. '*Non*, only after the meal. These are special chocolates.'

Lavender shrugged. She could wait. Smearing a slice of baguette with creamy cheese, she watched as Thierry expertly popped the champagne, managing to shoot the cork over into the nearby stream where it bobbed happily before being swept away. All pain was forgotten as dappled sunlight danced across Lavender's hair; she was sure her face was glowing with happiness and champagne.

'Feeling better?'

'Mmm, much better now,' replied Lavender, stretching her arms overhead, giving Thierry a good view of perky breasts straining against the material of her T-shirt. The champagne was buzzing in her head making her feel a little tipsy and wanton, and she smiled at his covert glance, the longing in his eyes.

Later, after they'd eaten their fill, Thierry reached for the chocolates. He presented them to Lavender with a serious look. She took in his handsome profile, his capable hands and finally his full red lips just waiting to be kissed.

Focus.

Thierry cleared his throat. 'Lavender Jones, these chocolates mean more to me than diamonds or champagne. These are the chocolates I was busy writing the recipe for. They are you, Lavender Jones…. you in a chocolate.'

A teenage Lavender would have giggled at the solemnity of it all. Yet, this older Lavender, who had experienced so much in her short life, realised that Thierry was not just offering her chocolates. This living, breathing, gorgeous man was offering her his heart, a heart that had been wrenched before. And now he was looking questioningly at her.

Lavender felt something lifting inside her. This funny, complicated, talented man who'd made her heart sing once again. Her heart, steeled shut for so long, was opening; it wanted to let him in. She sucked in a breath as he opened the box and placed a silky chocolate into her open, waiting mouth. An explosion of flavour zinged her tastebuds … strawberry first, then rich dark chocolate, until finally she caught the faintest hint of lavender.

She reached over and pulled him towards her, wanting his lips on hers. And when their lips met, it was all she'd imagined and so much more. Sensual and passionate, just as he was. Nothing like the kisses she'd shared with Jake. No, this was new and full of promise, different yet the same.

Later, she knew how lucky she was to have found not one but two men to cherish her in this lifetime. But now, she relished this new man and his lips – and the knowledge that her singing heart was big enough for love once more.

'I could stay here with you forever,' she said, finally pulling away from his lips and brushing a stray lock of hair from Thierry's forehead.

'I know,' he whispered, 'but look how dark it's becoming. I'm surprised *Maman* hasn't sent out a search party already.'

They made their way to the car, she leaning on Thierry's shoulder for support, even though she knew her ankle was fine. Every few minutes he'd stop, gaze at her in wonder and begin kissing her again.

'You are sure, Lavender? You know what you're doing? I do not give away my feelings lightly,' he whispered against her neck.

'Nor do I, Thierry, … but you and this magical place … it just feels right.' She cupped his face. 'I think we have both been sad for too long.'

As a long, slow kiss sealed the deal, tendrils of desire flared in Lavender's belly and she shivered. 'We'd better go,' she said, breaking away reluctantly.

When his mother greeted them back at the farm, Lavender could tell by her knowing look that she was no fool. She knew why they'd been so long. Lavender smiled to herself as Thierry's mother clasped his hands in glee.

Six months later there were two weddings for Lavender Jones and Thierry Boucleuse: one in a beautiful chateau in the South of France with the match-making Countess de Castile as their gracious host. Lavender laughed as she recalled Katerina's part in ensuring that Thierry and Lavender would spend a whole day together. The second wedding was on a lavender farm just outside of Heart Springs, Australia.

That day, the beautiful bride placed some lavender and custom-made chocolates on a grave high on a hill overlooking The Tea Lady Café. She shed no tears – they'd all been shed before. A sudden breeze whipped at her veil and she was encircled in the glow of the beaming sun.

'Thank you, Jake,' Lavender whispered as she heard the sound of a chopper approaching. It was Ayden, arriving to take her to the little chapel, she and Thierry had created on the farm. Theirs was to be the very first wedding on the lavender farm. First of many, Lavender hoped.

As she walked down the aisle towards her Frenchman, there was not a dry eye in the chapel. Silent tears slid down the faces of her bridesmaids – Izzy from J'Adore Travel Boutique and Brooke, who was now The Tea Lady Café's manager. Beside them, Becky and Regina looked on with shining eyes, resplendent in lavender-coloured bridesmaid dresses.

'You look gorgeous, my darling,' whispered Thierry, as she met him at the altar. She passed her lavender sprig bouquet to Izzy, and she and Thierry joined hands. 'I told you a little bit of lavender is magical and will heal almost everything that ails us.'

'And you were right,' she whispered. 'I am so blessed to have found you, my love.'

Thierry squeezed her hand and they both looked up to the sky before smiling at each other and turning as one towards the altar once again.

You never know where life will take you or from where the love in your heart will spring, she thought.

A London Minute

MICHELLE RULE

The Tea Lady Café is bustling. It's busier than I've ever seen it and (thanks to the free Wi-Fi), I've seen it a lot these past few months.

I first met the owner of the café, Lavender, in Mrs Ronald's Year Three class when we were both nine years old, so we go *a long way* back. When I told her about my employment situation, or lack thereof, she offered to run a tab for me so I don't need to pay for my lattes until I have an income stream again. I'm forever grateful to her – I don't know what sort of person I would be without my morning coffee; not the sort of person who would be getting out of bed and looking for job opportunities, I expect.

Lavender is standing behind the counter, with her brown hair tied in a messy bun on top of her head, and bright red cats-eye shaped glasses perched on her nose as she rushes to plate up golden scones and froth milk simultaneously. She doesn't look flustered but her usually flawless make-up is dotted with beads of sweat.

I don't know why her café is so busy this morning. I look around, trying to find a reason or explanation, but all I see is a constant stream of customers queuing well past the glass cabinets filled with home-made treats, that today smell like a delicious combination of summer and spice. People trail all the way to where I'm sitting in my usual spot, nestled behind a heavy wooden cabinet that displays shiny gift boxes of tea for sale.

I slowly lift the tall glass containing my morning vice, and swish the contents around before taking a sip. My concentration returns to the tablet screen in front of me. In a small town, jobs are a rare commodity and I'm not trained to do any of the jobs that have been advertised lately. It hasn't stopped me from applying but obviously, I've had no interviews. Unless you count the interview for Rockies Fish and Chip Shop, which I don't, because it wasn't based on the merit of my application; my parents set it up, and for that reason alone I turned it down. I don't need their pity, especially now that they are halfway around the world on their *fancy-pants* cruise. At least they left me their house to live in rent-free, until they return. Otherwise I might have been homeless.

The jobs advertised online are more of the same today. The local primary school needs a relief teacher and the dental clinic needs a dental nurse; neither fit well with my skill set of frying fish and battering pineapple rings.

I sigh as I close the tablet cover and push it to the bottom of my large satchel bag. Gulping the remaining lukewarm contents from the glass, I stand to leave, waving at Lavender as I push my way past women in crisp black suits and men in golfing polo shirts.

'Ruby,' I hear someone shout from behind me. I swivel around, looking for the source; Lavender is beckoning me with flailing arms that are adorned with jingling bangles.

'What are you doing today?' she mouths.

Nothing. I'm doing absolutely nothing. Shrugging my shoulders in response, I wonder why Lavender wants to know that.

'Can you help me?' she pleads as she casts her gaze over the waiting crowd in front of her.

'Okay,' I shout in response, before I have a chance to think too hard about it, and politely nudge my way back through the crowd to the black granite-wrapped counter.

She lifts open the hip height door that allows entry behind the counter.

'Why is it so busy today?' I ask her.

'Finance conference in town this week and Brooke has called in sick,' she replies, words tumbling from her mouth like rocks sliding down a mountain in an avalanche. Now is not the time for chit chat – that much is clear to me.

'I'll make the coffees, but can you please handle the orders and food preparation? It shouldn't be too different to what you used to do. I can't afford to pay you but I'll deduct earnings from your tab.'

I nod and study the till that is sitting in front of me. It is an old-style till, like the one we had at the fish and chip shop. All it does is work like a simple calculator so I don't think I'll have a problem operating it.

Lavender hands me a red-and-black dotted apron identical to the one she is wearing and a black cap for my head. I quickly accessorise and then take my place behind the till as she stands, dedicated, in front of the coffee machine.

The coffee machine has chrome sides and I can see my reflection in it; the thin face and large blue eyes that everyone says makes me look like my dad, and my cropped auburn hair poking out ever so slightly from beneath the cap.

'Hi, what can I get for you?' I ask the lady at the front of the queue, who is impatiently tapping her long French-manicured nails on the counter.

'About time ...' she grumbles in reply, followed by, 'short mac – topped up – and a slice of apple cake. Takeaway.'

I scribble down the coffee order on the notepad Lavender has left for me and then run my finger down the laminated price card sitting on the bench, finding the price of both items and punching the numbers in to the till.

She hands me a ten-dollar note and I carefully count out the change, returning it to her open waiting hand before wrapping the teacake and then directing her over to the right of the bench where she can wait for her coffee order. Lavender winks at me and it gives me confidence.

I can do this!

Over the next hour, we work in complete synchronicity. The long, winding queue has dwindled down to only a few customers now.

Lavender takes the opportunity for a small break from barista duties and sidles up next to me.

'I owe you!' she muses, grinning from ear to ear making her look like the school classmate I remember well.

'I'm not busy. I can stay for the rest of the day if you would like?' I reply.

'No, that's okay. But can you stay on the till for a few more minutes while I run to the corner store and pick up some milk? I'll wipe your tab clean, back to zero.'

I know I owe her more on my tab than an hour or two's worth of labour but I don't protest.

I can't make the coffees, but as more customers trickle through the door I take their orders, recording them in the notebook for when Lavender returns.

'A large takeaway cappuccino,' a deep voice booms as I'm re-arranging the cake display and spacing out the remaining stock so it doesn't make the cabinet look as empty as it is.

The voice takes me by surprise; I didn't hear the footsteps approach the counter, and my heart is racing as I look up at him.

I recognise him immediately. I've met him before, briefly, and once again I feel the same strange flutter in my stomach that I felt last time. He has piercing green eyes that are kind and cheeky in equal measure. He has a crew cut that is longer on the top and shaved on the sides and a five o'clock shadow even though it's nowhere near that time of day.

'Ruby?' he asks, confused. He probably didn't expect to see me wearing an apron and cap behind the counter of The Tea Lady Café, especially after turning down his offer of employment on the basis that I wanted to try my hand at something other than food preparation.

'So, is this where you are working now?' he inquires softly.

'Only for this morning – I'm helping out a friend,' I reply, my voice wavering. I know it's not his fault, or his family's fault, that I am unemployed and facing a future that makes no sense to me. It's not his fault that my parents sold our family business, the fish and chip shop that they ran for thirty years and I always imagined they would pass on to me to continue. It's not his fault … but it has been easier for me to blame his family, who put in an offer to purchase almost the second the shop went up for sale, when I had hoped no one would buy it and Mum and Dad would be forced to cancel their cruise and stay in Heart Springs forever.

'Oh, okay,' he nods, looking down at his hands that are clasped together.

I write Flynn's cappuccino order down in the notebook. Lavender has been gone for over ten minutes and the queue of waiting customers on the right-hand side of the bench is growing longer. I hope she returns soon.

'There is a little bit of a wait on coffees at the moment,' I advise him professionally.

'I don't mind waiting,' he whispers as he hands over the money and our hands brush against each other. The part of my hand, next to my right thumb, where we momentarily connect, tingles and it strikes a different beat to the flutters in my stomach, making me feel off-kilter.

'How is the fish and chip shop going?' I ask him nonchalantly as we continue to wait for Lavender.

'It's going pretty well, I guess,' he downplays.

I know it's going better than *pretty well* because I walk past the bustling enterprise every afternoon on my way to the walking track at the banks of the river, where I get my daily thirty minutes of exercise and ruminate over the latest photos my parents have sent me of the shoreline of Venice or the cliff-top towns of Santorini.

I've never been out of New South Wales; in family businesses, there is no such thing as annual leave. My school holidays consisted of wrapping greasy food in paper. Then one day, out of the blue, my parents decided they wanted a holiday; they wanted to see parts of the world they had never seen before and their plans did not include me. They wanted to retire early, and after spending so many years raising me, their only child, they wanted some time together to focus on their own relationship. In other words, I wasn't invited. The day after the business settled they had walked in to the J'Adore Travel Boutique and planned their six-month, daughter-free itinerary.

'That's good the shop is going well,' I mutter.

'We haven't hired anyone in that position we interviewed you for,' he continues, answering a question that I never asked.

Lavender rushes back in to the store, fabric shopping bags hanging from every available space on her arms.

'I'm sorry for the delay!' she declares and I know the customers will forgive her. It might be because she supplies the best coffee in town, but I prefer to believe it is because of her smile. It radiates like a rainbow, reminding me of sunshine after a storm. I feel a wave of affection for my friend as I realise the difference compared to a few months ago. New love definitely suits her.

'I'll hang around until you are caught up again on the coffee orders,' I offer, pushing the notepad towards her.

She gets to work, eliminating the orders one-by-one. The last coffee on her list is Flynn's and by the time she has reached his order I have removed my cap and apron, and placed them neatly on the bench, ready to end my volunteer shift at the café.

'You're an absolute gem, Ruby,' she smiles, oblivious to the pun.

'You're welcome, Lavender. I can help anytime, at least until I get a job. How long is the conference for? Do you need help tomorrow morning?'

'I'm not sure,' she ponders. 'But if you come in tomorrow morning at your usual time and I need help, I'll let you know.'

I nod and make my way to the exit of the café, reaching for the door just as Flynn does.

'Let me get that,' he offers, pulling the door handle towards himself as he holds the door open for me.

'Thanks,' I mumble as I walk quickly outside, hoping to be far enough ahead of him by the time he makes his exit that I won't have to stop and talk.

'Are you going home now?' he asks as he jogs up beside me.

I silently curse his athleticism. I should have walked faster.

'Yes,' I politely reply, but offer nothing more.

'I'm planning to walk until I reach the bottom of this coffee cup. Do you have time to go for a walk by the river with me?' he proposes.

It's a kind offer. The sun is shining, and there is every reason for me to say yes, but I stop short. Why would he want to spend time with me? We barely know each other and the only thing we have in common is that his parents bought something my parents sold.

'Well?' he prompts, humbly, as he takes a sip from the paper takeaway coffee cup.

I try to imagine what I would say if this were anyone other than Flynn; if he were a complete stranger. I haven't had a boyfriend since before my last dentist visit and I try to avoid dentist visits like the plague. I'm sure those two facts are mutually exclusive though.

'Okay …' I commit. 'But I can only spare thirty minutes. I have an appointment after that.'

Accepting a request to join someone for a walk while they finish their coffee is barely a date, but I still apply the golden rule of Dating 101; always have an exit plan.

We walk out of the town centre and down the sandy path that leads to the river bank. Brightly coloured wildflowers scatter their way through the landscape as if they are streamers, birds tweet simultaneously in a melody that sounds like an orchestra, and the bright blue sky is completely devoid of clouds. I am lost in the beauty of it all when it occurs to me that neither of us has spoken in a while. Is Flynn waiting for me to talk or is he simply the silent type?

'Do you walk this way often?' I ask him, awkwardly, before I realise that it sounds like a terrible version of a cliché pick-up line.

'Every day,' he replies, grinning.

'Me too,' I admit, despite myself.

'What time do you walk?' he asks.

'In the evening, usually.' *When you are working*, I think to myself, but I don't say it because I don't want to seem like a stalker.

'Do you listen to music or watch the wildlife?' he continues.

'No. Neither. I'm usually too busy thinking about the latest photos my parents have sent to me,' I blurt out and then instantly regret saying it. I don't want to talk about my parents with him.

'They're travelling, aren't they,' he mumbles, as if he's just remembered.

I nod and kick the sand on the path with my foot, causing a cloud of dust to plume in front of us. When I kick the dirt, I notice his shoes: black city-style loafers – the kind of shoe worn by a high-profile lawyer or a groom at a wedding. My plaited brown leather sandals look shabby by comparison, but they are comfortable for country living.

We are near the river now; I can hear the familiar rushing of the water.

'At least they are not trying to run your life,' he laments.

'Are yours?' I ask him, surprised by the honesty.

'Yeah. Constantly.'

'In what way?' I probe, realising that I might be crossing a line from offhand interest to outright nosiness.

'My parents moved here from Melbourne a year ago. A tree change, they called it,' he explains. 'I didn't need to move with them, I chose to,' he adds quickly, as if he thinks I am judging the decision of a grown man to move interstate with his parents. I *am* curious but I wouldn't judge him.

'I'd ended a long-term relationship and I needed a tree change too.'

'Do you like living here?' I ask him.

'Most of the time, I guess. Some days I wish there was more variety, more spontaneity. I wake up, I go to work, I come home and then I go to sleep; its rinse, lather, repeat. On the other hand,' he counters, 'I love the large, open fields filled with fresh air that makes it feel like I can breathe easier.'

My phone beeps in my pocket. I don't need to look at it to know the message will be from my parents; another message where they will enthuse at length about the latest postcard views, exotic food and luxurious hotel rooms. I've never been anywhere else than here. I don't know what it feels like to breathe foreign air. Is it really easier to breathe here?

'Do you have to check that?' he asks kindly, referring to the beep. I retrieve the phone from my pocket and read the message.

Hi Ruby. Your dad and I have a surprise for you.
Visit Maggie, she will arrange everything.

'It's from my mum,' I explain. He is very easy to talk to. 'I thought they'd be messaging to tell me their latest travel stories but this message is different.'

I show him the message and he reads it with a furrowed brow.

'Do they mean Maggie from J'Adore?' he guesses.

I nod, as that was my conclusion as well.

'Do you want me to come with you when you visit Maggie?' he asks.

This is something I should do by myself but at the same time I don't want to say goodbye to him just yet.

'I'll go see Maggie tomorrow,' I decide aloud as we continue to walk the winding path in front of us.

'This might seem very forward, but will you come for a walk with me again tomorrow?' he whispers as we reach the end of the river trail that bends back to the town centre.

Heat rises to my cheeks and I know I must be blushing. He looks confident but his fidgeting fingers give him away. Putting yourself out there doesn't get easier as you get older.

Why me? I wonder. But I've really enjoyed his company today when I would normally have been sitting in my parents' house wallowing.

'Okay, I'll wait for you at The Tea Lady Café,' I consent.

He smiles as he peels away from me and heads toward the fish and chip shop while I head home.

Maggie sits behind a large white circular desk, tapping away at the keys of a shiny silver laptop and pursing her bright red lips together in apparent concentration. I've seen her around town, I know who she is, but not in a familiar enough way to barge over and greet her with a hug. I am considering whether to interrupt when I sense someone standing behind me.

'How can I help you today?' asks a woman with short spiky blonde hair, as she walks in to my line of vision. A glossy white name badge, with the name *Izzy* displayed, is pinned to her blue dress. I've seen her around town, too.

'My parents told me to come here,' I mumble self-consciously. Spoken out loud, the words sound rehearsed and over-thought, which is exactly what they are. I don't know why I'm here, and I'm nervous.

'Okay,' she replies, giggling. 'You'll need to be a bit more specific.'

Her eyes sparkle when she smiles; she has a kind of warmth to her that instantly puts me at ease.

'My parents booked their holiday here. Our surname is Hunter. They told me to come here and talk to Maggie about some kind of surprise.'

'That sounds a bit mysterious, but I think I know what this is about ...' she says, appearing to glide across the room to where Maggie is sitting.

Maggie looks up as she approaches.

'This is Ms Hunter,' Izzy introduces, winking at Maggie.

'Ruby,' I add.

'Ruby!' Maggie exclaims, standing up from her desk and smoothing her red halter neck flared dress. It's like she has been waiting for me.

'Do you know why you are here?' she asks.

'Do I have a job interview?' I guess, coyly.

I've dressed up today in a striped pencil skirt and a white fitted blouse.

'No, that's not the surprise,' Maggie declares, smiling. That was the last surprise my parents sprung on me, when they sent me along to the fish and chip shop a month ago, so now I'm thrown.

'Guess again,' she prompts.

'I have no idea ...' I whisper, shrugging my shoulders.

'Do you have a passport?' she probes.

I *do* have a passport. It's brand new. My parents coaxed me in to applying for it, before they left – I think it was a *peace of mind* plan for them in case they died overseas and I had to be flown in to identify the bodies. I don't *think* that is the reason that Maggie is asking though.

'Yes,' I nod, grinding my teeth.

'Do you have any particular plans this Friday?' Maggie asks evasively.

I wonder if … 'Are my parents booking me a holiday?' I ask her curiously, as the metaphorical penny drops.

'Yes!' she enthuses. 'They want you to meet up with them in London for a week.'

I don't know how to respond. Different coloured emotions fire through my mind like Australia Day pyrotechnics – fear, excitement, confusion, wonder.

Why did they want me to join them? After all this time have they realised they hate being alone together? Do they miss me? Do they *pity* me?

Stop it, I berate myself. *Just stop it.*

'Can I think about it?' I ask hesitantly.

Izzy and Maggie exchange a glance that's as easy to read as a bestseller book. They think I'm crazy for not jumping at the opportunity. Maybe I am, but I need to process this in my own time.

'There aren't many seats left on the flight that your parents wanted me to book. I can put a hold on the ticket for twenty-four hours but that's the best I can do.'

I nod – that's twenty-four hours to decide.

J'Adore is on the same street as The Tea Lady Café. As I walk through the doors of the café I hear Tina Arena's mellifluous voice carrying through the speakers, competing with customer conversations and the high-pitched shrill of the milk frother.

The collective effect overwhelms me and for a moment I wonder how Lavender stands it; absorbed in this constant buzz all day, every day.

'The usual,' I mouth to her and she nods as I head to my favourite table and relax in to the cushioned seat. Lavender appears with a hot cup of coffee minutes later.

Normally I would have already started scrolling through employment websites, but not today; if I do agree to my parents' offer then my job hunting plans are on hold.

'It's quiet this morning,' she mutters in obvious relief. 'Thanks again for your help yesterday.'

I expect her to rush back to the counter where a customer stands waiting, but she doesn't. She taps her silver ballet flat shoe on the floor and blinks her eyes impatiently. What is she waiting for?

'So … are you going to tell me or am I going to have to pry the information from you?' she asks.

How does she know? Did Maggie or Izzy tell her already?

'I don't …' I start.

'Oh, don't be coy,' she interrupts. 'I saw the way he was looking at you. It was as if you were the only one in the room.'

Is she talking about *Flynn*?

'We went for a walk. That's all that happened.' I shrug.

As if on cue, he chooses this exact moment to walk through the door. Lavender winks at me and returns to her base behind the counter. The room is suspended in a state of slow motion as our eyes lock. I notice more about him than I did yesterday, as if I am slowly tuning in to a radio frequency where the static is being replaced with music. He is dressed differently today; wearing Nike trainers and casual cargo shorts with a black polo shirt. He does a double take as he observes my business attire and I suppress a giggle. I must be very confusing to him. He's dressed down to match my casual attire from yesterday and I have dressed up. Not purposely on account of him. It's just the way it happened because I came here straight from the travel agency where I thought I was going to be interviewed.

He slides in to the chair next to me and he is so close that I can smell his aftershave; an earthy scent that reminds me of snuggling in to Dad's old dinner jacket when I was a young child. Despite this making him seem familiar to me, I barely know him.

He is clutching a shiny pink gift bag in his hands.

'This is for you,' he declares bashfully as he pushes the bag along the table towards me.

'A gift? For *me*?'

'Yes, for you,' he replies smiling.

It's been a long time since I've been given a gift in a romantic context, and I'm still not entirely sure if this is a romantic context, but this is as close as it has gotten for me lately.

262

I open the bag slowly, peeling off the tape securing it, and my mind is in overdrive as I try to imagine what is contained inside.

'Champagne!' I exclaim, lifting out the large pink-labelled bottle.

'I was hoping I could drink it with you,' he explains.

'Now?' I ask incredulously. I am not really a shot-of-liquor-in-the-coffee kind of girl.

'No … later,' he explains. 'What are you doing this evening? Will you let me cook dinner for you?'

Isn't he *working* tonight at the fish and chip shop? Is that where he is going to make me dinner – at the fish and chip shop that is etched with my childhood memories and stolen dreams? My face feels like it is burning and I don't know what to say. He, of all people, should realise this would be a touchy subject for me.

Flynn leans closer to me. He is staring at me, with big green eyes that look hurt by my delayed response.

'You don't have to … there's no pressure,' he says, biting his bottom lip awkwardly.

I am suddenly so tired. Tired of my parents expecting that I will jump on the next plane to be with them. Tired of everyone thinking I should be getting over the whole future plan of my life going awry.

'I'm sorry,' I apologise. 'I just don't think it's a good idea at the moment.'

Silence hangs between us as if it has carved out its own zone amid the background buzz.

'What's not a good idea?' he probes eventually. 'Me? Or the offer of a nice meal at my house? Or both?'

His house? Not the fish and chip shop? I close my eyes, desperate to make sense of things and hot tears pool in my eyes for reasons that I can't explain to him or even myself.

'I don't know …' I whisper.

'Are you all right?' he asks with concern, as I try to imagine what he is thinking.

'My parents want me to meet them in London. That's the surprise. I saw Maggie this morning.'

My eyes are still closed so I can only predict that he must be looking at me the same way that Izzy and Maggie did; like I'm crazy for not having started packing already. But when I open my eyes, his expression catches me off-guard completely.

'Why do parents do that? Don't they realise that we are not five years old any more? They can't fix things for us like they used to.'

I'm not sure how he's done it but his words strike a chord so deep inside me that it's unsettling. Like he's seen straight in to my heart and soul. I've been trying to fix things for myself, I've been trying to find a new job and do things on my own, and this holiday offer feels like they don't trust me with that.

'On the other hand, you could take your free trip to amazing London and everything will still be waiting for you here to sort out when you return.' His eyes glint with mischief.

'Let me cook dinner for you tonight?' he asks again. 'I'm really good at helping with pros-cons lists.'

'Okay,' I agree. It might be nice to have an unbiased opinion and I really can't drink a whole bottle of champagne on my own.

He scribbles something on a napkin and pushes it across the table towards me. His address. The gesture makes me smile because we live in a small town and I already know which house he lives in. He still hasn't adjusted from big city living, even though his shoes today suggest he is trying.

As I knock on Flynn's door I second guess the outfit I have chosen for tonight. It's been so long since I've had to compile a date outfit that I wonder if things have changed; am I meant to wear something dressier or something tighter? The structured zebra-striped dress and white cardigan I have chosen suddenly seems so inadequate. I fidget with the hem of my cardigan, clutching the champagne bottle in my other hand as I wait for him.

The door opens but the dimly lit hallway is empty for a moment and then he appears; crisply ironed shirt, neatly brushed hair and missing the five o'clock shadow he sported earlier.

'How do you do that?' he asks me, grinning.

'Do what?' I reply, playing along.

'Yesterday you were dressed in casual gear, this morning professional and now ... well, just wow. You're a chameleon, you keep surprising me, Ruby,' he flirts.

He's been noticing me, I think, as he ushers me inside the hallway towards the kitchen and takes the champagne bottle from my hand.

His parents' house resembles the cover page of *Beautiful Homes* magazine: chic wallpaper, stainless steel appliances and, beyond the dining table, a sitting area with a white leather couch that has more scatter cushions than our local country Target.

'Your house is lovely,' I gush. It is unexpected decor for Heart Springs but exactly how I imagine a trendy Melbourne city apartment would look.

'They gutted everything,' he groans. 'I tried to convince them to keep the galley kitchen and bay windows but they wanted clean modern lines. Country charm is completely lost on them.'

He likes country charm, I note happily.

'Dinner is cooking,' he explains as he retrieves two champagne glasses from an overhead kitchen cabinet. He pops the cork with an almighty bang that makes me jump and carefully fills the glasses until the bubbles almost spill over the sides but then stop short as if on command. He hands me a glass and picks up the other for himself. 'Cheers,' he declares.

'Cheers,' I echo.

I take a sip, feeling the bubbles burst on my tongue, making it tingle. He walks across to the scatter-cushioned couch and takes a seat. In front of him, on the coffee table, is an open notepad.

'I thought we best get started on the pros and cons,' he declares stoically and I wonder again if he used to be a lawyer in his past city life. 'I've started the list with some ideas to get things flowing,' he says, pointing at the notepad.

I hadn't realised there was already some writing scrawled across the white paper. I lean across to read it more closely. It says: Pros – *Free Holiday*, Cons – *Flynn won't be there*. His list makes me giggle but at the same time I'm torn by an impossible choice; holidaying with my parents means leaving Flynn behind just as I'm getting to know him. Are there any other options?

'You can keep working on it while I get dinner ready ...' he suggests as he walks to the kitchen.

I've known him for months, since the business sold, but really, I've only known him for a day and what I am about to propose is ridiculous, I know that. His sleeves are rolled up as he removes a baking tray from the gourmet wide oven. Steam rises from the dish and encircles him.

'I can think of a way to conclude the pros and cons list,' I whisper.

Am I really going to go through with this? Once the words are said I can't take them back. On the other hand, the polar ice caps are melting and extinction might be just around the corner for all of humanity; so, what am I waiting for?

'How?' he queries, curiously.

'You could come to London with me,' I put forward.

The dish he is holding in his hands slips from the oven mitt and smashes on the tiled surface below. The look on his face is pure terror – he has just dropped the whole reason that he invited me over here tonight. That, and maybe the fact that the contents of the dish are scalding hot.

'Oh no ...' he mumbles, 'I'm so sorry!'

I feel terrible because I did distract him while he was carrying the dish. This is partly *my* fault.

'I'll get the pizza menu,' he asserts after a short pause, collecting his composure along with the glossy folded coupons, as he momentarily ignores the incredible mess travelling through the white grout lines towards us both.

While we wait for the pizzas to arrive, we clean up the floor with squares of floral-patterned paper towel, and we talk; about lasagne, about broken cookware, about our favourite dinner meals and about stained tile grout lines that neither of us have had to clean before. I reach for another square of paper towel as he does too and our hands meet, brushing against each other. I wait for him to move his hand first but he doesn't, and as I meet his gaze I feel his fingers intertwine between mine. The gesture is unexpected, intimate and I don't want to let go. His hands are smooth and strong and I realise how empty the spaces between my fingers have been.

He stands up slowly, pulling me upwards by my hand so that I am soon standing too and then he draws me forward, closer to him, until I think he is going to kiss me. I'm hypnotised by his slow breathing, and the mischievous way his mouth curves upwards in to a half-smile. I don't know how long the moment lasts before we are interrupted by a knock on the front door.

'That will be the pizza delivery,' Flynn whispers.

I nod.

'I should get the door now,' he declares softly, as much to himself as me. I don't want him to let go of my hand but I know the moment is inevitable.

He slides his fingers away from me slowly but an invisible energy remains behind, lingering, as a hard-edged thought nudges its way in to my subconscious.

Why hasn't he answered my question about London?

I clear space for the pizza boxes, moving the open notepad; hiding it in a drawer that rests underneath the coffee table because I don't want him to see it and have to awkwardly attempt to explain why he doesn't want to go with me, or perhaps pretend I never even asked it at all. And then I slide on to the couch and sink back in to the cushions until he finally appears, arms full, and places two boxes neatly in front of me.

He collects my champagne glass from the kitchen, which I notice has been topped up again to the brim, and then sits down beside me. I twirl the stem of the glass, spinning it around, as tension hovers between us like we are each waiting for the other to make the next move.

He slides open the pizza box and lifts out a slice of Supreme pizza that he passes across to me. 'Guests first,' he explains, breaking the silence.

Taking the slice of pizza from him, I start devouring the cheesy crust.

'I like a girl that doesn't count calories,' he murmurs.

A blush creeps across my cheeks – we are still at the stage of dating where I think I'm meant to pretend that I have the appetite of a pigeon. Is Flynn being sarcastic or sincere? I try to imagine the type of girl he would have dated in the past but I don't know him well enough yet so the picture in my mind is blank.

He smiles at me and I think he is being sincere.

'Does that mean you like *me*?' I ask him quickly, half-joking and half-not.

'I think you know the answer to that ...' he replies nervously and hesitates as he starts to say something else and then stops himself.

Is he trying to ask me if I like him too? I want to tell him everything but I don't want to hurt him. I want to lift the weight off my shoulders and take a risk, but I'm not sure if he can handle it, and then once I start the words will tumble out of my mouth and I won't be able to stop them.

'I hated you when we first met,' I announce softly.

His nervous giggle quickly changes to a frown and he looks away from me.

Rubbing my eyes, I exhale slowly. 'You bought something that I didn't want to be sold and, even worse, it wasn't my decision to sell it. I had to watch as my life changed in front of me and people told me I was supposed to adapt and be resilient but those are just buzz words – no one gave me instructions for *how* I was supposed to adapt or be resilient. But I'm learning that change isn't something to be afraid of ...'

With sudden clarity, I continue, '… and, despite any list that I might write, that is why I have to go to London.'

Ten kilometres overhead, aeroplanes circle the sky, preparing for their descent in to Heathrow airport; I watch the names of those flights light up on the large television screen as I wait to collect my bag. It's Friday afternoon and the arrival lounge is crowded with people waiting for their loved ones to disembark, ready to spend the weekend with them. I am here for a different reason; after I went to see Maggie she had my flights organised faster than 'a London minute', or so she said. I had to trust her on that one because I've only ever known Australian minutes, specifically Heart Spring minutes, where if you blink and then open your eyes *nothing* has changed.

Conversations surround me as I wait nervously by the carousel, pretending to look like I am a well-travelled tourist or at the very least somewhat-travelled. It seemed like such a fun adventure when I bought the floral pink suitcase from the only bag shop in town; and labelled the shiny black bag tags with a purple Sharpie. Right now, the idea seems less adventurous and more terrifying as my stomach knots with anxiety of what lies ahead of me, outside of these airport doors. London! What is it going to be like? I have no idea. Double decker buses, royal palaces and beautiful cathedrals? Will the city be filled with bright lights, dark rain clouds and falling snow like I imagine it to be?

I haven't told my parents that I arrived today but there are a lot of things that I haven't told them about lately; like about my new friendship with Flynn. It was his idea to delay meeting my parents for twenty-four hours so I could have my own London adventure before I joined in on their adventure. I have a hotel booked in Marylebone for tonight and then I will meet them at their hotel tomorrow evening. Maggie was surprised when I told her that I already knew which hotel I wanted to book. Flynn had recommended it to me, it being one of his favourites from his many trips here.

I recognise the edge of my suitcase as it snakes its way towards me slowly. A movement in my peripheral vision catches my attention and I can't help but shift my vision towards it; goosebumps prickle on the surface of my skin as a familiar figure leans forward across the conveyor belt and retrieves my suitcase for me. I smile without consciously deciding to do so, and he looks at me with those piercing green eyes that stop my heart for a moment. His brown hair looks too neat for just-landed and he waits for me to say something.

'What are you doing here?' I ask, stepping closer to him, confused and wondering if the stress of a long-haul flight has somehow tricked my mind, like a mirage in a desert.

'I'm your tour guide!' he exclaims, his eyes twinkling.

It is him. It really is him!

'Were you on the same flight as me?' I whisper, dumbfounded. Am I really that unobservant?

'No,' he replies as he smiles in a way that makes my heart start again and flutter at a manic pace. 'I landed a bit earlier than you. Maggie helped me to co-ordinate everything. I wanted to be here waiting for you.'

'Why?' I ask him. There are a million thoughts circling my brain and I can't make sense of any of them.

'Because you wanted me to be here,' he professes as he looks down towards his hands. *Those hands.* The ones I haven't stopped thinking about since they fitted my own hands so perfectly. So, he did understand the question that I asked him a few nights ago … the one that made him drop the casserole dish. I thought he hadn't understood what I was *really* asking of him.

'Are you ready for your tour, my lady?' he quizzes me.

I squeal with excitement and I sense that people are watching us: two Australian tourists making a scene at the baggage collection as I run towards him and wrap my arms around his neck. This might be the craziest thing that I have ever done. I place my lips on his as he wraps his arms around my waist and pulls me in tightly. His lips are warm and soft and I feel his heart beating through his shirt as it presses up against me; the kiss is innocent and delicate but promises so much more.

'You're beautiful,' he says as he tenderly brushes my fringe from my eyes.

'Even when I'm in desperate need of a shower?' I rebut, giggling.

'Well, there will be plenty of time for that later. For now, I have a plan.'

'A plan?' I ask curiously.

'A plan!' he repeats enthusiastically as he grabs the suitcase with one hand and my hand with the other, and leads me through to the exit of the airport, towards a waiting black taxi cab that is so *distinctively* London-shaped I have to pinch myself to be convinced this is not a scene from a movie.

Cold air rushes through my layers of clothing and I quickly climb in to the backseat of the cab, which the heater has made warm, as Flynn places the suitcase in the boot of the car and instructs the driver with details of our destination. My stomach flutters as Flynn slides in to the seat next to me and his thigh brushes against mine, accidently at first, and then rests there deliberately, intimately.

The cab starts to move and I can now see beyond the airport, to a long-stretching sky that is dull and grey and we are surrounded by several other taxi cabs, travelling in complete unison like a marching band. Red tail lights form a pattern of dots ahead of us and large white arrows on the road direct us forward. We travel past high-rise buildings and terraced townhouses, in silence, and as we get closer to the city I notice that the green grass lining the road is replaced by footpaths with pedestrians and cyclists. The silence is not uncomfortable, but rather perfectly necessary, as Flynn lets me see this beautiful city for the first time in my life. The taxi cab pulls up outside a brightly painted red building that stands in stark contrast to the otherwise monotonous greys and browns surrounding it.

'Stay here,' Flynn orders as the cab driver opens his door and I watch him remove my suitcase from the boot and disappear in to the building. I realise how vulnerable I am right now, trusting him, but I *do* trust him, and the cab driver keeps the cab running until Flynn reappears minutes later.

'You're all checked in,' he explains, and then I recognise that this is the front of the hotel he showed me the pictures of. I suddenly feel awkward; if he checked me in does that mean we are sharing a room? Everything is so new to me and I am not ready for that step in our relationship just yet, but I push the thought to the back of my mind – I will have to wait until later to find out.

The cab starts moving again and it is not long until I see straight ahead of us, rising out of the ground like an extraordinarily oversized version of the Heart Springs town hall clock, a structure that must be Big Ben, lit up against the night sky, and it takes my breath away.

The cab stops right outside it, and Flynn pays the fare as I am ushered out in to the cold air once again, but this time it is not within the confines of the airport. This time, it is on real soil, and for a moment I simply stand there absorbing the cacophony of voices projecting with foreign accents and sirens in the distance and the smell of smog and petrol fumes.

'I know you like walking,' he explains. 'I thought we could go for a walk tonight.'

He is carrying a backpack that I had not noticed earlier and he leans down and unzips one of the pockets, retrieving a coffee flask. He hands the flask to me and then retrieves another flask for himself as the sound of melodic chimes fill the air and the clock tells us that time has passed to the next hour. Is it even the same day that I left Heart Springs? With the time difference, I have no idea.

I slowly unscrew the lid of the flask and steam rises from the contents as the familiar aroma tickles my nostrils and reminds me of home; of Lavender and The Tea Lady Café and it all seems so far away from me right now. Sipping the coffee, I feel the warmth spread through me and then I follow him as we walk towards the river. An illuminated circle sits in the distance that is the London Eye, and then we meander through well-lit pathways leading us past iconic buildings that Flynn has seen before and he points them out to me as we pass them by. Everything is so different from home, supersized and glittery, like a fairy on steroids.

We walk until our feet are sore and the buzz from the coffee has worn off entirely, and then Flynn takes my hand and leads me in to a café that is still lit up despite the fact that it must be nearing midnight.

'I'm starving,' he confesses. 'Shall we order some food?'

I haven't eaten since the flight but the excitement of being here, of seeing Flynn here, has made me forget all about hunger.

'I'd love something to eat,' I remark as my stomach grumbles at the sudden reminder.

A waiter, carrying a menu, directs us to a rustic mahogany table-for-two nestled in the corner of the café, pressed up against the window that overlooks a cobbled street. Light rain falls gently, splattering tiny drops on the glass. The waiter scribbles furiously on a tiny white-lined notepad as Flynn orders an assortment of entrée platters for us to share, and I pause to observe the mural on the wall to the right of me. It is a collage of photos of old red phone booths, street signs and country flags.

'Where are we now?' I ask.

'Soho,' Flynn replies quietly.

'Did you enjoy the tour?' he asks, as he leans forward, with his elbows on the table and looks intrigued as he waits for my answer. He looks so happy, so carefree.

'It's been the best night of my life,' I admit.

His eyes seem to twinkle as he replies '… it's not over yet.'

Anxiety tugs at my chest. I have to tell him. He has flown across the globe for me and I am sure there is some sage advice in Dating 101 for this exact situation, but I can't remember it, and I don't want him to expect anything from me when we return to the hotel room. I really do like him, and it's not that I don't want to (or haven't thought about it, in fact I have probably thought *too much* about it) but this is really only our second date, albeit a totally amazing second date.

The waiter returns with plates piled with Turkish breads and colourful dips, platters of deep-fried squid rings and a tray of olives resting in oil.

'About that … I'm not really that sort of girl,' I confess feebly as the waiter retreats and Flynn leans in to tear off a corner of bread, using it to scoop up a pink dip that I assume must be beetroot.

I look down at the white napkin resting in my lap and start playing with the edge of it, to avoid seeing his expression.

'Ruby,' he says gently.

I don't look up at him.

'That's not what I meant when I said the night wasn't over yet,' he explains and something in his voice changes until it is lower and almost apologetic.

'I was going to take you to a park where we could watch the sun rise,' he continues.

The sun *rise?* What time is it?

The waiter returns to our table and pours wine in to two sparklingly-clear glasses.

'Cheers!' Flynn says as he clinks his glass against mine.

'Here's to surprises and adventures and love,' he declares.

Surprises. Adventures. Love. In that order, it makes sense.

'To surprises and adventures and love,' I reply, letting my eyes finally look squarely in his and allowing myself to get lost in them as if they were an ocean.

Beep ... beep ... beep.

As I reach over and press the snooze button, it feels like I have woken up in a dream. This isn't home.

I look around the room; white-and-navy striped carpet, long ice blue curtain drapes, a grey tub chair in the corner. The numbers on the bedside clock next to me reads 15:00. I've been asleep for only six hours. I sink further in to the bed and wrap the soft white blanket around me, grinning as I remember last night and the way it ended with watching the sun rise over London. It was the most surreal experience of my life; like I was floating in space, high and weightless, and watching someone else live that moment of my life. Like my life was just beginning – and all this time I thought that the sale of the family business meant my life was ending. Maybe this is what my parents have been searching for too, but I've been so busy caught up in myself.

There's a painful tug in my heart as I think about having to say goodbye to Flynn in a few hours. He is part of my new beginning and although I know he'll be there when I get back to Heart Springs, for now that isn't enough. My hand feels cold without his warmth.

An idea suddenly occurs to me ...

I open my suitcase and everything is neatly folded, exactly how I packed it when I left home a million years ago, or so it feels. I destroy the order as I rummage through the contents, changing in to a clean set of clothes, and brushing my short hair in front of the large gold-framed wall mirror. I rush to the wooden door that belongs to the room next to mine and I knock loudly.

Seconds later the door opens and he is standing there, smiling at me, like he knew I was about to knock.

'Good morning, sleepy head,' he whispers. He is dressed casually in tracksuit pants and a warm polar fleece jumper; he looks tired but happy, how I imagine I probably look too.

'When is your flight booked to go back home?' I ask him urgently.

'The same day as yours,' he grins.

'I don't understand ...'

'I am going to wait here for you, in case you need me. In case you decide you don't want to spend your whole holiday with your parents. I am your back-up plan,' he says, winking at me.

'Won't you get bored waiting for me?' I wonder aloud.

'Oh, that's a tough one! I didn't do a pros-cons list for this but I'm sure I'll find something to do in this city that never sleeps. And I'll never get bored waiting for you.'

Tears form at the corners of my eyes and threaten to spill down my cheeks. Tears of hope, gratitude, belonging.

'I don't need a back-up plan,' I declare. The look of hurt on his face is fleeting as he appears to regroup and his eyes drop to the floor. 'I do, however, need *you.*'

He looks up, frantically searching my face, clearly confused, but it appears he finds the answer he wants as he grabs the two ends of my knitted scarf and pulls me towards him. He hugs me and we are so close that I can smell his skin; a soapy scent, like he has just showered. His hands move from my waist to my shoulders and his breath tickles my ear as he brushes his fingers across my cheek, and then his lips are on mine and now I can taste him. I close my eyes and let my senses override my thoughts as I lose myself in the moment.

'I need to head to my parents' hotel room soon. They'll worry if I'm not there on time,' I finally whisper as I pull back from him. I don't want this moment to end but I know that it has to. 'Will you come with me?' I ask.

'Are you sure?' he croaks.

'I'm sure.'

'Okay then, I'll come with you,' he replies, nodding his head, beaming.

It takes only a few minutes for me to pack up my belongings, grab my suitcase, check out, and then stroll down the flight of stairs to the street where we hail a cab. Flynn carries my suitcase and I watch him do it effortlessly as if it is no burden at all. There is a freshness in the air that I didn't smell yesterday, a legacy from the recent rainfall, and the street seems quieter for some reason as if the city is pausing between rounds.

The cab winds its way through the roads, past shops, hotels and houses, all while my head is crowded with thoughts, imagining; what will my parents say? What will they think? Will they approve or will they disapprove?

I don't notice the cab get closer to the hotel until it has stopped and Flynn has opened the door, waiting for me to get out. In front of me is a brown brick veneer that stretches for as far as my eyes can see and, standing at the large glass doors, is a concierge waiting to greet us.

'Room 308,' I mutter to the concierge as he points his arm to the left and instructs us that way.

A long winding corridor, dimly lit with lanterns on the walls, leads us up flights of rickety stairs and then eventually to a door with a wooden number 308 printed on it and I knock.

The door opens and my parents stand there, sweeping both of their arms in to the air in unison, and a collective babble erupts from them as if they are being reunited with someone who has been away from them for years, not weeks.

'You're here!' Mum exclaims.

'Finally!' Dad continues.

'We've been waiting for you!' they both shout.

Amid hugs, and kisses on both cheeks, they don't seem to notice the figure standing behind me until I wave my arms toward him. 'Mum, Dad, this is Flynn. I'm sure you remember him,' I explain.

'Of course, we do …' Mum offers, stiffly, as Dad looks on silently.

How am I going to explain this? Butterflies tumble and dive in my stomach as I rehearse what I am going to say; it sounds insane, even to me.

'Why is he here? With you?' Mum asks, with a frown forming in the space between her perfectly shaped eyebrows. There is something different about Mum; she looks like she has been pampered. Despite the frown, for the first time in her life she looks relaxed.

I am happy for her but at the same time I feel tiny bubbles of resentment begin to inflate in my chest.

'I asked him to be here with me,' I defend, evenly.

'But … you didn't ask us if that would be okay …' Dad replies, dubiously.

One of the bubbles – filled with anger – bursts inside me.

'Why should I? You didn't ask me if it would be okay to sell the business! You didn't ask me if it would be okay if I was left on my own while you travelled the world! You didn't ask me if *I* would be okay …'

'Honey,' Mum affectionately coos, as she brings me in close to her head which is scented with her shampoo. I don't know why I expected her to smell differently now; maybe I thought that cheap country-town apple-scented shampoo wouldn't fit in with her reinvented well-travelled self but it makes me wonder if perhaps she hasn't changed at all. I wonder if she is still the same Mum that recited maths homework with me in between defrosting imitation crab sticks.

'You'll see, one day, that this is the right thing for all of us. You have to trust us,' she continues.

'I'll try…' I murmur.

Flynn coughs nervously before he says, 'Mr and Mrs Hunter, I am sorry for surprising you like this. I can go. It's no problem, really.'

'No!' I fight to release myself from Mum's embrace and turn to face him.

'Trust works both ways, and – Mum and Dad – now I am asking you to trust *me*. Flynn is my boyfriend …'

I pause as I ponder the word that I have just said out loud. Is that *right*? Is he really my boyfriend?

Flynn stares back at me with bright green eyes that are sparkling, as if in agreement with the definition that I have just given our relationship. Mum and Dad turn to look at each other, seemingly exchanging thoughts without words, as I reach for Flynn's hand. My hand melts into the warmth of his.

'I didn't know Flynn was going to be here. He surprised me too …' I explain to my parents as a grin spreads across my face.

'You know…' Dad starts to say, and I am expecting a lecture, 'my daughter wasn't part of a package deal, with the business.'

Flynn looks at the floor gravely as laughter erupts from my throat.

'Dad, stop it!' I giggle. 'You'll get used to his sense of humour,' I explain to Flynn, affectionately.

Stepping forward, I gesture to the amazing skyline visible from the hotel window. Mum, Dad and Flynn follow my lead as I point to the places that I want to visit. Today, now, it is time to start a new adventure.

Spoilt for Love

MONIQUE MULLIGAN

It's him!

Maggie's heart raced as she caught sight of a tall, red-headed man walking past Bob's Grill on the opposite side of the road. She stopped and willed the man to look across at her, for his eyes to burn into hers once again. Hope surged as he stopped in front of the busy restaurant, and then, as if he could feel the heat of her gaze, he turned around, squinting into the sun. Hope fled as fast as it appeared.

It *wasn't* him. Not even close.

She sighed. She saw him everywhere in Heart Springs lately. In Tarts Bakery, outside Bob's Grill, through the window at the Heart Springs Hotel, near The Tea Lady Café. Never up close. Always from a distance. He was everywhere and nowhere. And despite him being a figment of her overactive, undersexed imagination – not one sighting had ever turned out to be the real thing – he never failed to make her heart dance and pulse race.

For the past month, he'd visited her dreams. She'd woken more than once tangled in her sheets, flushed and disoriented from dreamy kisses and caresses that turned her into the wild woman she most definitely wasn't. Other times she would wake, arch into a slow feline stretch, and fall back on the bed with a contented purr. And then she would turn her head, regard the empty bed beside her and sigh with disappointment.

Why was she tormenting herself like this? The chances of ever seeing him again were a big fat zilch. She'd have more chance of winning the lottery, and she didn't even buy tickets.

Get a grip!

Maggie shook her head and headed for the zebra crossing, holding down her skirt against dress-lifting winds, willing away the image of the man she'd only ever seen once. This ridiculous daydreaming and fantasising had to stop. Not only was it embarrassing to get caught staring at random red-haired men, but if she was honest, the man of her dreams had well and truly spoilt her for love. No one else had ever come close.

Maggie looped JD's leash around the park bench and sunk gratefully into the bench facing the river. Her arm ached from being yanked from its socket by her friend and workmate Elle's crazy Border collie. Elle was having a romantic weekend with her latest fling, Tony someone, and it was Maggie's turn to look after JD. Lucky Elle, Maggie thought, not for the first time since Elle had mentioned the mini-break to the coast. She was always off here and there. Maggie counted on her fingers – each count a year, not month – it had been two years since her last loved-up getaway. And then her lover, Mike, had dumped her for Elle. Bastard. Thank god Elle had given him the finger when she realised her new Mike was Maggie's old Mike. Mike's betrayal had hurt – it wasn't the first time she'd been cheated on – but Maggie consoled herself that Mike was no match for her red-headed dream lover. No, Mike's lovemaking technique reminded her of the guy from Lily Allen's "Not Fair" song rather than Jamie Fraser's in *Outlander*.

Sipping her coffee and dreaming of romantic getaways with a Jamie Fraser lookalike while idly patting JD, Maggie didn't hear footsteps approaching. A voice like smooth whiskey cut through her thoughts: 'Nice dog,'

Maggie startled. The man looked up from patting JD and his eyes met hers. Recognition jolted her.

It's him!

His brow furrowed and hazel eyes focused on hers intently. Did he recognise her? The unspoken question was answered as words burst from them simultaneously: 'It's you!'

He laughed. Shock tingled Maggie's body. Was this another one of her dreams? Had he stepped from her daydream of roaming the Scottish highlands with a man in a kilt? Maggie reached out and pinched the man's arm. *Nope. Not a dream.* He was real.

'Ouch!' he said, half laughing, half grimacing. Maybe she'd pinched a bit hard. 'What was that for?' His accent was Australian, not Scottish as she'd always imagined. She'd 'met' him in Glasgow, after all.

Maggie coloured. She was willing to bet her face was as red as her patent peep toe heels. Or her lipstick. 'Sorry, I'm so sorry,' she managed. This was even more embarrassing than being caught sussing out random red-haired men. 'This is going to sound stupid, but ... I was pinching you to see if you were real.'

'Oh, I'm real, all right,' he said dryly. 'As are you, judging by the strength of that pinch. I'm probably going to bruise, you know.'

'What? No. Oh, this is embarrassing. I'm so sorry. I don't usually behave like this. It's just, I couldn't believe it was you.'

He grinned. 'It is.'

She titled her head sideways. 'You look different.' When he'd walked into the café she was waitressing in during her gap year in Glasgow, he didn't have the beard he was sporting now. And she would have remembered the intricate Chinese dragon tattoo that now swirled along his bicep and under his white T-shirt. She had never been a lover of skin art, but now she very much wanted to trace that design and feel where it ended.

'So do you,' he interrupted her tattoo-tracing trance. 'Your hair is longer than I remember.'

'You remember my *hair*?' Her hand went atomically to her head, where her shoulder-length hair was held back by a red and white polka dot scarf. Even *she* couldn't remember what her hair was like six years ago. Was that when she was going through her Audrey Hepburn pixie-cut phase? She made a note to look at her gap year photos and then decided not to. She'd finally found a style that suited her personality – anything 1950s – and she didn't need reminding about what a fashion disaster she'd been back then. She smoothed down her circle skirt, wishing for the umpteenth time her tulle petticoat wasn't so scratchy on her thighs, and waited for him to speak.

'I've never forgotten you.' He let the words sit. 'Okay, this time I'm not walking away without knowing your name.' He held out his hand. 'I'm Rafe.'

'Maggie.' She took his hand, relishing the warm feel of it around her smaller one. Their hands looked good together. They fit.

'Maggie? Can I have my hand back now? Only I'd very much like to add your phone number to my phone, if you'll let me.'

She reddened and released his hand, missing its warmth as soon as the cooler air blew over her skin. She told him her number and then added his to her phone. She stared at the entry a moment: Rafe. Such a strong, manly name. She loved it. Loved the look of his name on her phone. Would he notice if she took a quick photo?

'Maggie?'

'Yes?' She put the phone in her bag.

'Would you like to have a drink with me?'

They found a vacant table out the front of Grappa, an upmarket, dog-friendly café cum wine bar that catered mainly for photo-opportunity seeking tourists who came to see the famous Heart Springs falls in the nearby national park. Maggie preferred The Tea Lady Café, which was owned by her friend Lavender, but the alfresco area was full. While Maggie and Rafe perused menus, a thoughtful staff member brought a bowl of water out for JD. The dog lapped at it enthusiastically and then curled up under Rafe's feet.

'He likes you,' Maggie said, watching Rafe ruffle JD's hair.

'I'm a dog lover from way back. JD reminds me of my dog as a kid,' Rafe said. 'How long have you had him?'

'Oh, he's not mine. JD's my friend Elle's fur-baby. She's away at the coast for the weekend and I'm looking after him,' Maggie explained. 'Jamie, my cat, hasn't been too impressed.'

She held her breath. What if Rafe didn't like cats? That would be a nasty trick of the gods if the man of her dreams turned up after six years and he turned out to hate cats.

'A cat, hey,' Rafe mused. 'Never thought I'd like cats after growing up with dogs, but my sister Kate's cat won me over. I had to look after him when she went off to Europe with her fiancé about a year or so ago. Cheeky little bugger, he was. Used to jump on me at 5 a.m. on the dot and lick my ear. His way of telling me it was breakfast time.' He grinned at the memory, melting Maggie's cat lover heart.

Phew! No deal breaker yet.

'So, what brings you all the way from Glasgow to Heart Springs?' Maggie asked after the waiter brought their drinks – white wine for her and a boutique beer for him – and a trio of dips with toasted Turkish bread.

'I was in the UK for a gap year,' Rafe said. 'A belated one – I had to work a few years in my home town to raise the money. And then I had a year backpacking. What about you?'

'Same, but more of the working holiday variety,' she said, taking a sip of her wine. Her fingers trembled. She was sitting here, drinking wine with *him*. He was *real*.

'And where's your home town?'

'Eagle Point. That's in WA.'

'Western Australia? You're a long way from home.'

'Yeah. Well, I came here because my Dad lived here. He died recently and I came over for his funeral. Turns out he'd left his house to Kate and me. I'm between jobs, so I'm getting it ready to sell. Needs a fair bit of work.'

'I'm sorry.'

'I didn't really know him,' Rafe admitted. 'He left when I was three. Hardly had any contact with Kate and I. The house thing came as a total shock.' He shrugged, looking so much like a little lost boy – albeit one with a beard and tattoo – Maggie wanted to put her arms around him. Was it too soon? He caught her eye. 'Let's talk about something else. Um … how about, where were you when I went back to find you at that café? They told me you'd gone and weren't coming back.'

'You came back for me? Are you serious?'

'Yes. The next day. I wanted to properly meet the gorgeous Audrey Hepburn lookalike I'd glimpsed the day before.'

Maggie groaned. 'It was my last day. Izzy – my best friend – and I were doing the Heart of Scotland trail. We started a couple of days later.' She rolled her eyes. 'I can't believe you came back and I wasn't there.'

Maggie remembered the day she'd first seen Rafe. It was engraved on her memory, on her heart. Rafé – or The Man I'm Going To Marry, as she'd instantly dubbed him – had caught her eye as he walked into the café. What was it called again? *Fancy Cup? No. Fancy Coffee? No. Fan-Z Acuppa. Still sounds as stupid as it did back then.* She was taking an order from an annoying man who couldn't make up his mind, and her eyes had locked with the vision of manliness in blue jeans and a T-shirt standing just metres away. She'd never been able to explain the look that passed between them – it was knowing and intimate, as if their hearts had always been destined to meet. Izzy had laughed so hard she'd almost choked on a peanut when Maggie tried to describe that look.

'I can't believe I didn't stay when I first saw you.'

'Why didn't you?'

'My mate called. Said he had an emergency. Turned out he'd run out of money to buy pizza and beer. Bloody Dave.'

'Bloody Dave,' she agreed.

Rafe's phone beeped. 'Sorry,' he said, before glancing at the screen and cursing. 'Damn.' At Maggie's questioning look, he explained. 'You are *not* going to believe this. Seriously. It's Dave. The same *Dave.* He's come up from Sydney – he lives there now – to help me with the renos. Except he wasn't supposed to be here until *next* weekend. He's at the house wondering why I'm not there to let him in.' He showed her the text:

Where are ya, mate?

Hope ya getting pizza

I'm starved

'Bloody Dave.' He got to his feet. 'Listen Maggie, I've got to go, but now that I've found you, I want to see you again. I'll call you, okay?'

His bottom lip was all pouty. It was all Maggie could do not to kiss it. Would he at least kiss her on the cheek? Rafe's phone beeped again. 'Damn. I swear I'll throttle him,' he muttered. He shifted from side to side as if he was making a monstrous decision. 'I'm sorry. I'll call you.' And then he was off, power-walking to a late-model sedan that screamed hire car.

Bloody Dave. Just when we were getting to know each other.

Maggie and Izzy sighed simultaneously and slumped in their chairs as soon as the door closed. Monday mornings were always hectic at J'Adore Travel Boutique and today was no exception. Owned by Maggie and her best friend, Izzy Parker, the boutique was furnished with vintage travel posters and eclectic souvenirs collected over years of travelling, and was set along the Heart Springs café strip. Maggie had opened the boutique three years earlier to fill a gap in the market – ironically, the small town catered well for tourists, but for years had neglected to provide travel advice for people wanting to get out of town. It was a decision that had served her well. Heart Springs' older population welcomed the chance to organise their dream holidays with a real person, while younger people too busy to organise their own holidays were happy to leave the organising with J'Adore staff.

The need to find a replacement staff member was the reason Maggie and Izzy were mentally exhausted by 11 a.m. They'd been interviewing all morning, hoping to find someone to fill in for Elle while she was away for three months. Maggie looked at her watch. The final interviewee was due in five minutes. While Izzy topped up the water glasses, Maggie mulled over the candidates. Filling Elle's more than capable shoes was not going to be easy.

The first candidate had looked the part – professional, confident and well-spoken. She'd travelled extensively, courtesy of her wealthy father, whose name she was happy to drop more than once. But when she started live Tweeting the interview and made a snide comment about Maggie's dress, Izzy had drawn a cross next to her name on the shortlist. Strike one.

A harried-looking mother-of-three said she was available any days except Monday, Tuesday, Wednesday, Thursday and every second Friday. Strike two. The third candidate was Mary, whose resume boasted extensive travel agency experience. Questioning revealed she'd been a cleaner for a travel agent for several years and had never used one of 'those computer contraptions'. 'Would you mind paying me to do a training course in computers?' she'd asked, adding that her daughter was nagging her to learn Bookface. Strike three. And finally, there was Amanda, who was pleasant, well-groomed and had some retail experience. Her only problem was that she'd never left the state. She'd been to Sydney twice and stayed in Penrith, she said, with a measure of pride.

'Penrith, huh?' Izzy sat down next to Maggie and grinned, stretching her arms above her head. Friends since high school, the two had travelled together a number of times before opening the travel agency.

'Yes. Penrith. I haven't been there for … well, I may as well admit it. I've *never, ever* been to Penrith. Note to self: add the cosmopolitan metropolis of Penrith to my must-see list.' Izzy snorted. 'But still, Amanda was nice. I liked her,' Maggie continued. She poked at the pile of resumes Izzy had shortlisted. 'Who have we got next?'

'Ralph Peron. He's the last one.'

'Ralph. Well, we can only hope.' She pictured a mature man, balding at the temples and carrying a few extra love handles around the belly. *Don't judge!* 'Let's get this over with.'

Izzy ran her fingers through her short, platinum-blonde spiky hair before opening the door to their interview room – tea room, to be exact – in search of Ralph.

Maggie pulled out a vintage compact mirror and topped up her cherry-red lipstick while Izzy greeted their next candidate. Snapping the compact shut, she stiffened. Why did that voice sound familiar? It sounded like—

The door opened and Izzy walked in, followed by a familiar red-headed man.

It's him!

Maggie fought the urge not to rub her eyes. Surely her eyes were playing tricks on her. What was *Rafe* doing here? To be fair, he looked just as shocked to see her, but he managed to cover it before Izzy noticed.

'Hi,' he said, taking the seat Izzy offered him.

'Hi,' she said, pretending to be absorbed in reading his resume. How else was she going to hide her candy-pink cheeks?

Izzy lingered behind Ralph, waiting for Maggie to look up. 'He's hot,' she mouthed when Maggie finally caught her eye.

'Shall we start, Izzy?' She shot her business partner a no-nonsense look and cleared her throat. 'So, *Ralph*.' She paused, looked at him meaningfully. He nodded. Was that a twinkle in his eye? What was this Ralph-Rafe guy playing at?

Izzy looked at her, forehead creased.

Pull yourself together, woman. Maggie cleared her throat again. '*Ralph*. Why do you want to work for J'Adore Travel Boutique?'

The rest of the interview passed by in a blur of questions fired by Izzy. Maggie had no idea if Ralph-Rafe answered them well. She was lost in a barrage of internal questions. Why had Rafe called himself Ralph? Why was he here? Why did he have to smell so good? Did she have lipstick on her teeth?

'Maggie? Do you have any more questions?'

'Yes.' *Would it be okay if I kissed you?* 'No!' She ignored the amused expressions on their faces and dug deep for a semblance of professionalism. She was the owner of the travel agency, after all. 'I think we've just about covered everything, Izzy. Good job.' She didn't mean it to sound like she was patting a dog for good behaviour, but at Izzy's sharp look, perhaps that's exactly what it sounded like. 'We'll give you a call.' She nodded at Ralph-Rafe, as if to indicate that he was now dismissed.

He didn't move. Sat there looking adorable. There was no way he was getting this job. No way.

'You can go, *Ralph.*'

'Thanks Ralph. Lovely to meet you,' Izzy jumped in, reaching her hand out to shake Ralph's. 'We expect to make a decision in a couple of days.' She glared at Maggie, who reluctantly stretched her hand out to meet his. What Izzy didn't know was that if she touched him again, Maggie was lost. His hand, so warm and meant to fit perfectly with hers …

Pull yourself together, she told herself for the second time in half an hour.

Izzy rounded on Maggie as soon as the door closed behind him.

'What's wrong with you? Why were you acting so weird?'

'Nothing! Fine. I have a … heartache. *Headache!*'

'You're in a very strange mood today, Maggie. Stranger than usual.' Izzy shook her head, then tilted it to regard Maggie. 'If I didn't know better, I'd say you were in love. But, you my dear Maggie, are never in love, so unless you've been keeping secrets about some hunk-a-spunk …' She trailed off and changed tack. 'We *have* to give the job to Ralph. He's perfect. Better than any of the others, let's face it. And he's hot.'

'Yes. Yes, he is,' Maggie murmured. 'Wait, what? We can't. I can't.'

'For the love of donuts, why not? Maggie, he's better than the rest of them. And I think he likes you.' Izzy grinned. 'Just kidding. I tell you what, I'd show him my secret tattoo in a heartbeat, to be honest.'

'Izzy!'

'What?' Izzy pulled her I'm-so-innocent face, which turned just as quickly into pure mischief. She poked Maggie in the side. 'Oh, I see,' she teased. 'You've got the hots for Ralphy.'

'I do *not!*'

'Do too.'

'Not. And quit poking me!'

The sound of the door opening stopped them in their tracks. Elle stood at the door to their kitchenette, eyebrows quirked and arms crossed over her man-magnet chest. 'So, did you find someone?' Confusion marred her face at the simultaneous 'Yes' and 'No' that erupted from the boss and second in charge. 'You did but you didn't,' she guessed. 'Right. That clears everything up.'

'We did,' Izzy said, daring Maggie to stop her. 'His name's Ralph. We're going to offer the job to him, aren't we, Maggie? He was perfect in every way … except for his name.'

'Too right! He looks a bit like—' Elle stuck her finger in her mouth in a way that never failed to stop men in their tracks but pissed off Izzy big time. 'Wait, I've got it … I know! The guy in a kilt … Ron Weasley!'

What? Visions of a skinny red-headed, freckle-faced wizard took shape in Maggie's mind. *Ron Weasley? Are you serious?*

'Are you out of your flipping' mind, Elle?' Izzy bellowed. 'He looks like Jamie Fraser from *Outlander*. With a beard. And tatts. Not Ron bloody Weasley! Jeez!'

'Sor-ree,' Elle said. 'I get them mixed up all the time.'

Izzy snorted. 'How in the name of Hogwarts do you mix up Jamie Fraser and Ron Weasley? No contest, Elle. No flipping contest. Ron Weasley, my arse,' Izzy waggled her finger at Elle. 'I think it's time you watched Outlander and then you'll know the difference.'

Maggie looked between her friends. She wanted to laugh at their indignant faces, but a more pressing issue was at hand. Izzy was right – Ralph was perfect – except he was *Rafe*, the man she'd vowed to marry the moment she set eyes on him six years earlier. But if he worked here, how could they be more than friends? J'Adore Travel had a strict no-dating policy. She'd set that up after the hot mess of former employees Sharon and Tracy's on-again, off-again fiasco three years earlier. Not that it had been needed since, but still, bitter experience told Maggie it was best to keep work and love lives separate. But how in heck was she supposed to do that if Rafe worked here?

'Maggie?' Izzy was looking at her expectantly. Behind her, Elle was peering into a diamanté compact and topping up her lipstick.

'What? Sorry, I missed that.'

'Will I give Ralph a call?'

'I'll take care of it.' *Right after I get some answers.*

One cue, her phone beeped. Rafe's name flashed onto the screen.

I can explain

Got time for coffee?

Fine she tapped out.
Tea Lady in half hour
It better be good
The explanation, I mean
And make the coffee a double

Half an hour later, Maggie walked into The Tea Lady café and scanned the room for Rafe. He leapt to his feet when she walked in and her heart skipped a beat. How had this happened? How had this handsome hunk of a man walked back into her life ... and made it even more complicated?

'Maggie, I am *so* sorry. I was just as surprised as you. I didn't know you worked there. The ad said to contact Isobel. I had no idea—'

'I own J'Adore,' she said, sitting down in front of him. 'With Izzy – or Isobel. She's my business partner. We've been best friends since we were teenagers.' She picked up the menu. 'Have you ordered?'

'I have. Just coffee. What else would you like?'

She set the menu on the table. 'Nothing.' How could she eat when her stomach was flip-flopping all over the place?

'You sure? I have a hankering for a slice of cheesecake.'

'Fine,' she relented. She'd never been able to resist cheesecake. 'Just a little slice of the pecan salted caramel cheesecake.' She ignored his amused expression. So what if she knew every cake by heart here?

While he placed their order, she took a moment to suck in a few deep breaths. She felt like a giddy schoolgirl.

Breathe in and out. In and out. That's better.

'I guess you want to know about the Ralph-Rafe business,' he said when he sat down. She could smell the faint trace of his cologne. The giddy feeling returned.

'Well, now that you mention it, I do.'

'It's simple really.' He laughed when her eyebrows shot up. 'It is. Rafe is a variant of Ralph. It's embarrassing, but—' He paused and a bashful expression flitted across his face. Maggie wanted to reach out and bottle his face. 'I'm trying to change my name to Rafe but it's taking a while to catch on.'

'What, like by a deed poll?'

'Yes and no. You don't have to do that any more. You just fill out an application form and take it to the Registry of Births, Deaths and Marriages in your state, pay a fee, and then it's done.'

'So, that's what you've done? I'm confused. Why were you Ralph on your application?'

'I haven't done the paperwork yet. I've been caught up with other stuff. But I figured, over here, I could just assume the name Rafe and people would accept that. But my legal name is still Ralph on all my paperwork. You know, my qualifications and so on. Make sense?' The way he looked at her made her realise how much he wanted her to understand.

'Sort of,' she said. 'So … what do we call you in the agency?'

'Have I got the job?' He grinned. 'Seriously? I thought I had Buckley's after that interview.'

'Well, yes. I was going to mention that later.' Maggie decided to keep her misgivings to herself. 'Uh, can you start next week?'

'You bet. And I'd really love it if you all call me Rafe.'

Before she knew it, her lunch break was over. She stood. 'I've got to dash. Work calls. I'll see you next Monday, nine o'clock.'

'Maggie? Can we see each other on the weekend? My mate Dave's heading back to Sydney on Saturday.'

Every inch of Maggie screamed yes, but she kept her voice steady. 'I can't. I've got a few things on already.' She ignored the disappointment that flashed across his face. If only he knew how much it cost her to say that. And she'd taken the easy route, the cop-out, instead of telling him the real reason she had to say no. She stretched out her hand. 'Thanks for the coffee and cake.' The sound of her heels clopping on the polished concrete floor was like nails being driven into her heart. Truth was, there was no way she could date Rafe if he was working with her. She had Brodie Williamson to thank for that.

Maggie paced around the kitchen, waiting for the kettle to boil. After the morning's events, she'd been unable to settle at J'Adore, to the point where Izzy and Elle had started making fun of her. She'd laughed with them, pretended it was simply tiredness that was affecting her concentration, but eventually she'd given herself an early finish and driven home. For the next few hours, she tried to distract her churning brain, but nothing worked. Netflix, books, yoga, meditation, even going for a walk … all great in theory, as far as distraction methods went, but not so great in practice. At least, not now.

The idea of working with Rafe had triggered anxieties she thought she'd gotten past. Even though she'd given him the thumbs up, a flutter of panic had been her constant friend since she'd told Izzy, who'd promptly whizzed off a welcoming email detailing Rafe's job conditions. That meant it was real. No going back. And that left Maggie on edge. Because it wasn't Rafe who was the problem. It was her. And Brodie "The Bastard" Williamson.

Brodie. Maggie's shoulders tensed at his name. She hadn't thought of him in a couple of years, and now, he was an unwelcome resident in her thoughts. It was because of Brodie – *that vile sneak* – that she couldn't date Rafe.

She remembered her short and intense love affair with Brodie. It was before she'd bought J'Adore, back when she was working in sales for the regional newspaper. He was the boss's son and a junior journalist. Everyone called him a rising star. All the single women – and at least one of the guys – wanted to date him. And when he chose Maggie over all of them, she fell hook, line and sinker for his every single one of his lines. How she'd relished being the chosen one and all that went with it. The romantic dinner dates. The lust-laden looks across the office. The cheeky lunch breaks that were more like dessert. He'd lavished her with attention, ravished her with his young, fit body, and told her he loved her. And she believed him. For a time, Brodie made her forget the guy in the Glasgow café.

And then, by chance, she found out he was sleeping with the cadet journalist. And another of the sales girls. And the receptionist. Somehow the bastard had been able to dangle them all on strings, like brainless marionettes. When she confronted him at work one afternoon, her emotions getting the better of her, the boss – his mother – suggested Maggie resign or be fired, citing bad sales figures over the duration of the relationship. 'You let your emotions get the better of your professionalism, Maggie,' she'd said. 'And it's not good enough.' Maggie later found out the other sales girl had switched the figures to put herself in a better light, but it was too late. It wasn't fair. It probably wasn't even legal to fire her like that. But there was no fight left in her, so she moved on, heart-and-head-wiser, vowing never to date anyone she worked with again. The fiasco with Sharon and Tracy, which impacted on J'Adore's reputation, only reinforced her belief in separating work and romance. Hence the no-dating policy.

Until now, she'd lived up to her promise. Pouring hot water over the chamomile tea bag, Maggie laughed wryly. Of course she had. It was easy to keep a promise like that when she wasn't attracted to Izzy or Elle, the only people she worked with. But her comfort blanket was about to be ripped out from under her. She'd need extra strength to cope with Rafe being so close. And the Brodie-memories needed to get swept back under the rock they'd crawled from.

Monday swung around faster than a skipping rope in a schoolyard. Maggie had arrived early, twin coffees in hand for Izzy and herself. It was a longstanding habit to meet an hour before opening time for what was officially called a meeting, but always ended up a 'What did you do on the weekend?' update. Compared to Izzy, and her three-year lovefest with handsome helicopter pilot Ayden, Maggie never felt she had anything exciting to contribute in that department. Her weekends consisted of work on alternate Saturday mornings, catching up with family and friends, and reading. This weekend she'd binge-watched *Outlander* and consumed copious amounts of chocolate and ice cream in a lonely pity party. Rafe had left her messages but she'd forced herself to ignore them, telling herself she needed to start the way she meant to go on. She was the boss, he would be her employee. That was it.

No one had to know about the message she'd sent him after finishing a couple of glasses of red: **U wd look hot in a kilt**

Or his rapid-fire answer:

No kilt

Will tartan towel do?

She'd ignored that. That sort of flirtatious banter was unacceptable between boss and employee and she'd berated herself severely. *So much for keeping it professional, Maggie.*

As the minutes drew closer to Rafe's start time, her doubts returned. She should have stood up to Izzy and hired the Amanda woman. She wouldn't be in such a mess if she'd done that. She was fidgeting like a kid told to sit in a toy shop, and Rafe hadn't even arrived yet.

'Maggie, quick, check out this meme. It's made for you.' Maggie peered at the tiny image on Izzy's smartphone. It depicted Jamie Fraser in a kilt leaning against some rocks and read: 'Make mine a Scotch on the rocks.'

'Izzy!' Maggie giggled, resolving to download the image to her phone. *God, he was cute.*

And then Rafe walked in, all tousled red hair, black jeans, blue business shirt and brown belt. *Better* than a scotch on the rocks. Heck, those jeans were tight enough to leave little to the imagination.

'Hi, Maggie. Hi, Izzy,' he said, his eyes on Maggie, taking in her black wiggle dress, red-and-white headscarf and polka dot kitten heels. Or was he wondering why he'd bothered with her since she hadn't bothered answering his texts?

She cleared her throat. 'Good morning, Rafe …Ralph,' she said. 'Welcome to J'Adore. Uh, Izzy will run you through the paperwork and housekeeping before she heads out for a bit, and when Elle gets in, you can sit with her and watch what she does. I'll catch up with you later. I've got a nine o'clock I need to get ready for.'

She busied herself at her computer, preparing for her first appointment of the day. A young couple wanted to book their honeymoon. Where was it again? She looked at her notes and sighed. Scotland. Of course. It *had* to be Scotland. She looked towards Rafe, who was filling in employment forms, his head bent over the desk Izzy had cleared for him. Her fingers itched to run through his hair, to twist it between her fingers … as if he felt her gaze, his head lifted, and he winked cheekily. Maggie flushed.

This is not going to be easy.

Smack on time, her nine o'clock appointment walked in. The couple were wearing matching active wear outfits, and were flushed and perspiring, as if they'd power walked to J'Adore. It turned out they had. The young man apologised after he dripped on Maggie's desk, explaining that he and his fiancée were working on their fitness before their honeymoon. 'It's going to be a very active honeymoon,' he said earnestly. Behind him, Elle snorted and then pretended she was coughing.

'I see,' Maggie said, pressing her lips together in an effort not to laugh. 'It's always good to be prepared for such things.'

Elle made a strangled sound and disappeared to the kitchenette. From the corner of her eye, Maggie saw Rafe smirk, even though he was studiously looking down at his paperwork. His shoulders shook a little and Maggie squeezed her lips together tighter.

'Yes!' the man exclaimed, 'That's our motto. Be prepared.'

'I see,' Maggie repeated. 'Ah, do you have in mind a particular style of hotel for your, your um' – *Sex-fest! sex-fest!* – 'honeymoon?'

'Oh no, we won't be needing *hotels,*' the man said. His fiancée nodded, eyes shining on her husband-to-be. 'We'll be doing it in the wild. You know, stripping off our urbanity and connecting with nature. Wild and free!' He fist-pumped for emphasis.

Maggie swallowed and flicked her eyes to Rafe, who had his fist shoved against his mouth and eyes squeezed shut.

'Wild and free, stripping off, yes, got that,' Maggie said. Her mind raced with images, none of which contained a Scot in a kilt. She pinched herself under the table, hoping the pain would take away the giggles that hovered just below the surface. Get back on track, she told herself. 'So, how many nights are you looking at? Five? Sex? *Six!*' her voice trailed off as Rafe pushed his chair back and left the room.

'Oh no,' the man said. 'We'll need at least eleven nights of it. The Heart of Scotland trail will take *at least* that long.'

'Ohhh! The Heart of Scotland! Yes, yes, of course,' Maggie said quickly. *Not a sex-fest after all! Idiot!*

The woman peered at her. 'What did you think we meant? Don't you remember sending us the information on walking trails in Scotland?'

'I think that was my colleague,' Maggie said diplomatically. *Bloody Izzy!* Why hadn't she passed on that info when she'd asked Maggie to cover this meeting because of an overlapping doctor's appointment. 'But I've been on that trail. It's wonderful.'

The long-distance walk had been Izzy's big idea. She'd hooked up a guy who was making the trek with mates, and, convinced that he was the love of her life, was even more convinced that her life would be over if she – and Maggie – didn't follow him for a 'piddling 123-mile walk'. So persuasive was Izzy's argument – delivered mostly with generous side servings of alcohol – that Maggie found herself agreeing. For someone whose idea of fitness was climbing the stairs to the tiny apartment they shared with three others, the trek had been hard-going – following the River Tay upstream, trudging up and down hills and along ancient forest tracks, strolling down country lanes and meandering across foggy peat bogs. Maggie spent most of the eleven-day walk imagining she was hand-in-hand with her future husband, while Izzy mooned over the fickle wanderer who dumped her somewhere in the peat bogs for a haughty girl with no sense of fashion. And every night, Maggie bombed out in minutes, dreaming of a red-headed man running on the moors towards her, arms outstretched, with the dramatic mountain-scape soaring behind him.

'Excuse me?' the man said, waving his arm in front of Maggie's face. 'Anybody in there?' His fiancée sniggered.

'Right,' Maggie said, gritting her teeth. 'Let's get you booked in.'

Somehow Maggie got through the rest of the day, courtesy of a steady stream of appointments. Everyone, it seemed, wanted to book a romantic holiday somewhere, whether for honeymoons, anniversaries, or 'just because'. To Maggie's relief, Rafe – who'd explained the Ralph-Rafe situation himself – was kept busy with Elle, who had agreed to train him before heading off on her three-month European adventure. It didn't stop him stealing glances at her when he thought she wasn't looking, although, if Maggie was honest, it might have been the other way around. The busier the better, she told herself firmly. Having Rafe so close was testing her.

Strictly business. It leaves no room for awkward personal conversations. But a small part of her wished it weren't the case. And at the end of the day, when Rafe shouldered his backpack, called out a cheery goodbye and left right on five, Maggie couldn't help the small sting of disappointment.

You'll just have to get used to it. You made this bed. Now lie in it.

Without Rafe.

Over the next week, Maggie and Rafe barely had time to breathe as the appointments kept coming, one after another. The stolen glances, heated and lingering, continued. Maggie tried to stop but every now and then her eyes were drawn to Rafe's and she would tremble with wanting to touch him. Whenever he was close, Maggie surreptitiously breathed in his Rafe-scent – an intoxicating mix of an understated cologne and maleness. And when his body brushed against hers – accidentally when they exchanged files or passed each other coming and going from the tea room – she wanted to stop and press her body against his, heedless of time and place. The effort to keep things 'strictly business' exhausted her more than the constant stream of customers.

A few times, when Izzy and Elle were out of earshot, Rafe had suggested having a drink after work – each time Maggie put him off with a different excuse. She was beginning to think she'd have to resort to the 'I've got to wash my hair' fall-back. The first two times, Rafe looked disappointed and Maggie almost caved. The third time, he cocked his head and peered at her, as if he were trying to read her thoughts. As if he'd got her all wrong. And then he stopped asking. Maggie didn't know what hurt more – the fact that she had to stay professional or that he'd backed off.

Maggie and Rafe chuckled as they watched Elle flirt with a twenty-something hipster at the bar. They'd come to Grappa after work with Izzy and Elle, celebrating – or commiserating – Elle's imminent holiday and the end of her fling with Tony. The four of them had enjoyed tapas before Izzy had left them to it, citing other plans with Ayden. Now, Elle had dumped her workmates for hipster-dude, leaving Maggie and Rafe as alone as they could be in the busy wine bar.

A waiter delivered fresh glasses of wine – Pinot Noir for Rafe and Pinot Grigio for Maggie – and Rafe thanked him before patting Maggie on the arm.

'Is she always like that?' he asked, pointing to Elle, who was looking through lowered lashes at the hipster while stroking his bicep.

'Pretty much,' Maggie admitted. 'But it's just a game to her, you know. She's not as easy as she makes out.'

'Hmm.'

'She's not. Really. It's an act.'

Rafe nodded, then looked back at Maggie. 'People who play games aren't really my style.' His eyes bored into hers and she flicked her eyes back to Elle. Is that what he thought she was doing? Playing games?

He cleared his throat and she looked back at him. His eyes were softer and he sipped at his wine. She followed suit, hoping the wine would ease her leaping stomach.

'It's nice that we've finally got some time together,' he said, reaching for her hand. Pleasure-tingles shot up her arm and down her body. 'I've been wanting to go on a date with you all week.'

'We're not on a date,' she corrected, but didn't pull her hand away. It felt too good.

'Well, I don't know.' He looked around. 'There are candles. There's wine. There's soft background music. There's just the two of us now that Elle and Izzy have gone,' he said.

'Elle's still here,' she tried. God, she ached to kiss him.

'I think she's busy.' Maggie turned to the bar, where Elle was giggling as the hipster whispered something in her ear.

Rafe ran his finger up her arm and she jumped as her nerves went into overdrive. Knowing she should – must – pull away, she did the opposite and faced him, meeting his gaze, which hinted at games she most definitely *would* like to play. He reached out and traced her lips with his finger. She licked her lips, relishing the tingling feel his finger had left. Wishing his lips were closer.

He drew back. 'Do you want to go for a walk? It's a bit … hot in here.' He pulled at his shirt and fanned his face.

Damn right it is. A walk will cool things down. I'll be able to think straight if I get in the fresh air.

'Sure,' she managed. *Gotta cool down. I'm his boss.*

She followed him out of Grappa, stopping only to tell Elle she was leaving. Fortunately, Elle didn't seem to notice that Rafe was leaving, too.

'Do you mind if we walk in the park for a bit?' he asked when they reached the footpath.

'Sure,' she said again.

Taking her hand, he led her across the road to the riverside park where they'd met days earlier. She allowed him to lead, unable to speak with all the mixed messages in her head. And then he stopped walking and pulled her close that she could feel his heart beating through his cotton shirt. Could he feel hers leaping in time with his? He tilted her face towards his, grazing his lips against hers before trailing soft kisses down the side of her neck. *Come back*, she wanted to scream, as tingling sensations rippled through her body. As if he'd heard, he looked in her eyes for what felt like an eternity, before bringing his lips to hers again, not grazing, but tasting her lips with a hunger that matched her own. His hands roamed up and down her back and she arched into him, wanting no space between them. They'd waited so long for this moment.

'I've been wanted to do this since I first saw you,' he murmured against her ear.

'Me too,' she breathed, searching for his lips again.

'I get it,' he said when they came up for air. 'You're trying to keep things professional at work. That's why you backed away. It's cool.'

Work! The reminder served to douse ice water over the burning flame between them. Maggie pulled away sharply.

Rafe's eyes snapped open. 'Maggie. What's wrong?'

'This can't ... we can't ... I can't ... I've got to go.' Maggie took a step backwards, holding up her hands. 'I'm sorry, Rafe.'

Tears stung her eyes as she broke into a run, fleeing her dream.

'Maggie ...' he called. 'Maggie, stop.'

She didn't.

Maggie stared at her reflection in the bathroom mirror. She'd never been a pretty crier, but this was something else. A marshmallow with puffy, red eyes and a swollen nose stared back at her, blinking under the heat lamp she'd switched on out of habit. She shook her head in dismay. Somehow, she had to get her face together before work. She could not let Rafe see her like this.

Did putting cucumber slices on eyes work? Teabags? Checking the time, Maggie judged she had fifteen minutes to lie on the bed with cucumber eye patches. Moments later, lying on her bed, amid sheets as tangled as her mind, she winced as the cool vegetable discs contacted with her eyelids. Whose stupid idea was this? It probably wasn't even going to work.

Tears stung her eyelids once more. She wound the sheet around her fists as she lay prone, willing her body to relax, and the hopefully-not-mythical treatment to work miracles. Since running off on Rafe, she'd cried enough tears to fill Sydney Harbour twice over. The tears had begun as she sprinted to her car, ignoring Rafe's voice on the breeze. By the time she slammed the car into reverse, the trickle had turned to a cascade. She'd cried herself to sleep – crying for bad timing twice in her life, crying for a shattered dream. Crying because Rafe's kiss was the best she'd ever had and she'd gone and spoilt it. And when she woke on Saturday after dreams of reaching for a red-haired man but never quite being able to connect, the tears started again. She'd turned off her phone, unwilling to see if Rafe did – or didn't – message her and hibernated in her house, grateful only for the fact that it was her Saturday off. But no matter what she did, whenever her thoughts turned to Rafe, the tears welled anew. That was putting it lightly. She'd wailed and sobbed and beaten her defenceless pillow to a pulp more than once. Not even cuddles from a purring Jamie, two bottles of wine, an entire tub of Ben & Jerry's Chocolate Chip Cookie Dough ice cream, or the three Bridget Jones movies could stop the flow. As for *Outlander* – she might as well drown herself before her tears did. She hadn't even gone to farewell Elle at the airport. Some friend she was.

Now, as the tell-tale watering began behind the cucumber, Maggie gave herself a stern talking to. *This is all your fault.* She should never have allowed Rafe to hold her hand, let alone kiss her.

'You should have held firm,' she scolded herself, louder than she intended, and Jamie, who'd been nuzzling next to her, leapt off the bed at her no-nonsense tone. 'You should have made the no-dating policy clear to Rafe right from the outset. And as for the pathetic stealing-looks-across-the-office business, you should be ashamed of yourself. You're a businesswoman. Rafe's boss. Not a schoolgirl with a crush. Get yourself together, Maggie. And don't do it again.' Jamie meowed. In agreement, Maggie hoped.

In the office, she kept her head down, feigning great concentration on a website advertising a cooking tour of Iceland. Rafe's eyes burnt into the side of her neck, right where his lips had whispered soft kisses – *No thinking about the kisses!* – and she felt the cool loss of his gaze when he turned away. She managed to avoid anything more than polite exchanges about work until Izzy went on her lunch break.

Unsettled at being alone in the office with Rafe, Maggie headed to the photocopier to collect some itineraries she'd printed in advance for a customer. As she bent over to retrieve the duplicates, Rafe appeared by her side. He didn't waste words.

'So,' he started, 'are we going to talk about what happened?'

Maggie froze. This was it. Time to set him straight about the boss-employee situation.

'I'm so sorry,' she began.

'What happened?' he pushed.

'It shouldn't have happened. That … kiss. Us. We can only be friends.'

'Wait, what? Why Maggie? We've just—'

She held up her hand to stop him. 'It's probably best if we just keep it professional, don't you think, Rafe?'

'Hey, is this a private function or can anyone join?' Izzy barged past them, arms loaded with reusable grocery bags.

'I'm just trying to print something and the stupid machine won't work.' Maggie kicked the machine for emphasis. *Ouch!*

She hobbled away and sat down, pulling off her peep-toes, rubbing her foot.

'Maggie,' Izzy called. 'You forgot your copies.' She dropped them on Maggie's desk, her face quizzical, as if she wanted to ask something but it wasn't the time. 'I thought you said the printer wasn't working. Looks fine to me.'

Maggie rubbed her throbbing big toe, desperate to avoid eye contact with Izzy and Rafe.

Rafe placed an ice pack wrapped in a tea towel on her desk and walked back to his own desk without saying a word. 'Thanks,' she muttered, eyes down.

He was waiting for her in the car park, leaning against her red VW Golf, arms crossed. For a split second, Maggie considered running back into J'Adore and locking the door. Sucking in a shaky breath, she made herself walk towards him. Maybe if she started talking first.

'Rafe. I'm sorry. I didn't mean—'

'I don't understand,' he cut in. 'When did you decide to put me in the friend zone? We've just found each other again, Maggie. This sort of stuff doesn't happen every day. But it did. To us. And now you want to ignore what we both feel? I don't get it, Maggie.'

His words squeezed her heart. 'I'm your boss, Rafe. J'Adore has a no-dating policy.' As soon as the words were out, she wanted to take them back, to undo the heartache of the past week.

He stared at her. 'Why did you hire me then?'

'There wasn't any one else. You were the best of the lot. The only other person remotely suitable had only travelled to Penrith.'

'Great,' he muttered, kicking a stone on the ground. 'I feel so much better.'

'Rafe—'

'No, that's fine. You know, maybe you were right all along. Maybe this wasn't a good idea. Too good to be true and all that.'

She said nothing, too busy trying to hold her heart together.

He swung around, eyes glittery. 'You know, Maggie. I didn't expect to find you when I came to Heart Springs, but then here you were. And I thought it was meant to be. And now, I'm wondering whether it was better left as a dream. Because the reality isn't shaping up so well.'

Maggie didn't trust herself to speak. She was doing the right thing. So why did it feel so wrong?

He turned back. 'I was going to ask you to come with me to my sister Kate's wedding in Eagle Point. I wanted to show you where I come from. Guess there's no point now, is there.' It didn't sound like a question.

Two weeks earlier she'd have said yes without hesitation. She bit her lip, holding in the 'yes' that badly wanted to be heard.

Rafe sighed. 'Guess that's my answer then.'

The man who'd filled her dreams for six years walked away.

'What gives with you and Rafe?' Izzy rounded on Maggie. She'd sent out Rafe for takeaway coffees from The Tea Lady Café, which Maggie realised now was a ruse to get him away from J'Adore.

'What do you mean?' Maggie fiddled with her black and white wiggle dress, smoothing it over her hips.

'Come off it, Maggie. I'm your best friend. And even if I wasn't, any idiot can tell you two have got the hots for each other.'

'We do *not*.' She tried to cover up the squeak with a delicate cough.

Izzy grabbed Maggie's chin and forced her to meet Izzy's eyes. She looked like a banshee with her platinum-blonde hair spiked up, her eyebrows knitted together, her blue eyes piercing Maggie's faux nonchalance.

Harsh.

'Maggie? It's me you're talking to. You're acting the same way about that guy you once met in a café in Scotland. Yes, I remember. You were lovesick the entire time we did that walk and when we got back you were dead-set on finding him. Don't tell me you don't remember.'

'I do. Remember.'

'Good. You're acting exactly the same, I'm telling you. All dreamy and forgetful. And blushing and all that. You make me want to spew.'

'Really, Izzy? That's how love makes you feel? Like spewing?'

'Gotcha!' Izzy snapped her fingers triumphantly. 'I heard that. You just said *love*.' She paused and then clapped her hand over her mouth. 'Oh my god, you just said *love*. Maggie! What's going on?'

There was nothing for it. Time to 'fess up.

Maggie glanced around to make sure Rafe wasn't about to walk in. If she was going to do this, she'd have to be quick. 'You know that guy from the café all those years ago?'

'Duh. I just brought him up.'

'Yeah, well, Rafe's him. The one from the café.'

'Rafe? Our Rafe? Ralph-Rafe? He's *that* guy? Are you freaking serious?'

'Absolutely.'

'Well, if he's the same guy and you still have the hots for him – which you clearly *do* – then why aren't you two—' Izzy wiggled her eyebrows suggestively.

'Because I'm his boss, that's why.'

'So?'

'So? Izzy, you know our policy. No staff dating each other.'

'Oh that,' Izzy shrugged her shoulders dismissively. 'It's crap. If Rafe had the hots for me,' she continued, 'and I didn't have Ayden, then I wouldn't be paying attention to some *policy*. We're the owners. We make the "rules", we can break them. Or change them.'

'Maybe you can. I can't. Look how Sharon and Tracy worked out.'

'Piffle. They were always going to be tempestuous – fire with fire. No comparison. You and I both know there's more to it.'

'Izzy … don't make me say it.'

Izzy crossed her arms and waited her out.

'Fine! It's because of Brodie.'

'The bastard.' There was no emotion in Izzy's voice, just pure statement of fact. She narrowed her eyes. 'I can't believe he's still affecting you.'

'He's not! Not in the way you think. He was a bastard, still is, and I don't care about him. It's just that, well, I said I would never get in that same situation again. I would never let myself become attracted to anyone I worked with again—'

'Gee, thanks,' Izzy said. Catching Maggie's glare, she added, 'Just jokes, jeez.'

'I'm serious. I didn't keep things professional back then and look where that got me. Heartbroken, used, cheated *and* fired.'

'But you and Rafe, it's different. I've seen the way you look at each other. I tried to tell you about Brodie—'

'I know, I know, and I didn't listen. But it's not relevant now. What's relevant is that I have to look out for myself. Protect myself. Be a professional.'

'And throwing away a chance like this is looking out for yourself?'

'Yes! No! I don't know. I mean, I don't want to do this, but … but I have to. Don't I?'

Izzy rolled her eyes. 'Honestly, Maggie. I could just shake you. Didn't you once joke that he was the man you were going to marry?'

'I wasn't exactly joking …' One more look at the door. 'He was going to ask me to his sister's wedding in Eagle Point, but …'

Izzy grabbed her arm. 'Then don't push him away, you idiot. The guy's found you on the other side of the world. You might not get another chance! And isn't Eagle Point near Margaret-bloody-River! You're a numpty if you turn *that* down.'

Maggie poked Izzy in the arm. 'Look at you being all romantic, Ms love-makes-me-vomit.'

'Who'd have thought?' Izzy ran her fingers through her hair. 'Seriously, Maggie. Don't leave it too late. Now quick, put on your boss face. You don't want lover boy to think we're talking about him.'

They watched as Rafe, bearing a cardboard coffee tray in one hand and a paper bag in the other, pushed the front door open with his butt. He faced them, his eyes flicking from one woman to the other before shrugging his shoulders.

'White chocolate and raspberry muffins?' he asked.

'Rafe,' Maggie called, cursing the late afternoon wind that was stealing her voice.

Izzy had offered to close up – she'd practically shoved Maggie out the door when Rafe finished for the day – and now Maggie's short legs were in overdrive trying to keep with Rafe's longer ones.

'Rafe,' she called again. She leant against a brick wall and slipped off her black and white heels. 'Rafe!'

This time he heard her. He stopped and turned, his face quizzical. Maggie broke into a run – as fast as she could in a wiggle dress – and tried not to trip over anything. When she got to him, he was shaking with laughter.

'What's so funny?' She couldn't help feeling a little defensive. One minute the guy was giving her the 'What?' face and now he was laughing at her.

'You looked like …' his voice choked with laughter 'like a penguin!'

'A penguin? What?' Seriously? She was chasing after a guy to profess her love and he called her a *penguin*?

'I'm sorry, Maggie,' he tried to control the laughter and failed, 'the way you were waddling in that tight black and white dress – a lovely dress, by the way

301

– well, it reminded me of a … of a penguin.' He sobered when he saw her hands on her hips, but couldn't maintain it. 'You have to admit, it's not a dress made for running.'

'Hmmm. I suppose not.' Maggie knew he was right but she was still smarting over the penguin comment. Wiggle dresses were supposed to be sexy-femme fatale-bombshell dresses that made men's mouths drop. Not make them visualise penguins!

He cleared his throat. 'It really is a very … nice dress. It suits you.' He paused and swallowed. 'I suppose that wasn't very professional of me.' He paused again. 'You were calling me. Did you want me for something in particular?'

If only you knew how much. 'Yes, I do want you.' Maggie coloured. 'That's not what I meant.' He nodded, his eyes sad. Maggie wanted to kiss his eyes into happiness. Could she do this? *Just go for it.* 'Actually, that *is* what I meant. I do want you, that is, to be with you. I want to go to Eagle Point with you, to spend some time with you.' Now that she had started, the words spilled out. 'I've been such an arse, blabbering on about the boss thing. But I can't do it, I can't let you walk out of my life when you've just walked back in.'

His eyes gave nothing away. When he spoke, his voice was wary. 'I'm a bit confused, Maggie. First you were so happy to see me again and it looked like something was starting. Then, you were all about some archaic no-dating policy. You pushed me away. And now you've changed your mind?' He looked away and pushed his wind-whipped hair out of his eyes before facing her again. 'I don't like playing games when it comes to this kind of thing,' he said. 'You're either hot or cold with me. Not both.'

I deserved that.

Maggie bit her lip. 'I didn't mean to be playing games. That's not what I was doing. I was confused too. Trying to do the right thing. Except it wasn't. Right, that is.' Her heart thumped as she waited for his response. Could he hear it?

She thought his eyes softened a little. 'What changed your mind?' he asked after a moment.

'You. Well, and Izzy. She told me I was being an idiot.'

'I see. She could be right, you know.'

'She is! I *have* been an idiot.' She held her breath. Would he give her another chance?

302

'Maggie,' he reached for her hand, 'this wind is hurting my eyes. Would it be possible to continue this conversation somewhere else?'

'I'd like that.'

'Grappa?'

She nodded, slipped on her heels, and started walking through the alleyway leading to the café strip. Rafe lagged a few steps behind and the penny dropped.

'Are you watching me walk?' she asked, knowing the answer by his cheeky smile.

'I like that dress,' he replied.

Two weeks later, Maggie and Rafe boarded the plane for the Sydney to Perth leg of the flight. They'd already caught a plane from the nearest regional airport to Heart Springs – barely an hour in the air – and from Perth they'd catch a regional flight to Eagle Point. The wedding timed with the Easter long weekend, and Izzy had offered to cover the Thursday on her own, so they had five days together all up.

Five days to love it up, was how Izzy had put it. Maggie wasn't so sure about the loving it up part – they'd be staying at Rafe's sister's house, which wasn't exactly what she had envisioned for their first time. As she buckled her seatbelt, she cringed at the memory of Izzy's laughter when Maggie had brought up her concern about staying in Kate's house: 'You really think Kate will be thinking about what you two are getting up to in her spare room when she's about to get married? Jeez Maggie, what do you want? A castle with a four-poster bed? Servants to draw the curtains around the loving couple?' And of course, Izzy saved the best for last: 'I don't even get why you haven't jumped him already.'

Not that it was any of Izzy's business, but Maggie conceded she had a point. She wanted to make love with Rafe – and judging by the heat of his kisses as he pressed his body against hers, he reciprocated those feelings – but by some unspoken agreement, they weren't rushing things. Maggie didn't mind. They'd had to wait years to find each other. Surely a bit of extended foreplay was worth it?

'Are you all right?' Rafe asked, reaching for her hand as the plane taxied down the runway.

She blushed. If he were to read her mind, he'd know exactly what she was thinking about. 'Yeah, yeah, fine,' she said. 'Just thinking.'

'You looked a bit nervous.'

'Did I? Well, I suppose I am. Meeting Kate and all that.'

He smiled. 'Kate's a sweetie. For all she's a true professional in business, she's every bit warm and compassionate.'

'You love her a lot.'

'I do. After Mum died, Kate was all I had. I mean, I had my mates, but that's different. Kate always looked out for me.' He smiled. 'I can't wait to see her, to watch her marry Angus. He's such a great guy.'

'How did they meet?' Maggie loved hearing other people's stories, especially romantic ones.

'Now that was a fortunate accident,' he grinned, 'or maybe not so much of an accident.' He filled her in on Kate and Angus's romance and his sneaky part in getting them together in the first place, reducing Maggie to tears of laughter as he confessed how he'd set Kate up on a series of unsuitable dates.

'You're so cheeky,' she laughed, wiping her eyes with a tissue.

'You don't know the half of it.'

Over the next hour, they shared stories about their families – Maggie's extended and close one in Heart Springs, and Rafe's small but distant one in Western Australia.

'There's so much we don't know about each other,' Maggie commented as she peeled away the lid of her in-flight meal. Hopefully the vegetarian frittata tasted better than it looked.

'It will take years to find it all out,' Rafe said, swigging down his juice in one go. He poked at his in-flight meal – scrambled eggs and sausage – and then thumped the tray table with his fist. 'I know what we'll do!' At Maggie's questioning look, he stabbed the sausage with his fork and jiggled it around. 'Let's play Sausage.'

Maggie almost choked on her frittata. *Sausage?* Was there a double meaning in that? 'Um … Sausage?'

Rafe laughed, his eyes crinkling up like a boy's. 'It's like an either-or game. You have to choose between two options. Kate and I played it all the time. Like, I say "Sausages or Burgers", and you have to choose one. No judgement. Well … maybe a bit.'

Now it was Maggie's turn to laugh. This could be fun.

'Me first,' he said. 'Monopoly or Scrabble?'

'Scrabble.' She ignored his groan. 'Books or television?'

'Television.' She raised her eyebrows. 'What? No judgement, remember. And quit it with the eyebrows. Okay, um, beach or mountains.'

'Mountains. Wine or Beer.'

'Awww. Both.'

'You can't have both. Wine or Beer.'

'Beer? No, wine. Definitely wine. Unless it's … no, wine. Chocolate or ice cream?'

'What? What kind of choice is that? Both! Fine, *chocolate* ice cream. Glasgow or Heart Springs.'

'Now that's not fair. I think it's in the rules. Let me just check … Ouch!'

She relented. 'Okay, tatts or piercings.'

He quirked an eyebrow and let his eyes roam her body, taking in her pale pink '50's-style fitted cashmere sweater and black circle skirt with pink trimmings. 'Have you got a piercing? Is that why you're asking? Ouch! Tatts. Of course.' He flexed his bicep, sending Maggie into giggles. 'My turn. Kisses or cuddles.' He followed that one up with a lingering kiss.

Maggie could see the possibilities of this game. Perhaps it wasn't so innocent after all.

A mixture of weariness and anticipation hit Maggie as she and Rafe drove into Eagle Point. It had been a long day of travel and it was far from over. Yawning, she looked out the window as they drove down the main street, past a slightly more upmarket café strip than the one in Heart Springs, with Rafe pointing out various landmarks like a tour guide on fast forward.

'That's Serendipity Bridal Boutique, Kate's shop,' he said. 'And that's Vyntage, where Kate and Angus first met. And that's the supermarket where I used to work … that's my old school …'

'It's so pretty. And right across the road from the beach,' Maggie turned to Rafe, eyes shining. 'What a lovely place to grow up.'

'It was pretty idyllic,' he admitted. 'I learnt to swim at that beach – that's where we had swimming lessons every summer – and I went fishing and crabbing. Sometimes it was like being on permanent holidays.' A nostalgic note tinted his words.

'You miss it,' Maggie said.

'Yeah, yeah, I do. It's a great place. I can't wait to show you around.' He patted her hand and then pointed. 'That's Kate's house. We're here.'

They pulled up in front of weatherboard house framed by a charming cottage garden, an explosion of colour. As they opened the car doors, the front door of the house was flung open and a tall woman ran out. Maggie didn't need Rafe to tell her that the smiling woman with reddish-blonde hair knotted on her head, trendy black glasses, and the effortless chic of a white shirt, skinny blue jeans and boots, was his sister Kate. Maggie looked down at her ensemble, wishing she'd chosen something more classic.

She's so … so professional looking. I will never look like that. Not even if I tried for a million years.

Her insecurity fled with Kate's 'Hello' and warm hug, which was quickly followed by a sincere, almost wistful, 'I *love* your outfit, Maggie! I've never been confident to wear that style myself, but I've always loved it.'

Maggie straightened her shoulders and grinned at Kate. Nothing to worry about here.

Kate led them to Rafe's childhood bedroom, now the spare room. It was decked out in a romantic and eclectic vintage style, the kind Maggie adored. Art deco style posters adorned the walls, and a patchwork bedspread covered the queen-size bed.

'I'll leave you to freshen up. The bathroom's through there. You must be exhausted. Shall I pop the kettle on? Tea? Coffee? Wine? Two teas, great. Sugar and milk? No. Well, meet me in the kitchen when you're ready. Angus has just popped out to get some takeaway for us. I've been too excited to cook.' She disappeared down the hallway.

'Which side do you want? Of the bed?' Rafe asked.

'Um, right.' Maggie said. He dragged her suitcase around to her side and leant it against the wall. She watched him, mind reeling with the implications of staying in this room, this bed, with Rafe. Why was she so nervous? She felt like a blushing virgin bride on her wedding night.

Well, the blushing part is right.

Rafe clapped his hand on his head, breaking her thoughts. 'I can't believe I forgot to tell you.'

'What?'

'You know my mate Dave? Bloody Dave? Well, you'll never believe this, guess who he hooked up with in Prague? He Skyped me the other day, and he reckons it's love with a capital L.'

Maggie was at a loss. 'No idea. Elle?' she joked. 'Wouldn't that be funny? Imagine if your friend Dave and my friend Elle randomly bumped—' She stopped when she saw the strange look on Rafe's face. 'What?'

Rafe was staring at her strangely. 'Did she already tell you?'

'Tell me what? Wait. What? Do you mean to say—'

'Yep. Bloody Dave and Elle hooked up in Prague. And Paris. And—'

'Don't tell me any more. I can't deal with the visions. I mean, is Bl – Dave – really her type? He sounds—'

'Have you seen a picture of Dave? Here, let me show you the last one he sent me.' Rafe tapped at his phone, then turned it around so she could see the image. A ripped guy in low-rise jeans with no shirt and dark, finger-combed hair winked at her from the phone.

'*That's* Bloody Dave?'

'Yep. He's a model. Calls himself Daffyd, these days. He *is* Welsh, so it fits.'

'I've heard of *him*,' she took the phone back for a second. 'I pictured someone like that Spike guy in Notting Hill. You know, Hugh Grant's flatmate who had really bad taste in T-shirts.'

'Nope. Not Dave.' He nuzzled her neck, edging aside her sweater.

'Rafe!' she giggled, 'Kate's in the other room.'

'Hmmm. You're right.' He stood and pulled her up. 'Let's be sociable, Maggie-May.'

Light filtering through a gap in the curtains woke Maggie early. *Darn two-hour time difference*, she thought, knowing there was no way she'd get back to sleep. She rolled over carefully, so as not to wake Rafe, and gazed upon her sleeping lover. His pillow-smushed face looked relaxed. She was tempted to reach out, stroke the line of his jaw and trace his slightly pouted lips, but held herself back. Smiling, she recalled the night earlier, when Rafe had begged out of joining Kate and Angus in town – too tired, he'd said, but Kate's look was knowing – and she'd come out of the bathroom to find vanilla candles burning, and Rafe waiting, his face alight with hope and desire. He'd run his eyes, then his hands, over her vintage silk nightgown, which draped over her curves and made her feel like a 1940s screen siren, and she'd shivered at his silken caress.

'You look like a goddess,' he'd breathed between kisses that tingled every nerve in her body.

'You don't look so bad yourself,' she'd replied huskily.

307

'Morning, Maggie-May,' he said, startling her from her slow replay of their night together. He opened one eye and peered at her, his lips stretching into a half-smile. 'I can feel you looking at me.'

'I thought you were asleep,' she confessed.

He drew her in for a kiss. 'Not any more.'

'Well,' she said, a moment later, 'since you're already awake …'

Kate had prepared breakfast – hot cross buns, fresh fruit and locally made yoghurt – by the time Maggie and Rafe appeared at the table, hair wet from the shower, faces sheepish. Maggie thought she detected a hint of amusement in her eyes, but was grateful Kate didn't say anything about their tardiness. Instead, Rafe's sister suggested Rafe show Maggie around greater Eagle Point, bearing in mind nothing was open on Good Friday.

'All the wedding plans are taken care of,' Kate reassured Maggie, who felt guilty leaving Kate to everything.

An hour later, Rafe drove Maggie down a long gravel road to the Eagle Point lookout. Bushland gave way to dry coastal scrub as the road wound towards the cliffs. Wind buffeted them as they walked from the car park to the lookout, and Maggie's hands were glued to her side trying to hold her floral tea dress down. Her hair lashed at her face and she wished she'd thought to wear her hair up. Thank heavens she'd worn a cardigan.

'I should have suggested you wear jeans,' Rafe said. 'The wind can be pretty fierce sometimes. But you can walk in front if you like and I'll keep an eye on … the wind.'

'Mmmph,' she said, through a mouthful of hair.

The next stop, Hidden Pool, was less windy, but as they walked down a rocky gravel path, Maggie regretted her shoe choice. Pretty they might be, but her ballerina slippers weren't made for bushwalking. Why hadn't she packed something more suitable? Her remonstrations fled the moment she saw the natural rock pool, fringed by lush ferns and a canopy of graceful karri trees.

'It's beautiful,' she breathed. 'Can you swim here?'

'In summer people do,' Rafe said. 'But it's pretty cold. I used to do bombies off that rock over there,' he pointed.

'We have a similar place in Heart Springs. But more … rainforesty.'

'Rainforesty? With such an evocative description from an esteemed travel agent, I must see it.'

She poked him in the side and laughing, he drew her in for a kiss. And then she came back for more.

'You look beautiful,' Rafe whispered.

Maggie squeezed his thigh under the table. She'd worn a red dress – a timeless design with a boat neckline, half-sleeves and a full pleated skirt – that flared from her hips courtesy of a petticoat. Paired with pearls and adorable red patent shoes with cream spots on the cross straps, she *felt* beautiful.

Kate and Angus's wedding was perfect, Maggie thought as she sipped champagne. The couple had opted for a low-key garden ceremony in the early evening. Kate's back yard had been turned into a romantic paradise, with strings of fairy lights draped in trees and over two long tables that served for the wedding dinner. Paper bag candles lined pathways and candles in mason jars flickered between old-style milk bottles filled with flowers. Earlier, there had been a heartfelt exchange of vows under a bespoke wedding arbour of poles wrapped in ivy and white roses, a chiffon sheet floating above in the gentle breeze. Kate had worn an elegant but breath-taking gown designed by her business partner, Kyle. Maggie had almost swooned when Kate had glided into sight, wearing a slim cap-sleeved A-line dress embellished with exquisite lace appliqués. It skimmed her body and finished at her feet with a delicate scalloped hemline, and was equally as spectacular from behind, with a sheer back accented by crystal buttons. Maggie drank it in, hoping one day she would wear something as magnificent.

And the food. Aside from being gobsmackingly delicious, it was a real family affair, from what Rafe told her. Angus's sister Bianca, who owned the business Bianca's Bites, had catered the appetisers and main meal, while Kyle's partner, pastry chef Angelo from Angel Heart Bakery, had apparently outdone himself with his truly decadent desserts. The guests – an intimate group of about thirty – ate and danced under the twinkling lights. Maggie watched Kate glow as she basked in the love and attention from close friends and family – but never more so than when Angus smiled at her. Their love for each other was inspiring to behold.

When Rafe excused himself for a bathroom break, Maggie stood to one side. To cover up the self-consciousness she felt at not knowing anyone, she debated with a particularly tempting cupcakes the pros and and cons of eating said cupcake. She'd already had two, and her dress was beginning to feel tight around the middle, but—

'So, you're Ralph's girlfriend?'

Maggie spun around to face a twenty-something couple. Brett and Nat. Or was it Brent and Pat? Whoever they were, they were related to Angus. She hadn't heard them approach, so intently had she and the cupcake been communicating.

'Yes, I am.' Rafe had told her people in Eagle Point had trouble accepting his name.

'I hear you and R-Rafe are working together,' Brett said after a few moments' polite conversation.

'Yes, he's filling in for someone for a few months.'

Brett scratched his head. 'How's that working out?'

Maggie stiffened. Why was he asking that? 'Good. Really good. Uh, why do you ask?'

Brett laughed. 'My experience has been that it's never a good move for couples to work together. Last girlfriend and I did, and it was tragic. Like, a dead-set disaster. She was always getting her back up about something or the other. Having hissy fits. Refusing to talk to me. It was—'

'Ridiculous,' Nat put in. 'I had the same thing. Hooked up with a guy from work and then when we broke up – he was two-timing me – it was unbearable. Like, I had to quit.'

'It never works,' Brett said, more to Nat than Maggie. 'You always think it will—'

'But it never does,' Nat finished for him. 'Never.'

Brett seemed to remember Maggie was part of the conversation. 'Maybe you guys are different,' he said, considering her with his head to one side. He wiggled his finger at her. 'Time will tell, I guess.'

Rafe slipped an arm around Maggie's shoulder. 'Hey, what are you guys talking about?'

'Mate! Haven't seen you in ages,' Brett said. 'We were just getting to know your girlfriend, is all. So, what's been going on, man? We gotta chill before you go back.'

Maggie turned her attention back to the cupcake. It didn't look as tempting now, not the way her stomach was lurching.

'I'm going to sit down a bit,' she whispered to Rafe. He squeezed her arm and smiled, but kept talking to Brett and Nat. She left him to it, glad for some space. Thanks to Brett and Nat, her mind was bubbling – and not in a good way. In less than five minutes, they'd managed to tap into every worry she'd had about dating someone she worked with. For the sake of Kate and Angus, she kept it together. She smiled and laughed, danced and possibly drank a little more Prosecco than she intended.

But much later, when they were undressing for bed, Rafe asked, 'Are you okay, Maggie? Only I wondered if something was bothering you.'

'Just tired,' she lied.

The next morning, Maggie's head hurt. Not as much from the champagne as she pretended, but from spending half the night worrying. She sneaked a look at Rafe, who was chatting out by the barbecue with Angus as they cooked a fry-up. God, she loved looking at him when he was relaxed. He was in his element out there with Angus, chatting and laughing. Getting to know him in his home environment had been an eye-opener, and Maggie felt like she loved him even more, if that was possible.

Would working together ruin what they had? Were Brett and Nat right?

Izzy's words drifted into her churning mind: 'Honestly, Maggie. I could just shake you.'

Am I being an idiot again? If only Izzy were here to talk to.

Her internal debate went back and forth.

You're being an idiot.

I'm being realistic.

You're being an idiot.

I was right all along.

She tried to hide her turmoil, ignoring Rafe's questioning looks and going along with the general assumption that she was tired and hungover. She needed to get this sorted in her head, once and for all, but how could she with everyone around?

Late morning, Rafe drove her to a nearby bay where friendly stingrays swam to the water's edge and frolicked near camera-bearing tourists. Maggie was delighted – in all her travels, she'd never seen anything like this before – but as soon as he led her away from the crowd and down the seemingly endless beach, she fell quiet.

'Maggie? What's going on?'

'What do you mean?' She pointed at something a few hundred metres off shore. 'Is that a whale?'

'It's a rock.' He cupped her face in his hands and made her look at him. 'Maggie. Talk to me. I know something's wrong.'

'It's fine—'

'Don't give me that "fine" rubbish, Maggie,' he said gently. 'You went quiet last night after talking to Brett and Nat. And you've been distant ever since. I was hoping you'd tell me what was going in that whirling but brilliant mind of yours.'

She said nothing. Bit her lip. What should she say? That Brett and Nat had—

'I'm guessing it's something Brett and Nat said,' he cut in. 'Brett told me he was teasing you about working with me. Is that it?'

Teasing? Is that what they called it? Interfering, more like it. She hesitated and Rafe had his answer.

'Jeez, he's a dick. Sorry, Maggie, but that guy gets my goat. Let me guess. He gave you the rundown on working with his ex? About how she was a crazy psycho bitch?'

'Not quite in those words … but yes, something like that.'

He swore. 'Maggie. Don't listen to him. Let me tell you, there was a reason – and the reason was hanging off his arm last night – that his ex was somewhat pissed with him.' He cupped her face again. 'I am not Brett. Or bastard Brodie – yes, Izzy filled me in about him before we left. I love you. Whether we work together or not. Don't go having second thoughts, Maggie-May.'

Her heart swelled. He loved her. He. Loved. *Her.* 'Rafe—'

He kissed her before she could speak and she sank into the warmth of his lips, gasping when he pulled away too soon for her liking.

'Remember I was telling you about Dave and Elle? Well, there was something else I was going to tell you.'

That was a quick change of subject, she thought. She latched onto the Dave and Elle theme anyway, grateful to steer the attention away from herself, but wishing he were kissing her instead. 'More? Do *not* tell me they are getting married. Too soon.'

'Uh, no. It's about me actually. And us,' he reached for her hand. 'Um, I'm resigning. From J'Adore.'

'You're what? You're *leaving*?' Maggie's heart jack-knifed.

'Resigning,' he corrected, kissing her forehead. 'As if I'd leave you now. Anyway, turns out Dave – Bloody Dave – knows the guy who owns Grappa, and he put in a good word for me for a part-time job. I start next week, if that works for you. So, I can finish renovating the house, still have some funds, *and* you won't have to worry about how "Maggie and Rafe" will affect J'Adore.'

'But … I was just getting used to having you work with me,' she pouted. He pressed shiver-light feather-kisses along her neck.

'Too late,' he whispered. 'Now, I believe all impediments to pursuing our relationship have been dealt with?'

'Yes. I think they have.' She'd miss him at J'Adore and she'd have to get Amanda, the girl who'd only been to Penrith, to fill in, but at least his cheeky smile would no longer distract her at work.

'Rafe? Could you shut up and kiss me now?'

This time, his lips lingered on hers. For a long while.

Contributors

CAROLYN WREN

Carolyn Wren is a Perth-based author whose family travelled a great deal during her early life. This gave her a fascination with the world around her. Her eleven books have so far been nominated for nine national and international writing awards, resulting in three winner's trophies.

Carolyn doesn't limit herself to one sub-genre of romance, preferring to let her characters take control. The end results can range from light hearted, sweet comedic contemporary, through to sexy, action packed romantic suspense and emotion-driven urban fantasy. She is also a movie buff and makes video book trailers in her spare time.

Connect at www.carolynwren.com

TANYA KEAN

Tanya's love of romance stretches from her earliest memory: the day she picked up *Pride and Prejudice* she knew she'd found her passion. Austen's way with words had her enthralled. She vowed that if she couldn't be Miss Lizzy, she wanted to write like her.

Tanya writes contemporary, rural and historical romance with strong female heroines and men who are their equal. She writes about women triumphing over adversity to find their happy ever after (HEA). In 2016 she won first *and* second place in RWA's Selling Synopsis competition and progressed to the second round of the Emerald Award for unpublished manuscripts, with her historical romance, *A Reckless Heart*.

JEAN JENKINS

Jean started writing her memoirs and, in the process, discovered that she finds writing fiction far more rewarding. The memoirs lie in a drawer awaiting editing. In the meantime, she has written a number of short stories and is trying her hand at her first novel.

Jean finds any opportunity to drink champagne adds spice to life, as does going to the theatre or dining with friends. She is able to indulge in such activities as her many children are now grown and live all over the world. This also means she has a constant excuse to travel.

RENEE CONOULTY

Renee Conoulty is an Australian Air Force wife and mother of two who had a destination wedding in Thailand. She writes stories of dance, romance, and military life, including *Don't Mean a Thing*, short story "Catching Onix", and *Wife, Mother, Woman*.

If you run into Renee at the shops, make sure you wave to get her attention because she'll likely be listening to an audiobook or lost in a day dream.

LISA WOLSTENHOLME

Lisa Wolstenholme is a mum, wife, counsellor and ex-IT person hell-bent on getting her writing out into the literary world. No easy feat, but being a member of the Katharine Susannah Prichard Writers' Centre and Board Secretary helps. You'll find her loitering around KSP on a Tuesday morning facilitating the Tuesday Writers' Circle, and at most of KSP's events.

She swears (a lot), drinks (too much), is opinionated, and, like Uranus, spins in a different direction to most. She hopes this gives her a unique perspective on life and reflects well in her writing.

MELANIE PAGE

Melanie Page is in training for the competitive reading team, just as soon as it becomes an Olympic sport. If she doesn't have a book in her hand, she's probably holding a pen.

Married for more than thirty years and having raised three delightful human beings, she and her husband are now enjoying their empty nest. She teaches English at a large high school north of Brisbane and writes in the evenings. Melanie took the plunge and independently published her first novel, a Regency romance entitled *An Affair of Honour* in 2014. Two other books have since followed.

MEL A. ROWE

Mel A. Rowe is a writer and weekend wanderer, trying not to get too lost outback of North Australia. With an allergy to all things drawn-out and corporately serious, Mel A. Rowe is an internationally published, multi-genre word-player who takes common characters on uncommon journeys from boardrooms to billabongs, offering an entertaining escape to happily-ever-after.

Find her at www.MelAROWE.com

MICHELLE BEESLEY

Michelle Beesley is a Brisbane writer, wife, mother of three and occasional supply teacher. She is a regular columnist with e-magazine *She Society*. Michelle also writes romantic fiction and children's stories. When not writing, Michelle can be found reading, doing yoga, beside a footy field cheering on her favourite rugby teams, or in her local coffee shops chatting with friends. Michelle loves everything pink and sparkly (including champagne).

You can connect with Michelle at www.michellebeesley.com

MICHELLE RULE

Michelle lives in Perth, Western Australia with her husband, her primary-school-aged son and daughter, and a hyperactive puppy named Chuck. She works part-time as an accountant, so writing creative fiction and reading books is her escape. She's finished writing three novels (all unpublished) but has recently been focusing her efforts on short stories, self-learning, and submitting to writing competitions.

MONIQUE MULLIGAN

A former newspaper and magazine editor, journalist, children's curriculum writer, Monique has had a varied career in writing. In 2015 she turned to fiction writing, and the publication of "The Point of Love" in *Rocky Romance* was followed by children's picture books *My Silly Mum* (2016) and *Fergus the Farting Dragon* (2017). She has completed two contemporary fiction novels and is working on finding a home for them.

Connect with Monique at www.moniquemulligan.com

Thank you!

Thank you for reading *Destination Romance*.

We invite you to share your thoughts and reactions on Goodreads and Amazon, and also to spread the word among your writing and reading community.

For more information about Serenity Press titles, please visit serenitypress.org

While you're there, we invite you to sign up for our e-newsletter so you can keep up-to-date with new releases.

Printed in Australia
AUHW012041281118
305834AU00001B/3

9 780648 310617